My Aun there are two truths about **Southern belles: they survive and they endure.**

She's a Southern belle through and through—gracious, steadfast and honest. She's ready to offer you a tall glass of sweet tea, or a piece of her mind, whichever best suits the situation.

I suppose the Villa Magnolia is a Southern belle in her own right, too, because beneath her peeling paint and red tile roof that's mildewed green-black, she stands graceful and proud.

She is a survivor.

I could learn a thing or two from both of them.

Sarah rests her head against the passenger window as if it's too much for her to open her eyes and take a peek at our new home.

I want to turn to her and say, "Baby girl, I know you hate me for uprooting you, but it's going to be all right."

It has to be all right.

Nancy Robards Thompson

Award-winning author Nancy Robards Thompson lives and writes in Florida, where she spent three years serving on the PTSA board at her daughter's school. Along the way, she encountered a couple of "Stratford Wives" in the ranks of the general membership, but her overall PTSA experience was quite pleasant, thanks to the dedicated ladies with whom she served on the board. She holds a degree in journalism and has worked a myriad of jobs, including television-show stand-in; production and extras casting for movies; newspaper reporter; and several mind-numbing jobs in the fashion industry and public relations. Much more content to report to her muse, Nancy has found nirvana doing what she loves most—writing women's fiction full-time. Critics have deemed her books "funny, smart and observant." *True Confessions of the Stratford Park PTA* is her fourth NEXT novel.

TRUE
CONFESSIONS
OF
THE STRATFORD PARK
PTA

Nancy
Robards
Thompson

TRUE CONFESSIONS OF THE STRATFORD PARK PTA

Copyright © 2006 by Nancy Robards Thompson

isbn-13:978-0-373-88112-3

isbn-10:   0-373-88112-6

This edition published by arrangement with Harlequin Books S.A.

® and TM are trademarks of the publisher. Trademarks indicated with
® are registered in the United States Patent and Trademark Office, the
Canadian Trade Marks Office and in other countries.

TheNextNovel.com

HARLEQUIN®

PRINTED IN U.S.A.

From the Author

Dear Reader,

Isn't it interesting the different people we meet along life's path? Those with whom we bond instantly and others who remain distant enigmas. Sure, it's easier to feel connected to those with whom we share common interests and thoughts. But sometimes the "difficult" people teach us the most about ourselves—even though at times it seems as if they were simply put on this earth to annoy us.

That's the case in *True Confessions of the Stratford Park PTA*. Three women—Maggie, Barbara and Elizabeth—forge an unlikely friendship in the midst of personal storms too dark to weather alone. In the process, the bonds of their alliance are stretched and relationships are tested, but in the end, they emerge stronger women because of it.

I hope you'll find a piece of yourself in these three courageous women and come away knowing that through faith, love and friendship anything is possible. I love to hear from readers, so please visit me at www.nancyrobardsthompson.com and let me know what you think.

Warmly,

Nancy

This book is dedicated to my father, Jim Robards,
for being the best dad a girl could wish for. Daddy,
thanks for making laughter such a big a part of our lives.

Acknowledgments

I would like to thank Tammy Strickland for taking
time away from her own writing and nursing career
to advise me on high-risk pregnancy.

Hugs and appreciation—

To Sarah M., Sandy M., Evelyn S., Tyler J., Janet W.,
Cindy P., Debi W., Danella S., Donna S. and Polly R.,
who made my PTSA service an enjoyable experience.
Ladies, it was an honor and a pleasure to serve with you.
Your dedication to our school is what makes
it such a wonderful place.

To Beverly Brandt for sharing the Bob joke!

To Kathy Garbera and Teresa Elliot Brown, who always
know the next move when I'm stuck.

To Michael and Jennifer, who are my world.

Maggie

It's easy to look back and pinpoint what you should've done differently, to think of words you could've said, or a path you should've taken if you'd only trusted your intuition.

What's not so easy is looking forward, past the *shouldas* and *couldas*, straight into the eyes of the here and now.

I stop the car in front of the wrought-iron gates surrounding the Villa Magnolia, this place I visited so many times as a child, and I take a good look at the *here and now*, forcing myself to drink it down like bitter medicine.

Funny how you can look at something for years and never really see it. As far back as I can remember, my aunt Barbara has lived in the sprawling, lakefront estate, the home where Barbara and Mama grew up.

My granddaddy made and lost a fortune in the citrus industry, and the house was all he managed to hang on to. Due to family tensions I never understood, Mama was disinherited. Granddaddy left Barbara the Villa Magnolia, and left Mama and me to survive on our own the best we could. The only thing I know is that it had something to do with Granddaddy not approving of Mama's boyfriend, the man who would eventually get her pregnant with me.

All my daddy left me was his olive skin, lush lips and dark curly hair.

The trinity of his legacy.

Today, as I sit here, with the sun shining through the dense, leafy branches of the old magnolia tree, I realize I've come back seeking answers. I haven't quite figured out all the questions, but they'll come. Yes, as sure as the sword fern has invaded the grass between the driveway and the fence, the questions will come.

Barbara's the one responsible for my daughter and me moving back. She just wouldn't rest until she got us here. It took a year of her badgering me, but I lived in a daze for the first nine months after my husband Tim died. In that big old house in Asheville, just my daughter Sarah and me.

Sometimes I'd hear or read something that would make me think, *Oh, I have to call Tim and tell him*— and a split second later, the realization would set in that *I couldn't* call Tim and the only way I could cope was to take a sleeping pill and put a pillow over my head so I could obliterate the pain.

It was bad enough that sometimes I'd sleep until it was time to pick up Sarah from school; but the wake-up call came after he'd been gone five months—the morning the knife I was using to butter Sarah's toast slipped out of my hand and slid underneath the refrigerator. I got down on my hands and knees to fish it out and found a note in Tim's handwriting caught in the dusty coils.

Maggie, morning, hon, had to head out to an early meeting. Didn't want to wake you. Forgot to mention that my blue shirt needs to be spot-treated when you take it to the cleaners. See you tonight. Love you, Tim

No, I wouldn't see him *tonight*. He'd wrapped his white Infiniti around a telephone pole and was never coming home again. Not that night or any other.

In a stupor, I went upstairs to the spare bedroom and dug that blue shirt out of the boxes of his things I'd packed up but couldn't quite bring myself to take to the Salvation Army.

I put on that blue shirt and curled up into a ball, crying until the next thing I knew, I opened my eyes in a dark room.

I sat up with a start. Where was Sarah? How in hell could I sleep through picking up my daughter? There was no phone in the room so I had no idea if she'd called.

Oh, she had, of course. Several times. She was at a friend's house. The mom had tried to bring her home, but took her back to their house when no one had answered the door.

Sarah was worried sick that something had happened to me. Just as something had happened to her father.

I realized it was time I got myself to a shrink. The shrink, in turn, suggested that a change of scenery might be a good idea.

A few months later, I accepted Barbara's persistent invitation to come back to Florida and move into the guesthouse on the grounds of the Villa Magnolia.

It's been a long time since I last saw her, but my aunt Barbara is a Southern belle through and through—gracious, steadfast and honest. She's ready to offer you a tall glass of sweet tea, or a piece of her mind, whichever best suits the situation. She maintains there are two truths about Southern belles: they survive and they endure.

I suppose the Villa Magnolia is a Southern belle in her own right, too, because beneath her peeling paint and red tile roof that's mildewed green-black, she stands graceful and proud.

She is a survivor.

I could learn a thing or two from both of them.

Sarah rests her head against the passenger window as if it's too much for her to open her eyes and take a peek at our new home.

I want to turn to her and say, "Baby girl, I know you hate me for uprooting you, but it'll be all right."

It has to be all right.

She was such a daddy's girl, and there're times I think she wishes it were me in that grave instead of him. I want to tell her to be careful what she wishes for because Death listens. Death, that cold, hard bastard, waits in the shadows, hearing every fleeting impulse your heart utters.

The gate is open, but rather than pulling up to the house and unloading ourselves without warning, I press the intercom call button to let Barbara know we're here. She's expecting us, but it only seems right to announce ourselves instead of barging in.

"What are you doing?" Sarah scowls at me. These are the first words she's uttered since we crossed the Florida state line.

"Letting Aunt Barbara know we're here."

"Why do you think she left the gate open? So you wouldn't have to do that."

I ignore her haughty tone. She's been through so much, losing Tim and moving to a new state in the midst of middle school—as if that isn't an awkward time on a good day. Honestly, I don't blame her for being upset.

I never had a daddy. I suppose it's worse to lose a good one than to never have had one in your life.

It was always just the two of us, Mama and me. But sometimes when I was with her, that's when I felt the most alone. Probably how Sarah felt when I was going through my crazy spell.

Mama's been gone now for twenty-two years. In a way it seems as if she's been gone forever. In another way it hurts as if it happened yesterday. Maybe her living inside herself all the time was to prepare me for being alone. But I got soft being married to Tim. I got used to depending on him. He didn't give me any warning that he'd leave, too.

I know better than most anyone that Death

doesn't just happen to *other people*. But I can't contemplate it for too long. I can't let my mind creep to the edge of that vast canyon where Death lives and gaze down into his eyes. Because I don't want him to be part of my here and now.

Shaking away the thought, I press the button again and wait for Barbara's voice to drift through the intercom, inviting us in. I take a good look around, drinking in everything. It's been a long, long time, but everything looks exactly the same, a little more overgrown, a little weathered around the edges.

I always did love that old magnolia tree. The way it stands just inside the gates, all tall and proud, spreading its protective branches as if no harm would come to any who entered.

The tree was here before the house. In fact, they had to veer the driveway to the right because it was smack dab in the middle of the straight line between the gate and the house. I never realized it before, but I'm glad they went around it instead of digging up its roots.

A cool breeze wafts in through the open car window. It smells of magnolia blossoms, something basil-like and the aquatic mélange of the lake off in the distance beyond the old Mediterranean house.

I close my eyes and breathe in deeply. We will be strong like that old tree, my daughter and I. Strong and sure with roots growing so deep that Death won't topple us.

The iron gate will fortify us, protect us so that Death won't march his very own hateful self in and endeavor to dig up our roots.

"Mom, no one's answering. Just go in."

I shrug, gaze back at the rusting call box, mashing the button again. It doesn't buzz or squawk or give any indication that it's announcing our arrival.

I toss it up to fate. *If Barbara answers, that means coming back here wasn't a mistake.*

Sarah sighs. "If this is our home, why do we have to wait for someone to invite us in?"

I don't know how to answer that question.

Because it's the polite thing to do when someone takes you in?

Because if we proceed up that long, winding driveway uninvited, maybe Death will, too?

Sarah gazes at me, waiting for an answer.

Barbara didn't answer, is this a mistake?

Reluctantly, I put the car in Drive.

"You're not real glad to be here, are you?"

It's not a challenge so much as an observation.

She's an old soul, that daughter of mine. Always has been. Despite her rampant teenage hormones, there's always a glimmer of truth in those soft brown eyes, a way of viewing the world that astounds me sometimes.

"It's hard for me, too, baby."

She bites her bottom lip and stares out the passenger window, and as the car rolls toward the main house, I try to ignore the dark shadows I see in my peripheral vision.

Barbara

I love putting my hands in the dirt, potting flowers and tending them so they bloom bold and bright. There's no better way to set my mind right than getting elbow deep in potting soil on a clear, cool January afternoon. No matter what's bothering me—an argument with my husband, Burt—which seems to be a perpetual state of affairs—or if Mary Grace is having a particularly hard time of it at school—kids can be so cruel…

Mary Grace is a special child. Down syndrome. All that means is she was born with an extra twenty-first chromosome. As far as I'm concerned, that makes her extra-special. But nowadays, it seems as if kids have even less tolerance for those who are different. It takes all I have to ensure my daughter lives a normal life without others adding to the task.

When it's all crashing down on top of me, I come out here for a little earth therapy.

Today, I've hauled my supplies out here so I can work with my begonias—Rose Form Picotes, Ruffled Picotes, Giant Ruffled and my special favorite— plain ol' Rose Form. There's nothing plain about 'em. The blossoms look like huge roses, and I've grown them so big that they're almost the size of a dinner plate. Hiding all that green underneath so as alls you see is a beautiful flower.

The secret lies in a bigger, stronger root system. There are two methods you can use to get that big root system, but the more challenging method produces better results than the easier one.

Isn't that just like life? Nothing worth doing or having ever comes easily.

I remind myself of that all the time. When Burt's being a snot or the struggles with Mary Grace overwhelm me or the efforts to keep this house feel as if they're about ready to drop down on my head.

This is where my roots lie. Generations before me struggled to keep this place. I will not fail them.

So I set out flowers. It's an affordable way to make this old place look better. Lord, it needs a foundation-to-rafter makeover, but begonias are more in line with my pocketbook.

Begonias will shift the focus.

So begonias it will be.

As I'm lifting a bag of potting soil, a hitch in my chest takes my breath away for a few seconds. I drop the bag of dirt and fall to my knees and take some slow deep breaths.

My heartburn's acting up again. Or maybe I just tried to stand up too fast. *Lord have mercy....* I suppose I should get myself into the doctor, but I hate to complain about every little ache and pain. Besides, who has time for doctor appointments? It seems as though once you start, appointments cluster like aphids on a tender leaf. This doctor sending you over here to get this checked; that doctor sending you over there to get that checked. I may be sixty years old, but I'm not ready to give all my free time to the likes of medical monkey business.

And, see here—as always, after a few seconds, the pain passes and I feel just fine.

Probably just gas.

I draw in a deep breath. Pain-free.

There. Now that I'm standing and my dungarees aren't binding me in two, I can breathe. The doctor would just tell me there was nothing wrong with me that losing a good thirty pounds wouldn't cure.

The sound of car tires crunching on the gravel drive makes me shade my eyes. I don't recognize the blue car, but I realize with a start that it's probably my niece Margaret, my late sister Leila's girl. I'm expecting her today. But I didn't think she and her little one would arrive quite so early. I was thinking it would be late afternoon.

I glance at my watch and realize it's half past two.

For crying out loud, where did the day go? I'm embarrassed to admit that sometimes I lose track of time when I'm working out here.

Oh well, it makes no never mind. In fact, it's better that they're arriving now rather than later when Burt's home. I haven't told him that we're having houseguests. Because of certain circumstances that transpired with Leila all those years ago, I figured he wouldn't be thrilled about me inviting her girl to live in our carriage house until she can get back on her feet.

Bless his heart, Burt doesn't understand things like this. Mind you, I don't make a habit of going behind my husband's back and making plans without involving him. Manipulation was more Leila's style. Although, living with Burt all these years, there were definitely times when I could've benefited from employing a few of my late sister's techniques.

Like the time I came up with the plan to turn the Villa Magnolia into an elegant bed-and-breakfast. I discussed it with Burt, never fathoming he'd flat out refuse. I mean, with my knack for hospitality, cooking and decorating, I was just sure a B and B was the answer to our financial woes, especially seeing how that male ego of his wouldn't let me go out and take a job outside the home. I suppose he was afraid people would think he couldn't support his family. Well, there was that and the problem of Burt not taking kindly to strangers in his home. He pooh-poohed the B and B in no uncertain terms. No discussion. Not even an "I'll think about it."

So do you see why sometimes I opt for asking for forgiveness rather than permission?

He won't turn Margaret out now that she's here. The poor dear needs to be with her people right now, and other than her girl, Sarah, I'm all the people she's got. Despite all that's happened, I owe at least that much to my sister, to take care of her baby when she needs a hand. I shouldn't have let the silence between Margaret and me go on this long. Lord knows I had good intentions of keeping in

touch with her after Leila passed, but with Margaret
being all the way up there in North Carolina, it was
difficult and then I had Mary Grace and time just
flew. And I suppose if I'm honest, the bad blood
between Leila and me festered in the back of my
mind. It took a long time for me to finally face facts
that I was mad at her.

Mad at her for what she did and mad at her for
leaving us the way she did.

She always had to have the last word.

But I forgive her for what she did and any kind of
a decent human being with a lick of compassion would
not hold Margaret responsible for her mother's actions.

As the blue Toyota slows to a stop, a cool breeze
rustles the scarf anchoring down my straw hat. I bat
it out of my face with a grimy, gloved hand. *Land
sakes, I must look a sight.* I yank off the gloves, stuff
them inside the hat and toss the lot onto the porch
step, fluffing up my hair.

I suppose it's just been too hard for Margaret to
come back here to the place where her mama killed
herself.

I take a slow, deep breath and muster a big welcoming smile for them. I will not make this any
harder on that child and her little girl than it already

must be. Poor, poor Margaret, so young to be a widow.

I squint to get a glimpse of Sarah through the smoky glass of the car window. Land, that baby's a teenager by now. She was born the same year as Mary Grace.

When the door opens, a tall, skinny, blond-headed girl slides out of the car and squints at me as if she's tumbled out of a cave by accident. The sight of her steals my breath. There in her face is the whisper of Leila. The pale ghost of my sister. Flickers and glints of her in the valleys beneath the apple cheekbones; the curve of her nostril; the rosebud set of that pursed little mouth. Genes have slid down the years, skipping a generation to manifest in this beautiful young woman.

There's scarcely a hint of Margaret in her own daughter. Instead, it's as if Leila's reached out from the grave and claimed the child for her own.

"You must be Sarah."

The girl stares at her sneakers.

Leila's granddaughter. It's hard to reconcile that my sister would be a grandmother. I mean, I'm a grandma. I don't know why it's so hard to wrap my mind around the fact that she would be, too. That's what happens, I suppose, when one dies young. They are youthfully preserved for eternity.

Margaret rounds the side of the car and I shove Leila into the back of my mind, to the place where she resides.

Good heavens, it's been a long time. Margaret was just a few years older than Sarah the last time I saw her, which means I would've been round about Margaret's age.

"Just look at you." I hold out my arms. "It's so good to see you, honey."

I enfold her in a hug. As her bony shoulder pokes into my fleshy upper arm, the reflection of an old crone stares back at me from the car window. The image startles me.

Who *is* that? Not me. Surely not me. She's too fat, too gray, too wrinkled.

It's silly, how this passage of time takes me by surprise. But I suppose it's not just the dead who are forever immortalized. In our mind's eye we see ourselves in our prime, and it's startling to realize how much you've aged.

The reflection slips away as Margaret slides out of my arms and wipes tears from her eyes.

"Barbara, it's so good of you to—" Her voice

breaks. I'm afraid she's going to start bawling. And if she does, I will too. We can't have that.

"Don't you worry about a thing, baby doll. It is my pleasure. You girls stay as long as you like. As far as I'm concerned, you can stay *forevah*."

Margaret makes a noise like she's going to protest, but I wave her off and focus on Sarah. "Lord have mercy, child. You are the spitting image of your grandma, Leila."

Sarah's face remains blank, but Margaret flinches, or maybe she's just pushing a stray strand of hair out of her eyes.

All I know is awkward silence hangs in the air.

Sarah doesn't say anything, just stands there with her arms dangling down at her sides.

"Sarah, did you say hello to Aunt Barbara?"

The girl's expression doesn't change. She simply shifts her flat, dark gaze to her mother, looking up through lush eyelashes.

Margaret narrows her eyes at her daughter and gives a sharp nod in my direction.

"Hey." Sarah's single word is as lifeless as a humid August day, as if it took all she had to muster the single syllable. But that's okay.

"Hey, darlin'," I say. "I'm so happy you're here."

Margaret has sad eyes. And as this weary-looking, thin wisp of a woman in her baggy jeans and untucked pink button-down opens the trunk, I want to tell her that this is the prime of her life, that she's not supposed to look so worn out. But I suppose prime time does not include widowhood. Not by any means.

I muster the best smile I can manage. "Let's get your things out of the car. I'm sure you girls are anxious to get settled in."

As we start to unload the car, removing suitcases and boxes and bags, Mary Grace's school bus chugs to a stop at the gate. Since she's considered *special needs*, the bus picks her up and drops her off right in front of the house. She doesn't have to walk the three blocks down the road where the other kids catch the bus. It would be nice if someone would wait with her—someone like the Deveraux girl across the street. There's no reason she couldn't catch the bus here. In fact, I mentioned it to her mother, Elizabeth, once, but she said Anastasia meets her friends down the way and likes it that way.

People are creatures of habit. Once they're used to something it gets ingrained in their system and it's hard to do things differently.

The first day I put my baby on that school bus all by herself I thought I was going to die. I was used to taking her to school, but Burt got it in his head that Mary Grace needed to ride the bus, and well, since I'm always insisting that our daughter is no different than the other kids, I think he was calling my bluff.

Everything has to be a battle with that man. It's no skin off his nose if I drive our daughter to school every day. But he was so smug and superior reminding me that this was just one more example of how Mary Grace was not able to function in the real world.

What he didn't say, but it was there between the lines, was it's my fault. That I should've never gotten pregnant with her, being in my late-forties and all. Our other kids were grown and out of the house, and here I was with this unexplainable hankering to have another baby.

Burt adamantly opposed reverting back to diapers and middle-of-the-night feedings. He said I simply feared empty-nest syndrome—as if that could explain it all away. But the need to have this child ran deeper than that. Deeper than I could explain. It was as if this soul had chosen me to deliver it into the world, and I would just die if I didn't have another baby.

Two years later, when I got pregnant, Burt accused me of doing it on purpose, which I suppose was true, but I couldn't tell him that. Especially when Mary Grace was born with Down's.

That's when he started pulling away—from me and Mary Grace.

"Well, you got your wish," he said. "This child will never leave you."

So to prove him wrong, that this girl was as capable as the next child, I put her on that bus. He didn't know that I followed her in my car every morning for the first two months. In the afternoon, I'd drive up to the school and make sure she got on the right bus and I'd follow 'em home.

It made no never mind to him. And I certainly didn't mind doing it. It was better than sitting at home and worrying myself sick.

"Come on, Sarah, let's you and me walk down and meet Mary Grace. Margaret, honey, you go ahead and get settled in. We'll be right back."

I start off down the driveway. The girl falls into step beside me.

"Who's Mary Grace?"

"She's your cousin. She's about your age. What are you, 'bout thirteen?"

The girl nods.

As we approach, Mary Grace bounds down the bus steps. She stops in her tracks, scrunches up her face and looks at Sarah.

"Sugar pie, this is your cousin, Sarah. She and her mama are going to live with us for a while." The bus doors close with a hiss and the vehicle chugs away.

Mary Grace smiles. "Is she going to live in my room?"

"No, angel, in the carriage house."

My daughter's brows knit, as if she's considering the arrangement. "Does Sarah like to push people on the swing?"

"Well, I don't know. Why don't you ask her?"

From the window I watch Sarah push Mary Grace in the old board swing that hangs from the live oak. That swing's been there since my oldest boy, Stephen, was tiny. Over the years I've replaced the ropes, of course, but it's always been there, a constant friend that's entertained all my babies. But my older kids had each other. Being so much younger than her brothers and sisters, poor Mary Grace has essentially been alone, save for me.

It's an unexpected bonus that my sweet girl will have a friend in her cousin. The sight warms me from the inside of my overflowing heart down to my curled toes. Oh, yes, this does bode well.

But the warm fuzzies come to a screeching halt when I see Burt's car meandering up the driveway. I glance at my watch. Dammit, what's he doing home so early? What is this? He's hardly ever home and the day I could use the extra time to prepare a good meal to soften him up, he comes crawling in before the end of the workday.

"The place is just perfect, Barbara." Margaret comes in from the other room and stands beside me at the window as he gets out of the car.

"Is that Uncle Burt?"

"Umm-hmm." I wonder if I should warn her about Burt not knowing. Oh, on second thought, why give her something else to worry about?

Margaret crosses her arms as if she senses something's not right. "Should I go out and say hi?"

I smile and walk away from the window, circling around so that as Margaret follows me her back's to the glass.

"Oh, honey, give him a few minutes to transition from work to being home. You know how men are." I roll my eyes. "He's always an old bear when he first gets home. The girls are playing outside. You just relax a little bit while I go take care of my man."

Margaret gives me a strange look, but doesn't protest.

From the window I see Burt circle Sarah like a suspicious dog. I wonder if he notices Sarah's likeness to Leila.

How could he not?

I'm overcome by the urge to go outside and turn the garden hose on him the way I would to chase away an old scurvy stray.

"We'll have dinner at six-thirty. Just come on up to the house."

"Can I help you with anything?"

I wave her off and start toward the door. "Heavens no, just relax."

With that, I try to follow my own advice and relax as I prepare to inform my husband we have houseguests—indefinitely.

Elizabeth

What do you get if you take two consecutive months of missed menstrual periods multiplied by six miserable weeks of morning sickness?

Go on, you do the math.

Shit. What else could it be?

Still, I close my eyes and hold my breath before I look at the stick I peed on five minutes ago.

I know before I *know*, but still the two little blue lines on the stick come as shocking confirmation.

I'm pregnant.

Shit.

This cannot be happening. I am forty-three years old. I *cannot* be pregnant.

Andrew is going to flip.

Shit. Shit. Shit.

I fling the aberrant plastic stick with its damn

blue plus sign at the wall. It bounces off the gray marble with a *ping* and clatters on the floor as if it's doing a little happy dance. Mocking me.

Then I throw up my dinner—half a package of saltines and one cup of weak English Breakfast tea—in the toilet right on top of the pee that turned the plus sign the offending blue.

Blue.

I turn on the faucet and rinse my mouth, splash water on my face.

Blue. As in baby boy?

Pressing my hand to my belly, it occurs to me for the first time that there is a little life growing inside of me.

Interloper. Gate crasher.

Poor unwanted little…baby?

My wet hands leave a big handprint on my beige slacks as if marking the spot. I press my palms over my eyes, grinding the heels of my hands into the sockets, so I won't have to look at it, as if it will clear my vision so I'll see another color on the stick.

Oops! Silly me. I'm not really pregnant.

But I am. I flush the toilet, collapse the pregnancy-test box, careful to stuff all the remnants of my clandestine science experiment back in the Walgreens bag. I hide the evidence inside my briefcase under the file for the new "Who wants to be a television commercial star" show I'm publicizing.

How in the hell did this happen?

Wait. Don't answer that. I know *how* it happened.

Just tell me— How the hell did this *happen*? I punctuate the silent question by slamming my briefcase on the cold, hard floor.

Andrew and I met in college.

When we fell in love and knew we wanted to spend the rest of our lives together we devised a plan so that we could live the life we'd always wanted.

A simple ten-step plan that required some sacrifices along the way—such as not having a whole stable full of offspring.

One child was fine.

I hear so many of my friends bemoaning the fact that their first child is an angel, but the second or third or fifth is a hellion. I see so many women whose main objective is to find someone on whom she can pawn off her kids so she can have a moment to herself—so she can go to the bathroom without someone pulling at her, demanding something of her.

What possessed them to pop out so many puppies in the first place? Each couple does not have a moral responsibility to replace themselves with a child. So I have no sympathy for Suzy Birthmore, modern-day *Woman Who Lives in the Shoe*—or should I say, the *Open-Toe Pale Pink Prada Pump*—who complains that there's no rest for the breeder.

Life is much less cluttered with only one child; it's much easier to raise one child well.

Quality over quantity.

That would be a good contribution to society.

I rub my belly and realize it's anger and fear talking. I recognize it for what it is. Our Anastasia is a dream child. I just don't see how we could get so lucky twice. Not to mention it totally and completely screws up the ten-step plan we've mapped out for ourselves:

1. Graduate from college at twenty-two. Check!

2. Land great jobs—theme-park public relations for me, banking for Andrew. Check!

3. Ascend corporate ladder. Task well underway.

4. Marry at twenty-five. Check!

5. Buy perfect Stratford Park house. Check (even if it was a mid-sized fixer-upper and

wasn't directly on the chain of lakes. A house on the lake wasn't in the budget—see steps seven, eight and nine)!

6. Have *one*—let me repeat that—*one* child upon turning thirty. CHECK!

7. Work our butts off. Check!

8. Save diligently. Check!

9. Work harder/save more.

10. Anastasia will graduate from college when we turn fifty-five. Andrew and I will be free to enjoy early retirement.

Do you see mention of a second child?

No.

That's why Andrew got a vasectomy.

How in the hell am I going to tell him I'm pregnant?

Barbara

We're barely inside the house when Burt starts spitting words at my back. "What the hell is Margaret Woodall doing in this house?"

Lord, I knew he'd be in a snit. I keep walking into the kitchen, weighing my words as I open the refrigerator and pull out the potatoes I peeled earlier and the London broil I'd set to marinate this morning.

Only then do I turn and look him square in the eyes, putting on a cheerful face, hoping to set the tone.

"She and Sarah are staying with us for a while." I set the French-white Corning Ware baking dishes on the counter so the food can come to room temperature. "Won't it be lovely to have them here? Sarah and Mary Grace are already fast friends. So nice to have her cousin here to play with."

He knits his brows and glares at me as if I'm an idiot. "Why didn't you tell me they were coming?"

Instead of answering him, I pull my *Better Homes and Gardens* cookbook from the shelf over by the door and busy myself looking up a recipe for au gratin potatoes.

"How long are they staying?"

"As long as they need to."

"In other words, they're moving in? That's why you put them in the carriage house."

I close the cookbook and flash a smile at him as if the thought hadn't occurred to me, as if he'd invented the very idea himself and it was genius—pure genius. "I suppose they are." Then I stab the big hunk of meat with a fork and turn it over to distribute the marinade. The tang of balsamic vinegar, onion, garlic and rosemary fresh from my herb garden wafts up to comfort me. I inhale a steadying breath of it, hoping the aroma will quiet the palpitations dancing beneath my breastbone.

"When was this decided?"

I glance up and see him glaring at me, agitated, as if he's waiting for the punch line to an absurd joke that he's the butt of and doesn't appreciate very much.

I squat down and pull out the stockpot from the cabinet, then turn my back on him as I draw water to boil the potatoes.

His hand is on my arm, gripping me a little too tightly. "I asked you a question, Barbara."

I jerk out of his vice grip and glare right back at him, sending the message that this arrangement is not negotiable. No way. No how. But I soften my tone before I speak.

"All that matters is that Margaret and Sarah are here now. We're not turning them away. They need family after all they've been through losing Tim. Burt, we are Margaret's people. We're all the family she's got."

"Family? Since when? You haven't talked to Margaret in years. And if you're so damned concerned about *your people*, what about me, Barbara? I'm your family. In case you've forgotten, I'm your husband, the person who works his ass off to pay the bills."

I turn off the faucet and heft the big pot out of the sink. He has to jump out of my way to avoid me ramming into him as I make my way to the range.

"I cannot believe you didn't at least give me the courtesy of discussing this with me before you invited them to move in. It's all I can do to support us without you takin' in strays."

I look at him square in the eyes and a little voice deep down inside of me whispers, *I can't stand his face or the sound of his voice.*

"I beg your pardon. I will thank you to not refer to my niece as a *stray*. Burt, you're simply being ridiculous. They'll be out in the carriage house. You won't even know they're here."

I salt the water and dump the dish of peeled potatoes into the pot. The water splashes in a satisfying way that punctuates my statement.

"There is nothing ridiculous about my not wanting Leila's daughter in *my house*."

I crank the knob, coaxing the gas burner to flame. The old range clicks ten times before it ignites, as if it's reminding me to hold my tongue before I mouth off and say something rash like, *It's not your house, you jackass. It's mine. Or—*

"What's the matter, Burt? Afraid you might see something you like?" I point a finger at him and get right in his face. "Well, I'll tell you something right now, mister. Fool me once shame on *you*. Fool me twice—" I shake my head. "No, you won't fool me twice. There will be no third chances. That's all there is to it. And don't you forget that."

He takes a step back looking flummoxed, standing there with his mouth gaping wide open as if I've rendered him speechless. Imagine that, little ol' me shutting the mouth of this lawyer who always has an answer for everything.

The spell of silence only lasts a few seconds. Then his eyes narrow and darken. I see his jaw working as if he's grinding his molars to powder. "For your information, I had someone interested in renting the carriage house. Someone who actually wanted to give us money in exchange for the electricity they'll be using and the space they'll be taking up."

I put my hands on my hips.

"Well, fancy that, Burt. Are you the pot or the kettle today? Because just a few minutes ago you were pretty damn adamant about us giving each other the courtesy of discussing potential renters *before* we invited them to move in. I don't recall you giving me that courtesy."

He's picking at the grout between the tiles on the counter. As I take a jar of pickled beets from the pantry, I wonder if he even heard me.

"Property taxes are due, Barb. Do you have the money to pay them? Because I don't."

I shoot him a look suitable for how utterly ridiculous that question is. "Well, maybe I should get a job."

He ignores that one. My heart beats like a big bass drum.

"I'm strapped, Barbara. Maxed out with bills and upkeep on this place and college tuition for the kids. So unless you've stashed away several thousand dollars, Maggie has to be willing to match what this guy is willing to pay— Or is she expecting a free ride just like her mother always did?"

The bastard just doesn't know when to quit. To him this is a challenge. A line in the sand. A gauntlet he's thrown down to make me retreat. And you'd think that after forty years of marriage he'd know me better.

"Now you listen here. I'm only going to say this once—" A strange jarring sensation in my chest nearly knocks me off my feet. I grab the edge of the counter with one hand for support, the other holding steady to the jar of beets.

"What's the matter with you?" Burt asks, his words peppered with annoyance.

"Nothing. I just had a…a spell. I'm fine now."

Burt looks at me warily, as if he's assessing whether this is a ploy, if I'm being a big drama queen since he's fighting mean.

I draw in a slow breath through my nose, exhale audibly through my clenched teeth. I shake the jar of beets at him. "Your pigheadedness only makes me all the more determined."

"Of course it does."

He gets that look of his, where the corners of his mouth turn up into a thin-lipped smile, but his eyes are hateful. It's a creepy, passive-aggressive incongruence that makes me ill. Makes me think that this must be what it's like to talk to the devil.

But, no. It's just my husband. I want to wipe that vile smirk right off his face.

"You are not going to blame *your* mistakes on that innocent girl and her child," I hiss. "She has done nothing wrong and she is welcome in my home."

"She's not innocent. It's in her blood, Barbara."

That lowlife son of a— I see red. Literally. The fringes of my vision get all fuzzy and crimson and I nearly choke on it. The pressure in my face and chest is like a volcano ready to explode.

"Now, you listen here. Her background is my background. Her blood is my—"

A sharp pain erupts in my chest, making me gasp, pushing me forward. The jar of beets slips from my hands and shatters on the terrazzo. I grip the counter for support and stare down into the red-purple mess on the floor.

"Barbara? What's wrong with you?"

"Nothing." I spit the word at him, but he edges closer.

"Maybe I should call someone—911, or—"

"No." I wave him off. "I have guests in my home. There is no way I will be carted off to the hospital. It's just my heartburn kicking up. You make me so mad sometimes." Rubbing my chest, I feel a little foolish for putting on such a show.

"What do you want me to do?" He looks scared as he scoots a kitchen chair over for me to sit on.

I slide down onto the wicker seat, whipping the beads of sweat from my brow. "For once, just be on my side, Burt. Don't fight me over this. *That's* what I want you to do. Make Margaret and that little girl of hers feel welcome in our home. Can you do that?"

Maggie

What's the secret of long-lasting love? Does it mean that the lovers never wish for different lives? Never feel she or he made a mistake in vowing to love that partner until death separated them?

Or do they simply turn a blind eye to the nagging doubts intrinsic to marriage, dig in their heels and resolve to stay for the long haul no matter the cost or sacrifice?

I wish I knew the answer.

I met and married Tim within a year of Mama killing herself; a few years later I had a daughter of my own and tried my best not to look back. Like most marriages, our relationship had its share of challenges. Well, I suppose it doesn't matter now.

Last night, as I sat at the dinner table with Barbara and Burt, who have been married for as long as I've been alive, I wondered what our marriage would have been like in the later years had Tim survived. It's still hard to believe that he didn't trust me enough to confide in me about the problems he was having with the business. I found out in the months after his death as I sifted through the rubble of our finances.

How could I have not known?

Stupid me. Safe in my cocoon. I'd finally found someone to take care of me.

As Barbara and Burt sat at the dinner table as they have, I'm sure, many nights over the course of their long marriage—being there, but not really being in the moment—I couldn't help but wonder how does love, or more specifically marriage, survive the long haul, especially if one partner keeps secrets?

I sensed tension between them. Maybe it was just my imagination. Maybe was just a typical night in the life of the eternally pledged.

Burt was mostly quiet through dinner. He mumbled a cordial hello to Sarah and me, then sat hunched over the delicious meal Barbara had prepared, mentally closed. Barbara, however, chattered enough for both of them.

I heard somewhere that as couples age, they lose

the ability to hear each other. Maybe that's the key to survival?

Burt, present in body, but mentally absent. Barbara, animated and flushed, carrying on as if he weren't even there.

Tiny beads of moisture glistened on her forehead and perspiration stains seeped through her blouse. She blamed it on hot flashes and fanned herself as she talked about a life that seemed separate from her husband's—the spring-break trip she and Mary Grace would take; her garden; how she'd love to remodel her kitchen; the cookbook she'd love to write; the Stratford Park Middle School PTA, of which she's vice president/president elect.

I'm registering Sarah for school today—at Barbara's insistence, of course.

"Honey, there's nothing for you to do hanging around here all day," she said to an indifferent Sarah. "Heck, it'll be even worse boring than this dinner tonight. You'll have so much more fun at school. In fact, how 'bout if I drive ya? Y'all, me and Mary Grace'll just hop in the car and go get you signed up. It'll be fun."

I wanted to tell Barbara it wasn't necessary. Really. She needn't put herself out by driving us.

And she needn't make such an effort to fill the silence. Those quiet spaces in between sentences are my favorite part of the conversation. I've always thought the truth lies in those rests. It's in these quiet spaces that the truth manifests, that the mind registers a pure thought—*I agree with what she said*, or *That person is lying*, or *Yes, there's definitely tension in that marriage*—even if it's for a nanosecond—before decorum wrestles it to the mat and truth is replaced by what is socially acceptable.

Pinned by decorum, I decided Barbara and Burt's marriage was none of my business and that it would be rude to refuse her offer to drive us to school.

So here we are the morning after the first night in our new home, doing our best to establish a new routine—much to Sarah's dismay.

"Mom. We haven't even been here twenty-four hours. Why can't I wait until next week to start school?"

I pour some cereal that Barbara left us into a bowl and set it in front of Sarah for her to add her own milk. "Because today is Tuesday. You shouldn't miss an entire week."

She frowns. "I could help you put things away."

I waver on this one and turn my back to her as I

weigh the pros and cons of letting her stay home. But she must mistake my silence for an answer.

"God, Mom, why not? You're so mean."

Her words bore under my skin and threaten to push me into anger. But I won't go there. The old me would have. She would have turned around and put that little girl in her place—let her know in no uncertain terms that her attitude is not acceptable, but I can't do that now. I'm not going to start the first day in our new house with a fight. I can, however, insist it's better to get into a new routine.

"Well, if you believe I'm so mean, I suppose you'll have much more fun making new friends at your new school, than staying home with me."

She rolls her eyes and shoves the cereal bowl away. It spins in the middle of the table as she scoots back her chair with an abrupt motion.

"Aren't you going to eat? You're going to get hungry before lunchtime."

"I have no appetite." She slams her bedroom door. "And I have nothing to wear," she yells so I can hear it through the closed door.

I stand in the small kitchen straddling indecision. Am I doing the right thing? The movers won't be here until tomorrow. Maybe I should give her a day to get acclimated. But somehow I know that if I do, it won't make her any happier. Yes, better we both have some space today.

Twenty minutes later, we pile into Barbara's Volvo station wagon.

She looks better this morning, rested and refreshed. Her thick silver hair freshly washed and framing her fleshy face. Her pretty blue eyes, rimmed in liner and mascara, sparkle as she bids us a good morning and tells everyone to buckle up.

Back in North Carolina I used to love to watch cooking shows. I thought she looked like that Food Network host Paula Deen. The resemblance really was uncanny.

The school is farther away than what I expected. Barbara says the county built it to accommodate the influx of nouveaux riches moving into this area that used to be exclusively old money. As we drive along, things look strange. Underneath, it's the same place I grew up, but on the surface it's different. As if a brand-new generation of inhabitants have invaded the place.

"They tore down the old Stratford Junior High where you went to school." Barbara points at a vacant lot with a Conrad Contractors sign sticking out of the ground. "The city sold the property to a developer." Barbara shakes her head. "That's prime real estate. I heard he's gonna cram a bunch of huge houses on that lot and sell them for millions. And people are buying them as fast as he can build them."

I nod and gaze at the empty lot. If I squint my eyes, I can see ghosts of the past milling about the phantom buildings—the lockers, the old concrete basketball court. All gone now. Not that I'm nostalgic over it. In fact, it makes it a little easier to take Sarah to a different school. It just makes me realize how much Stratford has changed in my absence.

Barbara merges into traffic on Jewell Avenue. "It's a long haul out to the new school, but Sarah can ride the bus with Mary Grace. They pick them up right outside the house."

I glance back at Sarah, who is staring out the window as Mary Grace hums a little tune.

"The kids at school are mean," says Mary Grace.

Barbara adjusts the rearview mirror toward the back seat. "What kind of thing is that to say on Sarah's first day, missy?"

"It's the truth, Mama."

The school sits behind a tall brick wall with a wrought-iron gate. The two-story, early American architecture is unlike any public school I've ever seen; certainly a far cry from the concrete block, one-story institutions with open-to-the-element corridors that the county constructed when I went to junior high.

"We have arrived," says Barbara.

And how.

She pulls into a parking space, then leads the way to the reception desk, just inside the front door like a sentry guarding the main hall. Anyone who wishes access to Stratford Middle School must first gain entrance.

The gatekeeper, a fine-boned woman with short dark hair, regards me suspiciously until Barbara introduces me.

Her name is Judy. She's the school office manager. I have a feeling nothing gets by Judy.

Mary Grace hugs her mother and Sarah goodbye and kind of half waves at me, then heads to class.

"Have a good day, M.G. Maybe I'll see you around."

Barbara laughs. "M.G.?"

"Yeah," says Sarah. "She likes me to call her that."

"Well, I think that's just great."

Sarah wanders over to look at some teacher photos hanging on the wall across from the desk.

The place still smells new—that freshly built smell of construction, paint and floor wax comingling with simmering school lunch. There's a trophy case to the right down the hall a bit; on the left is a set of double doors with a brass plaque that says Library. At the end of the long main hall is an elaborate staircase with swarms of teenagers traveling up and down.

The place buzzes with snatches of conversation and laughter, movement and the sound of the glass front doors opening and shutting, letting in intermittent clips of car engines and the occasional honk of a horn. People are everywhere—kids hanging out and talking; adults who I assume are teachers rush about with purpose; a group of four blond women each wearing large diamond rings and expensive-looking tennis outfits.

My God, they all look alike. How do they do that?

Barbara follows my gaze to the women. "Oh, I see you've located the *Stratford Wives*."

I have to bite my lips to keep from laughing. "The *Stratford Wives*? Oh my God, that's perfect. Who are they?"

"They think they're the queens of the universe, if

that tells you anything. In reality, they're just a clique of spoiled rich men's wives who don't realize high school ended more years ago than they can probably count."

"Barbara!" I am completely taken aback by this side of her. "I had no idea you could be so catty."

Stratford Park was full of old money when I was growing up here, but we never had *Stratford Wives*. My, my, how things have changed.

"Oh, honey, stick with me. You ain't seen nothing yet. Oh! Oh, that one over there." She lowers her voice conspiratorially and nods to a heavyset mousy woman with brown hair and glasses who is logging something into a notebook on a table under a Volunteer banner. "That's Connie Claxton, archenemy of the *Stratford Wives* and anybody else who dares look crosswise at her precious little brat."

"Claxton? Any relation to the Claxton fruitcake empire?"

"No, I believe the Claxton company is actually named after the city in Georgia. But Connie Claxton is a fruitcake all right. Oh, and Chloe's a seventh grader, you'd best warn Sarah to steer clear. She'll probably try to glom onto her. She doesn't have any friends."

I raise my eyebrows at her and try to keep my voice light. "Isn't that a little harsh?"

Barbara raises her eyebrows back at me. "Chloe and Connie are like pit bulls, they seem nice and maybe even playful at first, but they turn on you in a heartbeat. Believe you me, I am the first one to stand up for a child, but Connie and Chloe are a piece of work. The rules apply to everyone but them, but she's the first to scream if she thinks she's been wronged. I've had my share of Connie encounters and she got Anastasia Deveraux, the little neighbor girl who lives across the street, called down to the principal's office claiming the girl was a threat to her daughter's safety. You know once anyone raises the safety flag the principal has a duty to act on it. Ana may be a little full of herself because she's a popular girl, but she's no more a threat to anyone's safety than you are. Her mother, Elizabeth, was *mad* as a wet cat. It turns out it was all over Anastasia not wanting to sit with Chloe in study hall. Anastasia simply doesn't like that child because she's a mean, spoiled little brat who always has to have her way. From what I understand, very few of the kids like her because of how she treats them. Her mother doesn't help matters. Connie thinks she can bully her way to making people like Chloe. It's really sad. Oh, God, here she comes."

Barbara turns and busies herself, but Connie marches right up to her.

"Barbara, I need a word with you."

I actually see Barbara bristle.

"Connie Claxton. What can I do for you?"

Connie pushes her glasses up on her nose. "You can get your daughter under control."

Barbara cuts her gaze to me for an I-told-you-so moment then looks back at Connie. "What, pray tell, is Mary Grace doing that needs to be controlled?"

Barbara's voice is dripping with sarcasm and I don't know whether to laugh or turn and walk away, the scene is that unbelievable.

"She was laughing at Chloe in the library. If I didn't know better, I might think this was harassment. But considering the source, I suppose that would be silly."

My jaw drops at this dig at Mary Grace's disability. I'm sure Barbara is seething.

"She's a child, Connie. Children laugh. Laughter does not hurt anyone."

"I know that. She's a *special* child, she's not capable of physically hurting anyone. What I'm saying, Barbara, is there's no reason you can't teach her some manners."

For a second I fear Barbara is going to slug her. I want to slug her. I can't believe someone could be so low.

"Why don't you set the example and teach your little Chloe some manners? Maybe it will help her get along better, bless her little heart."

Connie huffs off.

"So there you go," says Barbara. "That's Connie Claxton."

I start the paperwork to enroll Sarah. But there's a slight snag when Judy asks for an official document to prove that I reside in the school zone.

"Don't you have a lease agreement or an electricity bill?" Judy says. "Something that shows you're official?"

"Certainly not," Barbara snaps. "I will not charge my niece rent to live with me. You're just going to have to take my word for it."

Judy smiles apologetically, clearly at a loss for what to do, clearly wanting to accommodate Barbara.

"I'll have to make some calls. But let me see what I can do. Why don't you and umm…" she glances at the paperwork "...*Sarah*. Why don't you and Sarah have a seat over there? This may take a few minutes, Mrs. Woodall."

Mrs. Woodall.

The words knock the breath out of me. Since Tim's death, it feels as if *Mrs. Woodall* is someone else. I have no idea who I am. But I nod anyway.

Sarah sits on a sofa across from the desk.

Barbara touches my arm. "I have to go make some copies in the PTA office. Do you want to come with me?"

I glance at Sarah ensconced on the couch with her arms crossed defensively, her backpack at her feet.

"Thanks, but I'd better wait here in case they need some more information—"

"Good morning, Barbara." The only blonde in the building who is not wearing a tennis outfit walks up and touches Barbara on the arm. She's dressed in a smart black pantsuit and carries a slim briefcase, which is not big enough to hold a racket. She's almost pretty—if not for the pallor of her skin and the dark circles under her eyes that she's trying to cover up with thick concealer.

"Oh, Elizabeth, you're here. Good. I want you to

meet my niece, Margaret Woodall. She and her daughter just moved here yesterday from Asheville and will be living in the carriage house." Barbara turns to me. "Elizabeth Deveraux and her husband Andrew live across the street. They have a seventh-grader named Anastasia. I'm sure she and Sarah will just love each other. We'll have to get them together once you're settled in."

Elizabeth smiles. "We'll have you all over for dinner next week."

"Thank you. That would be wonderful."

"Barbara, do you have a minute for me to go over something before tonight's meeting? The music department changed their request for funds and I want to make sure you agree with my counterproposal before we put it to a vote tonight."

"Sure, I do. Margaret, honey, I'm going to talk to Elizabeth and then go make my copies. Hopefully, by then they'll have everything in order. She's enrolling Sarah in school. You know how those things go nowadays."

The two women disappear behind a door that's next to the front desk. I sit down next to Sarah, who is busy watching Stratford's middle schoolers stream down the main hall. My daughter looks so fragile sitting there in her pink blouse and slim denim capris; her fine-boned features devoid of makeup and enhanced by the way she's swept her blond hair off her face into a ponytail.

I have a sudden flashback of what it's like to be thirteen years old, on the outside looking in. It wasn't until Tim and I moved to Asheville that I began to feel part of something—part of a community. I want to hug her and tell her it won't always be this painful.

But I don't dare.

Soon enough she'll be in the flow, right there in the thick of things.

The kids at school are mean.

I blink away Mary Grace's words, but find myself scrutinizing the children as they walk by: a group of five girls dressed cute—one in a Hollister T-shirt, another in a Roxy—walking shoulder to shoulder, sporting pastel messenger bags slung across their chests, rather than backpacks.

They whisper and giggle.

One squeals, "No way!"

Then they whisper and giggle some more.

Mean or nice?

They're just girls. Girls being teenage girls.

Two boys stop five feet in front of us. I look to see

if they notice Sarah— Hey, she's cute and she's the new girl. There's value in being the new girl whether she realizes it or not—but they're too busy play-punching each other to look in our direction.

A man dressed in a white polo and khaki pants—probably a teacher—breaks up their roughhousing.

"Don't you boys have somewhere to be?" he says. "First bell rings in seven minutes. If you're not in your seats, you're tardy."

Strict. Not necessarily a bad thing.

The boys move on.

As the throng of children starts to thin, I can see out the glass doors to the car line where parents are dropping off the last-minute arrivals.

Mercedes.

BMW.

Jaguar.

Lexus.

This is public school? A different breed than I've ever known.

"Mom, if they don't hurry and figure this out I'm going to be tardy."

I touch Sarah's arm—that soft, smooth skin. "It'll be okay. The teacher will understand since it's your first day and all."

NANCY ROBARDS THOMPSON   61

She yanks her arm away. "How would you like it if you had to walk in in the middle of class?"

She's so angry and I don't know how to help her. It breaks my heart a little more because I know that feeling of just wanting to disappear. I wish there was something I could do to comfort her.

"I'll check on things."

By the time the administrators figure out what to do with us, school's been in session for more than an hour.

"You'll go right to second period since first hour is already over." Judy glances at Sarah's list of classes, then hands her the schedule. "Geography is your second class. It's in room 234. Just go upstairs and turn left, you'll see the room on the right. Your mom can walk you to class if you want."

Sarah flashes me a *don't even think about it look.* My heart sinks, but I bolster myself with the thought that at least she has enough confidence to navigate these strange halls alone.

"See ya." She turns to go without a hug. I reach out for her, but she's already gone.

"I'll pick you up right here after school, okay?"

She doesn't look back. Just walks straight ahead down that long, empty hallway.

CHAPTER 5

Elizabeth

I hadn't planned on telling Andrew about the baby today. But I awoke this morning knowing I couldn't put it off. Just as this child is growing in my belly, the need to tell him has gotten so huge, I feel as if I'm about to burst.

Before he left for work I told him I was going in late because I had some PTA business to take care of at school and asked him to meet me for lunch.

"What, like a date in the middle of the day?" he says, kissing me on the neck.

"Yeah, like a…date."

He slips his hands inside my robe. "Or maybe I could come home for lunch." Kisses me full on the mouth. Queasiness crests and rocks me like a little boat on the ocean. I pull away, weighing whether I'll need to make a run for the bathroom. But the rebuffed look on Andrew's face jolts me back to level ground.

Why wait until lunch to tell him? Just do it now.

But he's already walking out the door, murmuring, "See you at eleven-thirty."

I arrive at Dexter's a little early, feeling a little better until I get a whiff of the catch of the day. The lunchtime din is at an all-time high and I wonder if I'll be able to last. The server brings a basket of bread and water with the menus. I nibble on the bread and try to tell myself that it's mind over matter. I didn't have a lick of morning sickness with Anastasia. She's been a model child. I wonder if the way I feel is any indication of this child's personality—

The thought floors me and I realize that this is the first time I've actually thought of this little interloper as a…human being.

Oh, God, what are we going to do? I don't want another child.

I sip my water and watch Andrew materialize through the crowd.

Okay, here we go. This is it.

Two women at a nearby table turn their heads to watch him as he passes. They have good taste.

With his thick, dark, curly hair and lithe runner's

build, he just seems to get better looking with age. People have said he looks like a mature Orlando Bloom. I can see the resemblance in his handsome face.

"Sorry I'm late." He kisses my cheek and pulls out the chair across from me, glancing around the crowded restaurant as he sits down. "I was tied up on the phone. Clients in Paris."

He waves at a man across the room.

"Jerry Singer with Nicholas and Anders," he says looking at Jerry not me.

For a moment, I'm afraid Jerry Singer is going to come over to our table, but the woman he's sitting with says something and draws him into the conversation.

"This was a good idea." Andrew smiles, finally focusing his attention on me for the first time since he arrived. "I'm glad you suggested it."

All traces of this morning's misunderstanding have vanished and that puts me at ease. Well, until his brows knit and he touches my hand. "Are you okay?"

I smooth my hair with my free hand. "I'm fine. Why?"

He picks up a menu and opens it, glancing up at

me. "I don't know. You just look a little pale, I guess. A little tired." He pulls his hand away and picks up the menu. "What are you going to have?"

"Your baby. I'm going to have your baby."

I can't help it. The words rush up my throat and into my mouth, the same way the bagel I tried to eat for breakfast came right back up and I couldn't stop it.

Andrew looks momentarily amused, but all too soon that melts into confusion, as if he doesn't understand.

I sit frozen. *Oh God, why did I do that?* I didn't want to say it like that. I close my eyes a moment, trying to get my bearings.

"We're pregnant, Andrew." The words are softer this time. I open my eyes to gauge his reaction. "We're going to have another baby."

He closes his menu and lays it down. His entire face is now a dark, defensive question. "There's no way. This can't be."

He sits back hard in the chair, turns to the side, rests his arm on the back of the chair and pinches the bridge of his nose.

"I know," I say, trying to comfort him. "I had the same reaction because of your vasectomy."

I'm suddenly aware that a woman who is dining solo at the table next to ours is listening. I glare at her. She has the decency to turn away.

But my husband won't look at me. Still, I know that look, that closed body language. He's not just mad, he's livid.

I didn't expect him to jump for joy. I'm not exactly thrilled either, but I never imagined he would act this way. As if it's my fault.

"Andrew, come on. I'm just as shocked as you are, but we're in this together. Talk to me."

His expression is as hard as stone. "How can *we* be having a baby if I'm shooting blanks?"

"What? What are you saying?" The pitch of my voice rises, but I don't care. "Of course *we're* pregnant. Do you think I've been having sex with another man?"

He finally looks at me. Stares me straight in the eyes and shrugs.

The server arrives at our table, and I sit there flabbergasted as Andrew gets rid of him. The woman next to us is looking at us again, but this time I don't care. All I can focus on is the way my husband is looking at me as if he's caught me in the act of infidelity.

Something inside me snaps.

I stand and grab my purse. "I am not going to sit here and plead with my *husband* to believe that I'm carrying *his* baby."

Maggie

After we leave Stratford Middle School, Barbara drops me off at home and goes to run errands. I hope she doesn't think I'm unsociable for not going with her. I just need some time to put away the things we brought with us from the car and make arrangements for a storage shed before the moving van arrives tomorrow.

I'll have to store the majority of our furniture because the carriage house is furnished. I just don't feel right asking Barbara to move her things out.

Besides, it's better this way because it reminds me this arrangement is temporary. Sarah and I can't stay here forever. Just long enough to figure out what we're going to do.

It's the first I've been alone in days and I take a moment to savor the freedom. I walk through the rooms of our little three-bedroom dollhouse, getting a feel for our new home, letting it speak to me the way old houses do.

There's no foyer. The screened front door opens right into the living room, which is complete with polished hardwood floors and a fireplace, though why one would need a fireplace in Florida baffles me. Off to the left is a tiny galley kitchen and dining alcove; to the right, a squat hallway holds the lone bathroom and our bedrooms.

It's about half the size of our house in Asheville, but the place is bright and cheerful, furnished in white wicker and shades of yellow. Generous windows in the living room invite in an abundance of light.

I'm soothed by the hominess of the place.

It's such a beautiful day, I open the front door and windows to air out the closed-up musty smell places take on when they haven't been lived in. My bedroom window looks out toward the lake. I open the blinds and stand there a minute enjoying the quiet of the house, the way the green lawn slopes down to the lake. I love the huge live oaks, the way the Spanish moss that's draped on the branches dances in the wind.

I take a long, deep breath of fresh lake air and think about getting out of the skirt and blouse I wore to the school into something more comfortable, and taking a walk before I start organizing. I'm just about to tug my blouse over my head, but I'm overcome by the strangest sensation that I'm being watched. I whirl around toward the door and shriek at the sight of someone standing in my bedroom threshold.

My hand flies to my heart as I try to still the white-hot terror that spikes the split second before I realize it's just Burt standing there.

"Oh, I'm sorry," I say, a little breathless. "I didn't hear you knock."

"Guess not."

I fully expect him to offer up an apology for scaring me or make some excuse for appearing in my bedroom door unannounced. But he just stands there with one hand braced on the doorjamb, his gaze meandering down my body in a way that's almost...creepy.

An uneasy sensation, like fingers sweeping down my spine, shakes me. I shudder at this invasion of privacy.

How long has he been there? And, oh my God, what if I'd yanked off my blouse before I turned and saw him there?

I feel violated until irritation starts a slow burn

in the far reaches of my tolerance. I don't care if he does own the place, he can't just go walking in on people like that. We need to set some boundaries.

I push past him and walk into the living room, a thousand questions rushing through my head, such as whether I should mention this to Barbara and what I'd say if I did— *Please keep your husband out of my bedroom.*

Poor Barbara.

The only thing I know for sure is that I will make a point of keeping the doors locked.

But surely, he has a key.

He follows me, unbidden, into the living room. I have the urge to keep walking right out the front door, but I don't. *No, better to face him head-on, pretend like he hasn't flustered me.*

"So Burt, what do you need?" My voice is matter-of-fact, with a little chill injected into it.

"What do I need?" He arches a graying brow, as if he's ready to let loose some smart-ass comment. But instead, he scratches his head of thick silver hair and makes himself at home on the sofa. His gut strains the buttons of his short-sleeved madras plaid shirt as it laps over his khaki pants. Watching him sit there so nonchalantly makes my skin crawl, especially the way he studies me, his eyes grazing over me the same way he did in the bedroom.

He was never very warm when I used to come here as a kid, but I never remembered him being so creepy. My memories of him are neutral. Almost nonexistent. As if he were there, but not there.

More than a little unnerved, I cross my arms over my front.

"So, Margaret, what is it you're planning on doing with yourself now that you're back in Florida?"

His question throws me. "I beg your pardon?"

He smirks. "Now that Sarah's in school all day, what do you plan on doing with your time?"

I don't quite know what to say other than *None of your business.* So I say nothing.

"I just thought you might be thinking about getting a job. A friend of mine needs a pretty girl to work in his office. I'll bet you'd be real good at it."

The stream of light that was filtering in through the living-room window dims and the sheer curtains billow on a cool breeze that rolls in.

"Are there qualifications for the job beyond being a *pretty girl?*"

He snorts. "I have no idea. You'll have to call him and set up an interview and find out."

"Well, I probably can't help out your *friend* right now. I'm going to need some time to get settled in. In fact, I was just heading out. I don't mean to be rude, but—"

"I'll be frank, Margaret." He runs a hand over his close-trimmed beard. "I had to turn away a renter because my wife informed me after the fact that she'd promised this place to you."

Oh. So this is about money. It always comes down to money, doesn't it?

"It's amazing how much it costs for people to stay out here in this house. Seems like the cost of electricity and water just keeps going up and up. I don't know if Barbara told you, but it's all we can do to keep this place—it's so important to her, being in her family so long…"

It was my family, too.

"…that's why we generally need to rent out the carriage house."

My heart sinks. I didn't expect a free ride. At least not forever. I had hoped I'd have a couple of months to get my feet on the ground, find a job and an affordable place of our own. Tim left us in such a financial mess that I barely have anything left of the proceeds from the sale of the house. There was no insurance money. In the silence between the notes of sorrow, a different kind of ache surfaces. One that berates me for losing myself in Tim, for living inside my insular cocoon and letting him support me. For taking no interest in the finances and being oblivious to how much in debt we were.

"How much rent do you want?" My voice is even and cool.

A slow smile spreads over his face. He bites his fat bottom lip then makes a clucking noise.

"Well, now, I suppose we could negotiate a fair price that suits everyone involved."

It's not so much what he says but how he says it that makes me uncomfortable. I turn away from him and grab my purse and car keys off the table next to the chair.

"Right. What sort of *fair price* would suit you and Barbara?"

He doesn't even flinch at the mention of her name.

I open the screen door. "I have to go out for a while. When I get back, why don't we discuss a *fair price* with her, okay?"

"I'm leaving today for China. Business trip. While I'm gone, you think about what you're willing to offer."

I can't get out of that place fast enough. My old Toyota bumps and shakes as I drive a little too fast over the gravel driveway. I nearly bottom out as I turn onto the road.

I don't care. I just want to get away from him. I'm stopped at a red light about three miles away before I realize I have no idea where I'm going.

Getting Sarah enrolled in school today, I'd started feeling as if we might be able to make a home here at the Villa Magnolia, even if it was temporary.

With this conversation, all that vanished.

I glance at my watch. It's a few minutes before eleven. I don't have to get Sarah until three.

I have between now and then to figure out how much I'm going to tell Barbara about my encounter with Burt.

One thing's certain. I need to find us a new place before he gets back.

The car seems to drive itself to the cemetery where Mama's buried. Once inside the gates, I maneuver my way to the general area of her grave. I've only been here once. The day we buried her. I hope I can remember where it is.

I vaguely remember that it was about midway down next to a skinny flowering tree—crepe myrtle, maybe?

Who knows if the tree is even still there? I notice a mausoleum that wasn't there last time. And that they've started allowing standing headstones rather than the flat grave markers that were so much easier to mow over. I locate the crepe myrtle, which is full of deep pink blooms today, and make my way in a straight line to her grave.

I'm surprised by how easily I find it. I am alone in the cemetery, except for the sound of a lawn mower off in the distance. The smell of freshly cut grass perfumes the air. I lower myself onto the ground, tucking my legs up underneath my skirt, and finger one of the red silk roses from the large bouquet in the metal vase attached to the grave marker. Barbara must have brought them here.

Blades of cut grass are scattered over her name-plate like green confetti and I brush them aside so I can read it.

Leila Cambridge 1941–1982 Daughter, Sister, Mother.
The word *wife* is conspicuously missing and it makes me think first of Tim, the missing husband, and then of my missing father, whoever in the world he might be.

For one reckless second I wish I knew him. I wish he were here with me. If he was, maybe Mama wouldn't have done what she did and there wouldn't be a reason to be sitting in this cemetery.

Ah, but wishes, what good are they?

The last time I made a wish was on that hot August day of Mama's funeral. Right there in the season of heat and rain, I wished—no it was more like a promise—I *promised* myself I'd never, ever come back to the town where she died. That way, I could pretend she was just away. Gone on a long trip, somewhere fancy, with my father.

I suppose that's a trait I inherited from Mama, that ability to pretend. She always lived in her head too much. Sometimes I could be sitting right next to her and she might as well have been in Egypt.

When the bills needed paying, the dishes needed cleaning, the laundry needed minding—sorting, washing, drying, folding.

Endless.

Relentless.

Never ever done.

She would just slip away.

Pour herself a bourbon and drift away.

I made that promise to myself all those years ago, to never set foot in this town again, but here I am. If there's one thing I know now it's you should never say never.

Never is a wicked, unforgiving taskmaster. He slaps you in the face and makes you eat your words—every single stale crumb, sparing only a splash of humility to wash it down.

The sun is hot. So I don't stay at the cemetery long. I get in my car and head toward the hardware store with a mission of getting a couple of those slide locks for the doors.

I have to do something to ensure Burt doesn't make an encore appearance—especially after he acted like such a bastard. He'd know damn well and good why I put the new locks on the doors. Explaining to Barbara, however, would be another matter. I'll think of something. Unless I wanted to take a chance of her telling me I had to find a new place to live, I'd better not mention what transpired with Burt. I mean, what woman, even if she was as good as gold, would let an outsider stay if she knew it was going to cause problems?

Plus, he's the kind of man who would deny everything and, technically, I suppose he didn't come right out and say anything off color. It was all in the delivery, all in the subjective gray area.

I have to park on the other end of the avenue from the hardware store, but the walk will be good for me.

I'm about halfway to my destination when my cell phone rings. My heart lurches in my chest. The only ones who have the number are Sarah and the school.

I stop walking to fish the phone out of my purse. I check the number but I don't recognize the caller. I flip it open. "Hello?

"May I speak to Mrs. Woodall, please?"

"This is she."

"Yes, hello, this is Paige Farmer, the guidance counselor at your daughter Sarah's school. I think we have a little problem. Could you come in for a conference, please?"

Barbara

Sprinkled among the humdrum are defining moments that change our life. We're never given notice of them and often we don't even realize they've happened until they're long gone. But when I open Burt's suitcase to toss in the new tube of Crest I purchased today at the Winn-Dixie and find the black leather bustier with matching thong and the little vibrator, I recognize a defining moment is all but slapping me up the side of the head.

The goodies aren't exactly lying right on top, I have to dig a little to find them, but Lord have mercy when I do....

I have a little dizzy spell and have to sit down for a minute.

I've been married to Burt for forty years and have never once had the inclination to snoop in my husband's things. I don't know what possessed me, but I just knew if I looked I'd find all I needed to know.

I'm brokenhearted for about one minute. Then I get mad. Furious, vengeful mad.

A million ugly thoughts race through my head. I think about cutting little holes in the cups of the bustier or snipping the butt floss off the G-string. But that'd give him warning that I was onto him. And I want to blindside him when he gets home. Although, if I knew how to rig that vibrator to electrocute, I'd do it in a heartbeat. But since I don't know how, I do the next best thing. I decide to torture him with the unknown. I take the trashy things out of his suitcase so that when he gets to China and goes looking for them they'll be gone and he'll think, *Oh, shit, I could have sworn I put those things in my suitcase. God, what the hell happened to them?*

With my luck he'll probably think someone in customs stole them. But even if he panics for one minute worrying if *old-timer's disease* has set in and maybe he carelessly laid them out, say, on the foot of the bed, and *thought* he put them in his suitcase— Maybe he did. Maybe he didn't. Maybe he went off and left them on the foot of the bed but he can't remember because of his *old timer's*—it'll be worth it.

Because what's an old man like him doing with trashy lingerie and sex toys anyway?

Never mind. I don't want to know.

'Cause now I know all I need to know.

Elizabeth

It's been three days since I told Andrew about the baby. We haven't said much to each other since then. It's obvious he doesn't want this child.

Neither did I. Not in the beginning. But since I've had a chance to digest the news... I don't know.

I'm sitting in the lobby of my ob-gyn, Dr. Riggs, waiting for them to call me back for my appointment. The same ob-gyn I've been going to since we moved to Stratford Park after college.

Dr. Riggs delivered Anastasia. It's a comfort to have such an established relationship with him. He will be the voice of reason.

I glance around at five other women waiting. Three are in various stages of pregnancy. One looks as though she could go into labor any minute. The others aren't so far along.

I don't know about the remaining two. Maybe they're in the blissful beginning stages of a wanted pregnancy. They probably haven't suffered a lick of morning sickness. Their husbands are probably ecstatic.

Or at least talking to them.

One of the few things Andrew did say to me was that he'd meet me here. I pacified myself by trying to believe that was a step in the right direction.

If he shows.

I pick up a parenting magazine and thumb through it.

Of course he'll show.

If he said he'll show, he'll show.

An ad featuring a family of four gives me pause. A mother, father and older sister smile down at an adorable bald baby, toothless and grinning, all dressed in yellow.

If I squint my eyes, I see our family in that photo. But the squinting makes me feel vaguely nauseated. I toss aside the magazine, lean my head back, resting it against the wall.

Oh, this can't be happening.

Linking my fingers over my belly, I close my eyes and remind myself that it *is* happening.

This is real life. Andrew and I have to come to some sort of conclusion together.

I've always been a firm believer in a woman's right to choose, never wanting anyone to dictate what I can and can't do with my body. The government and the radical right don't know what's right for my family and me.

I open my eyes and glance at the expectant women. Faced with a decision where I actually need to exercise the choice, it astounds me that the choice seems very narrow.

My child is growing inside me. Our child. Like Anastasia is our child. Even though I wouldn't *choose* to have another baby, every time I've looked at Anastasia since that damned positive double-blue line appeared on the pregnancy test, I think this baby will grow up to be a person just like her.

Could I bear never to see her or him? Never to know that child?

Every time I saw a kid about the same age as this one, I'd wonder. Would it have been a boy or a girl? What color hair? Blond like Anastasia and me or dark like Andrew?

What about the color of the baby's eyes?

Why is this happening?

I am a wreck. Since this alien being has invaded my body, I've been reduced to a hormone-ridden wreck. Me, the one who has on occasion brought grown men to tears in the boardroom, sitting here getting all teary and sentimental at the sight of bald babies.

This can't be happening.

A door on the wall across from me opens. "Elizabeth Deveraux?" The nurse is calling me back. I turn and glance through the glass front doors out into the narrow strip of parking lot visible from my vantage point.

No Andrew.

As I stand up and gather my purse, preparing to march toward the smiling nurse, I look at my watch.

Four twenty-five. Andrew knew the appointment was at four.

He's not coming.

Oh, my God. I can't do this alone.

"Right this way," says the nurse.

Before the door closes behind me, I glance back one more time, hoping to see Andrew sprinting up the walk. But the view is as empty as the hollow in my heart.

The solid wood door shuts with a click.

He's not coming.

It's all I can do to keep myself from bursting into tears.

The nurse looks at my chart and beams at me. "So you think you're pregnant? Congratulations. How wonderful."

We go through the standard rigmarole of my peeing in a cup, the nurse weighing me and taking my blood pressure.

She picks up a small stick she'd dipped in my urine sample. "Yep, you've definitely got a baby on the way."

Ugggh.

She's in the process of ushering me into an examination room when I hear a voice behind me.

"Elizabeth, I'm here."

Andrew. *Oh, thank God. I can't do this without you.*

"So this must be a surprise," says Dr. Riggs, testing the waters. "It doesn't happen often, but vasectomies can reverse themselves even this late in the game."

I want to hug the doctor for bringing it up. The subject has been living between us like the elephant in the room that no one wants to talk about. *Just how did I get pregnant given Andrew's vasectomy?* Other than the comment about him shooting blanks, he never came right out and asked if I'd cheated, but isn't that what it boiled down to? If he was shooting blanks, then who did plant this seed?

"How long has it been since the vasectomy, Andrew?" The doctor flips through my chart.

"Ten years," Andrew supplies.

"Late vasectomy failure may occur because of persistent sperm and spontaneous recanalization. I'd like for you to make an appointment with a urologist to check into it."

Andrew nods, but doesn't look at me. Even so, I can see the set of his jaw starting to relax. I can virtually hear him breathing again for the first time in three days. That feeling that my husband wants to pin a big red A on my chest disappates as Dr. Riggs further explains how things like this do happen without adultery or immaculate conception.

After the routine pelvic exam, the doctor informs us that I am about ten weeks along.

I feel a bit more even-keeled with Andrew holding my hand as the doctor starts what he calls "genetics counseling."

"Because of your age, you are at increased risk of having a baby with a genetic disorder or other congenital problems. I'd like to perform a chorionic villus sampling or CVS to alert us to any potential problems. Amniocentesis is usually done at about fifteen weeks. I'd like to do the CVS because I can do it now and, worst-case scenario, should there be questionable results it will afford you more time to make any decisions you'll need to make."

Excuse me?

I've been so caught up in the shock of the unexpected pregnancy that I haven't even given any thought to the possibility of complications.

But I am forty-three. No spring chicken.

"If you'd like, we can do the test now or if you need some time to think about it, you can come back another day."

I glance at Andrew, hoping he'll throw me a lifeline, that look that says everything will be okay, we'll get through this together, but he's standing there, tight-lipped, staring at Dr. Riggs as he moves forward explaining the risks and benefits of the CVS test.

I'm still stuck back at the worst-case-scenario part…where he says *he's affording us more time to make any decisions we might need to make*.

He makes this baby sound so disposable. If the results aren't to our liking, we can just throw it away.

The thought makes me sick.

Andrew squeezes my hand. "Yes. We absolutely need to do this now. You see, we haven't even decided if we want to keep it. We decided early on that we only wanted one child, hence the vasectomy…and now our daughter is thirteen. So you can understand why we would hesitate."

A strange heat grows inside me, like a hot-air balloon of hysteria rising in my throat.

Andrew talks on and on and on "…I mean, I can't imagine starting all over again with the sleepless nights and diapers. We both work. I just don't know…"

I can't speak. I can't force words past the huge balloon that's now lodged in the back of my throat.

"Let's go ahead with the test," Andrew says. "We can decide if we're going to keep the baby after we get the results."

Dr. Riggs says it will take about ten days to get the test results. As Andrew and I walk out of his office, I make up my mind that during the wait, I will not put myself and my family through hell wondering what fate holds for us.

Andrew is just starting to come to terms with the reality that we're pregnant, that this is in fact his baby.

One step at a time.

As he walks me to my car, I say, "Let's just try and get back to normal, okay?"

He opens the door for me. "I'd like that." The words sound stiff, but it's a step in the right direction. I'll take it.

"I have an idea," he says. "Why don't we invite friends over for dinner this weekend? It'll take our mind off things and we haven't seen Rob and Blair in ages."

The thought of a dinner party feels like a one-thousand-pound weight, but I suppose we should do something to shift focus.

"There are new neighbors across the street," I say. "Barbara McMillan's niece and her daughter, who's Anastasia's age, just moved into Barb's carriage house. Let's invite them, too."

Andrew nods and then kisses me for the first time since this whole fiasco began.

Barbara

The girls arrived on Monday, and already Margaret and I are in the kitchen talking like mother and daughter as I ice a cake to take over to the Deverauxs' dinner party. More than twenty years have passed between us, but it's a comfort to know she's the same girl—save for some wear and tear around the edges and a little more wisdom in the soul. When she was itty-bitty, she used to sit right there at that table and help me roll out biscuits or spoon cookie dough onto a greased sheet when I watched her to give Leila a break.

Today, despite my mood, I've made homemade red velvet cake and my special cream-cheese icing. Cheerful, I think. I hope, because I have to do something to get my mind off what I have to do when Burt gets home. It seems we've come to the end of the line, but I haven't quite figured out how to get off the train. I only have a few days to sort things out. Tonight, I'm going to a dinner party.

Margaret watches me as I crown the confection with the sixth and final layer, slapping on a generous helping of frosting so it looks real pretty.

"I wish we could go with you tonight, Barbara, but Sarah's grounded."

I point my spatula at her. "Honey, cut that child some slack. It was just a harmless prank."

Margaret grimaces. "Lying to her teachers, claiming she only spoke French, was not a harmless prank. It made her look foolish and set her off on the wrong foot with her teachers. Do you know how mortifying it was to get called in for a conference on my daughter's first day of school?"

I suppress a smile.

"Frankly, I think it's pretty funny that she pulled it off for three hours. I'll bet if she hadn't had that dog ball of a teacher Bettina Swenson, Sarah would've fooled 'em all. Who knows how long she would've gotten away with it."

I laugh, but Margaret looks appalled.

"Barbara, this is serious."

I wave her off. "Where in the world did she learn to speak French like that anyway?"

Margaret bites her bottom lip and gets a faraway look in her eyes. "That was something she and Tim used to do. Tim said as soon as she was fluent, he'd take her to Paris."

I nod. "Honey, you've made her suffer for four days. That's long enough. Let it go. Come with me over to the Deverauxs' tonight. Burt's out of town, and I need a date. It'll give you a chance to meet the neighbors and will give that child a chance to meet the Deveraux girl and make friends."

I swirl the spatula through the icing, making pretty peaks and curlicues on the snow-white surface.

"You know what all this nonsense is about, don't you?"

Margaret gives a little sideways shrug and tilt of her head. "She misses her father. And she's mad at me for uprooting her. She doesn't want to be here—no offense."

"None taken. Sarah just needs a little extra attention. Give her a friend and you'll be doing her a lot more good than grounding her butt."

Margaret opens her mouth to say something, but stops. She sighs and messes with the fringe on the place mat. I can tell by the look on her face that there's more on her mind than Sarah's French masquerade.

I set down the spatula and lick the icing off my fingers. "You got something else on your mind you need to talk about?"

Margaret purses her lips, then smiles and she sits up straight. "I got a job."

I gasp. "You did what?"

Her smile broadens. "I got a job. Yesterday, I noticed a Help Wanted sign in the window of Jacobsons Department Store over on Park Avenue. I went in and filled out an application."

"Well, good for you."

"For once in my life, I was in the right place at

the right time. The store manager was there and I got an interview before I left. He called me this morning and offered me a job."

I rinse my hands and shake off the water. "Well, that's fabulous. What will you be selling?"

"Cosmetics."

"Oh! How fun! You'll make over three quarters of the population of Stratford Park, and you'll have to tell me all their dirty little secrets. Because you know how people start spilling their guts once you break the touch barrier."

I pull a chilled bottle of Estancia Chardonnay from the fridge and hold it up. "It's five o'clock and we need to celebrate. How about a glass of wine before we head over across the street?"

Margaret frowns. "Barbara…"

I arch a brow at her. "Do it for your daughter. So she doesn't feel like such a fish out of water."

She sighs. Rolls her eyes just like she used to when she was little.

"Okay, fine. You win. But I'll need to shower and get ready. What time do we need to be there?"

"Six-thirty. Plenty of time for a glass of wine."

I take two glasses down from the cupboard and pour the chardonnay.

"I didn't realize you were a makeup artist."

She smiles sheepishly. "I'm not. So this completely throws me. I may end up making three quarters of the Stratford Park population look like a bunch of clowns."

I set a glass in front of her. "Oh would you do that, please?"

We both laugh and I realize it's the first time I've seen her relax since she's been here. I raise my glass to her.

"To your new job. May you be very, very happy."

"Thank you."

We clink glasses.

"When do you start?"

"Monday. I wanted to take the weekend to be with Sarah. If she can ride the bus home after school, she shouldn't be alone for more than a couple of hours in the afternoon before I get home."

"I'd be happy to look in on her, or for that matter, she's welcome to come up here and play with Mary Grace— Oh, excuse me, I suppose children Sarah's age don't *play* anymore. She's welcome to *hang out* up here with us."

"Thanks. I appreciate your offer, but she'll have homework, so she'll be busy with that. Still, if she needs someone, it's nice to know you're here. We just don't want to put you out."

"Oh, don't be silly. Y'all could never put me out."

She swirls her wine and takes a sip. "While we're on the subject, I wanted to let you know that I'm looking for a place for Sarah and me."

"What?"

"I'm looking for a place and I hope to be out of your hair within the next couple of weeks."

I set down my glass. "Don't be ridiculous. *This* is your home. I know it's probably smaller than you're used to, but we have more than enough room up here and you two are always welcome."

Margaret sets down her glass, too. "Burt told me he had the opportunity to rent out the carriage house but had to let it go because of us. I'm sure I can't afford what you'd get if you rented out the place—"

Burt? "When did you talk to Burt?"

"The day I registered Sarah for school. I saw him after you dropped me off."

"*Umm-hmm.*"

Why that conniving son of a—of all the stingy, crass things to do. I get up and grab the wine bottle, so Margaret doesn't see the horns and fangs I'm sprouting. I cork the bottle and put it back in the refrigerator. He's lucky he's away on this trip to China. When he gets home, I'm fixin' to pitch one heck of a hissy fit. How dare he mention such things to Margaret?

She must sense my irritation because she changes the subject. "Now that I have a job, it won't be a problem getting a place."

"I don't want to hear another word of talk like that. You're staying right here and that's all there is to it. So don't you feel like you have to rush out because of anything ol' Burt said. He's just a man and sometimes men don't see the big picture of what's important."

I sit down at the table shaking my head, thinking about how life is always so much smoother when he's away. "Promise me, you hear?"

"But—"

"Uuutt!" I hold up my hand. "Promise me."

"I don't know. I can't promise you that right now."

We sit in the awkward silence and sip our wine.

"So are you excited about the new job?"

She shrugs. "They must have been desperate for help to practically hire me on the spot like that."

"Nonsense. They know a good thing when she walks through the door."

Margaret stares into her wineglass. "Barbara, this

is my first job." She darts me a sheepish glance. "I've always stayed at home with Sarah. Even after she got into school."

"Well, honey, I always stayed home with my kids, too. And when Mary Grace came along, well, there was no way I could work. It would have been too traumatic on everyone. Stayin' home's nothing to be ashamed of."

We're quiet for another minute.

I reach out and touch her hand. "Tootsy bell, you and me have lots in common, don't we? Stayin' home with our babies and both of us losing our mamas too early in life. I don't know about you, but it's made me a little more protective of my family. I kept my babies as close as I could for as long as I could. I wanted to be there to see all the happenings in my youngens' lives because my mama wasn't there for me."

Margaret frowns a little and picks at her cuticle. "How can two sisters be so different, Barbara? Death obviously didn't affect my mother the way it did you. Sometimes it seemed like she couldn't wait to get away from me. She finally did."

Oh, honey, there's so much about your mama you don't know. I just need to figure out how much of it I should tell you.

Maggie

I don't want to go to this dinner party tonight, but I feel as though I owe it to Barbara as much as Sarah.

I feel a little guilty for telling her about Burt asking me to pay rent. I guess I just wanted her to know what he did.

Or maybe it's more of a message to *him*, that any crap he tries to pull on me, I am not afraid to tell Barbara.

I have no problem paying rent. I just didn't like the way he went about it.

I shower quickly and twist my hair back with a clip so it looks a little more kempt than if I left it alone to let it frizz.

I turn my head to make sure the back is smooth and see a wiry sprig of white hair sticking straight out of my left temple like a faded arrow pointing west. I lean into the mirror and yank it out. *Uggh*. I need to get something done to my hair, but right now I can't afford it.

I look tired and I'm in no mood to party. Even so, I pull on a simple pair of black pants and a black tank with my silver chain belt. Do I really want to get to know the neighbors again, get involved in the community the way I did in Asheville? I don't know if I have it in me to invest that much again. Who knows where Sarah and I will end up?

But it's too late to back out now. At least tonight it is. Well, this is just dinner. I don't have to take home a doggy bag of friendship.

I knock on Sarah's closed door, hoping she's ready to go. As I feared, she's stretched out across the yellow gingham bedspread of one of the twin beds in her new room reading. She's still wearing the same jeans she's had on since this morning.

"Come on, sweetie, we need to meet Aunt Barbara and Mary Grace in ten minutes. We don't want to be late for dinner."

She doesn't look up from her book. "I thought I was grounded."

"You were, but it's been long enough."

She turns a page. "I don't want to go."

I walk in, stepping over her shoes and backpack that are littering the floor, and sit down on the edge of her bed. "I know. I don't either, but we need to do this for Aunt Barbara."

I lie down next to her and draw her close, half expecting her to squirm some space between us. But she lets her book fall to her chest and she snuggles into me. My heart swells at this unexpected closeness. I bury my nose in the crook of her neck and drink in the scent of fruity shampoo and something that smells like bubble gum.

I could stay like this for the rest of my life, Sarah and me safe in our insular cocoon where people don't leave and Death can't find us.

"Why do we need to do this for Aunt Barbara? Why can't she just go by herself?"

I breathe in one more time.

"Because Uncle Burt is out of town, and she doesn't want to go by herself." I lift up a little so I can give her a conspiratorial look. "But I think the real reason this is so important to her is that she wants you to meet the Deverauxs' daughter. Anastasia— I think that's her name. Do you know her from school?"

Sarah shrugs, pulls away a little. "She might be

in one of my classes. If I go, can I have my cell phone back so I can call Wendy?"

Wendy was her best friend back in North Carolina. The two of them practically grew up together. When I grounded Sarah, one of the things I took away was her cell phone. I lift the book off her chest and look at the cover—*Catcher in the Rye*—before I put it on the bedside table.

Pushing to my feet, I say, "Sure. Come on. Change clothes and let's go."

Sarah sits up, slumping round-shouldered as her legs dangle over the side of the bed. "I'm wearing what I have on."

I'm not going to argue with her. "Okay, fine, then come on."

Elizabeth and Andrew Deveraux live in the whitewashed, two-story brick house directly across the street from the Villa Magnolia. Elizabeth, who's dressed in a flowing black skirt and a white, V-neck tank, answers the red lacquered front door and greets us with a hearty, "I'm so glad you could make it. Come in, Andrew's just opening some wine."

She takes Sarah's hands and says, "Anastasia is so eager to meet you. She's upstairs with her girlfriends Katy, Emily and the Mallorys' son, Seth. I want you to meet his parents, who are in the family room, then I'll take you up and introduce you to the gang."

Mary Grace frowns and slips her arm through Sarah's. I'm proud of her for not pulling away.

I appreciate how Elizabeth is going out of her way to make sure Sarah knows everyone.

The house is decorated exactly as I expected: expensive-looking antiques placed strategically amid expensive-looking modern pieces all pulled together by expensive-looking window treatments, art and Oriental rugs. An eclectic mix that can only be achieved by a designer or someone with exquisite taste who has painstakingly tracked down just the right pieces.

We walk from the foyer past a formal living and dining room that is set for tonight's party, into a huge kitchen that is open to the family room.

And then I see him.

Rob Mallory?

My heart slams against my breastbone.

Yep. There he stands as tall, dark and gorgeous as ever. All the blood drains from my face right before it rushes and heats my cheeks as if they've been set aflame. I want to turn and run or disappear. Because suddenly I'm eighteen years old and transported back to my senior year at Stratford Park High School. To a hot night on a scratchy wool blanket under the stars, down by Lake Tindell when, to the strains of Rod Stewart's "Maggie May" playing from his car stereo, Rob Mallory and I did a whole lot more than study for the trigonometry test that threatened to keep him out of college if he didn't pass it.

We dated for a couple of months. It was one of those *Why is Rob Mallory dating her?* anomalies that made people scratch their heads and wonder why he'd gone fishing outside his designated pond. He passed the trig test, thanks to our passionate tutoring sessions, and went on to the University of Florida that summer. I went to the University of North Carolina.

And that was that.

I'm firmly jolted back to the present by the beautiful blond who walks up next to him in the Deverauxs' kitchen. She holds a martini in one hand and snakes her free arm around Rob's waist.

Blair Houghton. Homecoming Queen. *Every schoolboy's dream.*

And Rob Mallory?

Oh, God. I knew I'd run into people from high

school—Stratford Park is the place everyone moves back to after they've gotten out into the world—the perfect small town in which to raise a family with its upscale neighborhoods and good schools. I just didn't bargain on running into *him*.

Rob squints at me. Then I swear his jaw drops. "*Maggie?* Maggie Cambridge? Is that you?"

Elizabeth looks back and forth between us. "You know each other? Well, how about that. Small world."

Sarah's standing slightly in front of me. I step close behind her and put my hands on her shoulders as if she can shield me from the past. But she promptly moves to stand beside me. Mary Grace mimics her movement, standing next to Sarah, slightly behind her mother.

There's nothing quite like talking to the guy to whom you gave your virginity. Especially when 1982 was the last time you set eyes on him. What's a mere twenty-four years between lovers?

A man who bears a striking resemblance to Orlando Bloom steps forward, kisses Barbara and Mary Grace on the cheeks and introduces Rob as his fraternity brother.

Orlando turns to me. "I see you and Rob have

already had the pleasure, but I haven't met you. Hi, I'm Andrew Deveraux."

I feel myself blush all over again for some asinine reason.

"I'm Maggie Woodall, um, Cambridge was my maiden name." I steal a glance at Rob. "And this is my daughter, Sarah."

Andrew introduces us to Blair. But Barbara already knows Blair from the Stratford Middle School PTA. And in a flash, I realize Blair was one of the perfect blond *Stratford Wives* Barbara pointed out the day I registered Sarah for school.

I can't believe I didn't recognize her earlier. But she can do me one better. It's not that she doesn't recognize me. She doesn't even remember me. Period.

She pulls away from Rob and offers me the hand that isn't holding the martini. The rock on her finger winks at me.

"Hi, I'm Blair Houghton Mallory." Her Southern accent is a little too syrupy and I suspect this is not her first drink.

All I can think is, *I've slept with your husband and you have no clue.* Well, of course, it was before he was her husband.

God. Rob *married* her.

Rob looks a little sheepish, but I'm probably the only one who notices. "Blair, Maggie went to high school with us. We all graduated the same year. You remember her, don't you?"

She tilts her head to the side, sloshing a little of her drink. Peering at me as if she's trying to look back through the years. She finally smiles a perfect smile and she shakes her head.

"Nope. I'm sorry. It's been a long time and we had such a large graduating class."

You don't remember me because I was the invisible girl. The one on the outside, too proud to press her nose against the window. Full of that self-righteous dignity.

"You haven't been to any of the reunions, have you?" She tucks a strand of shiny blond hair behind her ear and I don't know where to look first—at the tennis bracelet sparkling on her tanned wrist or at the hefty diamond stud on her earlobe.

"No."

I want to say, *Of course not.*

"I didn't think so." She sips her drink. "I've been on the reunion committee every year since graduation. I would have remembered you if you'd come."

People like me don't come to your parties. I don't know what the hell I'm doing here now.

"Well, you know how it is. We've been in North Carolina all these years. It was hard to make it back."

Rob's gaze is trained on me. I can feel it, even though I'm not looking at him.

"Oh, is your husband here?" Blair looks around as if she simply overlooked him during the introductions.

I feel as if the rug's been yanked out from under me.

"No, Blair, Margaret is a widow," says Barbara.

The room falls silent and everyone gives me the pity stare. That's the part of widowhood that never gets any easier—that god-awful silence that comes just after they learn I'm a widow.

But along with that, I realize that Sarah has slipped away—into a black hole of sorts for a few moments while I was talking to Rob and Blair. I didn't even realize she was no longer in the room. Since Elizabeth and Mary Grace are gone, too, I assume she took them up to meet the other kids.

So Rob Mallory married Blair Houghton. And they have a son.

I feel a little stupid for allowing myself to slip back into the old high-school roles of when Blair was the girl who controlled the stars and turned the tide.

The girl who always got what she wanted has obviously grown into the woman who commands the heavens and earth— I can tell just by talking to her for five minutes.

I suppose when you have birthright, there's no question that you deserve everything you wish for.

My gaze flits over to Rob.

All that you wish for and more.

Within a half-hour of being in the Deverauxs' home, their love of good food and wine shines apparent.

Elizabeth sets out hors d'oeuvres worthy of a meal: artichoke and spinach tartlets; bacon-wrapped Gorgonzola and sirloin skewers; citrus-lump crab cakes and spicy shrimp spring rolls. The woman works all day as vice president of something or the other for one of the theme parks and whips up feasts like this in her spare time. I think I might have to hate her. But first I want her crab-cake recipe.

Andrew opens four bottles of sauvignon blanc so we can taste them and compare. He carries them to the patio table on the deck off the family room.

Elizabeth says the wine tasting is for Rob's benefit because he recently purchased the Wine Cellar, the wine and specialty cheese shop on Park Avenue.

"Andrew is jumping for joy now that he has a buddy he can talk wine with." She hands me a bowl of crackers to take outside. "I like good wine, but I don't want to get technical about it. I want to enjoy it. Not dissect it."

I carry the crackers out to the table in time to hear Andrew announce that all the wines are from the Marlborough region of New Zealand, an area that I'm not familiar with, so I listen intently as Rob describes it.

Elizabeth and Barbara stay in the kitchen fussing with the food, and Blair—where has Blair gotten off to?

In this group I seem to be the odd woman out, but I make no apologies for being more interested in listening to Andrew and Rob talk about the colors, smells and tastes of the different wines than helping in the kitchen. I've always enjoyed wine, always loved closing my eyes and swirling it around my mouth, trying to pick out the subtle flavors as they reveal themselves to the palate.

It's such a sensual experience.

I stand around the table with the guys and Rob slides a glass toward me. "Try this one and tell me what you taste."

I smile and hesitate a moment before I lift the goblet to my lips, inhaling before I sip.

"Umm, this is nice." I close my eyes for a moment and let the flavors come to me. "Passion fruit, green apple and something else I can't put my finger on...."

"Good instincts," Andrew says. "That's the Framingham Sauvignon Blanc."

Rob nods. "Now taste it again and think herbs."

I do and he's right, I taste something green and leafy.

We try the other three—Goldwater, Spy Valley, Cloudy Bay....

"Personal preference?" Rob asks me.

Both men gaze at me expectantly and I feel a little self-conscious, a little loopy even from the small amount of wine I've tasted. I laugh. "What is this, a pop quiz?"

"No. No, it's nothing like that." He pours another splash of the wines in my glasses and offers me the cracker bowl. "I want your opinion—call it research for the shop."

He smiles—oh, those warm brown eyes—and a flicker of why I fell for him in the first place breathes in the recesses of my memory. I chase it away with another sip of the first wine, finally deciding it's my favorite.

"Good taste," says Andrew. "*Wine Spectator* magazine rated it a ninety-one. It's the highest rated and least expensive of the four. Best tasting and best value."

Rob nods.

Elizabeth calls Andrew inside for help with something. It's just Rob and me, alone on the deck.

The night air is cool and fragrant with jasmine and some other sweet-smelling plant. I feel a little awkward standing out here alone with him, as if he can see through me to all my secrets, which wouldn't be so far-fetched. After all, we share the same secret.

I walk to the deck railing and lean against it looking out into the backyard. The lawn is lit with small lights strategically placed near bushes and around the perimeter.

He joins me at the rail, carrying two wineglasses. "It's nice out here."

"It is." I reach up to take the glass he offers me and my wedding rings wink in the dim light. It's been more than a year since Tim died and still I can't bear to remove them. It seemed wrong to take them off before the one-year anniversary of his death. As though I needed to endure the passing of each season without him before I could officially declare myself free of grieving. As if I'd ever truly be free.

"When did you get back?" Rob asks.

"Earlier this week."

In the silence, Barbara's and Elizabeth's voices drift from the kitchen out into the night air, but I can't hear exactly what they're saying. I tilt my chin up to drink in the few stars visible tonight, the ones that have fought their way through to outshine the city lights.

"Maggie, why did you quit talking to me? I mean you just disappeared…. Why…?" He tucks his free hand in his pocket and there's a touch of vulnerability in his eyes.

Something about the way he looks knocks the breath right out of me. I want to say that the way I remember it is exactly the opposite. He was the one who fell off the Earth. But Mama died about a month after I got up to North Carolina, and I suppose I sort of went inward, but at the time it seemed as if not only did I lose my mother, but I lost my boyfriend, too. It's too complicated to explain.

"It guess it was just one of those situations where we went our separate ways. Wrong place. Wrong time in our lives."

As soon as the words are out of my mouth, I regret them. They sounded cold and wounded and jaded.

Stupid, proud defenses.

"You know it took me a long time to get over you."

Oh, please. I was barely a blip on your radar.

"There you two are." Blair is at the French doors, her golden hair backlit by the family-room lights. I feel small and dark and shadowy. For a moment, I'm afraid of what she might've heard, but she doesn't look concerned and all she says is, "Come in. It's time to eat."

As we make our way to the dining room, tantalizing aromas linger in the air—some sort of beef with mushrooms and what smells like a ton of garlic. My stomach rumbles and I can't quite figure out if it's because of the food or nerves from the implications of what Rob said out on the deck.

Elizabeth makes no pretenses about the dinner.

"I am not a cook, so I ordered it from Stirellos. Believe me, if you knew what my cooking was like, you'd thank me."

Blair gulps the last of her wine. "Elizabeth, you don't tell people that. If you'd have kept it to yourself we'd never have known the difference. Take the credit, *honey*. That's what I'd do."

Blair wobbles, a little unsteady on her feet.

"I suppose that's the difference between you and me, *honey*. Now, sit down over there."

She points to the chair on Andrew's right, next to Barbara. I have to bite the insides of my cheeks to keep from laughing and decide at that very moment I like Elizabeth.

She seats me on Andrew's left next to Rob. It's a little awkward for the first few minutes, but Rob makes an effort regaling me with the full story of how and why he gave up practicing law to buy the Wine Cellar on the avenue. The shop's been there for eons—as far back as I can remember when I lived here as a girl. It's kind of nice to know some things endure.

I feel that old pull of attraction. Hating myself for it, I force myself to glance at Blair.

His wife.

The mother of his child.

I set my wineglass down and take a drink of water, because I must be tipsy—or worse—to think I feel what I think I feel. Never mind that things didn't work out all those years ago, Rob is a married man.

"Margaret just took a job down at Jacobsons on the avenue," says Barbara. I didn't even realize she was listening. "Isn't your shop just a few doors down?"

A totally unreasonable twinge of embarrassment over her announcing my new position as *shop clerk* racks me. Elizabeth has such a high-powered PR job and Blair doesn't work at all because she's too busy playing tennis— *Stop it!* I give myself a mental shake against such proud thoughts.

"No, the Wine Cellar is at the complete opposite end of the avenue," Blair says. "*Ugggh,* that shop…" She rolls her eyes in exaggerated disgust, but no one acknowledges her.

"So you're in sales?" Rob asks.

I push my rice around on the plate with my fork.

"Well, I haven't quite started. Monday's my first day."

I glance up at him and he's staring intently at me.

"I wish I would have known you were looking for a job. You seem to have a natural sense for wine. I'm getting ready to add an outside sales position. Some-one to sell wine to hotels and restaurants. Sort of a quasi distributorship that's connected to the shop—"

"*God!* I *hate* that shop." Blair sighs and rolls her eyes again before taking a long sip of Shiraz. "It's all he ever talks about. Don't let him sit here and bore you with it, Maggie." She swirls her glass with one hand and points with the other hand. "I'll tell you what, he'd better get a heck of a salesperson in there to sell lots of this stuff because we're hurting. Can you sell wine, Maggie? Because we need someone to sell lots of it for us or we're going to be in the poorhouse."

She slurs her words, and Rob glares at her. "That's enough, Blair."

She swats at him as if she's shooing away a fly. "You know what? I married a lawyer, not a wino. Lawyers are the ones who make money. Ya gotta sell a hellofalotta this stuff before you see the money a lawyer gets."

She holds out her glass for Andrew to refill.

He looks at Rob, who shakes his head.

"I *want* more wine. Goddammit, the least you can do is let me drink it if you're going to use it to ruin my life."

When Andrew sets down the bottle, Blair picks

it up and pours a hefty glass, dribbling some on the white tablecloth. "Oops... So sorry."

She takes her napkin from her lap and tries to dab at the spill, but ends up knocking over her glass. Red wine goes everywhere.

"*Ooooh*, God! I'm such a klutz. I'm *sooo* sorry, *Elissbeth*. I think I'm a little drunk. Rob was right, I probably shouldn't have had any more wine. *Oh, God!* I hate wine. It's gonna ruin my life."

She scoots her chair back from the table and exits the room.

Everyone is silent for a moment. Then Rob places his napkin to the side of his plate and stands.

"Andy, Elizabeth, it's been a lovely evening. I'm sorry. I'd better get her home."

"Did you have a good time with the girls?" I ask Sarah after we get home.

She shrugs and flops down on the couch in that bored manner she's perfected ever since she became a teenager.

I sit down next to her, curling my feet up under me. "So, go on. Tell me all about them."

Kicking the sole of one sneaker with the other, she frowns and looks as if she's weighing her words.

"All I can say is that they're mean girls, Mom."

"What? Why?"

Sarah shakes her head. "They were really, really horrible to Mary Grace."

I sit up straighter, alarmed until I realize, "Mary Grace seemed okay as we were walking home."

"Mom, she was oblivious. But they were making her do things and laughing at her. They're *that* kind of mean. The kind that think it's cool to make fun of a retarded girl."

I touch her arm. "Why didn't you come and get me?"

She sits on her hands and rocks from side to side. "I tried to tell Aunt Barbara. You were sitting right there, talking to that guy—Seth's dad. Aunt Barbara told me that Mary Grace was a big girl and could take care of herself. I think she's kind of blind about how the other kids treat her."

I feel a twinge of guilt that twice in one evening I zoned out on my daughter.

"Well they didn't hurt her physically, did they?"

Sarah shakes her head and the tender part in my heart swells because of this child who feels so much empathy for others. I reach out and brush a piece of hair out of her eyes.

"Maybe you'll be a good influence on them. Teach them that it's not right to have fun at someone else's expense?"

My daughter frowns and looks me square in the eyes. "No, Mom, all I know is after tonight I could never be friends with them."

CHAPTER 8

Elizabeth

It's six-thirty Monday morning and I'm in the office.
As I set my briefcase on my desk and sink into my chair
to boot up my computer, I realize just how exhausted
I am. You'd think I ran a weekend-long marathon
rather than giving a dinner party on Saturday night.
A dinner party for which I didn't even do the cooking
thanks to the magic of Stirellos' Gourmet Meals.

Anyhow, I am sick and tired of being sick and
tired so I came in early, employing the same mind-
over-matter philosophy I used with the dinner party
(which I did not feel like having, but made it
through with barely an upset stomach).

Yes, it's mind over matter. I don't know why I
didn't think of this before. Who knows how long
this morning sickness will plague me?

And having this baby won't change our lives. I

won't allow it because there's just no room for that. Dealing with unexpected events is what I do every day as executive vice president of public relations at Worldwide Studios. Why should this be any different?

Rather than lying in bed this morning, contemplating when I was going to get sick, I got up, got dressed and forged into the office.

Mind over matter. Really. If I tell myself I'm not nauseated, I'm not nauseated.

There. See.

I take a slow, even breath.

In through the nose.

Out through the mouth.

So far, so good.

Since I was out so much last week, I need to make sure I'm ready for this nine o'clock meeting on the Celestial Studios acquisition.

It's an important one—Worldwide is absorbing Celestial and there will be lots of layoffs when we restructure. If we don't handle this exactly right, it could become a public-relations nightmare.

It's all in the perception and I have it under control.

Gary Hillstead, Worldwide's director of PR and my right-hand man, sticks his head in my office door.

"Good morning, stranger. I brought you some coffee."

The smell of it nearly makes me retch. I hold up my hand.

"No, thanks. I'm giving up caffeine."

He sets the mug on the corner of my desk and sits in a chair. The smell permeates my office. I feel the bile in my stomach rise.

"So I had accounting run the numbers for—"

"Wait a minute." I stand and grab the cup, sloshing a little of the offending liquid as I rush out of the room and dump it in the bathroom sink.

I wet a paper towel and press it to my face, focusing on the floor because the pink-and-blue floral paper on the bathroom wall makes my head spin.

Mind over matter. Come on, you're okay. Pull it together.

A few minutes later, I return to my empty office. To my relief, Gary's not there. I sit down and gather myself, wishing I'd brought some crackers from home, deciding it might start people speculating if I asked Ruby, my administrative assistant, to go out and buy some for me.

I could tell her it was the new saltine-cracker diet, but something tells me she wouldn't buy it. Instead, I forage through the break room until I find a stash of club crackers. A little more buttery than saltines, but they'll have to do. I take the crackers and a can of Sprite back to my desk.

After my makeshift meal, I feel a little more human. I redo my powder, touch up my blush and lipstick and buzz Gary, who has the decency not to question my hasty exit earlier.

We spend the next hour getting our act together for the meeting. Gary's a good guy with a great future in PR. Sometimes I worry that I'm training him for the competition because someday someone is going to recognize his talent and steal him away. But for now he's mine—figuratively, in a work sense.

Ten minutes before the meeting starts, we walk into the conference room together and take our places at the big, glass-covered mahogany table. We're the first to arrive, other than members of the food-service staff who have brewed two large pots of coffee and have some kind of food items covered by large silver lids on a mobile warming tray.

It smells like eggs—quiche or something.

Ugggh.

One by one, executives file in and help themselves to quiche. Gary offers to bring me a piece when he gets up to get himself some.

"No, thank you."

I try to do the breathing routine, but the egg-coffee smell makes my stomach pitch. I break out in a cold sweat. All of a sudden the crackers and soft drink are talking to me.

Pushing to my feet, I say to Gary, "I'll be right back. I forgot something."

If I can just get some fresh air—

He frowns at me. "Are you okay? You look a little green."

"Fine," I croak.

I'm just about to clear the door when I run headlong into my boss, Herb Waters, Worldwide's CEO.

Shit.

"Ah, Elizabeth, there you are. I think you've met Harry Sanderson with Celestial Studios?"

I open my mouth to say, *Yes, I have indeed met Harry Sanderson.* But instead of words, the crackers and soda make a return appearance—

All over my boss's navy sport coat.

Maggie

What in the hell was I thinking taking a job in cosmetics? I do well to apply my own makeup, let alone try to make someone else look good.

I spent my first morning of my first day of my new job getting a crash course in writing up a sale—no cash registers. Can you believe it? The store is so small—and family owned—we write up the sales by hand on numbered tickets. They seem to think that this refusal to enter the computer age demonstrates *personal service*. Personally, I think they just don't want to invest in the computer system.

At least they let us use tax tables and calculators.

I am no math wiz and just when I think the worst is over, they throw me out onto the sales floor. No product training. Come to think of it, they didn't even ask me if I knew how to do a makeover. Horror visions of being fired on the first day of my first-ever job flash through my head.

The cosmetics department is small by regular department-store standards. In fact, it's sort of the equivalent of a galley kitchen; a long, narrow pass-through from the lingerie department to women's wear, with counters and shelves stocked with various upscale lines such as Lancôme, Chanel and MAC among others and a well-represented selection of fine perfumes lining both sides of the wall. It smells of a mélange of expensive creams, powders and perfumes. It smells rich and inviting and seductive.

A tall, good-natured redhead, probably in her fifties, looks up from her customer and greets me with a hardy, "Welcome! Welcome," as I venture onto the sales floor. Her name is Renata and she's worked in cosmetics at Jacobsons for fifteen years. "So you're Barbara McMillan's niece?"

"Yes, I am."

"How is Barbara? I haven't seen her in ages."

"She's very well, thank you."

Renata lifts her eyebrows in a *well-go-on* expression, but when I don't, she asks her customer to excuse her and herds me over to a stack of boxes sitting behind one of the counters. "We got in a large order of Clinique that needs to be checked in and put away. So why don't you get started on that?"

She turns to go back to her customer, who is waiting patiently, sitting at a desklike area, but I say, "I think it's only fair to let you know that I've never done this before."

She waves me off. "Don't worry about it. It's easy

as pie. Just check to make sure what's on the invoice is really there and you'll see where the stuff goes on the shelf."

"No, what I mean is I've never sold cosmetics before."

She smiles a gentle smile and I see that one of her front teeth is darker than the rest. "Well, that's not a problem. The companies will have training sessions for you—they'll either send you to a school, which is actually just a one- or two-day basic training—or they'll send in a rep to go over things with you. Honestly, once you learn the basics on one line, you can sell them all. In the meantime just listen in to what I tell customers. You'll catch on quick."

I must not look convinced because Renata adds, "Don't worry. You'll be fine. I'm just darn happy to have the help. The last girl who worked here with me just up and left. She left us in a real lurch. Look around, open drawers, play with the testers. All it amounts to is playing with makeup."

With that, she turns and goes back to her customer.

I appreciate her faith in me. But I wonder why they're so hard up to find someone with experience.

The hourly wage isn't so great—barely above minimum wage—but when you figure there's a four-percent commission on everything you sell, it makes the pay pretty good.

Especially for a first job.

I go about my business checking in the order, while Renata helps the steady stream of customers. I stop and offer assistance every time someone enters the department, but the general answer is usually that they're just looking or that they're waiting for Renata.

I soon realize she's somewhat of an institution at Jacobsons. More than a department-store clerk or over-the-counter makeup artist—she is the guru that women come from miles around to confide in.

Under the subtle greenish cast of the buzzing fluorescent lights, she advises a middle-aged woman named Pam to cut loose her louse of a boyfriend; she tells a mother named Angie how to get the upper hand over her teenage son who she suspects of selling drugs; she helps a bride-to-be decide between three wedding invitations; and to round off the collection, Renata consoles a blonde named Karen who sits at the consultation desk sobbing and yanking handfuls of tissue out of the Kleenex box that Renata seems to produce from thin air.

I listen closer to this conversation because I'm thinking I recognize Karen as one of Blair Mallory's tennis-playing, *Stratford Wife* friends. In fact, they kind of resemble each other, in that blond, blue-eyed, tanned and fit sort of way. But come to think of it, all the *Stratford Wives* look like that.

Today, it seems, Karen discovered her husband is having an affair with one of her best friends.

"It was awful, Renata. I just played tennis with her last week. This is my husband. How could she do this to me? How could he—" She buries her head in her hands and sobs.

Renata pats Karen's arm. "Are you absolutely sure about this?"

She nods her pretty blond head. "I drove up to Altoona Springs this morning because Macy's had the chafing dish I've been looking for." She sniffs and dabs under her eyes. "Before I get there, I pull up to a red light, you know, that one just before the Holiday Inn? When the light turns green, I see a car that looks like Bob's making a left turn into the Holiday Inn parking lot. When I see the license plate, I know it's him. I think to myself, what's Bob doing there? So I go down and make a U-turn…"

At that precise moment a customer walks up to

the cosmetics counter wanting a lipstick. I'm tempted to ask her if she wants to wait for Renata, but she seems to know what she wants.

By the time I find it for her and wrap up her package, Renata and Karen have moved to the Chanel tester at the opposite end of the department where Renata is redoing Karen's makeup.

The only other tidbit of conversation I hear is when Karen is paying for her purchase. "I don't know what I'm going to do. I don't want to confront either of them just yet because I have no idea what I'll do if he leaves me."

The feeling that washes over me is perverse because I realize I'm not the only one who put all my eggs in one man-basket. I don't know if it would be worse for the bottom to fall out of the basket because you lost your love to death or because he ended up being unfaithful.

It dawns on me that in the course of one workday, I haven't learned a darn thing about cosmetics, but I've acquired more dirt on the women in Stratford Park than I knew about the Asheville neighbors I lived with for more than two decades.

Jacobsons is the Stratford Park clearinghouse for gossip. It's kind of mind-boggling that no one seemed to mind me listening in on the conversations.

Is it any wonder the invisible girl would grow to be the invisible woman?

Only now, I don't mind.

Come five-thirty—a half hour before closing—the reason my predecessor walked off the job becomes a little more obvious. According to the sales tally sheets we keep to outline our daily sales—Renata reinforced how important it is to keep track of your sales, "So that you can be sure they don't cheat you out of one penny of your commission"—the grand total of sales stacks up like this:

Renata—$1,942 (and an appointment to do the bridal party's makeup on the day of the wedding).

Maggie—$15.

Renata's daily commission—$77.68.

Maggie's daily commission—sixty cents.

Granted it was my first day and Renata has fifteen years of building a loyal clientele, but how can a newcomer compete with someone who not only does a mean makeover, but offers free psychological services on the side?

Obviously, there's more to being a success at this job than simply slapping on makeup and writing up the sale. There's an element of investing yourself in these people.

I don't know if I want to invest that much of myself. I'm exhausted just listening in on their tales of woe.

Renata starts to explain how to close out the cash drawer, but one of her followers walks in.

"Go ahead and count the money—first count out the two-hundred-dollar bank, including the coins and as many ones as you can use to make a round number—that's what we'll use to open with in the morning. Put it in the green bank bag. Then count out the rest—that's the day's profits—and put them in the blue bank bag. I'll be right over here if you have any questions."

I've just finished counting out the two-hundred-dollar bank, when I glimpse a man walking into the department.

Rob Mallory.

My stomach turns a quick spiral.

My reaction to seeing him baffles me more than his actual presence in the Jacobsons' cosmetics department.

"I found you," he says.

I smile. "Which implies you were looking for me?"

He chuckles. "I was indeed looking for you. I wanted to see if I could tempt you away from this place."

Heat rushes to my face and my mind flashes to that night all those years ago at Lake Tindell. Our naked bodies moving together on that blanket under the stars. I blink, trying to erase the memory that has survived all too vividly after all these years.

If I were a flirt, I would say, *Why, Rob, that sounds like an indecent proposal.*

Instead I glance over at Renata and her current project, not wanting to become fodder for the Stratford Park gossip mill. But they're sitting with their heads together. So I'm safe.

For now.

I must do a poor job at hiding how he's flustering me. Because he backtracks. "What I meant is I'm serious about talking to you about selling wine for me."

I glance around to make sure the store manager—or anyone else, for that matter—is not within earshot.

"Rob, there seems to be one little problem. I don't know anything about wine. I am probably not your best person for the job."

He straightens and I see the muscles of his broad

shoulders move underneath his blue polo shirt. God, I always loved his shoulders. I used to sit behind him in math class—that's how I ended up tutoring him for the trig test—and dream of laying my hands on those shoulders—

"Maggie, answer one question for me. Do you like to drink wine?"

I fidget with the zipper on the blue bank bag that still needs to be stuffed with today's profits.

"Yes. I love to drink wine."

"Well, there you go. That's the only requirement for this job. If you've got the appreciation for the *vin*, I can teach you all you need to know to sell the stuff. In fact, it's safe to say around here it will practically sell itself."

I glance down at the uneven sales tally on the desk.

"If it sells itself, why do you need someone to do it for you? Why don't you do it and save the commission you'd have to pay me?"

"The shop is more than I can handle right now. But this distributorship is too good an opportunity to let go. I need you, Maggie."

I know what he means by that—well, that he doesn't mean anything by that. He needs me—or

someone—to sell his wine to make him a handsome
profit.

I watch Renata gathering an armful of Chanel
facial treatment for her customer. Probably another
five-hundred-dollar sale. It's pretty clear that if I
work here, I'll be working for not much over the
hourly wage because I will be unpacking boxes. But
Rob's dark brown gaze snares mine and my stomach
not only spirals, it does a shimmy the likes of which
I haven't felt in ages.

For the first time since I met Tim nearly twenty-
four years ago, I feel the magnetic pull of attraction
for another man.

I don't know what wrecks me more—that it feels
disloyal to my late husband who has only been gone
a little more than a year or that Rob is married.

I can't do this.

"Well, if it isn't Rob Mallory. How's that pretty
wife of yours?" Renata says.

I step away from the wrap stand to give Renata
some room to package her sale.

"She's just fine, Renata."

Renata smiles. "So you know *our Maggie?*"

Our Maggie?

"Yes, Maggie and I go way back. In fact, Blair and

I just had dinner with Maggie and her aunt Barbara Saturday night."

I work here one day and I'm *their Maggie?*

Don't flatter yourself. It was just Renata's subtle way of letting us know that Rob's coming into Jacobsons was duly noted and filed away under the category of married man paying a visit to single woman who is new in town.

No. I could never work with him. It would be an impossible situation.

"Promise me you'll think about it," Rob says.

Renata and her cohort watch as I accept the business card Rob hands me.

"Call me in a few days and let's talk about it, okay?"

CHAPTER 9

Maggie

After work, I stop by the grocery-store deli and
pick up fried chicken strips and macaroni-and-
cheese for dinner. It's one of Sarah's favorite meals
and some of the best comfort food I can think of.

I think we'll both need a little comfort tonight.
I'm a little worried about how Sarah feels about
being alone in the afternoon. She's always been used
to me being there when she gets home from school.
I know she's thirteen and a lot of kids are left alone
at a much earlier age, but Sarah's having a tough
time adjusting to life without her father and her
new school and surroundings. That's a lot of adjusting to do on top of your mom starting a new job and
being gone more.

Some day, we'll look back and know that this
made both of us stronger women, but in the mean-

time I'd be kidding myself to think it's not going to be a challenge.

Faced with losing Tim, I'm still fighting that shaky feeling that history is repeating itself. I lost Mama. Now Tim. I suppose I've never fully faced all my feelings over losing Mama, but watching Sarah grieve, I haven't been able to turn around and walk away from my husband's death the way I moved away and denied Mama's.

I suppose I lost that luxury—if you can call walking away a luxury—when I had a child. Too bad Mama never realized that. That when people love you, you can't just decide one day that you're through.

I'm going to make darn sure I'm a better mother to Sarah than Mama was to me.

Tonight, I try to give my daughter extra attention. I want her to know that even though I'm not home when she gets home from school, I'm still here for her.

We sit across from each other at the tiny kitchen table eating our dinner and I try to get her to open up.

"How was your day?" I ask.

"Fine."

She stares down into her plate, spears two pieces of mac-and-cheese and puts the miniscule bite in her mouth. "Did anything interesting happen at school today?"

She gives me a *yeah right* look as she finishes chewing. "No."

I set down my fork and smile at her. "Nothing? Not one single interesting thing happened at school today?"

Now she looks really annoyed. "I told you, no. It was just another lame, boring day. Just like every other lame, boring day since I started going there."

Her voice is singsong, but I let it roll off me like rain.

"What about Anastasia and her friends? You were just over at her house. Do you think you could be friends with her?"

I remember what she said about Anastasia being mean to Mary Grace and almost regret suggesting it. But you know how girls are at this age; one minute they hate each other and the next minute they're best friends.

Sarah levels me with her unwavering, too-grown-up, old-soul gaze.

"How am I supposed to be friends with those losers?" Sarah asks.

"Sarah, well, it's no wonder you're having a hard time if you're going to take that attitude." I say the words as gently as I can, but my daughter pierces me with an incredulous stare that conveys something between *you've got to be kidding* and *go to hell*.

"Mom, do you know what they did to me today, Anastasia and her band of merry morons?" She pauses as if she's daring me to venture a guess, but I'm afraid to breathe much less utter a word. "Tad Phillips, that's Anastasia's boyfriend, grabs my arm as I'm walking past them at lunch and says, 'adweebsayswhat?'"

"What?" I ask.

Sarah rolls her eyes. "Exactly."

"What? Wait a minute, I don't understand what you're talking about."

She studies me through narrowed eyes and shakes her head as if she's lost all hope for me. For a moment I do feel utterly hopeless.

She arches her left brow, looking so much like her father it almost breaks my heart. "He said, 'A dweeb says what?'"

"A dweeb says what? That doesn't make any sense."

"God, Mom, you're so—" She breaks off mid-sentence and something vulnerable flashes in her eyes, and I'm glad she doesn't say it—stupid, dense, pathetic—all of which would describe how I feel at that precise moment.

"Mom." Her tone is a little bit softer. "Mean kids do this thing where they say something like 'a dweeb says what,' and if the person says 'what' that means they're a dweeb—or whatever they called them because they said 'what.' You see?"

I do see, but I don't understand how kids can be so mean. My heart breaks for my daughter.

"I'm sorry. I can see why that would upset you."

I can almost see Sarah's guard slip—just a notch, but the look on her face, her posture, both of which were poised for a fight, soften a little.

"Do you want me to talk to Mrs. Deveraux about it?"

Sarah snorts. "No. Anastasia didn't actually *do* anything except sit there and laugh. I'm sure she put him up to it, but if you told her mom, she'd be all innocent like, '*I didn't do anything.*' I'm just so sick of them all."

Momentarily I'm at a loss for words.

When Sarah was born I so wanted the two of us to be close, because my mother and I weren't.

Like everything concerning child rearing, it's been a little more difficult than I'd envisioned.

Probably because we're so much alike. She was such a daddy's girl. When Sarah and I would butt heads, Tim would play go-between and help us smooth things out. When something went wrong, she always went to her daddy.

Tim was the levelheaded one.

I was the emotional one.

Sarah knows how to push my buttons. I was prone to freaking out when we were at odds. I'd yell, fling ultimatums and toss out harsh punishments that I later regretted—after Tim talked some sense into me.

You're grounded for the rest of your life, Sarah! Go in your room, Sarah, and stay there until I tell you to come out.

What I was really saying was, *Go to your room where you'll be safe, where nothing can harm you. Don't be a screwup like I am, Sarah. You have so much potential and if you'll only listen to me, I'll help you live up to it. You can be so much more than I am.*

Tim helped me see that it was okay—probably even better—for her to make mistakes. "Is there a better way to learn?" he'd say.

My voice of reason.

Oh, Tim, how am I supposed to do this without you? How could you leave me like this?

The catch in my throat threatens to explode into a full-blown sob. So I change tactics fast. Without even thinking, I say, "Well, I had an interesting day. I heard so much gossip I could blackmail half the population of Stratford Park."

I'm sorry the second I blurt the words. I shouldn't be talking to my daughter about gossip. But when the scowl melts off Sarah's face, and she sits up straighter, tuning in to what I'm saying for the first time since I don't know when, I tell her everything.

Well, most everything. I edit the parts that aren't appropriate—okay, which was most of it.

I tell her about Renata and her band of needy women.

"This one woman—I think her name was Candy Berg—came in for some heavy-duty concealer to hide the bruises of her plastic surgery. Apparently she had it all done from top to bottom."

Sarah's eyes flash. "There's a stuck-up eighth grader named Monica Berg. I'll bet it's her mom."

I lean in conspiratorially. "I don't know, but do you know a boy named Danny Higgenbothem?" I ask.

Sarah nods, rapt, then scrunches her nose. "He's in three of my classes."

"Well, stay away from him. His mom thinks he's selling drugs."

Sarah purses her lips and stares up at the ceiling for

a second. "Yeah, probably. He looks like a burnout. He's always sleeping in class and his eyes are always red."

This gives me pause, and even though my daughter and I are relating, having a real conversation for the first time in what seems years, it makes me realize this isn't just a game.

I push the last bite of chicken around on my plate with my fork. "Wow, a seventh grader involved in drugs? That's kind of scary. Do you think we should tell the principal?"

Sarah's defenses rise and I see the start of her retreating back inside herself. "No. If anyone found out it was you who ratted him out, I might as well change schools. I may not have any friends now, but if you did that, I'd be..."

Her words trail off and the door on our conversation officially closes.

Back in North Carolina at least she had some friends her own age. I ache for her feeling so alone, and I don't feel completely right about perpetuating gossip. At work, it was as if the mindless talk wasn't about real people. But Sarah knows some of them— or at least some of their kids.

She rises from the table and starts to pick up her

plate, but then the strangest thing happens. She walks over to me and plants a kiss on my cheek.

"Even if you do get all freaked out, this was kind of fun."

For the first time since Tim died, I see a glimmer of sunlight.

Propriety be damned. If my daughter responds to the *Renata Reports* even for a few moments, I'll dish until she's filled up.

Elizabeth

How does one recover from barfing on her boss?

Or maybe the more appropriate question is *does* one recover—professionally, personally?

It's been ten days since that horrifying event and I want to crawl under the table every time I see him.

After the meeting, I apologized and sent his coat out to be dry-cleaned. A few days later, I even tried to make light of it, but he hasn't been in a jovial mood since.

I finally decided all I can do is move forward as if it never happened.

The phone rings.

"Hello?"

"Mrs. Deveraux, this is Paula from Dr. Riggs's

office. He asked me to call and tell you your test results are in. Could you and your husband come in tomorrow at four to discuss it?"

My blood runs cold. He wouldn't call us in just to give us an all-clear. Oh, my God—

"Sure, but, umm…could you give me a hint as to the result?"

The nurse is silent.

"Is my baby okay?"

"I'm sorry, Mrs. Deveraux, the doctor has that information. There are no notes in your file."

Take a deep breath. Don't panic.

"May I speak to him, please?"

"I apologize, but he's at the hospital delivering a baby."

I close my eyes against the mounting anxiety and rest my head on my hand, quashing the urge to yell at the nurse. *It's not her fault.*

"Okay, then. We'll see him tomorrow."

When I hang up, Anastasia is standing in the middle of the kitchen looking as if she just saw a ghost.

"What do you mean *is your baby okay?*"

Oh, shit.

We didn't want to tell her yet, not until after we decide what we're going to do.

The thought rings a pang of guilt. *You can't just throw away a child.*

"Mom? What's going on?"

She's asking me. I have to tell her. But emotions collide: anxiety over the pending news Dr. Riggs is keeping from us; unease at being unprepared to have this conversation with my daughter.

"Come here, honey, sit down."

She stays rooted to the spot, her face screwed into a mask of utter disgust.

"You're pregnant, aren't you? That's why you've been sick so much. That's why you've been coming home early from work."

Instinctively, I lace my hands over my belly.

It's all in the presentation, Elizabeth. Smile. Say, "Yes, I am! Isn't it wonderful? We're all going to be so happy."

Before I can utter a word, she screams, "I don't want you to have another baby. You don't have enough time for me as it is and now you're going to have another kid?"

She runs out of the room. I go after her, but by the time I lug my tired body upstairs, her door is shut and locked, the face of some pretty-boy singer smiling at me from the poster tacked to her door.

I knock on pretty boy's pimple-free forehead. "Anastasia, please open the door."

"Go away."

"Please, let's talk about this."

"Go away! I hate you."

"Open the door right this minute! I'm not going to tell you ag—"

Rap music blasts so loudly I can't even scream over its impenetrable barrier. I feel the bass thump in my chest as some punk sings something about telling all adults to go fuck themselves.

What?

Anger roils inside me. Since when did she start listening to music like that? She knows I don't allow it.

Who is this imposter who's taken over my child? My sweet, smart, obedient child.

I am her mother. She will not treat me like this.

We are going to talk about this whether she wants to or not because in this house we solve problems by *talking*. We don't drown them out with that hideous excuse for music. And that music is grounded. Not, not just grounded. It's gone. I am throwing it in the garbage because I won't have it in my house.

I start downstairs to get a kebab skewer from the kitchen so I can spring the lock.

I am her mother and she will treat me with respect.

I repeat this mantra as I stomp down the stairs. But by the time I get to the kitchen, tears are streaming down my face and I sit at the kitchen table with my head in my hands and bawl.

Bad news. Bad news all the way around.

And here I am falling apart.

Me, of all people.

I do *not* fall apart.

Damn hormones. Why can't I turn them off?

How could I have made such a mess out of what should have been a wonderful exciting piece of good news for the whole family to celebrate?

With a shaky hand I dial Andrew's office number and plug my free ear to drown out the strains of ugly music drifting down from upstairs. My husband's assistant informs me he's in a meeting.

"May I take a message?"

Go get him. I need to talk to him now.

"No. Thanks. I'll talk to him when he gets home."

"Is everything okay, Mrs. Deveraux? I can go get him if this is an emergency."

"No."

I hang up the phone and get in the shower.

By the time I turn off the water, it's been running

cold for a long time, but the cold helped freeze my out-of-control emotions. As I dry off, I realize the thump of Anastasia's music has quieted.

I wrap my hair in a towel and pull on my big, white terry robe, intent on going downstairs to make a cup of tea. But when I emerge from the humid bathroom, Andrew is sitting on the foot of the bed, the first button of his shirt undone, the knot of his tie slightly askew and pulled away from his neck as if he's grabbed a big fistful and yanked.

"Are you okay?" he says.

I wait a few seconds before I answer. I listen inside to see if some foreign emotion is going to erupt like a criminal bursting through a door ready to spray gunfire on anyone in his way.

I really do feel like a marionette these days, a rag doll controlled by unseen hands. But the puppet master must be on break or maybe I simply cried myself out in the shower.

All I feel is exhausted.

Wrung out.

Limp.

Totally and completely drained.

"Dr. Riggs's office called. The test results are in and they want us to come in tomorrow to discuss them."

Elizabeth

There's a PTA meeting tonight and as I pull into the driveway after a long, difficult day at work, I tick off a mental list of all the things I have to do, but my mind drifts back to the bad news that Dr. Riggs gave Andrew and me when we went to meet with him

The test results point to complications. But sometimes the results give a false positive. There's no way of knowing for sure until the baby is born.

I have decided that rather than make myself crazy wondering, I will focus on the positive things in life. Such as the PTA meeting that starts in one hour for which I haven't yet typed up the agenda.

I make a mental note to make sure I add *elect new secretary* to the agenda. That and the Web site thing that Hal Brooks, Stratford's principal, called about.

He was in a tizzy over it. Finds something about it objectionable.

I was going into a meeting so I couldn't really talk to him about it, but he gave me the Web address so I could look at it when I got home.

I don't have the time or inclination to do much Web surfing. Now Anastasia, she would be on the Internet twelve hours a day if I let her.

I wonder if she's heard anything about this. She's still not speaking to me because of the baby and I made her get rid of that obscene music. But she'll come around. I've always respected her enough to trust that she'd do the right thing. She's a smart girl and pretty soon she'll see that copping an attitude is the last way to get what she wants.

I consider knocking on her door and feigning dumb about the computer so she'll sign me on, but come to think of it, Hal didn't say exactly what it was he objected to about the Web site. He just told me it was inappropriate and I should see for myself.

I should do that before I pique my daughter's curiosity. I get the notepad that I scribbled the Web address on, settle in at the computer desk in the kitchen and start to sign on.

When the Web site comes up, I have to suppress a laugh.

The Stratford Park Potluck—come here for the latest dish. Written by the Fabulous A.

The name of the blog is pretty clever. I have to give *the Fabulous A* credit for that.

Yes, it's creative and full of gossip and disparaging remarks about various students, teachers and parents. It uses initials only, but according to Hal, people have already discovered the blog and are threatening to go to the school board if he doesn't put an end to it.

I scroll through the list shaking my head and *tsking* after each allegation.

J.W. got caught in the boy's bathroom with L.M. Take a wild guess what they were doing.

Please. This is juvenile nonsense.

A teacher, I'll call the person "S.," has some funky extracurricular activities.

What? *Funky* as in *funky chicken*? *Funky* as in "Play That Funky Music"? Lame. Funky is not a crime.

H.P.'s mother is a kleptomaniac. She got arrested for shoplifting.

Huh... I actually find myself pausing and trying

to think of someone with the initials H.P. But no one readily comes to mind.

Oh, come on, Hal. Don't get sucked into this nonsense.

I read on, under the guise that it's my responsibility as PTA president to be informed—

J.F.'s father is a gangsta.

A *gangsta?* Oh, give me a break. It would be more likely that Stratford Park had a resident vampire than a *gangster.* This child is obviously an underachiever who can't even spell.

Hal has to ignore this. If he makes a big to-do over it, it'll just draw more attention. That's PR 101. I'd better get my act together so I can go in and talk to him before the meeting—

I do a cursory perusal of the remaining entries that talk about garden variety *jerk faces, biotches, virgins* and *hos.* Not that I'm in favor of those terms, but face it—it's all so junior high—or middle school as this case may be.

Freedom of speech, Hal. Tell the complainers that if they don't like it, don't read the blog.

I'm just about ready to sign off when I scroll past—and go back to—a scary entry that hits a little too close to home.

"Oh, my God. This changes everything."

Barbara

The telephone rings as I'm taking the chicken-broccoli casserole out of the oven. I let the answering machine pick up. Burt's coming home tonight and I fear he might be calling from the airport. I don't remember what time he's due in—or if he even bothered to tell me—but I really don't want to talk to him just yet.

I suppose that finding those treasures in his suitcase proves that our marriage is in trouble and I need to do something about it, like moving him out before he gets home. But the thought makes me tired. Makes me feel as if there's a great big mountain smack dab in front of me, blocking the way to my happily-ever-after.

"Hello? Barbara? It's Elizabeth across the street. I know you're probably getting ready to go to PTA tonight, but I was really hoping to talk to you before the meeting."

I set the hot dish on the stove burner, pull off my navy-blue oven mitts and pick up the receiver.

"Elizabeth, hey there, I'm here. I was just getting dinner together. The sitter'll be here in fifteen minutes—oh, don't you dare tell Sarah that Carrie's a babysitter. She's just a high-school girl who's coming over to *hang out* with her and Mary Grace while we're at the meeting—and I am rambling, so I'll hush up. What did you need to talk to me about, hon?"

There's silence on the other end of the line.

"Elizabeth?"

"Yes, I'm here."

"Is everything okay?"

The overhead light in the kitchen buzzes, reminding me I need to get an electrician in here to check the wiring.

"Did Hal Brooks call you?"

"No, why?"

"So you haven't seen the blog?"

"What's a blog?"

The plates clatter as I take them down from the cupboard and set them around the table.

"It's a *Web log*, a diary of sorts that some people post on the Internet."

"So that everyone can read it?"

I'd started to pull the utensils from the drawer, but stop so I can hear her.

"That seems to be how it works."

Margaret opens the door and sticks her head inside. I wave her in.

"Well, what the heck would people do that for? I thought diaries were supposed to be private."

"The Web site Hal's worried about has all kinds of inane gossip about people from Stratford Park—teachers, students, parents. Who's sleeping with whom, who's getting into things they shouldn't be into. That kind of nonsense. There's only initials, but still, it's not hard to figure out who they're talking about. Listen, Barbara, do you have access to the Internet?"

"Heck, no. I don't even own a computer. I do well to pick up messages off this darned answering machine."

"Does Maggie have one?"

"I don't know. She just walked in. Let me ask her."

I hold the receiver away from my mouth. "Do you have a computer?"

Maggie nods.

"She does."

"Let me talk to her."

I hold out the phone to Margaret, who looks as if I'm offering her a hot poker. "It's Elizabeth Deveraux. She needs to talk to you."

Margaret looks at me askance. I shrug, knowing Elizabeth can describe it better than I can.

158 TRUE CONFESSIONS OF THE STRATFORD PARK PTA

"Hello?"

I continue setting the table, keeping my ear tuned to their conversation.

"Oh. Hi, Elizabeth. Just fine. And you?"

Margaret is silent for a few moments except for some *mmm-hmms* and *uh-huhs*.

Then she says, "Well, we have a computer, but we don't have Internet service. I just haven't gotten around to getting that yet...."

More silence as she listens.

"I'm not sure. Hold on a second. I'll ask her."

Margaret puts a hand over the mouthpiece. "When will the sitter be here?"

I hold up my hand. "Not a sitter. A teenage girl to hang out with the girls."

Margaret smiles and rolls her eyes. "Okay. Fine. When will the *teenager* be here?"

"In about fifteen minutes. Why?"

"Elizabeth says it's important that we see something on the Internet before we go to the meeting."

I wonder what could be so God almighty important that it can't wait, but Elizabeth's got a level head. She isn't one to get all riled up without good reason. I don't know why, but for a moment, the possibility that this could have something to do with

Burt buzzes in my brain as loudly as the kitchen light fixture.

Gossip.

Who's sleeping with whom.

But then the voice of reason chimes in.

If this has to do with me, why would she involve Margaret? Surely Elizabeth'd be more discreet than that?

"Tell her we'll be there as soon as we can."

Maggie

The blog that was so urgent we had to go over to Elizabeth's before the meeting was about Sarah.

Oh, I'm calm now, but when I first read it, I just about went ballistic.

There was a definite lack of hard evidence: *S.W. the new girl had better watch her skinny little ass.*

S.W. = Sarah Woodall?

New girl.

Skinny.

Enough similarity at a glance to make me uncomfortable that someone would single her out. But Mr. Brooks didn't think it was necessary to keep her out of school tomorrow. Even so, I'm still not certain I won't.

Still, I do appreciate Elizabeth telling us about it before we went into the meeting.

We met with the principal beforehand. He assured us that Stratford Middle School had an exemplary record. They'd never had a single incidence of violence in the entire history of the school.

"These are good kids from good families," he says. "But I can understand your concern."

Good kids. From good families.

My mind drifts to what Sarah said about Anastasia and her friends picking on Mary Grace, and the boy whose mother was lamenting his drug problem to Renata.

These are *good* kids?

I think he meant rich kids from wealthy families.

"I assure you, Mrs. Woodall—"

"It's Maggie. Please, call me Maggie."

"I assure you, Maggie, that we will make sure Sarah is safe. Of course, I'll rely on you to explain the situation to her however you best see fit."

I contemplate telling them I can't work tomorrow and keeping Sarah home so I can figure out how to explain this gently, to get the point across without scaring her. Another anxiety nags at me. I don't feel right about calling in. Renata is depending on me. But Sarah comes first.

I experience a split second of anger at Tim for

leaving us, for making it so that I have to juggle responsibilities. For not being here to protect his daughter. But the feeling is like a small cloud passing over the sun. Everything dims and then the cloud passes. Not even a rain shower this time.

As we walk into the auditorium, I spy Blair Mallory and wave, but she doesn't see me. I could have sworn she was looking right at me. She chats with the other *Stratford Wives*, each of them blond and animated and beautiful, looking as if they're dressed for cocktails or dinner rather than a PTA meeting.

Hmm. Karen is missing and I wonder if one of the three here tonight is the one she caught with her husband. But the way they all laugh and chat as though they don't have a care in the world makes me think it couldn't be one of them. Beneath the polished and lacquered exterior, they're probably loving wives and caring mothers. They have, after all, cared enough to come to the PTA meeting.

I guess it's shallow of me to think less of them for being blond and perfect. I always hate it when people judge me by my appearance.

Barbara leans over and whispers, "I see the *Stratford Wives* are here in force. Leave it to gossip to draw a good crowd. The only time they bother to show is when there's a controversy. Or when they want something. Otherwise they can't be bothered."

Connie Claxton walks in. She does a double take and makes a beeline in my direction.

"Oh, Lord, what does she want?" Barbara says.

"Are you Mrs. Woodall? Sarah Woodall's mother?" Barbara elbows me.

"Yes. Sarah's my daughter."

Connie grimaces. "May I have a word with you?" Barbara sighs and Connie gives her a dirty look.

"Would you please tell Sarah to quit picking on Chloe? You'd think that being a new student in this school, Sarah would try to get along."

I glance at Barbara for a little moral support because I have no idea what the woman is talking about.

"Connie, the way I understand it," Barbara says, "is that Sarah has been asking Chloe to stop picking on Mary Grace."

Connie sticks out her chin. "I am talking to Mrs. Woodall, Barbara. Butt out. This is none of your business."

"When it involves my niece and daughter, it becomes my business."

Thank God Hal Brooks interrupts. "Is anyone

taking minutes tonight? We need to make sure we get this all down for the records."

Barbara turns her back on Connie and grabs a legal pad and pen, which she thrusts at me. "Can you take notes? I need to pass out these agendas for Elizabeth. Besides, my chicken scratch is so terrible I can't even read it."

Connie takes a seat in the front row as Elizabeth calls the meeting to order and turns the floor over to Hal.

"I know many of you are here tonight because you're troubled by this blog. I appreciate your concern and want you to know that I have conferred with the school-board's counsel as to how we should handle this situation. While it is a major irritation, the mystery blogger is not violating any laws or usage agreements with the site that hosts the blog."

An alarmed murmur ripples through the audience.

"Excuse me! Please—I ask that you simply consider this a childish prank and ignore it. The more we—"

"But Mr. Brooks." Connie Claxton stands up. "If you don't do something to stop this person, it's like you're condoning what they're doing."

Another wave of chatter erupts from the membership. This time, the tone is agreement. But Principal Brooks interjects, "As I started to say, the more attention we give this blogger, the more he or she will—"

"I'm sure I speak for everyone here when I say we don't want our dirty laundry published on the Internet," says one of the *Stratford Wives*.

There's a collective hush in the room, as if everyone is doing a mental checklist to see which of the blog listings applied to her.

She flushes. "Well, not me personally, of course, I'm speaking collectively. On behalf of everyone here."

Connie Claxton stands up again. "I've had it with this school. I am pulling Chloe out and I'm sending her to a private school."

Barbara

Since we had to rush over to Elizabeth's before the meeting and didn't get to eat, the three of us grab a quick bite at Paulo's over on the avenue.

The meeting ended pretty fast after Hal closed discussion on the blog. It was like watching ants scurry away after someone packs up the picnic.

"Can you believe how everyone left in such a

hurry? I am appalled that no one will step up and volunteer to serve out the rest of the year in these vacant board positions. Margaret, you did a super job taking the minutes. I hereby nominate you for secretary."

"I think that's a wonderful idea and I second the motion," says Elizabeth. "We'll have to replay this installation the next time we have a quorum."

"Don't I get a say in the matter?" Margaret asks.

"Sorry, too late, you've been officially installed," I say. "Now we need to quickly find someone to be the treasurer before Connie Claxton volunteers just to spite me."

"I don't think you'll have to worry about that since she's pulling her daughter out of school," says Margaret. "What is with that woman?"

"She's a fruitcake, just like you said."

"For the record, I believe *you* said that. I just brought up the Claxton coincidence. You christened her the Fruitcake."

I'm antsy sitting here knowing that when I go home I'll have to face Burt. I haven't told anyone about my plans to ask him to leave. I figure there will be plenty of time for that once he's out. Or, he's gone so much, maybe I won't even have to mention it. I can say he's on an extended business trip. I can't sit here and dwell on it all night or I'll be a nervous wreck.

"I know Hal says we shouldn't fuel the fire by talking about it," I say, trying to focus on something other than Burt. "But since it's just us, it couldn't hurt. Who do you think H.P. the kleptomaniac is?"

Elizabeth shrugs. "I don't know. That would assume that what the blogger wrote is true, and I don't want to give Maggie any added reason to worry about Sarah's safety."

Maggie fidgets with the paper sticky tab that held her napkin around her silverware. I can tell she's concerned.

"I am so sorry this is happening," says Elizabeth. "Has Sarah had a chance to make any friends?"

"She's having a hard time."

"I'll talk to Anastasia and make sure she looks after Sarah. I'm going to ask her if she has any idea who might do something like this. I'm with Hal on ignoring most of the nonsense on the blog, but it would be such peace of mind to find out who's doing it just so we can make sure there's no violence."

The food comes and the conversation shifts gears.

"Where are you from, Elizabeth?" Margaret asks.

"I grew up in Seattle, but I went to college at the University of Florida. That's where I met Andrew. After we graduated, I got a job with Worldwide and we settled here."

Elizabeth moves her pasta around on her plate. She's been doing that since we were served. Mine is so good, I don't know how she can resist.

"Is your dinner okay?" I ask. "If not, I'm sure they'll be happy to fix it."

Elizabeth frowns. "I'm just—" Her fork falls from her hand and clatters on the plate. "I'm pregnant. That's what's wrong with me and it feels so good to share it with people who will be happy for me."

She looks as if she wishes she could take back the words, but Margaret and I cheer and we raise our glasses of sweet tea in celebration.

"Who isn't happy for you, honey?"

She sets her fork down again, this time without making a sound. "Andrew and Anastasia for starters. She thinks I don't spend enough time with her and that the baby will just demand even more of me. And, well, Andrew is just not too thrilled about having another child. It wasn't in our plan."

She smiles, but I can tell she's hurting.

"Now, let me tell you something. That man may

think he doesn't want another baby, but once it's born, he's going to be just as crazy about it as he is about that beautiful girl of yours. You mark my words. Burt wasn't none-too-thrilled when I found out I was pregnant with Mary Grace. And look at him now."

Keeping up appearances comes in handy at a time like this. In her delicate state of mind, she doesn't need to know that Burt's a bastard.

In the midst of talking about baby showers—of course I'm going to throw her one—and guest lists, I thought I'd lay down my sword for the occasion. "You can even invite Blair Mallory and the *Stratford Wives* if you want."

Elizabeth's eyes widen. She blots the corners of her mouth with her napkin.

"No, thanks. We're not exactly what you'd call tight. More like friend by proxy of Rob and Andrew. I mean, she's fine, we just don't have that much in common. And, here's some gossip for you—Blair and Rob are separated. Can you believe it?"

I'm flabbergasted. "Oh, my good heavens! Well, after Blair's little outburst at dinner the other night, maybe that's not so hard to believe."

"Rob dropped by Jacobsons a couple of days after

the dinner and he seemed fine," Maggie says. "What happened?"

Elizabeth leans in conspiratorially. "Come to find out Blair's been having an affair with her best friend, Karen Stark's, husband, Bob."

Burt's home when I get back from the meeting. But he's already asleep

That's all right. It's better this way. I'll have more energy to do what I need to do after a good night's sleep.

CHAPTER 12

Elizabeth

When I get home from the meeting, the house is
quiet. Andrew is sitting in a chair in the family room
reading. As I set my purse and briefcase on the bar
that divides the room from the kitchen, he looks up
from his newspaper. "How was the meeting?"

"Fine." I don't have the energy to tell him about
the blog. He wouldn't see the big problem in it anyway. So I just leave the meeting debriefing at *Fine*,
and walk over to kiss him hello. As my lips touch
his, he flinches. It's a subtle withdrawal that cuts me
to the quick. He's been like this since I made up my
mind to keep the baby.

I straighten and stand next to him with my hand
on the back of his chair.

Andrew returns to his paper.

It feels like a brick wall between us. I want to bat

it down. I want to plead with him. *Please be happy about this. This is our baby. There's enough love in this family for one more little soul.*

Instead, I ask, "Where's Anastasia?"

"Hmm—? Oh, up in her room." This time he doesn't look up.

Talk to me Andrew. I'm scared, too.

He sits there silent, reading.

I climb the stairs, knock softly on Anastasia's door.

"Come in."

She's sitting at her desk. Signed in online, as usual.

The Stratford Park Potluck—come here for the latest dish. Written by the Fabulous A.

A as in Anastasia?

No. No way.

"Hi," I say.

"Hey." Her back is to me and she keeps her eyes on the screen as she types.

I can tell even from this distance she's instant messaging with someone. IM-ing, as she calls it.

I don't see the point when she could simply pick up the phone and dial her friends. She tried to explain once that via IM-ing she can have several conversations with different people going on at once.

Again, I miss the point.

"*Isn't it hard to concentrate? To keep up with what you said to whom?*"

"Oh, Mother. *You just don't get it.*"

"Did you have a good night?" I ask.

"Mmmm…."

She keeps typing. *Click. Click. Click. Click.*

"I need to ask a favor of you."

"Mmmm…."

Click. Click. Click. Click.

"Mrs. Woodall says Sarah's having a hard time making friends at school. Can you make a special point of being nice to her?"

"I *am* nice to her." Anastasia doesn't lift her gaze from the computer screen.

I edge closer, trying to see who she's talking to, but she minimizes the screen and whirls around to face me. She's still mad, but what she and Andrew don't know is that I'm content to let it ride. They can be mad for as long as they like and when they're done the baby and I will be right here.

"I'm sure you're nice to her, sweetheart, but why don't you invite her over or at least ask her to sit with you at lunch?"

"She's a loner, Mother. Solo gal. She eats lunch

by herself every day." She smiles, but there's no joy in her expression. "I think she likes it that way."

Anastasia's flawless complexion is scrubbed clean. Her hair is pulled back in a ponytail and she's wearing her pink Paul Frank monkey pajamas. I'm taken by how beautiful she is.

"She probably eats by herself because she doesn't know anyone else. Invite her to join you and Katy and Emily."

She gives me the eye roll and I know better than to push the issue. "Just think about it, okay? Think about what it must be like to be the new girl. You're lucky you've never had to be in that position."

"Mom."

"All I'm saying is it would be a nice gesture to reach out and—"

"Okay. I heard you the first time."

Maggie

"Want to play hookie from school tomorrow?" I ask Sarah as we walk home from Barbara's house.

"Really?" Sarah shines like a lightning bug, but immediately the glow dims with suspicion. "Why?"

I shrug. "I just have an urge for us to spend the day together."

The cicadas buzz in the distance and a cool breeze blows in from the lake.

"Are you off tomorrow?"

"No. Not exactly." I grimace and swat at an imaginary mosquito. "I was going to call in sick, but don't tell anyone."

Sarah frowns. "So if you call in, that means we can't go anywhere fun, right? We have to hang around here."

Hmm… I hadn't considered that. "We could still make it a fun day at home."

"*Umm…*" Sarah lifts one shoulder to her ear. "I dunno. I have a test tomorrow in math."

"Oh." I hadn't counted on this being so difficult, having to persuade my daughter to skip school. I should be proud of her being so conscientious. My heart tightens because I *am* proud of her. And I hate it that because she's been singled out by some bully I feel as if I have to keep her home so we can talk about it, but I don't quite know how to bring it up. Even though she hasn't made many friends, her whole demeanor is different than even a week ago. She seems lighter, as if some of the world's weight has been lifted off her shoulders.

God, I hate to spoil that and set her back to square one. It calls to mind the old tree falling in the forest theory—if a tree falls, but no one hears it, did it really fall? If I never tell Sarah about the blog, is it real?

Of course it's real. And it will really set her back if she hears about it from someone else.

"Ummm...."

She glances at me. "What?"

"Ummm... How did you like Carrie?" I ask as we step up onto the porch. *Chicken.* "Was she fun?"

The amber glow of the light bathes everything in a warm radiance.

"I'm thirteen years old, Mom. Why do you think I need a babysitter?"

"She wasn't a babysitter, she was just someone to hang out with you and Mary Grace."

As I unlock the door, Sarah smiles and shakes her head at me. "She was a babysitter and you know it, Mom."

"If she was, she was there to sit with Mary Grace. Not you."

"Whatever." Sarah plops down on the couch and hugs a pillow to her middle as I lock the door and slide the bar bolt. "How was the meeting tonight?

Anything interesting or just the same old boring stuff?"

Tell her. I walk over and sit down next to her on the couch.

"Oh! Guess who's going to have a baby?"

"Who?"

"Mrs. Deveraux."

Sarah straightens. "Really?" She wrinkles her nose.

"What does Princess Anastasia think about having to share her royal princessdom with a baby? She really doesn't seem like the kind of girl who knows how to share."

I have to smile at Sarah's insightfulness.

"You're right. Maybe this will be good for her. But believe it or not, it's Mr. Deveraux who's not very happy about it. He doesn't want more than one child."

It's not appropriate to tell her he wants Elizabeth to get an abortion. So I leave it at that.

"How come you and Dad didn't have more than one baby, Mom?"

Her question knocks the air out of me. I think this is the first time in a year that she's uttered the word *Dad* without breaking down, and I have to hold my breath for a second to keep hold of my own composure. I don't know which affects me more—Sarah's seeming to have reached a new milestone in her grieving process or the thought of making babies with Tim. He and I actually had a hard time getting pregnant with Sarah and once we did, it was a joyous celebration.

I blink away the thought before tears fill my eyes.

"I don't know, honey. It wasn't really a conscious decision to only have one child, like the Deverauxs made. I suppose that's just the way it turned out."

She nods, satisfied with that answer. Suddenly, I'm exhausted. Too worn out to open the can of worms about the potential threat in the blog. It might give her nightmares. Plus, everything seems worse than it really is when you're tired.

I'll tell her tomorrow. Because it's late and she needs to get to bed. Tomorrow when we're home and having our day together, I'll be able to tell her about the other absurd entries first. It'll be the substitute *Renata Report*—

Hmm.

For a few seconds I'm struck by the irony of the blog appearing just after she and I started our daily

Renata briefings. The timing is uncanny and the coincidence sends a shiver snaking down my backbone.

No. Sarah wouldn't do a thing like that.

How would she—?

No. It's impossible.

Besides, she wouldn't threaten herself. And our computer isn't even connected to the Internet.

"Do you have access to the Internet at school?" I ask.

"No, why?"

Momentarily, I'm at a loss for explanation, but then I manage to say, "I don't know, I was just thinking that maybe we should get Internet service in a few months. I was hoping you could teach me how to do all that online stuff."

She shrugs. "Well, I'll have to learn before I can teach you. I think I'm the only kid in Stratford Park who doesn't have an e-mail address."

Thank God for that.

The next morning, Sarah comes out into the kitchen dressed and ready for school.

"I thought we were playing hooky today," I ask, eyeing her over the rim of my coffee cup.

"So what's up with that anyway? Why today and not one of your days off so we can actually do something?"

"Honey, sit down." I walk over to the couch and motion her over.

Sarah looks at me with wary eyes before she comes over and plops down in the same spot she sat last night. "What?"

I weigh my words. You'd think I would have had a script memorized the way I lay awake all last night thinking about this, but my mind is blank.

"This is probably nothing, but Mr. Brooks learned about this blog—do you know what a blog is?"

"Who doesn't?"

"Well, remember how I told you that it was just boring school stuff at the meeting last night? Well, there was a little something out of the ordinary. I didn't want to bring it up last night. But someone at your school is keeping a blog and wrote something about you."

Sarah's brow furrows. "What? Like what?"

"It was nonsense, but Mr. Brooks and I both feel like it would be better to exercise caution."

"You're keeping me home from school over that?"

Yes. If I hold on tight maybe you won't slip away.

"I told you I don't need a babysitter, especially not at school. I'm not afraid. You shouldn't be, either."

"Sarah, there's no harm in being cautious."

She glares at me as if I've suggested she wear a clown suit to school.

"Don't look at me like that." She looks away. "Since Mrs. Deveraux has a computer, Aunt Barbara and I went over to her house before the meeting and she showed us the Web site."

I get up and top off my coffee. Through the window, I can see it's a beautiful day, clear blue skies— that Easter-egg blue I love so much—and I wish we could have a day where we could do something spontaneous and fun, like take a picnic to the beach and fly a kite. I remember a time when Tim and I did that.

Come on, Maggie. Let's just disappear for a day. It'll be fun. The world will be waiting for us when we get back.

Now I'm glad I went because all I have left of him are memories like that.

"Mom? So what was on the Web site?" Sarah's looking at me as if this isn't the first time she's asked the question.

"Oh, just a bunch of gossip. Kind of like the stuff I tell you I hear at work."

Ugggh! I can't believe I said that, but Sarah doesn't even flinch and that makes me feel better.

"So then they talked about it at the PTA meeting and all?"

"Yeah, Mr. Brooks was pretty upset over it. At first, he was all up in arms and was telling Mrs. Deveraux how he wanted to have the blog shut down and had met with the school board's lawyers, but there's really nothing they can do to close it down, because the blogger isn't breaking any laws. They didn't use the school name, only used initials for the people they talk about. Since they don't name names, it's not libelous. Basically, there aren't grounds to force the blogger to stop."

Sarah nods and starts gathering her things. "I need to get going or I'm going to miss the bus and Mary Grace will have to fend for herself."

She slings her backpack over her shoulder and pauses at the door. "If anyone needs someone to look after her, it's Mary Grace."

Oh. Is that why she wanted to go to school? Because of Mary Grace? A smile tugs at the corners of my lips. I long to tell her what a sweet, empathetic girl she is and how much I admire her for it, but she's already out the door.

I sit there alone, feeling a little sick panic at what my baby might be walking into, but the disease is tempered by a strange sense of pride in her strength.

Maggie

In college, I learned that chaos theory is how something as minute as the flutter of a butterfly's wings can set in motion changes in the atmosphere capable of preventing or causing a catastrophic natural disaster. The flapping wings create a small change in the condition of the system, which, in turn, causes a chain of events leading to large-scale phenomena. Had the butterfly not flapped its wings, the turn of events would have been vastly different.

As I sit sipping the last of my coffee, I wonder about the chain of events Sarah's wanting to go to school— this flutter of my daughter's wings—will set in motion.

Simultaneously, Elizabeth's news about Blair and Rob separating niggles at the back of my mind. I let the thought take center stage so I'll stop worrying about Sarah.

Blair was the one Karen caught with her husband. I'm ashamed at myself for the perverse mix of feelings that course through me, feelings I can't quite identify—not quite surprise, not quite shock, not quite satisfaction, because how could I feel satisfied by something so bad happening to a friend? Still, maybe it's a mix of all of those emotions?

I have my own personal chaos theory—let's call it Maggie's Theory—the same principle as chaos theory, only it happens in reverse: catastrophe strikes causing my entire world to stand still.

The thrust behind chaos theory is that there's order in seemingly random happenings.

Order in chaos.

I was trying to restore order to our lives by keeping Sarah home from school so we could figure out the best way to handle this blog situation. Because even though it's not probable that anyone would harm her, if someone did...

Oh, God, I can't even go there.

With her in school, of course, I have to go to work. No playing hooky for me, even though I'd gotten quite used to the idea of staying home today, sans Renata gossip, just a day with my daughter, secure in our cocoon for the span of twenty-four hours.

It takes all I have to drag myself into the shower and get ready for a much different day than I looked forward to when I'd opened my eyes this morning.

At work, the morning amounts to endless gossip about the *Stratford Park Potluck* blog. Speculations on who is on the list. It's like a mental scavenger hunt.

Even though Renata is largely occupied trying to help her customers answer the clues, I only manage to write up two sales to her ten.

I keep my ears trained for any word of Rob and Blair's split-up, but in between blog speculation and stories of Margie Crawford's alcoholic husband, Carina Barker's waning sex drive and Peggy Lawson's ongoing money problems (which didn't stop her from plunking down seventy-five dollars for night crème she *couldn't possibly live without*), I hear nothing about the Mallory separation.

I wonder how Rob is doing. Did he move out or did she move in with Bob?

Despite Renata's uncanny ability to endear herself to the women of Stratford Park and draw information out of them, she's not the type to stand around talking about them after they leave—or at least not with me. As much as I want more information about the Mallory marriage debacle, I can't bring myself to fish for information, much less come right out and ask.

By the time my lunch break rolls around, I'm ready to get out of the store for some peace and quiet and fresh air, and—if I can get up my nerve—maybe even a stroll down to the Wine Cellar.

I take my sandwich—ham and smoked Gouda with honey mustard on a croissant—and sit on a park bench under a giant live oak. I love the way the lacy Spanish moss drapes from the branches and floats back and forth in the breeze in harmony with the hum of cars driving the avenue, the steady flow of foot traffic, and the gentle trickle of the fountain that's sometimes eclipsed by the delighted squeals of toddlers chasing the squirrels that scamper across their picnic blankets.

There's such a sense of community here—people investing in people's lives, and I wonder what it would be like to have been raised with that kind of closeness? For belonging to come naturally?

The closest I came was when we lived in Asheville, and I never really realized I was part of the community. It was only after Tim died and I was on the outside again that I realized that by virtue of my family that I was indeed part of the community. Belonging to one group granted me automatic admission to the other.

I wonder if Rob feels the same sense of being on the outside?

Something tugs at me, urging me to walk down to the Wine Cellar and see him, but what am I supposed to say? I heard about Blair's affair and I'm so sorry.

Besides, he didn't call me about the job as he said he would—or was I suppose to call him? Either way, he's had a few things on his mind. I didn't want the job when all was well with him and Blair and I felt the magnetic pull of crazy, unattainable attraction.

There must be some deep psychological meaning attached to the first man who stirs my senses being unavailable.

So get over it.

Do you really think you'll be able to support your daughter working for minimum wage?

My stomach tightens with apprehension. I tip my face to the breeze to quell the uneasy feeling.

I will sit here for five minutes. If a green VW Bug drives by, then I should go down and see him about the job. If it doesn't then I will leave well enough alone and trust that the right job will come along.

Off to my right, a woman is playing catch with a little girl with bouncing blond curls. The big plastic ball rolls past the child and I stop it with my foot before it rolls past me onto the street.

I gently toss it back to the girl, who squeals with joy as she catches it with both arms, hugging it to her little body.

The mother—or maybe she's the nanny, but I doubt it because she has the same blond curls— smiles and waves her gratitude.

I wave back. When I turn back to resume my watch for the green-car omen, my stomach flip-flops because one is attempting to parallel park in front of me.

Okay. Okay. I'll go.

I stuff the remnants of my sandwich into the pink vinyl lunch box and herd the butterflies in my stomach toward Rob's wine shop on the other end of the avenue.

It takes me about five minutes to make the trek, including the time I take to linger in front of the window of the French Closet, a quirky little boutique on Park Avenue where I've been window shopping since I got here. Lured by the sumptuous window displays, I've been dying to go inside this shop since the first day I wandered by, but I haven't because I don't have the money.

I move on down the avenue glancing in the Wine Cellar's giant plate-glass window, forcing myself to go straight inside. If I hesitate, I will un-doubtedly chicken out.

The air is cool inside the shop. There is row after row of wine racks made out of blond wood sitting atop the light hardwood floor. Skylights in the ceiling give the place a bright, airy feeling. Beyond the last row of wine on the far left side of the shop is the wrap stand with a small cash register.

A young guy with red hair, who looks to be in his early twenties, is helping a woman make her selec-tions, carries three bottles to the counter and deposits them among the others that stand tall like soldiers at attention. I count twelve bottles in all—a case, I think to myself. *I'm not totally hopeless at this.*

"Hi," he calls. "I'll be right with you."

Good service.

I nod, glancing around, but Rob is nowhere in sight.

I spend the next five minutes perusing the various racks of Bordeaux, cabernet sauvignon, Syrah, Shiraz, sauvignon blanc. All sound familiar and I know I prefer say a big, bold zinfandel to a lighter, fruity val-policella. But there are so many different kinds and I'd be hard-pressed to explain why you should pay forty-five dollars for a bottle of Chateau St. Jean 2002 Sonoma County Reserve Chardonnay versus ten dollars for the Australian Buckeley's 2004 Chardonnay.

My God, do people really pay forty-five dollars for a bottle of wine? To drink?

"Hey, how's it going?" I turn and the redheaded guy is standing behind me. I replace the Australian wine in the rack. "Looking for anything special?"

His name tag reads Mark.

"Actually, I'm here to see Rob Mallory. Is he in?"

"Sorry, you just missed him. He's gone for the day. Is there anything I can help you with?"

Disappointment clinches my gut and a small voice inside me whispers that it's for the best that he's not here. Really, it is.

"No, that's okay. I'll catch up with him another time."

I turn to leave, and Mark says, "May I tell him your name?"

"Tell him Maggie came by."

Barbara

I have a secret that I can't bring myself to share with a soul: Burt and I haven't slept in the same bed since I gave birth to Mary Grace.

It started because he couldn't stand to be awakened in the middle of the night by a crying baby. So he moved into the guest room so that he could get his rest and be sharp for work, leaving me to tend to Mary Grace 24-7.

Over the years I've lied to myself, pretending the arrangement was okay. But what kind of married couples have separate bedrooms? I mean, what's the point?

I'm sure he's been asking himself that very question since the last time we had sex, which was probably the night I conceived Mary Grace. Good Lord, that's embarrassing.

I may be sixty years old, but I ain't dead.

Now that I've had a few weeks to comprehend everything, I really and truly feel a sense of relief. That's pretty strange, isn't it? To be glad to have discovered lingerie and a vibrator in your husband's suitcase? It's odd, but I truly do have this strange sense of calm about me.

Mary Grace has already left with Sarah on the school bus. So if this should get ugly—I'm betting it won't—we'll have plenty of time to settle matters.

I knew he'd sleep in late this morning—would probably saunter into the kitchen about nine-thirty—because he'd be jet-lagged.

I hear his footsteps on the back stairs right on schedule. Even though I am fully prepared to do this, I find myself tensing up as he enters the room.

"Good morning," he says, sounding all hearty and rested. Smug, I think. Because he has no idea that I know all about his dirty little secret. Thinks he got away with it.

One time that would have made me madder than a wet cat. But this morning, I'm calm.

Perfectly calm.

"Mornin'." My back is to him because I'm standing at the stove, flipping his eggs. Over easy, just the way he likes them. Grits, bacon, sliced tomato and buttered whole-wheat toast. I figured I'd give him a good send off. One last home-cooked breakfast. Unless Miss Pocket Rocket knows how to fry eggs. She'd better because Burt is about as chintzy as they come when it comes to eating out.

Why spend four dollars on eggs when you can buy a dozen for half that amount?

He walks over to the coffeepot, pours himself a cup. The chair legs scrape on the terrazzo when he pulls out his chair and again as he scoots it into place.

The plastic newspaper bag crinkles as he pulls the paper from it. With a crisp, snapping sound, he shakes it open and refolds it back and over so that he has a perfect rectangle that's manageable with one hand and he can hold his coffee with the other.

All these sounds of his morning ritual that I know by heart without even looking at him. But really they're an intrusion. I didn't miss him the weeks he was in China with his bimbo. When he's gone, I can pretend he's gone on a long, long trip.

I take a plate down from the cupboard, slide the eggs onto it, add bacon, grits, tomato slices, toast.

I stand for a few seconds with my back to him,

gripping the plate. This is it. Once I set the plate down, there's no turning back.

Ohhhhh, I should have done this a long time ago. Back when I found out about him and Leila. Maybe if I had, things would have turned out differently. If I'd left him back then maybe she wouldn't have found it impossible to forgive herself.

I just wish she could have known that I forgave her. If I could forgive him, I certainly could have forgiven her.

The way the eggs and bacon are arranged on the plate looks like a grim face staring back at me. For some reason it reminds me that if I'd left Burt back then, I'd never have gotten pregnant with Mary Grace. Mary Grace.

My little love.

My shining star.

He barely glances up when I set the plate in front of him. I'm glad because I have something in my eye that's causing me to tear up something terrible. But I blink it away.

"Burt?"

"Mmm?" He glances away from his paper to break the egg yolks with the point of his toast and takes a huge bite.

"Burt, I want you to pack your things and go. I want you to leave this house."

Maggie

Sarah did fine at school yesterday. In fact, she came home talking about a new friend she'd made—a girl named Gretchen who's in her second-period art class. Apparently, Gretchen read the blog and was talking to Sarah about how uncool she thought it was that someone would single Sarah out in such a mean way.

My first thought was, *I haven't even met this girl and already I like her.* I told Sarah to bring Gretchen home with her after school one day if she wanted to.

She shrugged and said she'd think about it.

This morning, there was no talk about her staying home from school. I'm taking my lead from Sarah. If she's not anxious over the situation, I'm trying not to be.

Despite Renata being the town shrink—or maybe because of it—I can't bring myself to confide in her. Don't think that she hasn't asked some leading questions. It's not that I don't trust her, it's just that it seems as if once you start spilling your guts, all the rest of your secrets come spilling out. I've always been a firm believer that when you tell your secrets, you give away your power. What kind of power, I'm not sure. But I'm just not that comfortable letting people in.

I go on about my business and leave the counseling sessions to the others.

This morning when I get in, I'm delighted to see we've received a particularly large shipment of merchandise. The stacks of boxes will give me something to do today.

I'm about halfway finished unpacking and putting away the first box of La Prairie treatment when I look up and see Rob striding across the marble floor. The rush of surprise makes me draw in a quick, sharp breath. As our gazes meet, my heart slams into my breastbone then stumbles into an uncomfortable thud.

I resist the urge to smooth my hair or glance at myself in the mirror to see if I still have on lipstick or if there is just an outline around the outer rim because I've unconsciously nibbled the rest off.

Instead, I scan the packing slip for the item number of the face cream I'm clutching, put a tally mark next to it and put the product on the shelf. By the time I turn around to greet him, he's standing at the counter smiling that lazy smile that always makes my blood hum.

"Hello." He looks way too good to be standing there so nonchalantly. I start to search for traces of sadness over Blair, but look away, grabbing another item from the box of new merchandise.

Cleanser, this time.

"Hey. Did you come to help me put away this stock?" I glance up from the packing slip in time to see him smile again, and I realize what I love most about his grin is the way it makes his eyes turn down at the edges.

"Mark said you came into the shop yesterday. Sorry I missed you."

Heat blossoms at the base of my neck and I turn to set the item on the shelf before the blush can spread to my cheeks.

"I did." I steal a glance at Renata who is on the extreme opposite side of the department, deep in conversation with an elderly woman. Just as I'm about to look away, she darts a sneaky glance in our direction. *Oh, God, I can't talk to him about the wine job. Not in here.*

"I hope it's about the job," he says.

"*Shhhh!*" I put my finger to my lips.

Renata looks at us more obviously this time.

Rob waves to her and murmurs under his breath, "So it was about the job."

Renata waves back and tears her gaze from us back to the woman.

"Have lunch with me."

"Are you sure you want to do that? With the way people love to gossip around here, that might not be such a good idea."

There's an uncomfortable beat of silence and now I do see the sadness in his eyes. "How are you?" I add, hoping it doesn't sound like an afterthought.

He shrugs, picks up a perfume tester, sniffs, grimaces and sets it back on the mirrored tray. "That's something else we shouldn't discuss here." He picks up another, sniffs and wrinkles his nose. "So have lunch with me and I'll tell you. Which of these is your favorite?"

"I can't today." As I set out the bottle of Chanel No. 5, I rack my mind for a reason why not—other than I'm afraid of you.

He sniffs the bottle and nods, setting it down. I spray a sample card and hand it to him. He inhales deeply, then puts the card in his shirt pocket.

"You're going to smell like Chanel No. 5."

"I'll smell like you."

He smiles again, but I can see that he's wounded. A little voice inside warns that he's hurting, grieving the loss of his wife just as I grieved Tim, only he has to live with the ghost of a living person.

Knowing that he's missing Blair makes it easier to take the job because there is no way I will get involved with a man who is still in love with another woman, a woman who isn't even his ex-wife yet. Loving a man who can't love you back is as futile as loving a dead man.

"Then if you can't come today, meet me tomorrow for an early lunch at Le Jardin so we can talk."

Elizabeth

I'm reviewing the final draft of the press release for the Worldwide/Celestial acquisition when Ruby buzzes me.

"Elizabeth, Hal Brooks is on the phone. He says he needs to talk to you about an urgent matter."

I silently curse the day I agreed to be the PTA president. I contemplate having Ruby tell him I'm not available, but calling him back will be more of a hassle than dealing with him now.

"Thank you, Ruby. Put him through. Hello?"

"Elizabeth, I'm terribly sorry to bother you at work, but when was the last time you looked at *The Stratford Park Potluck* blog?"

"Oh, Hal, are we back to this?" I take off my reading glasses, toss them aside and rub my eyes. "What now?"

"It seems our mystery blogger has confessed. She says her name is Anastasia."

I sign on to the notorious Web site because I refuse to believe that my daughter could be the perpetrator of something like this, something so ridiculous that has caused such a furor in the community.

But sure enough, the new heading reads *Anastasia's Stratford Park Potluck—come here for the latest dish.*

Still, I'm not convinced. What's to say someone else isn't just using her name. I really want to believe that and almost have myself convinced. Until I spy the latest entry:

Okay, so I've been spilling it on all you guys. Here's some dirt about two people very close to me: HINT— think parental units—I know a woman who's pregnant and her husband wants her to get an abortion. That's fine with me. I don't want another kid in the house.

Maggie

Rob and I are the only two people in Le Jardin.

I order quiche and a salad. He orders the duck-and-Brie sandwich on a baguette. He asks if I'll share a bottle of wine, but I decline since I have to go back to work.

Since I'm not drinking, he opts for iced tea instead.

"Blair and I were having problems for a long time." Rob fingers his knife, looking at it, not at me. "I just couldn't come right out and admit to myself that she'd actually cheat. It was only when the guy's wife came to me and laid everything on the table that I knew it was over."

I sit silently, letting him talk, feeling a little guilty remembering the day Karen Stark was in the store crying. I sink back into the safety of my memories of Tim.

My love.

My faithful.

What is it like to love someone with your heart and soul only to wake up one morning to discover you never really knew them at all?

I'm glad I don't know. As bad as it was losing Tim, what we had will never, never be tainted or tarnished or devalued.

The beginning mandolin strains of the song "Maggie May" start playing over the Muzak system. I rub away the responding goose bumps on my arms, hoping Rob doesn't notice.

I wonder if he remembers all those times we were driving in his car when he'd sing this song to me. I loved it. Because not only did it have my name in it, it was a sexy song about a guy who was desperately in love with this Maggie.

Back then, when things were simple, I fancied it was our song.

Wake up, Maggie…

Rod Stewart sings about needing a friend, but the friend turns into a lover, wrecks his bed and kicks him in the head.

Judging by the nostalgic smile in Rob's face, he remembers. Neither of us says a word until the song is over. That's when Rob asks, "Will you take the job? I can offer you forty-five thousand plus commission for thirty hours a week."

I have to bite the insides of my cheeks to keep my mouth from falling open. Currently, I'm making minimum wage—six dollars and forty cents per hour—plus the occasional pittance of a commission, which on a good week, might equal an extra five spot. That works out to about fourteen thousand per year for full-time work.

I'd be an idiot not to take the job.

"That's to start," he says. "If you meet the plan I've outlined for the first six months then we can negotiate. So what do you think?"

Elizabeth

All day, I've been preoccupied by this ridiculous blog. I know the only thing I can do is talk to Anastasia and hear her side of the story. Even so, it's been hard to think of anything else.

Until my boss, Herb Waters, calls at two-thirty and asks to see me in his office.

When I get there, his administrative assistant says, "Go right in. He's waiting for you."

"Ah, Elizabeth, come in. Close the door so we can talk."

I do and take a seat across from his desk.

His hands are steepled in front of him and he's leaning forward in his chair.

"Elizabeth, how long have we worked together now—nearly twenty years?" He sits back in his chair, clenches and unclenches his fists, picks up a white envelope that was lying to the side and centers it on his desk blotter. I have the eerie sense something ominous is about to happen.

"You know, with the absorption of Celestial, we're faced with a reorganization." He shakes his head, looks down at the envelope. "Oh, there's no easy way to do this. Elizabeth, I'm sorry, but the board has decided to eliminate your position."

That's really the last of his words I hear, except for something else about a severance package: he hands me the white envelope, and says that I should leave and they will send my things to me. When I insisted on packing everything up myself, Herb says *no*, that he hates for it to come down to this, but security will escort me out if I don't leave the premises immediately. As if by theme-park magic, a uniformed security guard is waiting for me in the hall, holding my purse, and walks me all the way to my car.

Do you know how humiliating it is to take that last walk through the halls when everyone knows you've just been fired?

I drive around in a daze for about an hour wondering what we're going to do. We rely on my income and with the baby coming, I don't know how in the world I'll be able to get another job.

I remember the white envelope and pull into a shopping-center parking lot to look at the severance offering. One year's salary.

That's it? One stinking year and a uniformed escort to my car after I gave them twenty years of my life?

Barbara

My very own personal motto has always been, If You Can Laugh At Yourself, You'll Always Know Where To Find A Smile.

But smiles have been scarce around these parts the last few days. Burt left without as much as a cross word. He knew he was caught.

Even though he wasn't home much when he lived here—and when he was, he was usually a million miles away—there's something about knowin' it's over that makes me sad. Deep down-in-my-bones sad.

I failed.

But I had no other choice. There's just no explaining away the things I found in his suitcase. If he's giving them to someone else, it's bad; if they're not for someone else it's worse, because that means they belonged to his very own self and, well, I don't even want to go there.

I suppose if I had to choose, I'd rather my husband was giving trashy lingerie to other women than wearing it himself.

But it just doesn't matter now.

At least he didn't try to deny it. I went all these years turning a blind eye to his doings, but when I saw that lingerie with my own eyes... Well, no sense in dwelling on it now.

I think what makes me the saddest is that Mary Grace hasn't asked after him. All these years I thought I was sticking it out to give her the same kind of normal upbringing I gave her brothers and sisters, but I think it's best for everyone involved to move along.

That girl is giving me fits today. She's been a real pistol. One minute she's clingy, the next minute she's sassing me. I just sent her up to her room for a time-out because I couldn't take any more.

I'm frying up a mess of chicken when someone knocks on the door. I'm thinking it's Maggie. I haven't told her about Burt yet. I suppose I have to give myself some time to get used to the idea, but I need to tell her.

"Come on in. Door's open."

I just about fall over when Elizabeth Deveraux walks into my kitchen and bursts into tears.

"Honey! Honey? What's happened?"

I hug her until she calms down a bit. I grab a paper towel and hand it to her because I don't want to leave her alone while I go out and fetch a box of tissues from the other room.

I pull out a chair and ease her down onto it, then pull out another for myself so I'm sitting right across from her.

"I'm sorry." She blots at her eyes. "I can't believe I lost control like that. But today's been one of those days where everything fell apart."

Elizabeth leans her head on her hand. "I lost my job. I don't know how I'm going to tell Andrew. He's so uncertain about the baby. It's like I've lost control of my entire world."

I get up to turn the chicken. "You know sometimes losing control isn't altogether a bad thing, honey. Cook him a good dinner and he'll be fine."

She shakes her head. "How can I cook when the sight of food nauseates me?"

"Don't you worry about a thing. I'll fix you up a nice meal to take home with you. Chicken and biscuits, a little corn and mashed potatoes and he'll be just fine. You've been through a lot today. You need someone to take care of you so that you can be strong for that baby."

"It's generous of you to offer, but I can't take your dinner, Barbara. What will you feed your family?"

I can't bring myself to tell her that my family is less one person. That's a talk for a different day.

"Honey, I always cook enough for an army so don't you worry about a thing. There's plenty here."

I pour Elizabeth a glass of tea and go on about getting dinner, throwing in a few extra potatoes to boil.

"I don't mean to pry, but why is Andrew unhappy about the baby?"

"He's just afraid."

"What's he afraid of?"

"The test results show that there could be problems."

We're quiet for a minute. I see where this is going.

"Barbara, don't you ever feel resentful having to give up so much because of Mary Grace's condition? I mean you gave birth to five other healthy children. Don't you ever feel a little cheated that this had to happen to your child? To you?"

I remember what it was like to be in her posi-

tion. Scared and unsure when the doctor tells you
there might be problems. And then to have every
mother's nightmare come true when the doctor
confirms the diagnosis.

"I suppose there are a lot of things I could feel that
way about if I let myself. But I won't. I think everything
happens for a reason. Back before Mary Grace was
born, I wanted to turn this place into a bed-and-
breakfast. If we would have done that, we probably
would never have had another child— Who knows,
maybe I still would have gotten pregnant, but it's
unlikely. But once she was born, I gave up that dream
for her, because it would have been pretty much impossible to do that with a baby. So I suppose I sacri-
ficed one dream for another. She's my angel and I
could no more resent her than I could any of my other
children."

Elizabeth twists the paper towel.

"You're so much stronger than I am. At least
Andrew can admit his doubts. But one of the hardest
parts of this has been realizing that I'm not sure I can
handle it if the baby is less than perfect. I'm a terrible
person. I've made Andrew out to be the bad guy, but
despite the front I've been putting on, deep inside
I'm no more certain I can have this baby than he is."

"Honey, before I got pregnant with Mary Grace, my soul longed for a child. I thought if I didn't have another baby that I was absolutely going to keel over and die. Burt was furious when I came up pregnant, but we made it through okay."

Liar.

Actually, not really. Burt and I are not splitting because of Mary Grace. Our reasons are a completely different matter. But I don't need to worry her with that right now.

Elizabeth

When I get home from Barbara's house, I put the food in the warming oven and go upstairs and knock on Anastasia's door.

"Come in."

I can see she's been crying and I don't even have to ask, I just know she didn't do it.

Still, she starts right in defending herself. "Mom, it wasn't me. I swear it wasn't. You've got to believe me—"

"I believe you."

I sit down next to her and she's eyeing me warily as if she's waiting for me to start yelling at her anyway.

"Who do you think it is?"

"I don't know. But please make them stop."

"Let's talk to your father during dinner and see what he recommends."

Anastasia frowns. "You're the big PR expert, don't you know how to fix this?"

I shake my head. "No, I'm sorry, I don't."

"Why would they print something like that about Dad? That's not what he wants you to do, is it?"

"I know this baby has been a shock to all of us. But I think it's just taken us a little time to get used to the fact that we're going to welcome another person into our family."

Anastasia shrugs, not looking entirely convinced.

At dinner, Andrew promises to call the blog provider and see what can be done.

When Anastasia excuses herself from the dinner table and retreats upstairs, it's time to tell Andrew what happened today.

Why am I so nervous about this? It's not as if I quit. It was beyond my control.

But that's no comfort.

I don't like things beyond my control. I always thought the phrase *it was beyond my control* was a cop-out.

He helps himself to the last of the mashed potatoes. "This is delicious. Tell Barbara thanks."

She was right. He does seem a little more relaxed thanks to the good meal. It's a shame to make him bristle.

"Remember me telling you that this merger with Celestial was going to be tricky because of all the layoffs that were going to happen?"

"Right." He's scraping the potato bowl with his spoon and seems perfectly pacified.

"Well, the first round started today."

"Really? Who got the ax?"

"Me."

He stops, spoon in the air, and looks at me as if I'm kidding. "You've got to be joking—"

"Andrew, don't. Just don't. This is hard enough without you beating me up. So if you can't say something nice, don't say anything at all."

He blinks at me. Once. Twice. Sets down the empty bowl, but he doesn't say anything.

"They offered me a package with one year's salary. At least we're not out in the cold."

He reaches out and takes my hand, which almost floors me. "With the baby coming, maybe this is divine intervention."

Now I'm the one who's speechless. "What…?"

He leans in and kisses me, light and soft on the lips.

The whole world disappears for a minute.

Forehead to forehead he says, "I'm not saying this

will be easy. I'm scared to death, but we're a family and we will get through this together."

Maggie

According to Elisabeth Kübler-Ross, people who grieve go through five stages on their way to coping: denial, anger, bargaining, depression and acceptance.

Makes it sound so clean, doesn't it? As if you pass a test and are promoted to the next level.

Okay, let's see, you've met the requirements for denial; you did a smashing job with bargaining; but depression— Nope, I don't think you've wallowed enough. Come back and see me on this one later.

What's not always clear is that these emotional stages aren't clean-cut. In fact, the whole process can be downright messy—zipping back and forth between them as if you're caught in some sort of viscous emotional loop.

I've denied and bargained myself dry. Anger and depression are the ones that have tripped me up.

I'm tired of it. I'm tired of it draining all my energy. Maybe that's the first step toward getting past it? Maybe it's the new job or spring fever—but the good days are starting to outnumber the bad so much so that when I have a bad one, it really knocks me off-kilter. I've found it's best to keep busy. Not give myself time to think too much.

I'm off this morning because we're having a special tasting at the Wine Cellar tonight. Sarah and her friend Gretchen are helping Barbara at the Special Olympics out at the university after school. Barbara's going to look after Sarah tonight. So it feels as if I have an entire day.

That can be dangerous. Too much time to think.

So I busy myself with errands that need to be done, household chores and grocery shopping for the week.

I'm on my way to the store when I pass Palmetto Avenue. We've lived in Stratford Park a few weeks now and I've probably passed Palmetto every time I've ventured out to go shopping because it's not far from Barbara's house. Back in the day, Palmetto was the low-rent area, just over that invisible line where property values plummeted and the "neighborhood" went from good to bad.

Not anymore. Renewal has spread and upgraded the quarter. In fact, Barbara told me that the average price of a house in the Palmetto area is now upward of half a million dollars.

Until today, I could never bring myself to turn

down that street. But today the car makes a smooth right, and I'm taken down a different street than the one I used to live on with Mama all those years ago. The tired old houses have blossomed into a shiny row of two-story mini-mansions.

We rented the duplex we lived in and I wouldn't even venture to guess how much Mama paid per month. It couldn't have been much because she didn't make much at her job at the bar in the bowling alley.

I drive up and down the street twice before I pick out the lot where our place used to stand. It's replaced by a brand-new monster of a dwelling that's fabricated to look old. I stop the car across the street from where our place used to be and squint my eyes, willing the area to look the way it used to.

After a minute, it all comes back. The brown duplex with its twin jalousie doors the color of polished sea glass, the sparse front lawn with more brown patches than green, the window boxes with no flowers.

If I close my eyes I can hear Mama singing. I can see it, too. She drags out her record player and those old Bob Dylan LPs; she's singing along and swayin' to the music, a bourbon and water in one hand and a cigarette in the other. Dylan's wailin' about...*not wanting to work on Maggie's farm no more*.

"Maggie's Farm." It was her favorite.

In one of the rare moments she let down her guard, she stroked my hair and said she named me for the song.

Won't work on Maggie's farm no more...

"It wasn't actually *Maggie's farm*. It belonged to your granddaddy—his orange groves. His money. His way or the highway. But that's okay, because I never actually worked there, either. But I know *someone* who did...."

Then she caught herself and the wall went back up and that was the end of it.

I'll never forget the faraway look in Mama's eyes. I've always known deep in my heart that *someone* who worked on the farm was my daddy.

To this day I can't hear Bob Dylan without it conjuring memories of Mama and the smell of Wild Turkey and the phantom image of my daddy. A man I imagine was tall and dark and devastatingly handsome, who left me a blank space on my birth certificate and the template of his genes as the only clue to who he was.

I was standing right there in that yard the last day

I hugged her goodbye. I remember it so clearly, as if it were ten minutes ago. I loaded all my things into the back of that old white Volkswagen Rabbit, ready to start a new life at the University of North Carolina. I'd gotten an academic scholarship and she was so proud of me. She hugged me as if she didn't want to let me go. Then she stood on the lawn in her pink dress and bare feet waving goodbye until my car turned the corner. That image of her getting smaller in my rearview mirror as I drove away is burned into my mind.

It dawns on me with crushing clarity that Mama was my age now when she killed herself. The realization sends a shiver coursing through me.

I think of Tim and wonder if I can hold on to anyone in my life.

No! I can't go there because that makes me want to lock Sarah away so that no harm ever comes to her—and push away Barbara and Mary Grace, and Elizabeth and Rob…anyone who might make me care for them.

Because life is a ticking clock, a meter that's running. And just as certain as there is a beginning to all relationships, all things come to an end. We just don't like to think about it. It invokes darkness. Sadness. Emptiness. Aloneness.

Still, when it comes right down to it, aren't we really alone in this world?

That's the one thing Mama left me when she killed herself—the dawning that no matter how deep you fancy your connection to another human being, you really do walk alone in this world.

When I open my eyes, three women—one whom I recognize from school—have gathered at the foot of a driveway a few doors down. They have that casual, preppy air of the upper-middle-class homemaker. The one I recognize, the skinny brunette, bounces a baby on her hip, a little girl, with a big pink bow in her curly brown hair.

I try to imagine Mama standing out there like that with me when I was little. But what I see in my mind's eye is us a few years down the road. She takes my hand and pulls me up off the couch to dance with her.

"Dance with me, Maggie."

Bob Dylan's blaring, the house windows are wide open because we don't have air-conditioning and it's the dead heat of summer. Sweat glistens on her beautiful fair skin and her blond hair is streaming down her frail shoulders. She looks so alive, smiling and happy.

In my mind's eye that's the way I want to remember her.

Even if I never know *why* she did it.

Even if I never know what could have led her to that decision to just slip away.

Even if I never know if she hesitated for a single moment to think about the fallout of what she was doing.

The shrink told me she was probably too broken for rational thoughts.

Only sick people take their own lives.

Sick.

Thoughtless.

Careless, mother of mine.

I pound the steering wheel.

Just let it go.

Just let her go.

Wake up, Maggie.

The image of Rob singing "Maggie May" to me pops into my head and takes my breath away. It was just a few days ago when it was just him and me in the Wine Cellar. He played the song on the CD player in the shop, singing—no, more like growling—the song in a raspy, gravely Rod Stewart impersonation that made me laugh and left me weak in the knees.

What am I doing? Opening myself up for more pain? I just wish I had a sign pointing me in the right direction. Am I on the right path or is my internal compass so screwed up I've veered dangerously off course? Which is how it feels.

I look around for a plausible sign, but see nothing. Nothing.

Maybe that's the sign.

I start the car and I'm just about ready to pull away when my cell phone rings. I put my foot on the brake and fish it out of my bag, wondering if it's Sarah or Barbara calling, but when I don't recognize the number, an absurd thought pops into my brain:

If it's Rob, then I'm on the right path.

"Hello?"

"Hey, Maggie May. It's Rob."

I nearly jump out of my skin as I try to push ridiculous thoughts about right paths and second *chances* over the edge into nothingness.

"Hi. What's up?"

"I was just calling to touch base…wondering how your day's going."

As I pull away from Palmetto Avenue with my past behind me and Rob's voice in my ear, I can almost see Mama in the rearview mirror waving as I drive off.

Barbara

I'm proud of Burt. He didn't do anything stupid, like close out our joint checking account. Of course, I stashed away a little money just in case. But I'm hoping this bodes well that he'll behave himself out here today. When I told him what we were doing today, it surprised the hell out of me when he said he wanted to meet me out here at the Special Olympics, wanted to watch Mary Grace do some of her events. Let me tell you, you could have knocked me over with a feather.

It's noisy and crowded and not at all a good place for discussing particulars, but I wasn't about to say no.

I'm a little nervous because it's the first time I've seen him since that day I tossed him out and I'm ashamed to admit, I'm a little skeptical about what he wants. Why he'd give up his afternoon to come all the way out here to an event like this when he could barely give his daughter the time of day when we lived as a family.

I sense him before I see him clear the crowd. Mary Grace's first event is the four-hundred-meter-walk race and I asked him to meet me here. I only half expected him to show up. But here he is.

Sarah and her little friend Gretchen are goofing around, laughing about something. "Why don't y'all go over and make sure Mary Grace is stretching out?"

"After that, can we go to the concession stand for a soda?"

I nod, watching Burt approach. "As long as y'all stay together. I'll be right up there in the stand with your uncle Burt."

Calling him that stabs at my heart because it makes it seem as if nothing's changed: Even though Maggie and Sarah don't know it, too much has.

Irreparably, I fear.

"I thought Uncle Burt was out of town."

He sees me, but holds off to the side. I hold up my index finger signaling I'll be right there.

"Well, he's back now. Here, y'all are going to need some money."

I give Sarah a five-dollar bill, and she and Gretchen go running over to the roped-off area where Mary Grace is with her team.

It's the craziest thing, but my heart starts pounding against my rib cage so hard it hurts. When I get over to him, he tries to give me a hug, but it turns out to be more of an awkward squeeze. He starts to say something just as the starting signal begins another race. The crowd goes wild and I can't hear him.

"What?"

That old familiar look of annoyance contorts his features and a little voice deep inside me says, *Same old Burt. Nothing's ever going to change.*

It must be a short race because there's one last crescendo of applause and then the noise dissipates to a dull roar.

"Look, I realize this is probably not the best place to talk." His tone is brusque. "I want to come home."

He just doesn't get it, does he? He can't bully himself into everything he wants.

"I don't know, Burt. I'm going to have to think about it."

Maggie

Rob called. Just to see how my day was. Just as I was sinking into another funk, he turns up the dimmer switch and makes me realize I don't have to live in darkness.

Of course, I'm ignoring the rational part of me that's screaming, "Hello? He may be separated, but he's a married man. And he's your boss. And…"

I ignore that voice of reason because the world seems brighter and I hear Mama saying, *Dance, Maggie*, and Rob singing "Maggie May" and it eclipses the reason right out of my mind. For this moment, I'm looking forward, past the *shouldas* and *couldas*, straight into the eyes of here and now.

Maybe it's not just him. Maybe it's me. Maybe I had to drive down Palmetto Avenue right up to that phantom house that isn't even standing anymore and stare Mama's ghost in the face and—and by proxy Tim's, too—and tell them to rest in peace.

To give me some peace.

Please.

Tomorrow I may feel differently, but today—*here and now*—something's in the air.

After the grocery store, I dance myself all the way to the French Closet and splurge on a new dress to wear tonight. It's a silky, butter-yellow chemise that hangs just so and skims my body in all the right places. It makes me feel sexy and sensuous and alive. It'll go perfectly with my gold strappy sandals, the ones that are still in the box because I've only worn them once. They look as though they were made for this dress.

Then I go home and take a long hot bath with orange blossom and jasmine bath salts and spend extra time getting ready to go in and set up everything for the tasting.

As I'm sitting at my dressing table putting on my makeup, my wedding rings wink at me in the mirror.

A voice deep in my heart says, *It's time to take them off.* For the first time since Tim and I got married, I slip them off and leave the house with bare fingers.

When I get there, we're the only two in the shop.

Mark has gone out for a long dinner break and will be back just before the tasting starts.

"You look gorgeous," Rob says. "New dress?"

"It is." I walk behind the bar area where we'll be setting up the various wines.

He carries over a case of the wine we're sampling tonight, and we work side by side, unpacking the bottles and arranging them on the bar.

There's a charge in the air zinging between us, a type of silent communication that words can't match.

He stands so close to me, I could list to the side and touch him. I flex my hand, then fist it into the skirt of my dress and inhale the scent of him. It's like sunshine on skin. I glance up at his jawline peppered with whiskers and a shuddering panic quivers in my belly.

Shouldn't do this.

But I'm going to do this.

Not yet. Not right now, but I feel it in my blood that before this night is over something's going to change.

He glances over at me and smiles as if he can read my mind and we keep working silently in sync.

After the last person walks out the door with a

case of wine on his shoulder and an order for several cases of the other godly nectars we sampled, Rob turns the lock on the door and once again, it's just the two of us in the store.

I went easy on the wine since there were so many different varieties. One of the most valuable lessons I've learned since I've been working here is the necessity of pacing myself.

But as he uncorks a bottle of zinfandel, just for him and me to share, I feel an inevitable discarding of inhibitions as if it's been...well, inevitable.

He stands on the other side of the bar and pours two glasses of zin. I'm vaguely grateful for the two-foot barrier between us.

Handing me one of the wineglasses, he says, "Here's to a great night."

We clink glasses. Sip.

I savor the jammy blackberry flavor. "It was good, wasn't it?"

"I'd say that by all measures and standards, it was a pretty big success."

He raises his glass to mine and looks into my eyes for a long moment, during which I feel the bottom of my world open up, leaving me dangling over the edge of a vast abyss. He runs a finger down my cheek, over my lower lip before he takes my chin in his hand and starts to lean in—

Bambambambambambambambambambam

We jerk apart. One of us, I don't know who, connects with a wineglass and red wine goes everywhere, including down the front of my brand-new yellow dress.

Bambambambambambambambambambam

I look over and see Blair giving us the look of death through the glass door.

"*Shit.*" He spits the word through clenched teeth and goes over to let her in. As I dab at the maroon stain on the front of me like blood, I feel like the poster-woman for wicked, husband-stealing whores.

No, wait, that's Blair. I haven't slept with her husband, whom she left for her best friend's husband. Nothing's happened with Rob. Thanks to her impeccable timing.

"What do you want?" He's opened the door, but has blocked her from entering. But the way the door is angled, I can see her through the glass.

"What are you doing?" She sounds like the betrayed wife and I really can't believe she'd have the nerve to play the victim after what she's put him through.

"I'm having wine with Maggie." I hold my breath waiting for the qualifier, waiting for him to downplay *what he was doing*. But he doesn't. "Listen, Blair, this isn't a good time—"

"What? You think you can stand here in front of this big window and carry on with her in front of God and everyone. I saw you from the street."

"Yeah, I think I can. You made that clear when you set the standard."

"You—!" Screaming obscenities and crying, Blair starts beating on him with both fists and for a second, I wonder if I should do something to help him get her off him, but somehow Rob manages to close the door and lock it. Blair reverts to beating on the glass so hard I'm afraid it will shatter.

"She's drunk," is all Rob says as he walks away from the door.

Most of the shops on Park Avenue roll up their carpets at six o'clock. By eleven o'clock there's not much traffic outside because even the restaurants close up tight by ten. But just as I'm wondering whether we should call the police, she stops.

She runs to her black Lincoln Navigator, which is parallel parked in front of the shop a few empty spaces ahead of mine. We hear the engine grind, the squeal of tires, and the crash of metal and breaking glass as the big SUV flies backward into my Toyota.

We rush out onto the sidewalk as the truck lurches onto the empty street and peals through the cool night, leaving my sad little car in a mangled heap.

"I'm going to call the police."

The sickening feeling that he's out to punish her wraps itself around me like a constrictor.

"Isn't that a little harsh? If they stop her, she'll get arrested."

"She took that chance when she got behind the wheel."

"Rob, don't do this for me. And I certainly hope you're not just doing it to punish her for…"

"We have to stop her before she hurts someone." I know he's right. He goes inside and phones the police as I stand looking at the remnants of my car.

It takes about three minutes for an officer to respond and a good half hour to explain the situation and write up the paperwork.

We don't ask if they picked up Blair before she made it to wherever she's been staying. I half expect Rob to get a call asking him to come bail her out of jail. Maybe she'll call Bob Stark to do the honor.

"Well, this car's not going anywhere," says the officer. "Do you need a lift somewhere?"

"Thanks for the offer, but I think it's a nice night for a walk."

It's after midnight and as much as I hate waking the house, I give Barbara a quick phone call to tell her what happened.

"Well, I declare. I'm just glad you're okay. Do you want me to come get you?" she asks.

"No, don't wake the girls. I'll be okay."

"Well, why don't we just let Sarah sleep up here tonight and you can get her in the morning. It's been a long day. There's no sense waking her."

As Rob locks up the shop, it dawns on me that I could ask him to go back in and get that half-full bottle of zinfandel and bring it to my house to drink it. But I glance at my car and the magic of the evening is lost.

I feel myself sinking back into Tim. Into the cocoon of widowhood. Tim loved me. Tim will always love me.

A little voice inside says, *But Tim would hate it if you put yourself on a shelf. You're too young to cut yourself off.*

Rob's married.

He's been married to Blair for nearly twenty years. I can't expect him to lose those feelings overnight, and I sure don't want to get in the middle of it. Come to think of it, I don't even know what he plans to do. Divorce? Marriage counseling? Time out to figure out what he wants to do?

If we come together, we need to do so cleanly.

We walk for the first five minutes in silence. Side by side, but not touching. It feels as if there's a ten-mile canyon between us.

"I'm sorry about your car. And your dress. I'll replace it. And we have insurance—"

We. The *W* word. I can tell it catches him by surprise, too.

He sighs. "We *are* still married. For now. Until one of us files for divorce."

I know I shouldn't ask, but I have to. "Are *you* going to file?"

He stuffs his hands in his front pockets, bites his bottom lip, then nods.

"Yes. I don't see how we can save this."

"Have you even tried?"

Shut up! What are you doing trying to talk him into marriage counseling?

But I know deep inside that I have to ask these

questions or suffer the consequences when he breaks my heart telling me he's still in love with his wife.

"We've been in marriage counseling off and on for the past six years." We turn up the Villa Magnolia driveway. "When I found out about her affair I realized there's nothing left to save." He stops and looks at me. "And you know how I realized that?"

I shake my head.

"Because——" He groans and runs his hand over his face. "Because when Karen Stark told me, I felt nothing. I didn't go into a flying rage. I didn't feel hurt and betrayed or even surprised. What kind of a relationship is that?"

We start walking again, down toward the lake. I try to read him, try to see if he's just telling himself this or if he really is at the end of the line with Blair.

"She was furious when I gave up my law practice to buy the Wine Cellar. I think that was pretty much the last straw. She said she'd married a professional, not a shopkeeper. Which translated to 'she married someone who made a lot of money.' I wanted her to work with me. In the shop, side by side, sharing a passion. But, no——"

I'm glad it's dark because I feel my cheeks flame,

thinking about the way Rob and I work so well together.

We stop at the top of the retaining wall and he turns to me. "You know what? I don't want to talk about her anymore. She's not going to ruin what's left of this night."

Rob slides his hands around my waist and I feel the heat of his palms as he lifts me down from the retaining wall. My body skims his and he sets me down a fraction of an inch in front of him.

A patch of clouds clears the moon and his gaze meets mine in the soft glow and I see the heartrending tenderness in his eyes.

"It all started to crystallize that night you walked into Andy and Elizabeth's."

My body responds in swift and powerful awareness.

He takes my hands, lacing his fingers through them. Tension hums between us.

No urge to look away or look down. Not even the cool breeze blowing in off the lake or the nocturnal call of a distant animal or the splash of something wild in the lake breaks the spell.

In the lingering seconds before he pulls me closer, an image of Tim flashes in my mind. I gently shut the door as Rob closes the scant space between us.

It's no longer a question of *if* or *when*...

But *now*.

As his lips brush mine for the first time, the unspoken feelings spill over into wordless confession.

Together, we cross the line from *just friends* to lovers with a kiss that starts slow and soft, then blossoms to ravenous greed. He tastes like wine and cinnamon and something exotic. That familiar hint of yesteryear, yet a taste of the forbidden.

He slips his hands between us. His fingers linger on my stomach, work their way up to my breasts. I melt at the feel of his hands on me, in this place that hasn't known his touch in years.

He slides them around to my back and pulls me tight against him. I feel the hardness of him, out here under the stars, and I feel like *some other woman* caught up in the rush of sexual fantasy.

He kisses my neck. My head lolls to the side in appreciative ecstasy.

In my peripheral vision, I think I see the flash of a light from the direction of the house, and it sobers me, propels me backward. "W-We can't," I stammer. "Not here. Not like this."

He stands there breathless, closes his eyes, then rakes a hand through his hair.

Off in the distance I hear a creature of the night scamper through the leaves and I wonder if it might be Sarah or Barbara.

He blows out a breath as if he's blowing away all the tension built up between us tonight. But then he smiles, steps toward me, puts his arms around me again.

"You're right. Not here. Although, it's pretty damned romantic." He squeezes me tight and laughs and sighs. "I've wanted this since that first day I saw you."

"The first day back then, in high school, or the first day you saw me this time, as adults?"

Immediately, I wish I hadn't asked. But he nuzzles my neck, kisses it. "Both."

Both. I want to ask, *Why did we let it slip away?* But I don't. It was a long, long time ago and we were kids. I file it away, along with mental images of Tim, and questions about Rob's plans to file for divorce. And we walk silently to the house, hand in hand.

About ten yards away, he backs me up against a huge oak tree and murmurs, "Until next time."

He kisses me again.

A kiss that's slow and burning and holds promises of what's to come *next time.*

And because of that kiss, I know in an instant

next time I won't be able to say no. Spirals of longing and fiery need unfurl in my belly and it's only because we're less than ten yards away from the house that I can say no right now.

I hear the screen door slam, the porch light comes on and Barbara's voice says something, but her words don't register.

Rob and I jerk apart, but stay in the tree's shadow.

"It's all right, Sarah," says Barbara. "Your mama will be right back. We'll sit out here on the porch until she gets home."

Uugh. God, Sarah.

In a rush of guilt, I smooth my hair into place, run the back of my hand over my mouth, hoping it's not red from the burn of Rob's whiskers. I don't dare glance at the porch for fear that Barbara and Sarah will be staring back. I feel like a teenager who's narrowly escaped being walked in on as she made out with her boyfriend.

The word *boyfriend* makes me draw in a sharp little breath, despite the guilt. Is that what Rob is? My boyfriend? But how can he be when he's someone else's husband?

A stone takes up residence in the pit of my stomach. My gaze flits away from his handsome face and studies the bark of the tree as if searching for an answer.

It's too complicated to sort out now, especially given that I need to figure out how to explain my entrance from the shadows—with a man.

We were just taking a walk.

After midnight? A romantic, moonlit stroll? Maybe he could just slip quietly away, sight unseen, while I present myself at the front door alone.

The screen door whispers open and closed. No slam this time. Hope that both of them have gone inside propels me out from behind the tree. Rob follows at a safe distance.

Shock flows through me when I see Sarah sitting on the wicker settee, hugging her legs to her chest, a scowl firmly affixed on her face. She stares at me, but doesn't utter a word.

Uh-oh.

I turn to Rob. "Good night. Thank you for walking me home." I sound way too businesslike for what we've just been doing.

His equally platonic "Good night," indicates he understands.

He turns toward the gate, but turns back. "Do you need me to pick you up in the morning?"

"No!" My response is a little too sharp.

"But your car—"

"It's okay. I'll manage. Thank you, though. Good night."

As I turn away and start up the stairs, Sarah glares at me. I feel so guilty and have the beginning of a dull headache pounding in my temples. I hear Rob's shoes crunching on the gravel, but I don't look back.

"Hi, baby." My lips feel heavy and abraded. My mouth feels like cotton.

Barbara comes outside before Sarah can answer. "There you are." Her tone is light and lyrical, but she looks exhausted. "Your little girl was a bit worried about her mama— Who was that?"

I turn as if I need to look at him before I can answer. "Oh, that's just Rob Mallory. My boss. He walked me home. We didn't want to drive because of the tasting."

Barbara tussles Sarah's hair. "See there, Sarah, your mama is a good, responsible person. She didn't want to hurt anyone and that's why she and Mr. Mallory walked."

The unspoken question of what happened after he brought me home hangs in the air like a midnight fog.

Barbara gives me a look. Maybe I just imagined it. Who knows, maybe it's real and I deserve it?

I don't want to hurt anybody. Not Sarah. Not Blair. What is wrong with me?

"Well, thank you, Barbara. I really appreciate you looking after Sarah tonight."

"It was my pleasure. I think Mary Grace might have worn her out. They sure did have a good time."

I glance at my watch and see with a start that it's nearly one-thirty. Too late for a thirteen-year-old to be out on a school night.

"Come on, Sarah," I say. "We need to get you in bed, too, or you won't want to get up for school tomorrow."

She pierces me with a defiant stare, and for a minute I think she's going to start shouting. I can see it bubbling up inside her.

Oh, dear God, please tell me she didn't see Rob kissing me. For a second, I have a sick feeling that those rustling noises I heard might have been her following us down to the lake. But I comfort myself with the thought that it couldn't have been—that Barbara wouldn't have let Sarah go down to the lake by herself after dark.

Would she?

Barbara offers Sarah a hand and pulls her to her feet then enfolds her in a hug.

"Good night, honey, tonight was fun."

"Night, Aunt Barbara."

We start down the garden path toward our house, where the porch light beacons us home. We walk in silence about half the way, until I can't stand it anymore.

"Did you have fun at the Special Olympics?" I ask.

Sarah crosses her arms over her chest, that defensive posture that I can't quite get used to. My heart pounds a little faster when she doesn't answer.

What did she see?

She didn't see anything. She's just tired.

"Mr. Mallory is Seth Mallory's dad."

"Yes, he is. Is Seth a friend of yours?"

Sarah rolls her eyes. "Yeah, as if. Where's your car?"

I unlock the door.

"There was a little accident tonight."

She gasps. Her face goes pale and her eyes get large.

"Don't worry. I'm fine. I wasn't even in the car. Someone backed into it. Going really fast."

"Who was it?"

"Seth Mallory's mother."

Sarah narrows her eyes, and I could kick myself for blurting that out.

"Why, Mom? Was she mad at you or something?"

I'm not going there tonight.

"Look, it's after one-thirty in the morning. We're both tired. Let's get a good night's sleep, okay?"

At three-twenty I awaken with an uneasy feeling. It's more than the headache that's finally kicked in full throttle. It's an anxious apprehension gnawing at my bones.

My car. The wine. No sleep. Rob's kiss (well maybe not the kisses).

No wonder I'm restless.

I get up to take an aspirin and hear a faint voice coming from Sarah's room.

"No! Don't write it like that. If you do everyone will know it's me. Say—"

I open her bedroom door and she immediately snaps her cell phone shut.

"Who were you talking to?"

She sits up and opens and closes the cell phone in rapid succession. A nervous tick. "Wendy."

Her best friend back in North Carolina.

"Sarah, it's almost three-thirty in the morning.

It's too late to be on the phone. Have you slept at all?"

She shrugs. "Can't sleep. I just wanted to talk to Wendy. I miss her, Mom."

I sit down on her bed, trying to process what I just heard. "I know you do. I can't sleep, either. How about if I make us a cup of herbal tea?"

Walking to the kitchen, I weigh my words. *Don't write it like that. If you do, everyone will know it was me.*

"What were you talking to Wendy about?"

"What?" There's a look in her eyes I can't define.

I've just set the teakettle on the stove when we hear the sirens. Both of us flinch at the sound.

"Sounds close," Sarah says. "I hate hearing that in the middle of the night. It's never good news."

The sirens keep getting louder, until flashing red lights pulsate through the blinds.

"What in the world?"

Sarah's at the window.

"Mom! It's a fire truck and an ambulance! It's up at Aunt Barbara's house."

I don't even bother to put on a robe over my sweatpants and T-shirt. I just turn the flame out from under the teakettle and follow Sarah, who is already out the door.

The minute I hit the door, I smell smoke. Then I see the flames shooting out of the roof of the Villa Magnolia.

"Oh, my God! Mom, the house is on fire. Mary Grace and Aunt Barbara! They've got to get them out. They've got to save them." Sarah takes off running toward the house.

"Sarah, get back here! Don't get too close. The firefighters will save them." She doesn't listen. She keeps running toward the house, which is now surrounded by various fire trucks and rescue vehicles.

The gravel hurts my bare feet, but I run, too, choking on the acrid smoke, nearly blinded by panic over Barbara and Mary Grace. As I get closer, I see a firefighter stops Sarah and refuse to let her get any closer. I also see amid the hustle and bustle of rescue workers running here and there with water hoses and various pieces of equipment, that Barbara's strapped to a gurney and they're loading her into the back of an ambulance. Mary Grace is bawling hysterically at her side.

"Barbara?" I scream, but she's already inside the

vehicle. I run as fast as I can to get there before they close the doors.

"I'm her niece," I say to the paramedic. "What's happened?"

"Potential cardiac arrest, ma'am. Can you take care of the child?" He motions to Mary Grace. I nod but I see Sarah already has her arms around her cousin, trying her best to comfort her.

The paramedic says, "We're taking her to Stratford Hospital over on Gatlin." With that, the ambulance pulls away, lights flashing, siren wailing.

As soon as the vehicle clears the driveway, I see Elizabeth and Andrew Deveraux running toward us in robes and slippers.

"Oh, my God, Maggie. What's happened?" Elizabeth hugs me and this is the first time I realize I'm shaking, but I won't let the tears fall, not in front of the girls.

"It's Barbara, she's had a heart attack. I have to go to her." I motion to Sarah and Mary Grace. "Elizabeth, can you take the girls in the house and stay with them while I go...? Oh, God, I just remembered, I don't have a car. It's a long story."

Andrew puts a hand on my shoulder. "Elizabeth can take care of the girls and I'll drive you."

Elizabeth

By the time I get the girls across the street and out of the smoke and craziness, Sarah has managed to calm down Mary Grace. I don't know what she said, but at least Mary Grace is not screaming anymore. I'm grateful because honestly, I don't know how I would have handled it. Anastasia's still asleep and I'd rather not wake her.

From what I can see from my living-room window, it looks as though they have the fire under control, so I settle in a chair, across from the two girls who are huddled together on the couch.

Sarah's comforting Mary Grace, who is quietly sobbing for her mother.

"Sarah, do you know what happened?"

Sarah shakes her head.

Mary Grace lifts her head from Sarah's shoulder. "I call 911."

"You did?" I ask.

Mary Grace nods. "When Mama saw the fire she got sick and I call 911."

I lean forward in my chair. "Mary Grace, you're a heroine. You saved your mother's life."

A pang of guilt stabs me because I don't even

know if Barbara is alive, but if she is, it could very well be because of this child's clear thinking.

Oh, dear God, please. Please, let her be alive. For the sake of her child and for… Well, for the sake of us all please bring that wonderful woman back to us.

As I sit and watch Mary Grace and Sarah dozing, snuggled together on the couch, a slowly dawning realization passes over me—this child with Down syndrome actually *may have* saved her mother's life. This is a different picture than the one I'd painted in my head.

I've let my need for "perfection" prejudice me against this very capable child, this *human being*. I rub my little mound of belly and say a prayer for the baby growing inside of me.

If he or she is born with Down syndrome, maybe it wouldn't be as tragic as I feared.

Just like Barbara said, maybe these little angels do come into our lives for a reason.

Maggie

I'm going crazy sitting in this hospital waiting room waiting for word on Barbara. Terrified that she's dangling over death's canyon and I can't help her.

Deep in my cocoon, all I can think is, *If I lose one more person I love, I don't know if I can cope.* But then I look up and see Rob standing in front of me like an angel of mercy. That's when I begin to cry. I finally let loose and all the tears that I've kept bottled up pour out of me.

Rob holds me, until I'm finished.

"Andy called me," he says as he strokes my hair. "I thought you might need someone."

I blink at the mention of Andy. "Oh my gosh, Andy. Where is he? I hope he went home."

My eyes sting and feel tired and swollen.

"He did, after I got here."

I sit up and stretch, glancing anxiously around the emergency room, willing a doctor to materialize and give us good news. Only now do I notice it's light outside and the person I recognize walking toward us carrying a big flower arrangement is not a doctor, but Burt, looking put-together and shower-fresh in his crisply starched white shirt and khaki trousers.

"I got here as fast as I could after Andrew Deveraux called me."

I stand up and hug him, introduce him to Rob. "Burt, I'm so sorry. We don't know anything yet, but maybe since you're her husband you can get some information out of someone. How far did you have to travel to get here?"

He starts to turn toward the triage desk, but stops and looks back at me, puzzled. "Just across town."

The look on his face makes me feel stupid, as if I've missed something. "Oh, I thought you were out of town."

He shakes his head. "Barbara didn't tell you? She won't let me live at Villa Magnolia anymore. Kicked me out. Hmm. Maybe since she didn't tell you it means she's going to let me move back in." He shakes his head. "I really hate being manipulated."

Barbara

Land sakes, I don't know which makes me feel worse, my house catching on fire like that, or causing such a scene and scaring Mary Grace while they hauled me off to the hospital.

The doctor just left. Said I had an angina attack. That's not a heart attack, thank the Lord. It's like a warning signal that I'm a prime candidate. Well, believe you me, this has gotten my attention.

From what he can tell, mine is what they call *stable angina*. The least risky variety, but it's nothing to sneeze at. He said I have to make a lot of changes: eat less fat, get more exercise, lose thirty pounds (see there, what did I tell you?) and eliminate stress from my life.

So it was ironic that not fifteen minutes after the doctor told me all this, who should come sauntering in, but ol' Burt, carrying a big vase of flowers, always ready to put on a good show.

He sets them on the bedside table. "Maggie is out in the waiting room. She's been worried sick about you. But the doctor set her at ease when he told us you were stable."

The machines beep and wheeze and the fluorescent light box at the head of my bed buzzes.

"Why didn't she come in here with you?"

He stands with his arms folded across his chest and, the way the sun is streaming in through the window, he really does look handsome. Too bad he's such a cad.

"She wanted to give us a little time before she came in. She didn't know I'm not living with you."

"I hadn't quite gotten around to telling her."

He shifts from one foot to the other. "Does that mean you want me to come home?"

He peers at me expectantly.

I look away and finger one of the purple irises in the vase. "Beautiful flowers…. Did you call the kids? Be sure and tell them I'm all right. I don't want them rushing down here making a fuss. With the house all damaged I won't have a place to put all of them—"

"Barbara, I can't believe it took a scare like this for me to realize how important you are to me. If something would have happened to you without me being able to tell you how much I love you… If you will just give me another chance. I promise you I'll change. I'll be a better father to Mary Grace and a better husband to you. I want to come home."

I just stare at him for a long time, standing there all earnest and contrite-looking.

"Burt, I appreciate everything you've just said, and I would love to see you be a better father to Mary Grace because you certainly haven't been present for the first thirteen years of her life. So why don't you prove that to me in actions, not words?"

He starts to say something, but I cut him off.

Less stress.

"'Cause you know, it's funny you bring up Mary Grace. 'Cause I've been lying here wondering and worrying who would care for her if something happens to me. I'm not talking about sticking her in a home, Burt. I'm talking about who would love that little girl?"

He touches my leg.

"That's right, she needs two parents living at home."

I wonder how many other women he's touched over the years. Even with the blanket as a barrier between us, I don't want him putting his hands on me, so I pull away.

"See, Burt, I didn't have a heart attack. And this feels like a second chance. Like I have a brand-new lease on my life. Burt, I'm not going back to the same old life with the same old ways. For now I think it's best that you keep living wherever it is you're living. You can come and see Mary Grace, spend quality time with her, but as for you and me, it's time we move on."

His jaw drops, then snaps shut and I can see him grinding his teeth as he's thinking. Then his mouth curves into that hateful smirk that I detest.

"How in the world do you think you're going to support the two of you?"

I close my eyes so I don't have to look at him.

"Mister, that's exactly what I'm talking about, that nasty tone you're taking with me. When things

don't go your way, you start pulling that nasty, bully
voice. That's one of the things I'm not living with
anymore. But to answer your question, of course,
we'll appreciate the alimony and child support you'll
be paying, but in addition to that, I have a few ideas
up my sleeve. But it's time you go. Bye-bye, Burt."

Maggie

Now that Barbara's home from the hospital, she and Mary Grace are living with us out in the carriage house. It's close quarters, but that's okay. Barbara and I each have our own bedroom and Sarah and Mary Grace are sharing a room. Sarah's been great about it. I told her if she needs privacy, she can go in my room and shut the door.

At first, Barbara insisted on she and Mary Grace sharing a room, but I wouldn't hear of it. I told Barbara if that was the case then Sarah and I would just have to go out and find a place of our own. Who knows, maybe we will eventually. But for now, it's nice living with Barbara. Kind of like a big slumber party.

I want to keep things nice and light—on an even keel. That's why I have to take Sarah aside and talk to her about something that's been nagging at the back of my mind since the night of the fire. The telephone conversation with Wendy that I overheard.

At first, it didn't hit me, but the more I thought about what I heard her say, *No! Don't write it like that. If you do everyone will know it's me...* The more I think about it, the more it bothers me.

So this afternoon while Barbara has Mary Grace at the dentist, it's the first real chance I have to talk to Sarah.

She's lying on the queen-size bed in my room reading *The Great Gatsby.* I'm so glad she inherited my love of the classics. Even at this early age, she's read a bunch of them. *Gatsby* is one of my favorites. I go in and lie down beside her.

She glances up from the page. "Hey, what's up?"

"I was just thinking...just wondering, do you really think Anastasia is the *Mystery Blogger?*"

She doesn't answer me. She goes back to reading her book.

"I mean if it was Anastasia, do you think she'd confess like that? I find it really hard to believe."

Sarah glances over at me. "I don't know, Mom. Anastasia does a lot of things I don't understand."

I turn over onto my side and prop myself up on

my elbow. "But really, I mean, think about it. What would she have to gain by confessing? She makes the entire school mad and most of the community, too. So what does she gain out of this? I don't know about you, but I'm not buying it."

Sarah is staring at her book again, but I don't think she's reading. "I don't know Mom, she's a mean girl."

"Well, let's just say—hypothetically—that someone has set her up to take the fall. Do you think that's fair? I mean, hypothetically."

Sarah shrugs.

"So don't you think it would be better if this *Mystery Blogger* could somehow tell everyone she, or he—of course, it could be a boy. What if this *Mystery Blogger* posted that he or she was just trying to make a point and the point has been made, that Anastasia is innocent and the blogger wants to end this thing before anyone else gets hurt?"

Sarah closes her book. "What are you getting at, Mom? Do you think I'm the *Mystery Blogger* or something?"

"I said I was speaking hypothetically. Frankly, Sarah, if you were the one doing this, I wouldn't want to know because if I knew, it would make

NANCY ROBARDS THOMPSON 261

things pretty hard on both of us. I don't know about you, but for the first time in a long time, I feel like I've found a place in the community.

"So what I'm saying—hypothetically—is don't you think it would be best if the *Mystery Blogger* quit while *he or she* was ahead, cleared Anastasia and logged off for the last time? That way everyone involved could save face. Because if *he or she* keeps it up, posing as Anastasia or not, before too long *he or she* is going to get caught. It could happen as easily as someone *overhearing a conversation and putting two and two together*. Hypothetically speaking."

She picks up her book and flips to the page she was reading.

"Whatever."

I'm so frustrated with my daughter, I want to shake her. And I'm frustrated with myself for not knowing how to handle this. Maybe I *should* just ask her straight out, but I can't. It may not be the right thing to do, but I can't do that until I have proof positive.

I lie there for a few minutes listening to the gentle *wrrrr* of the ceiling fan, pondering why this has to be so difficult.

It's a relief when I hear Barbara call out, "Hey y'all, we're home."

I hear Mary Grace running down the hall calling, "Sarah! Sarah!"

Her footfalls stop, probably at their bedroom door, and then resume again until she appears at my bedroom door.

"Sarah! Look! I brought you toothpaste. They let me have two so I can bring one to you."

She's at the edge of the bed, holding out the small prize.

"Thanks, M.G., that's really nice of you."

Mary Grace beams. "Will you push me in the swing? Will you, please, Sarah?"

Sarah sighs and gives one last wistful look at the page she was reading before she puts down the book and follows the girl out of the room.

It's things like this—her old-soul insightfulness, her kind, patient way with Mary Grace—that make me hate myself for thinking that she could ever be responsible for something like *The Stratford Park Potluck*.

I lie there on my back staring at the fan until Barbara appears at the door holding a plate.

"Knock, knock. Take a look at these beautiful peaches I found at the produce stand next to the dentist's office. I don't how in the world peaches can be so ripe and beautiful in April. They usually don't look like this until August. So I grabbed up a mess of 'em and I'm gonna experiment with recipes for low-fat and low-sugar cobblers. It's gonna take something as luscious as these to make it work. I sliced one up. Here, have a taste."

I swing my legs over the side of the bed as she walks over with the plate and sits down next to me.

"What's the matter, honey? Are you sick?"

Oh, if you only knew.

"Nope, just..." I shake my head and take a slice of peach and bite into it. The sweetness explodes in my mouth, reminding me of a summer day. Reminding me of the taste of Rob's kiss.

Barbara reaches out and takes my hand. "Anything you want to talk about?"

I shrug. "Are we obligated to tell everything we know?"

She blinks.

"Well, honey, you don't have to tell me if you don't want to."

I stare at her weathered hand on top of mine and she gives me a little squeeze.

"No, that's not what I mean. I'm talking in general terms. If someone does something wrong, but is able to make the bad situation right without others knowing, is it really necessary for that person to confess to God and the world?"

There's a certain look in her eyes that makes me think I've hit a personal hot spot. She lets loose of my hand and starts fidgeting with the peach plate.

"I suppose if you're Catholic, confession makes a difference," she says tentatively. "But I'm not Catholic so it's always been my philosophy that some secrets are better kept as secrets. So long as you're not hurting anyone."

We're quiet for a minute. Then she looks at me with guilty eyes.

"I think I know what you're getting at here. It's about your mama, isn't it? Burt told you, didn't he? When you saw him at the hospital? That lousy son of a…"

Oh, my God. What is she talking about?

She sets the plate on the bed, gets up and walks over to the window.

We're obviously off on two different tracks of conversation. But this is something big, I can feel it. Bigger than *The Stratford Park Potluck*.

"What did he tell you?" She spits the words like stones.

"About you kicking him out..." *Think, Maggie....
Don't let her close this door.* "Oh, God, Barbara...
Umm. I was so upset over you being sick and the fire
and I'd had no sleep—what he said was all a jumble.
You tell me, Barbara. This is about my mama. I need
to hear it from you."

She stares at me, almost through me, as if she's
weighing what she should say, what should stay a
secret.

"I'm not sure you want to hear this, darlin'. I'm
not so sure you don't just want to leave well enough
alone."

I know what she's going to say. I know it and I
know I have to hear it if I'm ever going to put these
demons of my mama to rest.

"I have to know. I just want to make sure you're
up to this. We don't have to do this right now if it's
going to upset you and set you back."

She laughs a dry little chuckle. "Honestly it'll be
a load off my heart.... *Hmm.* I never thought of it
that way. All this ugliness hangin' on my heart for
all these years. No wonder I've had pain. *Hmm.*
Well, I suppose it's time you knew the truth. Come
on, let's you and me take a walk."

We head out the front door, past Mary Grace and

Sarah who are still playing on the swing. Mary Grace is laughing and flying and Sarah seems quietly content pushing her cousin higher and higher.

"Look at me, Mama! Look how high I am."

Barbara waves to her. "Now you hang on tight. Don't you fall off that swing. And no jumpin'. You hear? Margaret and I are going for a walk. We'll be back in a little while."

Then we're mostly silent until we get to the far side of the burned house. The air still smells like smoke and when the wind gusts, it picks up little pieces of soot.

But down by the lake, upwind from the house the air smells fresh and clean.

Barbara motions over toward two Adirondack chairs and we sit there.

"I left him one other time before this, you know? A long time ago, back when being a wife and mama was my whole identity. That's why I came back to him. My baby, Davis—this was way before Mary Grace—Davis was still at home and I'd never worked a day in my life. I had no faith in myself, and was just sure I couldn't support us and keep the house without Burt. I had this crazy notion that if I left him, Burt would take the house away from me and I'd end up just like Leila…."

She trails off, her voice breaking a little bit.

"I always felt guilty living up there in that big old house with you and your mama out there on your own, barely making ends meet. I wanted to at least offer y'all a roof over your head. But Leila refused to live in a place that had once been her home and had been unrightfully *ripped out from under her*. That's what she used to say."

Barbara chuckles, but there's no humor in it. I'm not used to seeing her so grave. I wonder for a split second if I really want to hear what she has to say. But whether I want to or not, I need to know. For my own peace of mind.

"A few years, after Daddy died and the wounds quit stinging, your mama saw just how hard it was to live on her own, I think she would have acquiesced, but by then Burt wouldn't let her stay here.

"I could never figure out why. You see I wanted to deed over half the property to y'all. I felt like it wasn't right, Daddy disinheriting her. Leila had just as much right to this place as I did. I thought Burt was afraid that if your mama got back in this house she'd convince me to do just that. The sorry thing is, we could've used someone to share the property-tax burden. But your mama was barely able to support you, and old business-minded Burt maintained that if I gave Leila half of the house, given your mama's unstable mental state, she'd probably force us to buy her out. We didn't have the money for that, and I certainly didn't want to sell the house. It just about killed me to admit to myself that Leila was unstable, but honey she was. You know that. I felt like I had no choice but to take Burt's advice and leave well enough alone."

She stares at her hands for a minute, then at me.

"Looking back now, I don't know if I did the right thing."

Barbara sighs and stares out over at the horizon across the lake, takes another deep breath. "But that's not the real reason why Burt didn't want you and Leila to live with us. Nope, not at all…"

The breeze whispers through the branches of the huge live oaks and she shifts her gaze to me.

"Are you sure you want to hear the rest of this, honey?"

I nod.

"Well then, okay. But I'm getting ahead of myself here. Let me go back and start from the beginning."

She bites her bottom lip and is silent for a moment before she starts.

"You know your granddaddy was in the citrus-growing business. He was a 'good ol' boy,' wasn't very polished, but he sure did pull himself up by his bootstraps. He was a self-made man and appreciated all the fine things money could buy."

She arches a brow at me and I recognize the expression. Sometimes I do that and Sarah does, too.

"At one time we were rich. *Obscenely rich*. Land, I figure we had more money than just about anyone around these parts. Mama died before Daddy made good on his promise to make a fortune and keep her in the style he thought fitting. I think he spoiled us rotten just to make up for what he couldn't give her."

She shakes her head.

"Leila and I were his pride and joy. She was the beauty. I was the good girl. And oh, how Daddy loved throwing around his money, using it to get us places hardly anyone could go. I remember one night he bought out an entire carnival—had them close it to the public so that it could be just us and whoever we chose to invite. But the one thing he discovered his money couldn't buy was the respect that's the birthright of those of old Southern fortune."

She nods.

"Now, keep in mind it was the late 1950s—early sixties, and times were different back then. It used to eat him up that certain doors of society were closed to us. He decided that come hell or high water, his baby girls would marry *right*. We'd marry into 'proper old money' so that we could enjoy the respect his fortune never earned him. Of course, he nearly had a heart attack when Leila fell in love with his foreman, Jose Salinas. When he discovered Leila was pregnant and planned to elope, he paid off Jose to get him out of her life."

My father's name? Jose Salinas. I sit there reeling at her words. *Leila was pregnant. Jose Salinas. Paid off.*

I want to stop her and ask questions, but I don't dare, not yet, for fear that I won't hear the end of the story.

"After a long time of hoping and believing he would come back, Leila eventually believed Jose accepted the payoff. That nearly turned her off men altogether. What she didn't know was that Jose refused the money, and…and, well…"

Barbara stiffens.

"Daddy had him…*umm*…taken care of, then sent Leila away to have the baby and give it up for adoption." Barbara turns to me apologetically, her expression and words pleading me to understand. "When your mama went away to have the baby, she never knew. She thought Jose had taken Daddy's money and left her pregnant and alone. But obviously your mama didn't give you up. She came back to town with you as a slap in Daddy's face for paying off the man she loved, for going to such great lengths to prove Jose never loved her. I suppose Leila needed someone to blame and Daddy was the one."

Barbara sighs and shakes her head. I feel a little woozy, trying to digest the fact that she and my mother knew who my father was all along but never told me.

"They were always so much alike in temperament that they fought like ol' junkyard dogs, but it had never been this bad before.

"When Leila first came back to town with you, Daddy wanted nothing to do with the two of you, but I talked sense into him and persuaded him that it was better to take y'all in than to have the whole town talking. So Leila and you lived in Villa Magnolia until Daddy died two years later. This is when it gets really ugly."

She pauses as if she's having second thoughts about whether to carry on.

"So what happened?" I urge.

She closes her eyes for a moment. "As a way to get in the final word, Daddy left everything to me, which by that time only amounted to the house— once it was all boiled down and everything was settled, the house and property was all Daddy had left to his name.

"You see, once the problems with your mama began, Daddy started a slow spiral. He started drinking and ran into hard times with the business—I told you he spent money like we had a never-ending supply. We had a couple of harsh winters back to back, ruining the crops. He made some bad deals and the combination bankrupted the business. All that was left was the big old house."

Barbara turns and looks at me with conviction.

"After the reading of Daddy's will, Leila took you and left the Villa Magnolia in a rage. I would've gladly let you all live here. Like I said, I would've even given Leila half, if not for Burt."

She's silent for a long time. I'm so numb I can't speak. My grandfather had my father killed. What kind of a man would kill the father of his grandchild, the man his daughter loved, because he thought he wasn't good enough?

"Jose Salinas, my father, what was he like?"

Barbara smiles a sad smile. "I never knew him very well, but he was tall and handsome. Cuban, from what I remember. He was a kind, hardworking man. He was Daddy's foreman for years. Daddy respected him, trusted him. Until Jose crossed the line and started messin' around with his daughter. But hearing Leila talk and knowing how it all panned out in the end, you have to believe Jose was a man of strong character if he risked death over taking a payoff. Though, really, he probably had no idea that Daddy was capable of that. I don't think anybody did. If Jose knew he was going to die, he should have taken the money and taken your mama away with him. But he had no way of knowing that. He was a man of honor and wanted to do the best for you and your mama, wanted to marry her and give you and her a good, proper life. He just never got the chance."

As I wipe away tears, a bubble of anger gurgles up to the surface. "Barbara, why didn't Mama ever tell me this? She made me think that my father ran off, that he couldn't care less about what happened to either of us. How could she lie—"

"Honey, your mama didn't know that Jose was dead until just after you left for school."

"What?"

Barbara squeezes her eyes tight for a few seconds and murmurs under her breath, "I just don't know... I just don't know... I just don't know if I can do this." But she opens her eyes and looks at me as if her heart is about to break.

"I always maintained that you and your mama were welcome in my home. And that carries right on up from the roots to you and Sarah now, and you know that, right?"

I nod, holding my breath waiting for what she's getting at.

"Things were better than ever right up until after you left for college. Then something happened. One day when Leila was over here, she and Burt got into an argument and he spilled the beans about Daddy killing Jose Salinas. He positioned it that I'd made a huge sacrifice by shouldering the burden of this secret all these years."

"But how did you know about this?"

"One night when Daddy was drunk, he told Burt what he'd done and Burt told me. I made him promise not to tell Leila because I knew it would destroy her worse than thinking Jose was a callous jerk.

"And it did. Once your mama found about this,

she went into a fighting rage and told me about the affair that she'd been carrying on with Burt for years."

I sit up stock-straight in my chair.

"What? No... Not Burt."

Barbara nods, tears streaming down her cheeks. "Yep. Just like that. And he didn't even deny it. Just broke down and cried like a little baby telling me it was over, begging me not to throw him out on his ass. Leila was so hell-bent on hurting us. She said she was sick and tired of me getting the best of everything. By sleeping with Burt she was taking a little something for herself. It was just days after that that she..."

Barbara buries her face in her hands and sobs.

That she killed herself. It all makes sense now. I don't like it, but it all makes sense. The way Burt used to always come around doing handy projects around the duplex. The way I used to catch him looking at her...but Mama was careful, though.

"I never had an inkling that anything was going on between them, Barbara. What about you? Didn't your radar go off?"

Barbara wipes her eyes, shakes her head. "Honey, I was so overwhelmed raising five kids and he was gone so much..."

She looks defeated. Absolutely defeated.

"How could you stay with him? I mean, I'm not judging you. I just—"

"Like I said, Davis was still at home and I was clinging to the notion of keeping this house. Didn't think I could do it by myself. My sister died. Killed herself because of—"

Sobs shake her body and I get up and comfort her, swiping away my own tears. Ancient tears that had gone unshed since the day I learned Mama was dead.

"Then," she continues in a shaky voice, "then I got pregnant with Mary Grace. You see, honey, I was always the 'good girl' who did everything everyone expected of me. Married the man Daddy approved of, had lots of babies, cooked and cleaned and took care of everyone. Divorce was not part of who I was. But you know what, to this day I don't know who was the better—or worse off—for it. Leila for being her own person and ending up with nothing or me for being the puppet and ending up with everything…because sometimes it felt like I didn't have anything that was really mine."

I sink to the ground, hollow and shaken to the very root. Everything I thought I knew turned upside down.

"I don't want this to color your feelings for your mama. I forgave her for what she did and for a lot of years I forgave Burt, but as of now he's in the red in my forgiveness bank. And that doesn't have anything to do with your mama."

Elizabeth

I realized something about myself today. I have a hard time sitting still. I never noticed it in the office. I didn't have time to stay in one place for very long. What I've realized is I have to find things to occupy myself so I don't end up trying to micromanage Andrew and Anastasia.

This afternoon, I'm making a chocolate bowl to fill with fresh berries to take over to Barbara as a welcome-home present. She's been home a few days now and even though I brought her flowers when she first got there, I thought something like this might cheer her up.

I'm following directions from a *Martha Stewart Living* magazine. It seems fail-safe. Easy and elegant, just my style. Dip a large balloon into melted dark chocolate; refrigerate on wax paper for a half hour;

carefully pop the balloon; peel it off and *voila!* Instant chocolate bowl.

Ha! This will prove I am not hopeless on the home front. In fact, I think I'll use smaller balloons and make personal-sized bowls for us to have for dessert tonight.

I'm breaking the Toblerone chocolate into the top pan of my rigged double-boiler when Anastasia walks in from school.

"Hi," I say, reading the directions to see what I'm supposed to add to the chocolate to flavor it.

"Hey."

She lingers in the kitchen doorway.

"How was school?" I ask.

"Interesting," she says.

She sets down her backpack on the floor, takes a folded piece of paper out of her purse and holds it out to me.

"What's this?"

I lay the wooden spoon I was using to stir the chocolate across the top of the pan and take the paper. When I unfold it, I see it's a new install-ment of that damn blog, I feel anger starting to simmer.

Just Stop.

The Mystery Blogger has a confession to make. My name isn't really Anastasia. It's not even "The Fabulous A." I just said that to give a certain mean girl a dose of her own medicine. How does it feel to be the victim for a change, Anastasia? Maybe you'll think twice before you torture your next prey?

It seems this blog has gotten a little out of hand. I never intended it to hurt people. I only wanted to hold up a mirror. If you saw yourself, well, maybe you should think really hard about why it was so upsetting for everyone to know those things about you. There's the face we show to the world and there's the face that's really us. Can you look at yourself in the mirror?

I have another confession to make. The majority of the things I wrote weren't even true. Or at least I didn't think they were. Most of them were just made up. Things I pulled out of thin air. Obviously, my made-up gossip hit a little too close to home. Some of the things were true. I got that information by listening. It's amazing what you hear if you just shut up and quit gossiping and talking about yourself for a while. I guess some would say I've been gossiping. But that's a whole different blog entry that will never happen because this will be my last.

Let's just stop being mean to each other, okay? That goes for the adults as well as the kids. Let's just stop trying to get the better of each other, stop trying to outdo each other. Just stop. Because aren't we all really after the same thing? Yeah, we are, and there's enough to go around for everyone.

With that I'll stop.

Peace,

Mystery Blogger

I've never been a person to overthink things, to read what's not there into an otherwise rational situation. It's always been black-and-white—trust your gut. It is or isn't. You act or you don't act. You don't muddy the waters by second-guessing yourself.

Standing here, I'm so glad I believed in my daughter.

"You see, I didn't do it. Just like I told you."

"Yes, and it looks like you've been vindicated."

I take both of her soft, smooth hands in mine. Hands that are no longer child's hands, but still not quite grown enough to be woman's hands. She lets me, and this in itself almost makes me weep.

"They think I'm a mean girl, Mom. I don't want to be thought of that way."

She has tears in her eyes, just like me. My daughter is my mirror. Maybe we could both take a softer stance.

I fix her a soda, and she sits at the table drinking it while I stir the melting chocolate. After a few minutes, she seems more like herself again.

She sighs.

"Come over here and I'll let you in on a secret. Watch how easy it is to make something that makes you look really good."

I dip the large balloon in the chocolate. It explodes on contact, flinging the mixture everywhere—all over Anastasia, all over me, all over the kitchen. It looks as if a chocolate bomb exploded in the kitchen.

"God, Mom, you really are a disaster in the kitchen. When the baby is old enough, you really should get a job doing something you're good at."

We both break out in hysterical laughter. Big guffaws that make my stomach hurt.

I don't care about the chocolate mess; I hug her

as tight as she will allow and savor this moment, this feeling that everything is going to be all right. As I lick the chocolate off my lips, I realize for the first time in months that my stomach is not threatening to revolt.

And then I feel it. A subtle thump in my belly. She sees it on my face. "What's wrong?"

I put her hand on my stomach and watch the wonder in her face as she feels the baby move.

Barbara

If God didn't have a sense of humor, the rapture would have come a long time ago. The God I know is a loving, forgiving God full of second chances.

I beam at Maggie and Elizabeth. "I can't tell you how happy I am that we could do this."

"I can't tell you how happy I am that you are doing so well." Elizabeth reaches out and squeezes my hand.

"I have a lot of changes to make, such as with my diet which isn't so much fun and with my lifestyle— Oh, I was going to wait until after we ate to tell y'all this, but I just can't wait. I have a business proposal for the two of you."

I watch the curiosity shine in their eyes before I lay everything out on the table. It almost makes me giddy.

"Well, good news the insurance is going to pay to fix the house back up. It's going to be a job, too, since old faulty wiring was what caused the fire in the first place. If they're going to invest, they're going to do it right from the inside out. So I was thinking, just like I'm getting a second chance at life, that old house is, too.

"I don't know if you know this, Elizabeth—Maggie does—but I've always had this dream to turn the Villa Magnolia into a bed-and-breakfast. A real first-class place. So I was thinking with your public relations and business background, we could all three partner to turn this dream into a reality. I can't do it by myself. And the good thing is we can work it around our families."

They stare at me, kind of half-dazed almost as if they aren't believing their ears.

"Well?" I ask.

You've never heard such a rush of laughter and squeals and talking out of two grown women.

After Elizabeth leaves, Maggie and I stay at the restaurant for a few minutes so I can finish my tea— it's unsweetened and I guess I'll get used to it in time, but there ain't nothing like a big ol' cold glass of sweet tea to quench your thirst.

"There's more pertaining to this partnership that I need to talk to you about. I just wanted to wait until it was just the two of us. You remember what we talked about the other day about how I never have been at peace with how your granddaddy cut your mama out of her half of the Villa Magnolia?"

Maggie nods.

"We'll, I've fixed that. I saw my lawyer—not Burt, incidentally—and I had him draw up papers deeding over half of the Villa Magnolia and the grounds to you."

I think that child is about ready to fall out of her seat. "Barbara, that isn't necessary—"

"Now you just hush up. It *is* necessary, and it should have been done a long time ago. Of course that means you're going to have to swing your share of the property taxes. But your part will only be about fifty thousand a year."

Her jaw drops and I can't go on teasing her.

"I'm just trying to get your goat. Property taxes will come out of the corporation and I'm looking into some tax incentives that the city might be able to offer since we'll be bringing business into the area. Honey, this means just as much to me as it does to you. In a way it feels like I'm making restitution to your mama. Thank you for letting me do that."

I watch her eyes tear up and just seeing the look on her face makes me know I've done the right thing.

One Year Later
Maggie

Rob and I walk on the shores of Lake Tindell. A warm breeze skates across the water, and I lift my chin to greet it, savoring the aquatic mélange of cypress knees, tannins and water grass, and the feel of his hand in mind.

As we walk silently side by side, Barbara's words from more than a year ago resonate in my heart—*Some secrets are better kept as secrets.*

But not all of them.

Before coming back to Stratford Park, I couldn't deal with Mama's death; in turn I couldn't come to terms with losing Tim. I'd anesthetized the festering wounds of loss and abandonment and let them scar over. Now that I have these answers and can look down the long path I traveled to get them, I realize I was heading down the same self-destructive road Mama had. Only by staring down Death's ugly havoc I have managed to set myself free, to have the courage to come back to the place I started...and start again. I wonder if Mama would've had a chance to deal with her problems in a healthier way—if she would've let people in—maybe she could've come to terms with everything? I'll never know the answer, but somehow, having all the pieces of the puzzle makes it easier to believe she didn't leave *me* as much as she left the life that made her so unhappy.

A lot of things happened over the past year. The same lawyer who handled Blair Houghton's DUI case (which resulted in a hefty fine and community service) handled her divorce.

When Bob and Karen Stark reconciled, Blair moved to Hollywood to pursue her thwarted dreams of acting. It was a surprise, but once I considered her penchant for being a drama queen it made sense. Good for her for realizing it's never too late to pursue your dreams.

Repairs are complete on the Villa Magnolia. Barbara and Elizabeth are ready to open the bed-and-breakfast.

I'm mostly a silent partner since I concentrate

most of my efforts at the Wine Cellar, where, I'm happy to report, business is booming.

Working together, Rob and I have steadily increased business—and rekindled our romance, too. Neither of us is in a hurry to get married. We've decided to take it one day at a time and enjoy rediscovering each other and to give the kids a chance to adjust. Rob's son, Seth, stayed with him in Stratford Park and he needs a little time to come to terms with his parents' divorce.

Sarah has made friends and finally feels like she's a part of the community. One step at a time. There's no need to rush things.

That's Barbara's philosophy with the bed-and-breakfast, too. Elizabeth is working very part-time right now because of the new addition to their family: a healthy baby boy. All the red flags that flew during the tests ended up being false alarms. Anastasia still has her moments, but overall she's a great big sister.

Speaking of having moments—Burt McMillan has made good on his promise to be a better father to Mary Grace. Even though he and Barbara will probably never reconcile, they remain on good terms working together for the benefit of their daughter.

It's hard to believe that a little over a year ago life seemed so flimsy and uncertain. Now as Rob takes me in his arms and places a gentle kiss on my lips, I know that instead of dwelling on the past, I am happy to be firmly rooted straight in the here and now.

* * * * *

Experience entertaining women's fiction
about rediscovery
and reconnection—warm,
compelling stories that are relevant
to every woman who has wondered,
"What's next?" in their lives.
After all, there's the life you planned.
And there's what comes next.

Turn the page for a sneak preview
of a new book from Harlequin NEXT.

CONFESSIONS OF A NOT-SO-DEAD LIBIDO
by Peggy Webb

On sale November 2006,
wherever books are sold.

My husband could see beauty in a mud puddle. Literally. "Look at that, Louise," he'd say after a heavy spring rain. "Have you ever seen so many amazing colors in mud?"

I'd look and see nothing except brown, but he'd pick up a stick and swirl the mud till the colors of the earth emerged, and all of a sudden I'd see the world through his eyes—extraordinary instead of mundane.

Roy was my mirror to life. Four years ago when he died, it cracked wide open, and I've been living a smashed-up, sleepwalking life ever since.

If he were here on this balmy August night I'd be sailing with him instead of baking cheese straws in preparation for Tuesday-night quilting club with Patsy. I'd be striving for sex appeal in Bermuda shorts and bare-toed sandals instead of opting for comfort in walking shoes and a twill skirt with enough elastic

around the waist to make allowances for two help-
ings of lemon-cream pie.

Not that I mind Patsy. Just the opposite. I love
her. She's the only person besides Roy who creates
wonder wherever she goes. (She creates mayhem,
too, but we won't get into that.) She's my mirror
now, as well as my compass.

Of course, I have my daughter, Diana, but I refuse
to be the kind of mother who defines herself through
her children. Besides, she has her own life now, a
husband and a baby on the way.

I slide the last cheese straws into the oven and
then go into my office and open e-mail.

From: "Miss Sass" <patsyleslie@hotmail.com>
To: "The Lady" <louisejernigan@yahoo.com>
Sent: Tuesday, August 15, 6:00 PM
Subject: Dangerous Tonight
Hey Lady,
I'm feeling dangerous tonight. Hot to trot, if you
know what I mean. Or can you even remember??
Look out, bridge club, here I come. I'm liable to end
up dancing on the tables instead of bidding three
spades. Whose turn is it to drive, anyhow? Mine or
thine?

XOXOX

Patsy

P.S. Lord, how did we end up in a club with no men?

This e-mail is typical "Patsy." She's the only person I know who makes me laugh all the time. I guess that's why I e-mail her about ten times a day. She lives right next door, but e-mail satisfies my urge to be instantly and constantly in touch with her without having to interrupt the flow of my life. Sometimes we even save the good stuff for e-mail.

From: "The Lady" <louisejernigan@yahoo.com>
To: "Miss Sass" <patsyleslie@hotmail.com>
Sent: Tuesday, August 15, 6:10 PM
Subject: Re: Dangerous Tonight

So, what else is new, Miss Sass? You're always dangerous. If you had a weapon, you'd be lethal. ?
Hugs,
Louise
P.S. What's this about men? I thought you said your libido was dead?

I press Send then wait. Her reply is almost instantaneous.

From: "Miss Sass" <patsyleslie@hotmail.com>
To: "The Lady" <louisejernigan@yahoo.com>
Sent: Tuesday, August 15, 6:12 PM
Subject: Re: Dangerous Tonight

Ha! If I had a *brain* I'd be lethal.

And I said my libido was in hibernation, not DEAD!

Jeez, Louise!!!!!

P

Patsy loves to have the last word, so I shut off my computer.

* * * * *

Want to find out what happens to their friendship
when Patsy and Louise both find the perfect man?

Don't miss
CONFESSIONS OF A NOT-SO-DEAD LIBIDO
by Peggy Webb,

coming to Harlequin NEXT
in November 2006.

Solitary confinement never looked so good!

Instant motherhood felt a lot like being under house arrest, until somewhere between dealing with a burned bake-sale project, PTA meetings and preteen dating, Kate realized she'd never felt so free.

Motherhood Without Parole

by Tanya Michaels

HARLEQUIN®

Ne xt™

HN65

Available November 2006
TheNextNovel.com

It's all a matter of perspective

Grace Campisi has lived her whole life according to plan. But when her sister runs off, leaving behind a six-week-old baby girl, Grace's plans are thrown a curveball.

So in order to stick to her plan, Grace could either

a) track down her wayward sister
b) put her niece up for adoption
Or c) formulate a new plan?

Which End Is Up?

Patricia Kay

Available October 2006
TheNextNovel.com

HN61

Some secrets are meant to be shared.

For a group of friends, this summer will be remembered forever as the year when Rose's family became complete, Doris became the woman she was always meant to be and Mercedes finally found her man. It's never too late to give the rest of the town something to talk about.

The Gossip Queens

by Kate Austin

HN67

Available November 2006
TheNextNovel.com

HARLEQUIN®
Next™

REQUEST YOUR FREE BOOKS!

2 FREE NOVELS PLUS 2 FREE GIFTS!

There's the life you planned. And there's what comes next.

If only Harvey the Wonder Dog could dig up the dirt on her ex!

The last person she expected to see at her
husband's funeral was his other wife! Penny
can't bring herself to hate his "wife" or toss his
amazing piano-playing dog out on his rump. But
thanks to her ex's legacy and Harvey's "amazing"
trainer, Penny's ready to run with whatever
curveball life throws at her!

The Other Wife

by Shirley Jump

Available November 2006
TheNextNovel.com

HN68

HARLEQUIN®
Next™

A stunning novel of love and renewal...

Everyone knows sisters like the Sams girls—
three women trying their best to be good
daughters, mothers and wives. Then in one
cataclysmic moment everything changes...
and the sisters have to uncover every shrouded
secret and risk lifetime bonds to ensure the
survival of all they love.

Graceland

by Lynne Hugo

Just like a blue moon, friendship is a beautiful thing

Hoping to rekindle a sense of purpose, Lola resurrects a childhood dream and buys a blue beach house. When she drags three of her fun-loving, margarita-sipping friends out for some gossip and good times, they discover the missing spark in their relationships.

Once in a Blue Moon

by Lenora Worth

Available October 2006
TheNextNovel.com

HN64

HARLEQUIN®

Next™

A RAKE'S INTENTIONS

"You are the fairest maiden at the ball," Lord Lucan told Diana.

"Except that I'm no maiden," she murmured, then blushed at her own boldness.

Surprised, the earl's eyes narrowed a little. "No," he agreed. "A poor choice of words, perhaps," he added, grasping her chin in one hand so that she was forced to gaze into his eyes.

"You are so beautiful," he said huskily. "Diana the goddess, the eternal virgin. Maiden or not, that is how I view you."

She pushed his hands away, but his eyes still held her captive. "You must not say such things, Lord Lucan. There is no purpose in this."

He turned her words around. "On the contrary, there is a purpose. I am a man who always has a purpose in mind, Diana."

Suddenly, he knew he could not wait, that he meant to ask her here and now to be his wife. When she knew he wooed her in earnest, she would not be so reluctant.

"You know what I want, don't you?" he began gently, pulling her closer. "I want you, Diana, in every sense of the word . . ."

Change of Heart

Julie Caille

ZEBRA BOOKS
KENSINGTON PUBLISHING CORP.

ZEBRA BOOKS

are published by

Kensington Publishing Corp.
475 Park Avenue South
New York, NY 10016

First printing: January, 1991

Printed in the United States of America

To my parents
Priscilla and Robert Burns
with all my love

Chapter One

Of the seven Farington offspring, only the two eldest daughters bore their mama company the cold March afternoon the letter from Great-aunt Serena arrived. Warmed by the dancing fire not five feet away, the three women were comfortably grouped about a low table in the Small Saloon, a room whose once-plush seat coverings and faded carpet hinted at the impoverished state of the rest of the house. Yet it was hardly a gloomy place, for the Farington family kept the house scrupulously clean and well-lit, and their many domestic doings filled its chambers with, if not continual noise and mayhem, at least a close approximation thereof.

Diana, the elder daughter, watched her mother slit open the letter with outward dispassion, but beneath her cool exterior she was far from calm. Her sister's future hinged upon their great-aunt's reply, and after her own appalling experience, Diana could feel nothing but dismay at the thought of her darling sister being paraded before the overcritical eyes of the London *ton*. Of course, Great-aunt Serena might well refuse to sponsor Aimee, for not even the most doting relative could claim that their great-aunt was anything but capricious. A refusal was something that Aimee would deem a calamity of the first magnitude, but Diana, having already experienced the deepest of pitfalls during her own London Season, could not agree.

She said nothing, however, but shot a veiled look at her seventeen-year-old sister, Miss Aimee Farington. From the expression on Aimee's face, one might think the letter merited the same degree of veneration that might surround, for example, the creation of new mountain ranges or the shifting of continents. Her heart-shaped little face was flushed with anticipation, and her lovely blue eyes sparkled as if some long-awaited treat were about to be bestowed upon her. Her small hands gripped each other convulsively as she leaned forward, her dark hair tumbling from its fastenings as if it, no more than her emotions, could be contained.

"Oh, Mama, do hurry!" breathed the younger girl, bouncing with impatience. "I simply cannot *bear* the suspense! I cannot *think* what I shall do if Aunt Serena does not agree to present me—die of despair, I suppose! But she must do it, mustn't she? After all, she took Diana, didn't she? Oh, I know she'll do it! I know it!"

Mrs. Farington had thrust the newly arrived missive out at arm's length in an effort to bring the spindly handwriting into focus. "It's of no use," she said at last, heaving a disgusted sigh. "My eyes just are not what they used to be. Diana, you must read it, for I cannot make heads or tails out of this blur."

Perfectly willing to perform this office, Diana rose from her chair and moved gracefully across the short space to her mother's side. Ignoring Aimee's moaning appeals to read it aloud, she returned to her seat and scanned the letter, reviewing one section in particular with a startled frown.

At four-and-twenty, Mrs. Farington's eldest daughter was a striking young woman. She was of medium height and very slender, with an elegant carriage, a straight little

8

nose, and sweet, finely molded lips. Where he[r?]
hair was black as jet, Diana's hair shone like [...]
honey, and her eyes were some curious mixture of b[...]
and gold. However, it was not these attractions which
made one stare, though they should have been reason
enough. It was the look in, or rather *behind* those unusual
eyes that piqued the interest, for there was such a
shuttered look, such a vulnerable quality in their depths,
that one could not help but wonder what could have been
its author. As it happened, she was a widow, having
married one Edmund Verney at the age of eighteen. His
death, however, was not the cause of that look.

"Aimee is quite right," stated the young widow when
she finished reading. "Great-aunt Serena is quite willing
to finance Aimee's Season in London. She does not agree
that she should wait another year. She says my notions
are poppycock." Concealing her distress, Diana glanced
at her mother. "The whole letter sounds just like her,"
she added dryly.

Aimee looked ecstatic. "Then it is settled!" she cried,
clasping her hands to her bosom. "I shall go to London! I
shall see Cousin Charles!"

A troubled frown touched Diana's brow as she took in
the flush of color in her sister's pretty cheeks.

"Apparently so," she said, allowing a tiny ripple of
disquiet to creep into her voice. "I don't agree with Aunt
Serena, however. Are you absolutely set upon going this
year?"

Aimee widened her blue eyes. "Well, naturally, Diana!
I think it beyond everything that I shall have a Season
when I will not even be eighteen until next Christmas. I
cannot wait to tell Eliza—she will be mad with envy! But,
of course, that's not why I wish to go," she amended,
noting her sister's frown. "I shall have the whole Season
with Charles, you see. It may be the only chance I will
ever have to make him notice me. *Really* notice me,

9

mean."

Diana was unimpressed. "Yes, well, likely he will still be there next year," she coaxed. "Listen to me, Aimee, dear, if only just this once. London is huge and strange—not at all comfortable like our little village. There will be scads of people, none of whom will care a rap for you or your feelings. You will have to conform to a rigid pattern of behavior. And that is something you will find difficult, I assure you, for I found it nigh to impossible myself."

She might as well have been addressing the small potted plant on the table beside her for all the heed her words were given. "No lectures, *please*," begged her sister, adding brightly, "Yes, I do want to go, and no, I don't want to wait until I've grown a little older. It is boring in the country, Diana!"

Diana sighed. She honestly did understand her sister's feelings, for she remembered experiencing almost identical sentiments—once. It was really, she thought, her own emotions which were the source of the problem. It seemed so long since her own lips had curved into the light-hearted smiles that came so easily to Aimee. She knew most people assumed this was because she was still mourning the death of her husband. Her lip did curl a little at that absurd thought.

"When does she wish Aimee to come?" inquired Mrs. Farington, fussing with the folds of her skirt. As Diana raised the letter and opened her mouth, her mother added quickly, "Only the bare facts, if you please, for I've no desire to listen to Aunt Serena's sarcastic form of wit, if I can avoid it. Will she pay the travel expenses? For I'm sure your Papa's carriage will never make the journey in one piece, and we cannot afford for her to travel post, and—"

"And I absolutely refuse to ride the Mail!" declared Aimee, secure in the knowledge that she would never be asked to do so.

10

Diana's gaze went to her sister. "She says she will p
for us both to travel post, and to bring either a maid, or
Miss Tilden."

"Both!" echoed Aimee and Mrs. Farington at once.

The first to recover from surprise, Aimee clapped her
hands in delight. "You are coming, too, Diana? Oh, how
famous! We shall have such fun!"

Diana's leaden silence caused her mother to eye her
uneasily. "Why, how . . . how kind of Aunt Serena," she
ventured. "I think it might be good for you, Diana. Will
you consider it?"

Having steeled herself to resist an entreaty, the
tentative question put Diana at a loss. "I . . . I don't
know, Mama," she answered, staring past her mother at
some memory from the past. "You know how I feel about
London."

Mrs. Farington's rosebud mouth turned down sadly.
"Yes, Diana, dear. But all that was long ago. Edmund has
been gone now for three years. People will have forgotten
all about what happened."

"I have not forgotten," her daughter reminded her
softly. "I shall never forget."

Her mother sighed. "Of course not, love, but you must
learn to live again. You are too young to want to bury
yourself in the country like this. With Edmund's money,
you could have been living in town somewhere, enjoying
yourself, making friends, perhaps meeting another
gentleman who could—"

"Who could make me as miserable as Edmund
managed to do!" interrupted the young widow with her
first flash of impatience. "Look, Mama, if I did go to
London with Aimee, it would be simply to bear her
company and keep her from falling into scrapes! I have
absolutely no intention of marrying again."

"Or of ever having any fun," inserted Aimee daringly.
"Oh, Diana, I *am* sorry, but it is difficult to remain

11

cheerful when you talk so. And I do not intend to get into any scrapes."

Diana forced a smile. "One never does. Oh, I know how I must sound to you, dear. And, believe it or not, I am not trying to cast a damper on what must seem to you the ultimate good fortune. But as for my coming with you, well, I would have to give that a great deal of thought."

Recognizing the obstinate set of her eldest daughter's jaw, Mrs. Farington tactfully abandoned the subject, and turned her attention instead to the younger girl.

"It would be foolish for us to depend upon it, of course, but if you *were* able to attach the interest of your cousin Charles, your papa and I would be excessively pleased. He is such a fine, steady sort of man, so exactly what one would wish! And so very well set up in the world! Of course, I am the last person on earth to push you to marry for such a vulgar reason as money, for only look at your poor papa and me! And we, as you know, are as happy as two ducks on a pond—despite the fact that the roof is sadly in need of repair." Struck by this melancholy thought, she heaved a long, regretful sigh. "Well, there is no denying it would be a great comfort to know you were married to a man who could provide for you. Aunt Serena will not be here forever, after all. And there are Elizabeth and Dorothy and Louisa still to consider, and Jeremy's school fees, and little Nick's, when he is older."

"Do you think Cousin Charles will remember me?" inquired Aimee, rather anxiously. "It has been nearly three years since we visited the Perths. He may not even recognize me."

"Well, you have changed a great deal," agreed her mother. "It is quite possible he may not, so you ought to be prepared if that turns out to be the case. But that may be all for the best, for you were sadly plump in those days,

12

were you not? And correct me if I am wrong, my dear, but did you not have spots?"

Aimee scowled. "Only a few," she retorted. "Both Elizabeth and Dorothy are far worse! It is only people like Diana who can escape them altogether. You have such glorious skin, Diana."

But Diana was staring at the carpet, her thoughts far away. They were neither new nor pleasant, these thoughts, but over the years she had learned to distance herself from them. Objectively, she knew that, yes, she ought to get away from home. She was feeling only half-alive these days, as if a portion of her soul had died along with Edmund. But that was ridiculous. Escape from her role as Edmund's wife had been one of the most providential releases of her life. Not, of course, that she would have wished him to die, but since he had gone and gotten himself killed in a vulgar tavern brawl, there was really no more to be said. If he had not died, she would certainly have left him by now. Of that she was certain, even though she was sure of little else.

"She doesn't hear me," said Aimee. "She's woolgathering, again."

Diana glanced up. "I'm sorry?" she murmured, her attention returning to the present. "I'm afraid I didn't hear what you said."

"Never mind," said Aimee. "I was just saying that you never had spots."

"Oh?" replied Diana vaguely, missing the worried look her mother and sister exchanged. "Goodness, look at the time. I'd best get back, for Tildy will be missing me. Let me know when you're going to write to Aunt Serena. I must think this over very carefully."

When she had gone, Mrs. Farington shook her head. "You know, when she came back to live near us after

13

Edmund died," she confided, "I thought it was a wise decision. I thought that for her to be near us would be good for her, that it would help her grow away from her misfortunes. I never thought she would just stay on here, growing older and more unhappy. I really think she ought to go to London with you, Aimee. She has no future here."

Aimee chewed her bottom lip, hesitantly forming the question preying on her mind. "Just what was it about Edmund she hated so, Mama? What was it about him that was so beastly?"

Mrs. Farington patted her lace mobcap nervously, and glanced down at the letter on the table. "Oh, Edmund was all wrong for our Diana. She should never have married him. She *would* never have married him, were it not for his . . . ungentlemanly conduct. When a lady is forced into a compromising position and the gabble-mongers get hold of it, well, there's really no alternative. She marries the man in question, or retires from society forever to live in disgrace." She cleared her throat, and continued firmly, "It is unfair, but true. The sad part of it is, your sister married Edmund to avoid scandal, then hid herself away in the country as if she were still in disgrace. But our Diana has never had a reason not to hold her head up. What happened was not her fault."

This was the first Aimee had heard of the true circumstances of her sister's marriage. Her blue eyes very big, she protested, "But, Mama! I cannot imagine Diana allowing a . . . a man to impose on her in such a manner. She is the most poised, controlled person I have ever met!"

Her mother smiled slightly. "Yes, well, you have not met a great many people, my love. The Diana of today is not the Diana of yesterday. You've forgotten, haven't you? She used to be so carefree, so spontaneous, so full of life—oh, how can I explain it? She was young, Aimee and

14

he was such a horrid young man. He cared nothing for her feelings. She has never said, so I draw my own conclusions, but I fancy he did not treat her well in private. *That* part of marriage is not easy for some women, my dear, and if the man is not gentle . . . but I should not speak of it to you! You are so young, so innocent!"

She dabbed at her eyes with her handkerchief, struck anew by the enormity of what her first daughter had suffered.

For a few moments, Aimee studied her mother, then said, rather suddenly, "She *shall* go to London, Mama, for if she does not, *I* will refuse to go, and then she must change her mind. And once we have her there, why, I shall look about and find her a proper husband. And don't think I cannot, for I know what suits Diana better than anyone in the world."

"So selfless! Such an angel!" sobbed her mother, still dabbing.

"Oh, pooh!" said Aimee. "That's farradiddle, Mama. I'm shockingly selfish and you know it. But I do love my sister and I hate to see her unhappy. So I shall find her another husband, only one who loves her this time. I daresay that will solve everything."

If Diana had heard these remarks, she would have been quite touched. She was closer to Aimee than any of her sisters, and had long been determined to prevent her from being hurt. And remembering how easily it could happen sent a shiver of foreboding running down her spine.

There was no dismissing the feeling. It gripped her, and what before had been a mere ripple of disquiet became a positive tidal wave of worry. What if a man tried to do to sweet little Aimee what Edmund had tried to do to her? The thought made her ill, and her expression grew bleak as she wended her way along the dirt road leading to the small house she had been leasing for the past three years.

It had not been quite as easy to come back as everyone imagined. Just the notion that others might know what Edmund had tried to do to her, the reason for her strange marriage, was enough to bring a flush of humiliation to her cheeks. When one was very private and very sensitive, such a sordid chapter in one's life was almost beyond endurance. Just knowing her name had been bandied about the drawing rooms of London was enough to make Diana want to curl up and die. Even here in this sleepy little corner of Wiltshire, she had never been completely comfortable.

When people asked, as they occasionally did, why she had never returned to London after her period of mourning was over, she could hardly think of a civil reply. Does one venture to return to the place where one has suffered the ultimate mortification? Does one seek out the very people who whispered about the scandal behind their hands? No, one does not. But, of course, she could not say this. And so she let them assume that town life had not suited her, and that she preferred the country. It was the simplest solution.

In fact, nothing could be further from the truth. Diana had loved London. She had reveled in the crowds, the color and excitement, the very busyness of it all. She had loved seeing the street vendors and the merchants, hearing their boisterous cries rising above the rumble of rolling carriage wheels and the clopping of horses' hooves on the rough cobbles. Every part of it had made her feel so alive, so a part of the rest of humanity. The balls, the plays, and the parks had been but an added bonus. But Edmund and the hypocrisy of the life had spoiled it for her.

So-called friends had turned her misfortune into the latest *on-dit*. Congratulations on her marriage had been extended by those who were aware of how much she detested her betrothed. The fact that he was a lecherous beast who tried to paw every girl he met made no difference. His uncle was an earl, and so, of course, he was rated a fine catch. She must be pleased with her achievement.

Her wedding night had been a nightmare. Even now, she closed her mind to the memories of Edmund's roughness, his utter indifference to her terror. The number of times they had been intimate had actually been very few, for she had quickly grown adept at avoiding his embraces. Fortunately, he had not appeared to care, for among various other outlets for his lust was a mistress in Chelsea. Like a good wife, Diana had stayed in the country and turned a blind eye to his infidelities, an action that had, ironically, earned her praise from Edmund. She had laughed scornfully when he had told her that the marriage was not turning out so very badly after all. And then she had thrown a Sèvres vase at his head. Not so badly, indeed!

By the time Diana arrived back at her house, she was thoroughly chilled by the stiff March wind. Hurrying upstairs, she threw off her dress and unpinned her hair, quickly drawing a comb through its long mass of tangles. Since she did not reside in town, she did not conform to the modern practice of cropping one's hair into short curls. As she retwisted it into its neat coil, she wondered whether going to London would mean having to cut it all off. She shuddered at the thought that any eccentricity on her part would give rise to gossip. She still recalled the awful, naked, helplessness of being a victim, and having others look at you as though you had brought all your

17

troubles on yourself.

Although she was quite alone, Diana still cringed when she thought about it all. She had never dared tell anyone how it had all come about, that she had purposely crept upstairs at the Edgerton's ball to peer out the upstairs window at Sir Henry Neyle walking with one of her rivals on the balcony below; that she had cherished some very warm feelings for Sir Henry and that jealousy had prompted her to eavesdrop upon the pair of them; that she had dared to believe the handsome blond baronet had looked at her differently, that his smile meant so much more than his actual words. And through her own foolish actions, she had managed to bring about her own downfall.

Edmund Verney, loathsome creature that he was, had followed her up the stairs and caught her spying on Sir Henry. He had laughed at her, then forced his horrid mouth onto hers, digging at her lips with his revolting tongue. She had kicked and bitten like a wildcat, but Edmund had proved surprisingly strong for such a thin young man. When their hostess walked into the room half a minute later, he was already half atop her, one hand clamped over her mouth, the other fumbling beneath her skirt. Though Lady Edgerton pretended sympathy, the scene was utterly damning in the eyes of such a malicious gossip. It mattered not that Diana was still chaste. To their hostess, it was simply too good a story not to tell.

By the end of the following day, their betrothal had been announced. Oh, Edmund had not been honorable enough to make the offer himself. He had sulked like a little boy when, like an avenging fury, an outraged Great-aunt Serena had descended upon his uncle, Lord Bathurst, and flung animadversions at him while brandishing her cane like a dueling sword. It was she who demanded that Edmund make amends for his despicable

18

action, she who had the wit to fight rumor with counterrumor. When Diana wanted only to hide, Great-aunt Serena took her to the opera, flaunting her great-niece as if nothing in the least untoward had transpired. Within hours, the story was diluted into some nonsense about a secret betrothal and stolen kisses, which most people accepted simply because they disliked Lady Edgerton. The fact that the woman was well known for her tendency to exaggerate was largely what saved Diana from complete social disgrace.

Yet even in private, Edmund was so far lost to all sense of decency that he had the effrontery to deny the whole of it. Then, when he finally admitted his misdeeds, he declared that he had no wish to marry Diana. However, in the end, he had succumbed to Aunt Serena's verbal thumbscrews, for it was the easiest way out of the hornet's nest he had created. One thing Edmund had always lacked was backbone. He had no shame either, for he never displayed, either in private or in public, any contrition or embarrassment over the entire episode. Indeed, Diana had been mortified to hear that he had bragged of his easy conquest in one of the men's clubs.

Was it any wonder that she was reluctant to return?

Wearing a fresh gown, Diana entered her small dining room to find that Miss Tilden, the nurse of her childhood years, and, more currently, her companion, was already seated at table, calmly engrossed with her knitting.

For as long as Diana could remember, Miss Tilden had been a knitter. In her sixty-six years of life, she had made an incalculable number of garments, both for charity and for people she knew. Her current project was stockings, vast piles of woolen stockings, which she eventually intended to donate to the Foundling Hospital in London. To Diana, the clicking of knitting needles was the most

19

comforting sound in the world, associated as it was with blurry childhood memories of warm milk, buttered toast, and the drowsy crackling of hearth fires.

As soon as she crossed the threshold, Miss Tilden's amiable face wrinkled into a welcoming smile. "Ah, there you are, Diana. I was just wondering where you might be. Did you have a pleasant visit with your Mama?"

Diana hesitated. "Oh, well enough," she said evasively. "I am sorry to be so late. You must be famished."

Her elderly companion put aside her knitting and Diana rang for her maid to bring in the soup. While Bess ladled the steaming liquid into their bowls, Miss Tilden cast a shrewd look at the girl she had known all her life. "Something's troubling you, I think. Did they hear anything from your aunt? I do hope it's not bad news."

Diana smiled what Miss Tilden called her bright, false smile. "On the contrary, everything is splendid. Great-aunt Serena has offered to frank Aimee's entire season, as well as the cost of traveling post. For both of us."

Miss Tilden, who had just picked up her spoon, put it down abruptly. "Both? My dear, what can you mean?"

Diana's own spoon dipped determinedly into her soup. "I mean," she said, after discovering it was too hot, "that I am invited as well. And you, for that matter. I suppose that Aunt Serena imagines enough time has passed now. She wants to try to auction me off again."

Miss Tilden looked pained. "Dear Diana, pray do not speak in that cynical way. It is most distressing! You cannot truly believe that is her only motive? Surely she is just being kind?"

"Oh, no, I doubt it," Diana responded coolly. "If the invitation had come from you, Tildy, then I would have said the same. But dear Aunt Serena is far too didactic a personality for that. She's probably bored and has forgotten how much trouble I caused her the first time."

"I see." Miss Tilden gave a delicate cough. "So, ah, are

20

we going?"

Diana shrugged. "I have no wish to see the place ever again."

"Diana," said the older woman quietly, "when you were a little girl, I could always tell when you were lying by the way you would shrug your shoulders in just that way. This time, perhaps you are lying to yourself."

Diana shut her eyes, one hand flying up to touch her head as if it hurt. "Oh, Tildy. I'm such a coward. Just the thought of seeing some of those people again throws me into a quake. Just talking of it makes my heart begin to pound."

"Stage fright," pronounced Miss Tilden, with less sympathy than Diana expected. "Good heavens, love, of course you're nervous. But surely it will pass."

Diana's hand fell limply to her lap. "It must pass," she said tonelessly. "Because I'm going, Tildy. I made up my mind while I was walking home. I have to go for Aimee's sake."

Miss Tilden looked blank. "Aimee's sake?" she repeated uncertainly.

"Yes. I have to protect her from men like Edmund. I must guard her, as must you, Tildy." Diana's mouth was set in a firm, stubborn line as she spoke.

Without hesitation, her companion assumed her meekest expression. "You are perfectly right, of course," she murmured. "We must go to protect Aimee. Now, why did that not occur to me, I wonder? To be sure, it is perfectly obvious. So sensible! I must be getting old."

"I'll go on one condition," Diana told her mother the following afternoon. "I will not stay with Aunt Serena. I want to hire a house for the Season."

"Hire a house?" repeated Mrs. Farington faintly. "Mercy, Diana, think of the expense! Particularly when you can stay with Aunt Serena in Arlington Street. Such a distinguished address!"

"Distinguished or not, I won't stay there," said Diana flatly. "I've enough money to do it. And since you persist in refusing to take any of it for your own needs, I may as well spend it on this. Oh, Mama, I don't want anything grand! Just a small respectable place where I can have some privacy. I'm *used* to being my own mistress, Mama. I cannot imagine spending several months under Aunt Serena's roof. You know what she is."

"Yes, but will Aimee like it?" wondered Mrs. Farington.

"Aimee will love it. And you need not worry about respectability because, after all, I *am* a widow, which, thank the Lord, gives me some level of freedom. And dear Tildy has consented to bear me company. We shall go on very well. I trust Aunt Serena will still sponsor Aimee, even if she resides with me?"

Her mother sighed, unable to argue with her strong-willed daughter for any length of time. "I trust so, my love. I shall write to her on your behalf, if you like. Will you write to Edmund's man of business as well? I'm sure he will look into the matter of the house for you, if you request it."

Diana's brow furrowed thoughtfully. "Yes, that's an excellent idea. I can describe specifically the sort of house I am looking for. Perhaps he can find something near Aunt Serena so as to pacify her. But not too near," she added, with a grimace.

"As you wish," said her mother. "I know your papa will not object." She paused, her caring gaze resting upon her daughter's face. "Are you sure this is right for you, Diana? I want you to go, but believe it or not, I do have some understanding of how you must feel."

The concern in her voice threatened Diana's control. Catching up her mother's hand, she gave it a loving squeeze. "Oh, Mama, I am a little scared to go back," she confessed, swallowing the lump in her throat. "I'm afraid all the gossip will be revived, and I'll have to face them all down again. And I don't want Aimee exposed to their maliciousness. It's difficult to know what to do."

Mrs. Farington pulled her daughter close, one hand stroking her hair tenderly. "You've decided to go, why don't you let it go at that? Aimee will be fine. You want to go, Diana. There's no shame in admitting it, and nothing to be frightened of, either. Just don't lump all the people you meet into one category. And remember, some of the best people are the ones who don't try too hard to impress. Try not to judge too quickly or too harshly. That's my little piece of motherly advice."

Eyes bright with unshed tears, Diana pulled back her head and managed a small laugh. "I'll try, Mama, but you know what a suspicious nature I've developed."

"You've changed," agreed her mother gently. "Life does that, I'm afraid, but it seems to me that too much of the old Diana went away. And despite her very quick temper, I miss my other Diana very much."

Diana sighed. "Oh, she's still right here, believe me— only a little more in control. I fear her shocking temper is never very far from the surface, though. No doubt it's only waiting for just the right person to set it aflame."

Chapter Two

In entrusting the selection of a house to Mr. Perkins, Diana was making a wise decision. A capable man, Perkins had served not only her husband, but her husband's uncle, Lord Bathurst, and was quite unfazed by her request. With his typical dedication to duty, he spent several days viewing a large number of the various dwellings available for hire, and after much peering about into bedrooms, kitchens, and attics, he narrowed the list of candidates down to three. His letter detailing the location, rent, and floor plan of each establishment arrived the following week.

To Diana's dismay, the cost of hiring a house was a trifle more than she had anticipated, but after carefully checking her records, she found the expense to be within her means. Each of the houses was located in the fashionable part of town. The first, in Clarges Street, had a great many advantages, but on the whole it sounded too large, and since it was the most costly of the three, Diana quickly eliminated it as an option. Of the remaining two, one was situated in Jermyn Street and the other in Clifford Street. The latter's proximity to Bond Street weighed heavily in its favor, but after more debate, she selected the Jermyn Street address. It was within walking distance to both Aunt Serena and the mews where she kept her carriages, an advantage when one considered the expense of purchasing and maintaining any sort of equipage. It seemed a reasonable assumption that since Aunt Serena owned both a barouche and a landaulet, as well as an elegant town coach and a large traveling chariot, she would allow them the use of one of these conveyances. As for riding, Diana shrugged that aside. Aunt Serena kept nothing but carriage horses.

Mr. Perkins's letter assured her that all three houses were adequately furnished, so that all she need be concerned with was the hiring of domestic staff. If she was desirous that he should look into that matter as well, he would be more than happy to oblige. He recommended, as a minimum, the employment of a cook, a butler, and either a footman or a pageboy, as well as at least one abigail. Since he had already demonstrated to her satisfaction the excellence of his judgment, it was with some relief that Diana decided to leave the business of interviewing and hiring servants completely in his hands.

Another week passed before she heard from him again. This letter informed her that the four menials she had requested had been engaged and were prepared to commence their employment on any date she chose. Since the Season was fast approaching, Diana wrote back to tell him they would be leaving at the end of week, and she would be pleased if the house was open and ready when she arrived. She then put on her bonnet and gloves, and left the house to inform Aimee and the rest of her family of the date of departure.

Diana's steps were light as she trod the short distance to Farington Place. It was a glorious feeling to be so in charge of one's life, she reflected in a sudden burst of optimism. There really was something to be said for being a widow. To be able to make one's own choices without

25

male interference, to have the freedom to set up one's own establishment, this was what she found most tolerable about widowhood. And since she had not loved Edmund, she had not been forced to suffer the agonizing sense of loss that normally accompanied such a bereavement.

True, she had had to settle some of Edmund's gaming debts, but on the whole, she had come out of it very well, Edmund had not been complete master of his own purse strings, and so had not been able to squander his money in the manner he would have liked. His uncle had been delegated trustee of the small fortune her husband had inherited, a responsibility Lord Bathurst had made sure to take seriously. He had insisted that Edmund make a will in Diana's favor, which later proved a fortuitous precaution. Thanks to that will, Diana had inherited all her husband's money rather than the half-share the law would have allowed her if he had died without a will. As long as she was not extravagant, it was enough to make her financially independent for the rest of her life.

Naturally, Diana's first impulse had been to try to assist her own family with their pecuniary problems, but her parents stubbornly refused to accept anything other than the odd gift or two for the children. Perhaps they felt their eldest daughter's sufferings entitled her to whatever profits she eventually reaped. Whatever the case, they insisted that Diana's money remain her own, that it made them breathe easier knowing she had it. And then, of course, there was the hope that Great-aunt Serena would remember them in her will.

The Dowager Lady Torrington was the matriarch of the family. She was shockingly rich, having been an heiress in her own right before her marriage to a wealthy viscount. Neither she nor the viscount had approved of gaming or improvident spending, and so their combined fortunes had increased over the years, endowing the viscount's widow with the power to rule over the family with an iron rod. Her despotic temperament made her a positive terror to those members of the family within swinging distance of her cane. Diana could recall times in her childhood when she had been quite frightened of Great-aunt Serena, but as an adult she saw her differently. In her own way, Diana had just as much steel in her as the dowager, and did not shrink from the prospect of facing her displeasure. If only she could face the London *ton* with as much fortitude, she thought wistfully.

The journey to London via post-chaise was accomplished with a minimum of discomfort, although Aimee chattered so much she eventually gave poor Miss Tilden a headache. And then, rather to Diana's amusement, she took such great care to keep silent that she did not, in fact, speak again until they rolled past Hyde Park Corner more than two hours later.

"Look, Diana! There is Hyde Park!" she exclaimed, pressing her face against the glass in wonder. "We are here! Oh, you must look, Miss Tilden! I am sure it will make you feel better."

In spite of the way her palms had begun to perspire, Diana found herself smiling. "Yes, Aimee," she said softly. "We are here."

Everywhere there were people. Aristocrats and beggars, ladies and ladies' maids, footmen and pageboys, thieves and pickpockets, errandboys, street hawkers, flowergirls, jarveys, sedan chairmen—these and a host of others were what made up this seething pocket of life that Diana remembered so well. She had not been in London since the day she had married; just knowing she was back made her realize how greatly she had missed it.

From then on, it seemed only a short time before they

reached their destination, 30 Jermyn Street. As Diana paid off the postboys, excitement went charging through her, supplanting the calm she had been trying to sustain. The tall narrow brick house was very like every other house on the street, each attached to its neighbor like so many links in a chain. Without speaking, she studied it eagerly, heartened by her own unexpected surge of elation. Here was where she was going to live, she told herself wonderingly. It was *hers,* at least for these next few months.

Drawing a deep breath, she glanced at Aimee, who stood watching her out of alert blue eyes. "Well," she said, making her tone brisk, "let us hope Mr. Perkins was right, and there is someone inside to let us in!"

As it happened, that good gentleman's assurances had not been in vain. The door was opened by Lawrence, her new butler, and their trunks and valises were fetched in by a tall, well-muscled footman named Felix. Within the hour, the ladies were well on their way to being settled into their new home.

Diana explored the house with a great sense of satisfaction. It was not at all commodious, yet it had the requisite number of reception rooms. The ground floor had a small, neatly decorated morning room, a slightly larger dining room, and a tiny back room which was meant for a study. Most of the first floor was devoted to the drawing room, although another tiny room at the back had been allocated for a boudoir. There were three bedrooms on the second floor, and the attics above that, while the kitchen, servants' quarters, pantry, and scullery were relegated, in the usual manner, to the basement. It was just the sort of house she had envisioned, Diana thought contentedly.

The first thing she did after supervising the unpacking of her trunk by Meg, her new abigail, was to sit down and compose a carefully worded note to the dowager

28

viscountess informing her of their arrival. This was borne off to Arlington Street by a cheerful Felix, who returned half an hour later with a rather curt response from that imperious lady. This dispatch contained the peremptory statement that she wished to see them the following morning, and she trusted they could find the means to get themselves there. She would expect them at eleven o'clock.

Diana rubbed her suddenly burning eyes, relieved that at least Great-aunt Serena had not demanded to see them at once. It was too late in the day to be making calls, and they were all tired and in need of a good night's rest. Though her optimistic mood lasted for most of the evening, later, as she slipped into her nightdress and crawled into bed, Diana was struck with another rush of anxiety. Had she made the right decision? How would she feel when she began to meet people she had known six years before, people who had known the disgraceful reason for her marriage to Edmund? Her eyes squeezed tightly shut, Diana prayed that her self-control and ability to hide her true feelings would be enough to get her through whatever was to come.

Diana awoke the next morning feeling extraordinarily refreshed. Whatever dreams she had dreamed must have been pleasant, she mused, as she stretched her slim arms above her head and yawned. Swinging her legs over the side of the bed, she glanced toward the clothespress, wondering what she could wear that would be both elegant and subdued. Having no desire to call attention to herself, she would leave Aimee to cut her swath in the paths of fashion alone.

However, the celestial blue walking dress she finally selected was hardly subdued, for in truth, Diana adored bright colors. Her spencer, too, was rather dashing,

composed as it was of white striped lutestring orna-
mented with braiding. The brim of her bonnet was not
large enough to be truly fashionable, she reflected, but
her matching blue kid shoes and straw-colored gloves
were very smart. But when she surveyed this costume in
the mirror, her brow furrowed. Instead of making her
appear dignified and sure of herself, it made her look
young and a little frightened. Well, perhaps this was
because her hair was not yet dressed, but hung loosely
down her back in a thick wavy mass. Laying aside the
spencer, bonnet, and gloves, Diana rang for her abigail,
who had assured her the previous evening that she knew
just the way the mistress's hair ought to be arranged.

Meg soon proved her contention to be no idle boast.
She seemed to possess just the knack for getting Diana's
thick hair to do what she wanted, combing and twisting
her honey gold tresses into an attractive, intricate style,
while leaving some wispy curls to soften the perimeter of
her face.

" 'Twould be a shame to cut all this off," remarked her
pretty young abigail. "Still, the modern styles would suit
you just as well. Miss Aimee says she wants to have hers
cut. You'll be wantin' to bring in one of them fancy
coiffeurs, I reckon. I couldn't undertake to do that for
you."

"I suppose so," said Diana, thinking it was just as well
Aimee wanted to follow the conventional road. She did
also, but somehow that did not extend to a willingness to
change the way she wore her hair. She had always kept
her hair long; it was a part of her.

After partaking of a light breakfast in the dining room
with Aimee and Miss Tilden, Diana went to the study to
make a short list of things she needed to do. Shopping for
Aimee headed the list, as well as sending a polite note to
Lord Bathurst, Edmund's uncle. She knew a visit from
him would not be too traumatic, for although his lordship

was a pompous sort of man, he had always been kind, and had written her a most conciliatory letter when Edmund had died. Mulling for a while over which shops they should visit, and in what order their purchases should be made, Diana made notes in her neat, concise handwriting. She was nearly finished when Aimee came to remind her it was time for them to visit Aunt Serena.

Diana had decided that they would walk. It was perfectly respectable for them to do so, and the distance was not so very great, even for Miss Tilden. Moreover, although it was a trifle windy, the sun was shining, and the sky was clear and bright. It would have been a shame for them to have taken a carriage when the weather was so fine, she told Aimee cheerfully, while pulling on her gloves.

As they strolled along the street, Aimee began to twirl her parasol in what she told them was meant to be a coquettish manner. "For I quite intend to make a stir among the gentlemen," she confided. "Oh, of course, I mean to have Charles in the end, but first I intend to enjoy myself. In my bones, I feel sure that I will be very good at flirting, Diana. And I want to practice as much as possible, so I can make Cousin Charles jealous. It will be so romantic!"

Miss Tilden looked quite shocked, and Diana said quickly, "I hope you will do no such thing, Aimee. It is not at all the thing for a young innocent girl to flirt, no matter what that hoydenish Eliza Fingleshaw may tell you. Honestly! If you'd told me that before we left, I should have done everything I could to keep you at home."

Aimee gave her a sidelong glance. "Well, that is why I did not tell you, Diana," she pointed out, rather blithely. "Oh, now, do not be working yourself into a fidget! I won't do anything to embarrass you or bring shame upon myself. I simply want to have a little fun. Surely you can

31

understand that?"

Diana was about to answer when two figures rounded the corner some distance ahead of them, advancing in their direction. Her heart skipped a beat. *Surely* that could not be . . . oh, dear Lord, could it actually be Sir Henry Neyle? It was beginning, she thought, in a sudden panic. Her hard-won poise was deserting her. Would he recognize her? If he bowed, should she speak? Nearly dizzy at the prospect of seeing him again, Diana barely glanced at his companion, a tall, strong-featured gentleman whose cool gray eyes had already locked upon the three women.

Carefully averting her eyes so as not to be caught staring, Diana turned to make some idle comment to Aimee. Aimee answered, but Diana did not hear, for the two gentlemen were getting very close and all her attention was focused on the laughing blond baronet. At the last possible moment, she turned her head, as if to give them a bare, uninterested glance. To her gratification, she saw Sir Henry's eyes widen in recognition, and instead of passing by, he stopped short and swept off his hat.

It seemed the most natural thing in the world to greet him. "Good day to you, Sir Henry," she said, hoping her voice did not quiver with the self-consciousness she was feeling. "How good to see you again."

Sir Henry bowed, his smile so angelically sweet Diana felt her heart turn over. "Why, it's . . . Mrs. Verney, isn't it?" he inquired. "It seems like years since you've been to town, ma'am, I'd quite given up hope you would ever again grace a London drawing room with your fair presence."

His gallantry brought a sweep of becoming color to Diana's pale cheeks. "Six years, to be exact," she told Sir Henry shyly. "May I introduce you to my sister Miss Farington? And, of course, my dear friend and com-

32

panion, Miss Tilden."

As the ladies acknowledged the introduction, Sir Henry clapped a hand on his companion's shoulder. "Do you know Lord Lucan, Mrs. Verney? If not, pray allow me to bring him to your notice. Make your bow, Geoffrey, old boy."

Unoffended by this remark, the gray-eyed gentleman looked straight into Diana's eyes. "Actually, Mrs. Verney and I have met," he said, his voice low and pleasantly masculine. His gaze extended to Aimee and Miss Tilden. "Ladies," he added, with a bow.

With some effort, Diana pulled her senses together and looked more fully at the man she now remembered was an earl. "Ah yes," she replied, a trifle flustered by the frankness of his regard. "How do you do, my lord."

"Well," said Sir Henry, "how absolutely delightful that you have returned! Dare I hope that you are here for the entire Season?" At Diana's affirmative, he went on, with flattering alacrity, "Then, may I call upon you sometime soon? I should very much like to renew our acquaintance. Where are you staying?"

As Diana answered, she was suddenly conscious of Lord Lucan's wandering gaze. What on earth was he— Good heavens! The man actually had the audacity to stand there and study her figure! How *dared* he, she thought furiously. The fact that the wind was whipping her thin muslin gown rather revealingly against her frame was absolutely no excuse!

Speechless with indignation, Diana shot the earl her frostiest dagger look, which the outrageous man feigned not to notice until his perusal was complete. Then, up went his brows as he flashed her an oh-so-innocent smile. Unhappily aware that she was beginning to blush, Diana raised her chin disdainfully and answered Sir Henry's next pleasantry—a polite inquiry about the health of her family—with enhanced cordiality.

Though she favored Sir Henry with her most dazzling smile, Diana's parting nod to Lord Lucan was distinctly cool. As the three women moved off down the street, Diana's emotions were chaotic. How dreadfully unfortunate that Sir Henry had been with that particular man! The earl was one gentleman whose acquaintance she had no wish to renew. Now that she saw him again, she recalled very well the few occasions they had been together. He had the annoying tendency to stand too close, that was it, so that when they talked she was forever wanting to take a step or two backward. He always made her feel as if she were threatened in some way, though by what she was unable to explain.

Although Diana would later puzzle over a reason for her next action, she would never produce one that made any sense. Surreptitiously, she glanced over her shoulder at the two men. To her horror, the insufferable earl looked around at precisely the same insant. His eyes met hers, and with a grin that to Diana seemed brimming with wickedness, he raised his fingers to his lips and blew her a kiss.

Aghast, Diana's head snapped back to the front so fast it almost hurt. Dear God, why had she done it? Overwhelmed with embarrassment, she fixed her eyes rigidly on a point somewhere in the distance and increased the length of her stride. And of course, she thought savagely, he would think she had been looking at *him!* The man obviously had an inflated opinion of himself.

"Diana," gasped Miss Tilden suddenly, "must we walk quite so fast? I find I am quite out of breath. Are we late, my dear, that we must hurry so?"

With a murmured apology, Diana relaxed her pace, but unfortunately the damage was done. The brief surge of confidence she had experienced while talking to Sir

Henry was already beginning to ebb. Had she learned nothing in these past few years? she wondered miserably. Surely marriage and widowhood should have had given her some veneer of sophistication, some ability to recognize and prevent potentially unnerving situations. Yet perhaps not, for it seemed that she was as impressionable as she had been at the age of eighteen.

The memories were sweeping in now, like the gathering wind before a storm. That man had always tried to stare her out of countenance, hadn't he? And wasn't he married? Yes, he was, to a very beautiful woman by the name of—was it Laurette? And here he was, up to his old tricks again. Heaven help that poor woman who was forced to bear his name! He was probably another such as Edmund, out chasing women while expecting his wife to sit chastely at his hearth, waiting for him to crook an arbitrary finger in her direction.

Well, she might still blush as easily as a schoolgirl, but Diana knew a great deal more about men now than she had at eighteen. In particular, she knew how deceptive were their smiles, and how selfish their lusts. This time around, she promised herself grimly, Diana Verney would no longer play the easy target. With all the contempt she could muster, she would snap her fingers in Lord Lucan's smirking face next time they met!

"What a perfectly exquisite creature," remarked Sir Henry languidly, as the two men continued along Jermyn Street. "I always admired her, you know. I even thought of making her an offer once."

"Oh?" Lord Lucan's deep voice was noncommittal. "What prevented you?"

"Oh, well, I was madly in love with Denise at the time. You know, that ravishing little French actress playing in some of the Drury Lane farces? And I thought to myself,

35

really, Henry old boy, two such beautiful women, and how is one supposed to divide oneself, you know? I'd wear myself out between them. And I remember asking myself, why should I get married when *la petite* Denise is so charmingly accommodating? And then, of course, there was that nasty business with Edmund Verney. I was a bit surprised at that, I must say."

His companion's expression grew a little hard. "Yes. Edmund Verney was the last person I'd have expected her to marry."

"Well, she's free of him now," sighed Sir Henry, negligently swinging his cane. "And since I have no Denise to amuse me at the moment, I really think I may try my luck with the fair widow. I'd say she's ripe for the plucking, wouldn't you? Who knows? I may be lucky. She seemed to look favorably upon me just now."

"She did, didn't she?" mused the earl. "Still, I think she liked me a little, too."

Sir Henry let out a chortle. "You? No, no, Geoff, old boy, you've got it all wrong. You haven't quite learned the knack of pleasing the ladies, have you? I mean, ladies of quality, of course," he added with a small guffaw. "If you must study the more interesting parts of their anatomy, my dear fellow, you simply *must* learn to do it when they're not looking. That's what they want, don't you see? If they catch you at it, then they must needs look insulted and *that* spoils all the fun. You bungled it this time, old boy." He laughed again. "I'll wager she won't even give you the time of day next time you meet."

Lord Lucan gave him a quizzical look. "You think not? How much would you care to wager on that? She'll give me far more than the time of day before I am through."

Sir Henry's eyes lit. "Oh, I say! You mean it? Oh, this *ought* to be amusing! No, *really*, you choose. What shall it be? A contest between us? Winner gets the widow *and*

36

the gold."

The earl hesitated. "I think not," he said finally, a curious glint in his gray eyes. "I never wager on anything serious. You see, Harry, I'm after the lady's hand."

"Her *hand?* Egad, do you really want to go and get yourself leg-shackled again? She's a widow, old boy. You don't have to *marry* her!" Sir Henry looked askance at the thought.

"You think not?" retorted the other, rather musingly. "I wouldn't be so sure. She doesn't strike me as the sort of woman who'd accept a carte blanche, and at any rate, I've a fancy to marry again."

The baronet laughed and gave him a sidelong look. "A fancy so strong you've never so much as mentioned it before, eh? It sounds as if the hard-hearted Geoffrey Trevelyan has been struck by one of Cupid's darts. Or should I say the fair Diana's arrows? Oh, this is *marvelous!* I wish you luck, old boy, but to be frank, I wish *me* even better luck. You don't object to a little rivalry, do you?"

The earl raised his brows. "Rivalry? You're not suggesting you want to marry her, are you?"

A derisive snort hissed from between Sir Henry's teeth. "Not unless she's an heiress, and as far as I know, she's not. Anyway, what's the point? She knows what's what by now." He gave a small laugh. "Married to Edmund Verney, she'd have to."

"She won't accept you."

It was a statement, flat and sure, and it goaded the other man.

"Oh? Well, we'll have to see about that, Geoff, old boy. I've a certain way with the ladies, don't y'know? Boyish charm, and all that. *Ma chère mère* tells me I'm perfectly irresistible."

The earl's lip curled. "Odd. My mother says the same

about me, Harry. But I don't make the mistake of believing her."

The three women were ushered into Great-aunt Serena's drawing room fifteen minutes later by a tottering and extremely stiff-lipped butler. As regal as a queen upon her throne, the dowager sat in the center of that huge salon, her voluminous blue skirt spilling about her like water around a peninsula. The gnarled fingers of her left hand were tightly wrapped about the silver head of her long ebony cane.

"You're late!" barked the old woman, before they had taken more than a step into the room.

"Nonsense," said Diana, moving forward to kiss her scowling relative on the cheek. "It is precisely eleven o'clock. It cannot be that which has you miffed."

Her aunt glowered at her. "You're still as saucy as ever, I see. Well, go ahead, sit down, sit down! Barclay!"—this was addressed to the lingering butler— "Pull over those chairs for my nieces and Miss, ah, Tilden, is it? They're too far away from me. Now, Diana. I suppose it's too much to expect that I might be given an explanation?"

Sinking into the chair nearest her aunt, Diana raised her delicate brows questioningly. "An explanation, ma'am? What can you mean?"

The dowager had obviously been nourishing her complaints. "To start with, I want to know why you must waste good money setting up a household of your own when you could be staying here under my roof! What's wrong with my house?"

"Nothing," answered Diana calmly. "But I felt I would prefer to be on my own, having been accustomed to it for so long now. I thought Mama explained all that."

38

"And *my* feelings do not enter into the matter, I suppose?"

Diana smoothed her skirt, irritated by the dowager's accusing tone. "I did not think you would object. Indeed, I can think of no reason why you should."

Her aunt reached for her sherry. "You can't, eh?" she said, taking a hefty sip.

"No, and what's more, my dear ma'am," retorted Diana baldly, "I've purposely chosen to live nearby, thinking it would please you. But it seems I set myself an impossible task."

The response fared well with the dowager, who had always preferred spunk to spinelessness. "Hrumph! And so you could use my carriages, I'll hazard a guess!" she threw out, in a slightly less peevish tone.

Diana studied her fingertips. "Only if it suits you, madam," she said evenly. "Otherwise, I will gladly purchase my own."

The dowager peered at her for a moment, then let out a cackle. "Oh, hoity-toity! Aren't we the proud lady now! *Madam,* indeed! You used to call me 'Aunt Serena,' for land's sake!"

"And I still shall, if you like," said Diana, with a reluctant laugh. "But when I am in your black books, Aunt Serena, I don't dare take such liberties."

"Liberties, be damned! I'm your aunt, Diana. Oh, now I've shocked your Miss Tilden. Haven't you told her I'm a plain-spoken woman?"

This time Diana's voice quivered in amusement. "I rather fancy she knows it. But as for my setting up house on my own, are you truly that put out by it?"

The dowager finished her sherry, and reached for the hand bell to ring for tea. "If you were to ask me, Diana, you're no more fit to be on your own than little Aimee, here," she pronounced. "Just look what a hash you've

39

made of your life already."

"Oh, no, Auntie Serena," protested Aimee, quick to intervene. "That is unfair. Diana has done very well, and we have the snuggest little house in Jermyn Street. Diana knows just how everything ought to be done, I know she does."

Pleased by this mark of sibling loyalty, the dowager merely sniffed, and said, in a conceding tone, "Well, it ain't a bad address, but why the devil you must bury yourself alive since that rascally husband of yours died, I cannot begin to understand. If I'd had my way, I'd have had you up to London years ago to find you a decent mate."

Diana opened her mouth to reply, but as Barclay chose that moment to bring in the tea tray, she closed it again, and cast a speaking glance at her sister. When he was gone, she continued, in a more moderate tone than she had meant to employ, "But I don't wish to remarry, Aunt Serena. I'm perfectly happy as I am. I am here to assist you with Aimee's Season."

"I didn't pay for you to come all this way to help me play chaperon," retorted the dowager, a trifle sharply. "Now, what I want to know is this: did Edmund leave you well enough set up to meet this ridiculous expenditure? I won't have any niece of mine getting herself behindhand in the world."

A little surprised, Diana said mildly, "Oh, I can afford it, Aunt Serena, but, as you guessed, I would prefer not to have the additional expense of buying and stabling a carriage and horses."

The dowager waved her hand dismissively. "No, no, there's no need for that. It would be a shameful waste of money when you can use mine. But we'll have to purchase a couple of nice ladies' hacks for you to ride, eh?" As if reading Diana's thoughts, she continued,

"For God's sake, don't look so amazed! What an old lickpenny you must think me!"

Blinking, Diana remarked, "No, I never thought you that, Aunt Serena. It is simply that I find you so unpredictable!"

Taking this as a compliment, the dowager snorted. "It's a damned good thing to be! Take my advice, Diana, and always keep 'em guessing! That way, you won't ever be called a dead bore. Now then," she said with evident relish, "let's get down to business. I've picked a date for the ball and made up the guest list. No sense in wasting time, I felt. Let us hope, Aimee, that we can fire you off without starting any scandals."

Again, Aimee deflected the barb. "That is kind of you, Auntie," she responded, with her sweetest smile. "Perhaps I should warn you, though. I have already quite made up my mind to marry my cousin Charles."

The dowager cocked her head. "My grandson? Oh, aye, that would be a fair enough match—*if* you can bring him up to scratch! The young fellow's been devilish slick at avoiding the altar." She grinned ferociously. "I've been trying to put some spirit into the boy for years, but it's no use. He's terrified of me, did you know?"

"I can't imagine why," said Diana dryly.

The dowager gave her a suspicious look, then allowed her mouth to relax. "Never mind him. What's this nonsense about not wanting to remarry?"

"Just that, Aunt Serena," replied Diana shortly, her mind on something else she wanted to say. "About the ball. Did you by any chance include Sir Henry Neyle on your guest list?"

"Why?" Her aunt's tone was equally abrupt. "Don't tell me you're still hankering after *him!*"

Diana stiffened. "I'm not *hankering* after anyone, Aunt Serena. But we met him in Jermyn Street a short while ago, and he was most courteous. I think it only civil that he receive a card."

Aimee, exchanging a swift glance with Miss Tilden, said ingenuously, "Oh, and do not forget Lord Lucan, Diana. I think he has an admiration for you, also."

The dowager's small brown eyes snapped with interest. "Eh? What's this? You've already caught *his* eye, have you? Well, I'm not altogether surprised. "Now, *he* would make you a fine husband!"

"But I don't want a husband," wailed Diana. "And I don't care a straw for the odious man. Anyway, Aunt, you know perfectly well he is already married."

"No, he ain't. That wife of his ran off with some American two summers ago and drowned herself. Oh, no, not on purpose. There was an accident at sea—she fell overboard, or some such thing. They rescued her, but it was too late. Anyway, he's well rid of her! She was a wicked, faithless woman, and a poor excuse for a wife!"

"Well, I'm very sorry, I'm sure, but that does not mean I'm interested in taking her place. I don't even *like* the man!"

The dowager's tones were tart. "At least he's a man and not a mincing Jack-a-dandy like Sir Henry Neyle. Why, the man's as pretty as a girl, Diana. You cannot seriously expect *him* to make you happy!"

Diana eyed her aunt in growing exasperation. "No, I don't. Because I—am—not—looking—for—a—husband!" she ground out, through clenched teeth.

"All right, all right," said her aunt, changing her tactics. "No need to fly up into the boughs about it. You like being a widow. Why, so do I, for that matter! Just as long as you understand that widows as young and attractive as yourself are considered by some to be *fair game*. I trust I make myself clear?"

Diana's expression turned bleak as the meaning

behind these words sank in. "Fair game," she repeated with effort. "I see."

The old woman watched her for a moment, and was pleased to see the resolute tilt return to her chin.

"Well," replied Diana, the light of battle entering her eye, "I shall be very much on my guard. But I still must request that you invite Sir Henry Neyle to the ball."

"Very well," agreed the dowager blandly. "And the Earl of Lucan, as well."

Chapter Three

If he were asked, Lord Lucan would have said he was not a romantic man. He had never been in love, and, if he thought about it at all, would likely have said that falling in love was not a very practical thing to do. Remarriage, however, was eminently practical, and choosing a woman who suited his exacting taste was high on his list of priorities. Once he had decided that Diana Verney was that woman, it was typical that he wasted no time, and set out to commence his wooing the following day.

He had never been given to mulling over decisions for vast lengths of time, but this was not because he was impetuous. His thought processes might be lightning quick and his decisions seldom subject to reconsideration, but this did not mean the earl had not given serious thought to the matter of choosing a new wife. The truth was that having met Diana six years before, she had registered—and remained—in his mind as the most intriguing woman he had ever met.

In appearance, she was his ideal woman—soft and feminine, neither too short nor too tall, with a lovely face and wonderful figure. Astonishingly, her demeanor and disposition also attracted him. In fact, he could recall quite clearly the searing effect she had had on him at the time of her come-out.

He had noticed her immediately, for she had stood out from the other girls like a candle in a throng of rushlights. He remembered experiencing quite a pang of regret that he was already married, there being something about the way she held her head, something in the proud tilt of her chin that had caught his fancy. Curiosity had driven him to converse with her and his interest, he recalled, had quickly heightened. Though she had been a little shy, her responses had been intelligent, and as for her spirit . . . *that* he had found amusingly evident in the flash of her eyes and the slightly disapproving tone in her voice. Of what she had disapproved he was still unsure, but he had longed to further the acquaintance and find out. Such a fascinating young woman had been utterly wasted on a man like Edmund Verney, he thought with a frown.

But now she was back, and he lacked a wife. When fate offered a second chance, only a fool would fail to take advantage of it. He would begin his courtship without delay.

Having been granted the use of the dowager's town coach, the two sisters had spent the entire morning shopping, and had managed to make a fair dent in the monumental task of supplying Aimee with the items of fashion she would be needing for the London Season. Miss Tilden had accompanied them, and as she had become quite exhausted, was soundly asleep upon her bed when his lordship arrived.

Downstairs in the study, Diana was halfway through a letter to her parents when the clang of a bell brought her head up with a jerk. Her expression alert, she found herself paying unusual heed to the firm tread of Lawrence's footsteps as he went to the door. Though she tried to remain calm, her pulse began to flutter in an odd anticipation. Could it be Sir Henry? Surely it must be he, for the odious Earl of Lucan would not dare have the impertinence to come here . . . would he? Rising from her chair, Diana was nearly to the door when a deep male voice brought her to a halt.

He *had* come! Her worst fears confirmed, Diana froze, her hand just inches from the knob. The door was ajar, and through the crack she caught a glimpse of the earl as he stepped into the hall and followed Lawrence up the creaking wooden stairs to the floor above.

As if transfixed, she stared at the spot where he had been. Though she could not think him a handsome man, she was forced to admit his presence was imposingly masculine. He was very tall and very solid, at any rate, with a wide pair of shoulders and a broad chest. It was impossible not to be aware that most women rated such features high on their list of ideal male attributes; as for Diana, she could not recall ever having given the matter a great deal of thought. Why was it, then, that she abruptly (and rather perversely) decided she preferred fair men? This, of course, could have nothing to do with the fact that her uninvited caller was very dark, both of hair and skin. His features, too, were too harsh to please, and there was a certain arrogance in his stride that she disliked.

Stalling for time, Diana raised an unsteady hand to smooth her hair, while casting her rose-colored gown a critical glance. It would not do, she reasoned, to appear to disadvantage, since there was little doubt she would need all her confidence to survive an encounter with this man. She hesitated another few seconds, catering to her reluctance to face what was sure to be a difficult interview. She would be very cool—no *cold*, she corrected, so that he would be quite put off and— But where was Aimee?

The question effectively shattered what little poise she still possessed. Terrified that her innocent young sister was upstairs alone with a man of libertine propensities, Diana rushed up the steps to the next floor with an energy seldom displayed outside a cavalry charge. Her fears, however, were quite unwarranted; when she burst breathlessly into the drawing room she found the earl to be alone. Indeed, he looked distinctly taken aback by her unconventional entry.

Knowing how foolish she must look, Diana made a hasty attempt to salvage her dignity. Arching her brows daintily, she said, "My lord" in a tone just icy enough to suggest that there could not possibly be a rational reason for his visit.

The earl bowed. "My dear Mrs. Verney, there was no need to run," he assured her, with an irritating smile. "I had no intention of leaving before you arrived."

"I was *not* running!" she responded hotly, entirely forgetting that a dignified person would not respond with such vehemence.

How dared he laugh at her!

"Weren't you?" he inquired, his amusement annoyingly evident. "Then I can only say you are the most energetic woman of my acquaintance!"

It took all her resolution to ignore this. "Just why are you here, Lord Lucan?" she demanded.

"What, weren't you expecting me?" He surveyed her, his black brows rising in apparent surprise. "I thought I made it quite clear I wished to know you better."

So Aunt Serena was right . . . !

"No, of course I wasn't expecting you," she lied. "I hoped you would have the decency to leave me alone."

"Decency?" His head cocked to the side. "No, really. That's doing it too brown, my dear. What's indecent about paying you a visit?"

Diana eyed him suspiciously, then gave a slight sigh.

"Nothing," she conceded, yielding to his logic against her better judgment. "Pray, be seated, my lord. I will ring for refreshment."

"Now, that's better." He stepped forward, then waited for her to take a seat before he did likewise. "I was beginning to think you didn't like me," he added with what she felt was far too satisfied a smile.

"Your remarks," said Diana, nervously smoothing her skirt, "are most improper. I must ask you to refrain."

"Refrain from being improper?" He looked amused. "Very well, I'm willing to give it a try, at least for a bit. What shall we talk about? The weather?"

Since at this juncture Lawrence arrived with a tray laden with wine and cakes, Diana was forced to bite back her response. She dismissed her butler at once, however, so as to allow herself the pleasure of saying, as waspishly as possibly, "The weather, my lord, is very probably the only subject upon which you and I could agree!"

"Now, why on earth would you say a thing like that?" he responded, helping himself to a biscuit. "You certainly seem to be in the sullens. Did I do something to offend you?"

Diana glared. "Lord Lucan, my extremely brief acquaintance with you is enough to assure me that you are being deliberately provoking. You must know that your behavior yesterday was excessively impertinent. I am amazed you had the effrontery to show your face here today."

She said it with such stiff dignity that he ought to have been firmly put in his place. However, Geoffrey Trevelyan, sixth Earl of Lucan, only stretched out his long legs and regarded her with what could almost have been called a twinkle. "You're supposed to offer me some sherry," he pointed out in a kindly manner.

Biting her lip, Diana reached for the decanter and poured him a drink. "Aren't you going to answer me?"

she inquired, resisting the powerful urge to hurl it in his face.

As if reading her thoughts, he hurriedly accepted the glass. "Thank you. So you think I was impertinent. How so?" He gave her a quick side look as he sipped his sherry.

Diana clenched her hands into fists, convinced she was on the verge of a strong spasm. "I wonder if it will rain this afternoon," she remarked, in a pointed manner.

Although a gleam of humor entered his gray eyes, her aristocratic caller showed no sign of taking the hint. "Surely you did not take exception to the fact that I saw fit to admire you?" he persisted.

Diana's bosom heaved indignantly. "In far too blatant a manner!" she snapped.

"I see. Then I assume you did not care for the kiss, either?"

Eyes flashing, Diana lifted her chin in just the manner he remembered. "I care nothing for your kisses," she informed him, in the most withering accents she was capable of summoning. "I may as well tell you, my lord, that I found such a vulgar display the veriest epitome of insult. And I shall take leave to inform you that I am *not* the sort of female you seem to imagine!"

"Ah. I see we have a little misunderstanding," said his lordship, setting down his glass. He leaned forward, and dropped his bantering tone. "Now, why do you instantly assume I rank you low? I meant only to flirt with you, but if you deem it an insult, I must certainly apologize. I assure you, Mrs. Verney, I don't view you as anything but a lady of unimpeachable virtue. We seem to have gotten off to a bad start, I am sorry to say." He paused and gave her one of his direct looks. "When you came in just now, I thought you looked a bit worried. I only sought to make you smile. Perhaps it was presumptuous of me."

"Oh." Somewhat appeased, Diana eyed him uncertainly. But then . . . why are you here?"

His lordship sighed ruefully. "I see we have come full circle. My dear Mrs. Verney, although you hardly know me, you may believe me sincere when I say that I have long admired you. My purpose in coming here today was merely to beg the pleasure of your company tomorrow. I should like to invite you to drive with me in the Park."

"Oh," repeated Diana, her emotions in a jumble. "I'm sorry, my lord, but I cannot."

"Why not?" he said. "I'm a competent whip; I won't overturn you."

A rebellious sparkle crept back into Diana's eyes. "Lord Lucan, when a lady declines an invitation, she is not required to give an explanation for her refusal."

"Is this one of those interminable rules of etiquette? I never abide by 'em, my dear. They're far too confining." A sudden glint entered his eyes. "That one about not receiving gentlemen alone, for instance. *Most* confining."

Diana was suddenly assailed with a vexing urge to giggle. She controlled it, however, and managed to say, with only a trace of a gasp, "Miss Tilden is sleeping, my lord, and anyway, I am far too old to require a chaperon."

"Quite in your dotage, in fact," he agreed. "Come, I have no wish to be at outs with you. Shall we be friends?"

"Very well," said Diana, wondering how on earth he had managed to maneuver her into a tractable mood.

Her answer obviously pleased him, for he surged out of his chair with a twisted grin. "Capital! Then I'll come for you tomorrow a little before five."

"What?" she exclaimed, rising with him. "I did not mean . . . You know very well I did not mean . . . Oh! Where are you *going?*"

"I think I can find my way out," he explained, his long legs carrying him swiftly to the door.

"It is extremely rude," said Diana, her voice gathering strength as she spoke, "to walk out of a room when someone is speaking to you!"

She was but two steps behind him, and he startled her by turning suddenly and reaching for her hands. "If I stay any longer," he said, with an odd little curl to his rather hard mouth, "I really will kiss you. And since you barely know me, and care nothing for my kisses, I think it best that I go. Unless you've begun to feel differently?" His flaring nostrils belied his playful tone, leaving Diana no doubt that given the slightest encouragement he would do it.

"Go!" she gritted, trying to pull away. "Go, before I have a fit of the vapors! Impossible man!"

He grinned, and his grip tightened. "Until tomorrow, then. Be ready."

Then he released her and rather to her surprise, favored her with a formal bow. "And in the meanwhile, Mrs. Verney, rest assured that I remain your most obedient servant . . ."

"That man is simply too much!" she told Aimee a few minutes later. She watched Aimee adjust the tilt on the saucy little bonnet she had purchased that morning. "I am glad you had the excellent sense not to join us. There are some gentlemen, my dear, who do not know how to behave themselves in the company of innocent young girls."

Her back to Diana, Aimee was watching her sister's face in the mirror. "You like him, don't you?" she said suddenly.

"Like him!" Diana gave a careless laugh. "Don't be ridiculous! He has the manners of a country bumpkin. He is far too bold, and those gray eyes of his stare too hard for my comfort. He makes himself entirely too free in my

51

house, and purposely misinterprets my words to gain his own way! I detest him."

Aimee swung around and stared at her sister. "Gracious, Diana, you sound so unlike your usual self! Are you all right?"

Diana shrugged. "Just disappointed, I suppose. I had hoped it was Sir Henry come to call."

Aimee removed her bonnet and went to sit near her elder sister on the edge of the bed. "Tell me about Sir Henry," she prompted with interest.

"Oh, there is really nothing to tell," replied Diana uncomfortably. "Except that he is the most complete gentleman, the very opposite of Lord Lucan. If *he* calls, it will be perfectly safe for you to meet him."

"I see," said Aimee. Her speculative gaze rested on her sister's face. "He is very handsome, isn't he? Once, long ago, did you perhaps cherish a *tendre* for him?"

Diana looked at the floor. "Long ago," she answered, with a long sigh. "I was very foolish then. Things worked out so differently."

"Mama told me a little. I am so sorry, Diana."

"Then you understand why it is so important for me to be here with you. It would kill me, Aimee, if anything like that were to happen to you. We must be so careful."

Aimee covered her sister's hand with her own. "I shall be careful, dearest."

"What you said yesterday about wanting to flirt, well, it frightened me," Diana confessed, rather abruptly. "It's a dangerous game, Aimee. You can have no notion how the slightest encouragement can affect a man. All noblemen are not gentlemen, you see. Think of Edmund!"

"Wouldn't it be better if we did not think of Edmund?" Aimee suggested wisely. "He is best forgotten, Diana. You owe him nothing."

Diana's hands slid over her face, as if to erase some

unpleasant memory. "I know it. But marriage to him changed me, somehow. I just don't want that to happen to you."

"Oh, it won't," Aimee assured her confidently. "I promise."

The following afternoon, Diana decided to take an inventory of her own clothing to see what she would need to purchase to see her through the Season. Since she subscribed to several ladies' magazines, she had been able to keep up with the latest styles, but she suspected that her gowns were far fewer in number than what she would require. She had made most of them herself, in some cases meticulously copying the fashion plates, in others, improving upon them. Although she disliked embroidery, she had always enjoyed making her own dresses. There was a sense of accomplishment in completing something one could wear that she did not feel by merely covering a pillow with some frivolous pattern. She had made gowns for her sisters as well, which was a large part of what had kept her occupied for the past three years.

Staring into the clothespress, she wondered what to wear for her drive with the Earl of Lucan. While she had no intention of making any effort to impress the man, she could not forget that it would be her first public appearance, and her pride demanded that she look her best. There were members of the *ton* who would be only too eager to label her a dowd; things would be bad enough without that, she knew.

Fashions had changed since she had made her comeout. After Waterloo, skirt bottoms had widened and become much more decorated, and the waistlines seemed to have come up even higher than before—a difficult feat, one would have thought. Gone were the plain, columnar, figure-revealing frocks which had reigned so popular before the time of Napoleon's exile. Trimmings of every sort were increasingly the mode: ribbons, bowknots, ruffles, flouncing, lace, artificial flowers—the possibilities were endless. Diana was just as well satisfied that this was so. Some of the thin muslin gowns she had worn at age eighteen had revealed a great deal more than they had concealed, making her feel decidedly uncomfortable when in the company of gentlemen. Besides, she thought the various trimmings quite attractive, as long as they were not carried to extreme.

After much debate, she pulled out a very pretty round dress of dove gray bombazine, a fabric which was still considered very elegant. It would do very nicely, she reflected, for its high collar and long sleeves would shield her from the wind, while its subdued shade and design would surely provide her with an aura of mature dignity, something the brighter colors did not seem to do. She had completed it only a month earlier, and was pardonably pleased with the results. Its severity was alleviated by a band of peach-colored satin under the bust, and a double rouleaux of the same at the hem and base of the sleeves.

Without bothering to ring for Meg, Diana slipped out of her morning dress and into the handsome carriage dress. She had added peach satin trimming to the jaunty cottage that she had purchased to go with it. Placing this upon her head, she assessed the effect in the mirror. She found the style of the bonnet's crown, which resembled a man's, to be quite dashing, and a new confidence flowed through her. No, she decided defiantly, Diana Verney was not going to be labeled a dowd. She was going to take the shine out of them all!

Nor would she allow Lord Lucan to bring down her defenses. Her topaz eyes held a militant gleam as she mulled over all the things she would say to him. She would tell him, quite calmly, that he was insolent, that he was overbearing and rude, that she disliked being manipulated and that she was not going to put up with it.

54

Someone scratched on her bedchamber door, interrupting these delicious plans to put Lord Lucan in his place. Sounding apologetic, her abigail's voice floated through the thin wood.

"Sorry to bother you, mistress, but there's a gentleman to see you."

Could it be Sir Henry at last? Or would this prove to be another disappointment? "Meg," she said in agitation, "come and help me with the fastenings to this gown. Oh, do hurry!"

Aimee peeped into the drawing room, and, recognizing the blond gentleman within, tripped happily in to join him. "Hello," she said, her guileless smile tilting the corners of her pink lips in just the bewitching way she had been practicing. "Aren't you Sir Henry Neyle?"

Sir Henry bowed, his golden-lashed blue eyes moving over her in an appreciative manner. "I am. And you are the little sister, if I remember correctly. I *do* beg your pardon, my dear, but I've quite forgotten your name."

Knowing full well the man must know her as Miss Farington, Diana's young sister favored the handsome baronet with a single provocative bat of her long black lashes. "It's Aimee," she revealed in her most flirtatious voice. "Aimee Farington."

Sir Henry's smile altered subtly. "Well . . . Aimee . . . what a very pretty creature you are, to be sure. You don't resemble your sister much, do you?"

This time Aimee's lashes fluttered several times. "I fear not," she admitted with a deeply regretful sigh. "I take after Mama's side of the family, you see. Is Diana not the most beautiful girl? If I weren't so prodigiously fond of her, I would be quite green with envy. And she is the strictest chaperon, is it not unfortunate?"

His fancy tickled, the baronet studied her from head to

toe. "I see. And you are a little minx, aren't you? Here to be presented into society, like your sister."

Aimee regarded him soulfully. "It is so. Will it be too dreadfully dull for me, do you think?"

"It can be as dull or as exciting as you wish it, little Aimee. Your fate lies in your own hands," Sir Henry told her with an intent look.

"Oh," Aimee responded, dramatically clasping her hands together at her bosom, "I must have excitement, Sir Henry. I simply *crave* excitement."

The baronet's hand lifted for an instant, then dropped to his side. "Remind me of that some other time, Aimee dear. I think I hear someone coming."

As Diana entered the room, Aimee abruptly ended her experiment. She watched Diana calmly greet Sir Henry, and struggled to evaluate the entire episode.

It had been her first taste of flirtation, and she could not deny that it had been an exhilarating experience. As she had expected, Sir Henry had seemed to flirt back, but not quite in the manner she had anticipated. While she had not completely understood the underlying meaning to his words, she was aware that he ought to have been more formal with her. Was he a rake? If so, he would definitely not make a good husband for Diana, for Aimee had come to the conclusion that if a gentleman were right for her sister, he ought not to flirt with other ladies, and most especially not with herself. This was the gauge of measurement she had decided to use, and in her youthful mind, it seemed a good one.

"Have I caught you at an inconvenient time, Mrs. Verney?" Sir Henry was inquiring. "You look as though you were about to go out."

"Actually, no," Diana explained. "I was just trying on the dress to see if it fit properly. I may wear it later."

"I can see no flaw in the fit," he said smoothly. "Whoever made it for you did an exquisite job of it."

She smiled. "Why, thank you. Since I made it myself, your words are music to my ears."

"Did you really?" Sir Henry put up his quizzing glass. "How extraordinary! Mrs. Verney, I find you an amazing woman."

Feeling a little embarrassed by his scrutiny, Diana gave a self-conscious laugh. "Hardly that, unfortunately. Sewing is merely an outlet for my energy." Seeking to change the subject, she said, at random, "Have you any interesting news to tell me? I fear I've been sadly out of touch with practically everyone since . . . since my marriage." This was not what she had meant to say, and the sentence ended rather flatly.

But Sir Henry took no notice. "Gossip, you mean?" His fair brows went up. "Oh, *loads*, my dear. But I cannot remember six years worth this instant. Why don't you drive out with me later? Then we can have a cozy little chat about it all."

Diana opened her mouth to accept, when, unbidden, a vivid and thoroughly disconcerting image of Lord Lucan entered her mind. "I—I cannot, I am sorry to say," she heard herself respond. "I have a prior engagement."

A master at the game he had chosen to play, Sir Henry did not press the issue. "Well, perhaps another time, then," he offered carelessly. "And when is Miss Farington's presentation, if I may ask?"

Aimee smiled sunnily. "It is to be in two weeks, Sir Henry. Aunt Serena is sending out the cards for my ball this very day."

Sir Henry shot her an enigmatic look. "And shall I be invited, do you think?"

"Our aunt intends to invite some of my own friends, as well as the younger set," Diana put in quickly, unsure what Aimee's response might be. "I believe your name was one of those included. Naturally, I—we—will be

57

pleased if you will join us."

The baronet's lazy eyes did not miss the quick, involuntary rise and fall of Diana's bosom. "Why, I would not miss it for the world," he said easily. "You are both such lovely ladies, one would have to be addled not to attend what promises to be a most diverting affair."

It lacked but one minute to five o'clock. Diana, garbed in the dove gray ensemble, stood tapping her foot, her serenity gone, her temper more on edge than it had been in months. Where was that exasperating man? The prospect of facing the *ton* had put her nerves on such a fray that the additional delay was pure torture. How could he be so inconsiderate?

It was another ten minutes before Lawrence's footsteps told her the earl had arrived. "Lord Lucan awaits you in the drawing room," her butler informed her with a wooden countenance.

Diana swept into that room with every intention of starting a battle. Putting on her most wrathful expression, she began, "I thought that perhaps you had found something better to do today, my lord!"

The earl's brows flew up. "Something better?" he repeated, sounding quizzical.

"I mean," she said tartly, "that you are late. But perhaps it was foolish of me to expect punctuality. I am sometimes afflicted with the strangest notions."

The earl consulted his timepiece. "You baffle me, my dear. Look, it is just five now."

"It is more than ten minutes past that hour," she corrected, gazing significantly at the clock upon the mantelshelf.

"Oh, no. My watch always keeps perfect time," he said, quite kindly. "Your clock must be fast. I recommend you have it checked."

Irked by the knowledge that he was laughing at her,

Diana retorted, "Well, you should have been here well before the hour. You must know how crowded the Park becomes."

He must have heard something odd in her voice, for his steel gray eyes studied her thoughtfully. "Something's bothering you, isn't it? Will you tell me?"

Diana gave her gloves an unnecessary tug. "Nonsense! I was simply—Oh, never mind! Shall we go?"

His eyes narrowed a little, but he did not pursue the matter. "Very well. My carriage awaits, my dear," he said, with a courtly gesture of his hand.

For some unaccountable reason the gallantry erased Diana's other concerns, replacing them with a raw, dangerous awareness of the six-foot man in front of her. "I am not your dear," she replied, stammering a little. Annoyed by her weakness, she whirled away so that he could not see her face. "And I beg you will remember it!" she snapped.

It had little effect on the earl. "Not yet," he murmured. "But that is easily remedied." He had moved forward so that his mouth was close to her ear, which startled her nearly as much as the brush of his finger as he pushed back a stray golden curl.

The touch of his hand, and the warm breath upon her cheek combined to send a startled shiver down Diana's spine. Obviously, she decided, the only thing to do was to pretend she had not heard. Head held high, Diana sailed out of the house, her mind completely unable to come up with a suitably scathing response for this new outrage.

Outside, Lord Lucan handed her into his curricle with amazing cheerfulness. "Well, at any rate, I'm pleased you did not forget our engagement," he said. "I half-feared it might slip your mind."

"It was a temptation," Diana told him coldly, watching him swing his long body into the open, two-wheeled carriage.

A glint of humor warmed his eyes. "Ah, now, if we are

59

to speak of temptation, Mrs. Verney, perhaps we should dispense with my groom."

Diana's hands clenched. "Don't you *dare!*"

He laughed softly. "Very well. James shall play duenna, if it makes you more comfortable. Although, of course, you are far too old to need one," he reminded.

The groom, responding to a motion from his master, released his hold on the horses' bridle and made a deft leap for his perch. The carriage rolled forward over the cobbles, but Diana soon realized that James's presence made little difference to the earl.

"You look quite charming in that gown," was his next remark, "but I liked the other one better. Blue becomes you a little more, I think."

"That seems to be less a compliment than a piece of advice," she pointed out. "Are you always so clumsy with words, my lord?"

His quick look was difficult to read. "On the contrary, I make it a practice to say exactly what I mean."

"I see. Then should you care to criticize anything else whilst you have the chance? My hat, perhaps? Or my gloves?"

His teeth flashed white against his bronzed skin, and Diana was conscious of a curious jolt of gratification that her response had amused him. "No, everything you wear is completely *sans reproche*, Mrs. Verney. Rather, I would like to compliment you on your failure to cut your hair— an admirable piece of restraint, in my view. However, as I suspect my doing so will cause you to immediately rush home and hack it all off, I believe I will refrain."

A sudden urge to giggle poked holes in her gravity. "Well, as long as you do not mention it, I promise I shall not," she assured him, with only the slightest quiver in her voice.

He grinned at that, and a short, surprisingly companionable silence prevailed between them for several minutes. They reached the entrance to Hyde Park, and the earl guided his curricle through the gateway with the careless skill of one who was renowned as something of a nonpareil. Once inside, his curious gaze immediately shifted to probe Diana's expression. She was looking extremely pale, he observed, when but a moment before her creamy skin had been aglow with confidence, the healthy, rosy hue he so admired.

Indeed, Diana's mouth had gone completely dry. Sprinkled all along the winding road ahead of them, in droves of carriages, was the *ton*, come to parade its finery like so many cocks in a barnyard. The moment had finally come when she was to face them, but somehow none of the stern little self-lectures she had prepared for just this occasion came to mind. All at once the scene blurred, and the ladies were proud, chattering harpies darting sly glances in Diana's direction, their escorts sharing the joke with typical male crudity. During her repartee with Lord Lucan, Diana had been able to forget her fears, but now they resurged, dominating her so completely that her palms grew damp and her stomach churned with nervousness.

"Easy, now," soothed her companion. "They don't bite, you know."

Too upset to remark his perception, Diana swallowed hard and answered automatically. "I know that, but it—it doesn't help, somehow."

"Would it help if I held your hand?" he inquired, his lazy eyes watching her keenly.

Diana's head turned in confusion. "Hold your—*what* did you say?" A small sparkle entered her eye. "Did you say what I think you said?"

"I don't know. What do you think I said?"

"Did you just ask to hold my hand?" she demanded.

"Not at all," he assured her, a suspicious tremor in his deep voice. "You could not have been attending, my dear

Mrs. Verney. I merely asked if it would help if I did so."

"Oh, you are impossible!" she exclaimed, her complexion heightening. "And, if I might add to the list, arrogant and presumptuous and overbearing—"

"Oh, come now," he protested, rather mildly. His shrewd gaze swung away from her face to scan the carriages in the immediate vicinity. "Look, there is Lady Jersey and Mrs. Drummond-Burrell waving to us from that barouche. Now you must nod and smile, very graciously. There's a good girl. You're quite marvelous, did you know that?"

Startled by this praise, Diana gave him a puzzled look. "I don't understand you. You're doing this on purpose, aren't you?"

"Doing what? Flirting with you? But of course I am," he said smoothly. "The temptation to do so is quite irresistible."

Diana felt the betraying warmth seeping into her cheeks, and decided to give voice to what was to have been a highly satisfactory set-down. However, at the instant she opened her mouth, her horrified gaze fell upon a certain person not thirty yards ahead of them.

The set-down flew from her mind. "Lady Edgerton," she whispered, barely knowing she spoke aloud. "Oh, Lord."

Supreme among her apprehensions had been this—the moment of meeting with the malicious woman who had found her that night with Edmund. Suppressing the urge to clutch at his lordship's sleeve, Diana gave him one wide, frantic look before assuming what she prayed was an expression of total indifference.

Until now, the earl had not made use of his quizzing glass, a fashionable frivolity which the average cynical nobleman would have classed as a virtually indispensible weapon. Diana's entreaty for help, though mute, was neither to be misunderstood nor ignored. Without hesitation, his lordship leveled his weapon upon the rapidly approaching Lady Edgerton.

"An odiously fat woman," he pronounced, inspecting his victim pitilessly. His dark head gave a mournful shake. "She reminds me of an overfed orangutan. How in the world do you think she gets into her corset in the morning? Or out of it at night, for that matter?" His glass swiveled suddenly, and his large magnified eye hovered over Diana. "Speaking of which, my dear Mrs. Verney, you appear to have preserved your own figure very nicely, despite your extremely advanced age. I'll wager you don't even wear a corset. You certainly don't need one, and that's something very few females can claim!"

"My lord!" gasped Diana, very much shocked. "I'll thank you not to— Oh! You're trying to make me laugh, aren't you?" And she shocked herself even more by giving way to a nervous giggle.

Glancing down at her, Lord Lucan's mouth twisted into that same curious half-smile that she had noticed before. "Perhaps I am," he acknowledged. "Still, I happen to find the topic of some interest—for future reference, you understand. You don't wear them, do you? Come, you can tell me." Lady Edgerton's fleshy countenance, angled for the moment away from them, was but a horse's length away.

"I certainly will not!" Diana retorted with asperity. Almost absently, she found herself giving Lady Edgerton a cordial smile and nod as that astonished lady's eyes came to rest upon her face. "Such a question is completely improper, my lord," she admonished, hardly noticing Lady Edgerton's attempt to stare her out of countenance before Lord Lucan's gargantuan eye forced her to look elsewhere. "I have never been so shocked in my entire life!" she finished, with less heat than might normally have accompanied such impassioned words.

Then it was over. Lady Edgerton had passed on, and Diana realized that the first—and probably the most dreaded—of the ordeals was painlessly concluded. Gradually, her tension began to abate. Things were going to be all right after all, she reflected. And she owed the man beside her a great round of thanks.

Observing her relief, Lord Lucan knew he had accomplished his objective. But just to be on the safe side, he lowered his lips to whisper in her ear. "Sooner or later," he said in a devilish whisper, "I'll find out, you know. I'm determined on that score, Diana."

"Oh!" she sputtered indignantly, her complexion now completely restored to what his lordship considered its proper shade of rosiness. She clenched her gloved hands into small fists, and tried very hard to ignore her companion's wolfish grin. "You . . . you . . . *Oh!*"

But scowling was strangely difficult, for at this precise moment Diana was making a staggering discovery. How could it possibly be, she wondered? How was it that such harsh features as Lord Lucan's could suddenly seem so amazingly attractive?

Chapter Four

As Diana entered the room, Aimee snapped shut the book of poems she had been endeavoring to read. It had failed quite dismally to engage her interest, for something had occurred which overrode any desire she might have felt to escape into the idyllic world of odes and sonnets.

"Oh, I am so glad you are back, Diana!" she exclaimed, her words pouring forth as they invariably did when she had worked herself into a dither. "Did you enjoy yourself? Was Lord Lucan pleasant? Did you see anyone you knew? Come and tell me how it went!" She patted the chair next to her invitingly.

Diana sat down, unaware that Aimee's sharp eyes were taking in the flustered twisting of her fingers. "Well," she said slowly, "it went better than I expected, actually. He does tend to make the most unconventional remarks." She hesitated. "But all things considered, I suppose it went very well."

Aimee's curiosity was roused. "Why, what sort of things does he say, Diana?"

"Oh, well—" Diana gazed pensively at her fingertips. "He is a shocking flirt, of course, but in a kindly sort of way. That doesn't make much sense, does it?"

"Not much," agreed Aimee, diverted by this explanation. "Did he try to kiss you?"

"Of course not!" Diana gave her young sister a reproving look. "Whatever put that notion into your head?"

Aimee shrugged. "Eliza Fingleshaw says that is all the gentlemen really want." Belatedly recalling her sister's opinion of Eliza Fingleshaw, she added hurriedly, "Well then, what does he do?"

"Nothing really," insisted Diana uncomfortably. "He just talks about things he knows he should not. Like, er, corsets." At her sister's incredulous stare, she added quickly, "I think he only did it to make me laugh. That horrid Lady Edgerton was there and it was she, you see, who spread those awful rumors about Edmund and me . . ." Her voice drifted off in a faint shudder of remembrance, before surging vibrantly back. "Evidently, he realized I was very ill at ease and decided to come to my rescue. He stared at that woman through his quizzing glass in *such* a way, Aimee. It was really quite comical, now that I think about it."

The undercurrent of laughter in Diana's voice caused Aimee to give her a considering look. "Well, that was extremely obliging of him," she remarked. "You cannot now say you detest him!"

After a pause of a few seconds, Diana met her sister's inquiring gaze. "Yes, well, I suppose that word is a bit too strong," she admitted. "Rather, let us say that I am *wary* of him, my dear, for there is no disputing the fact that he is very much a man of the world. You see, I know what he . . . what he wants from me, and I am not about to agree to it. To my sorrow, I have already discovered how easily one's reputation can be damaged, and I have no intention of allowing anyone to sully mine ever again."

"No, of course not." Aimee's expression sobered for a respectful instant, before she plunged once more into

66

ebullient speech. "Well, let me tell you who was here while you were gone! No, *not* Cousin Charles, I can see that is what you are guessing. It was only Aunt Serena. She arrived just twenty minutes after you left, and I rather fancy she was not at all pleased to find you gone— until I told her who you were with, that is," she added, with an arch smile. "Then she laughed in that odd way of hers, and said she might have known. I do not know what she could have meant by that."

Diana made a small grimace. "Aunt Serena is the most *managing* female alive! That, as you are probably aware, is the real reason I did not wish to live with her."

Almost too airily, Aimee replied, "Yes, well, I intend to turn her managing nature to very good account. In fact, I have already done so, and you will never guess how, Diana! I have convinced her to have us to dinner tomorrow evening, and to invite Cousin Charles!" She sat back triumphantly. "Now, wasn't that clever of me?"

Diana could not refrain from laughing. "Yes, very! Next you will be telling me Aunt Serena has agreed to frighten Cousin Charles into making you an offer!"

"Now, Diana, you know that is not what I want! Arranged marriages may be very much the thing, but that will *not* do for me! It is essential that Charles fall in love with me. He must offer for me because he wants to and not because he has been coerced into it." Aimee beamed. "I explained all this to Aunt Serena, and she agreed."

Diana stared in disbelief. "She did? Are you sure you understood her correctly?"

Aimee's dark curls bobbed as she nodded. "Absolutely. Auntie can be very reasonable, I have found."

"I do not think," said Diana carefully, "that we can be talking about the same woman. There must be something you're not telling me."

Aimee's eyes grew round with innocence. "Why, what can you mean? Goodness, Diana, you *have* grown

67

suspicious all of a sudden."

"Now, Aimee, you know I can always tell when you're trying to cut a wheedle with me." Diana studied her sister suspiciously. "Out with it, now."

"But I promise you, there is nothing!"

Unconvinced, Diana eyed her sister for one long moment, then gave a tiny shrug. "Very well, Aimee. We shall let it go at that."

"I need you both to help me decide which gown to wear, for I simply *cannot* choose. Should it be the pink, the lavender, or the white?" appealed Aimee, the following afternoon. "Which is most likely to impress Charles? Which becomes me more?" She whirled away from the mirror and looked expectantly at her audience. "I cannot think how I will choose when all the other gowns arrive!"

Diana cast a deliberative eye over the three choices, then exchanged a glance with Miss Tilden. "Well, the white does make her look a positive angel doesn't it, Tildy? But I am not the one to ask since in the end I will always choose a color. You'd better leave it to Tildy."

Aimee turned eager eyes upon Miss Tilden, awaiting her verdict.

"What about the lavender?" suggested Miss Tilden musingly. "With that coal black hair and those eyes—! And the little white lace collar so demure! And yet," she debated, "there is a great deal of favor to be found in the pink. A perfectly delicious dress, my dear. It reminds me of some sort of confectionery!"

Aimee's nose wrinkled. "Well, I am sure I do not wish Charles to view me as a confectionery! Perhaps it should be the lavender, then. But won't it make a better impression if I wear white? Or does white make me look too young?"

Diana laughed. "Never that, dearest. All three are extremely lovely, which makes it difficult to advise you. But I do think Tildy is right. There is something about the lavender that appeals to me. Pink and white are so commonly worn. The lavender is distinctive, and we can thread a matching satin ribbon through those beautiful curls of yours. *Not* that you would not stand out in any color, for you always look a picture in anything! I'm persuaded you'll have no trouble at all catching Cousin Charles's eye. And I plan to wear mauve, so we shall harmonize."

"But, Diana," grumbled Aimee in mock distress, "you forget I may have to compete for Charles's attention. There will be someone else present whom he might find more interesting than my poor self."

"Oh, who?" said Diana, looking surprised.

Her sister dimpled. "You modest creature, don't you know?"

"Oh, for heaven's sake, Aimee!" Diana's brown-gold eyes warmed with affection. "You are far more vivacious than I, besides being of marriageable age, which I am not! I *do* hate to discourage you, but your difficulty is more likely to lie in the fact that our cousin appears to prefer being a bachelor. Aunt Serena will have it that he has been at considerable pains to remain so."

"Yes, she told me that, also," retorted Aimee, in a more subdued voice. She glanced a bit anxiously into the cheval mirror, as if to seek reassurance that she had some small chance of attracting such a determined bachelor. She was not beautiful, but she was certainly a far cry from being unattractive, she told herself stoutly.

Reaching for the lavender gown, she held it up and surveyed it critically. "Perhaps," she mused aloud, "what I need is a more sophisticated gown. Something with a lower neckline so as to show off as much of my bosom as possible. Eliza says the gentlemen just adore

69

seeing a little glimpse of—" She broke off, catching sight of her sister's horrified expression. "Well, it was only a thought," she added quickly.

"I should certainly hope it was only a thought!" said Diana feelingly. "If Eliza does not know any better, at least you should. Such an indecorous notion should never even cross your mind!"

Aimee looked dismayed. "Truly, Diana? Didn't you *ever* consider doing such a thing? Even to attract Sir Henry?"

"Aimee," interposed Miss Tilden sternly. "I think your sister should be spared such prying questions, don't you?"

Noting her sister's silence, Aimee realized that she had inadvertently stepped into forbidden territory. "Oh, I *am* sorry, Diana," she said unhappily. "Forgive me?"

Diana forced a small smile. "Of course, dearest." She rose to her feet. "I think I will have a bit of a rest now. I have the oddest feeling this evening with Aunt Serena is going to be very wearing upon my nerves."

Diana returned to her room feeling a trifle guilty. She should have answered Aimee's question, she thought, hating herself for being such a coward. It was just that anything to do with attracting men in a physical sense made her uneasy. Of course, there was little harm in what Aimee had said, but she found the mere idea of her sister pulling such dangerous tricks alarming. Was Aimee going to be more difficult than she had anticipated? She *did* tend to get herself into scrapes, but thus far each of them, in the final evaluation, had been fairly harmless. Here in London, however, it was far easier to attract real trouble.

Diana yawned suddenly, knowing her sleep had been restless the night before. What on earth could she have dreamt that had so interfered with her rest? Knowing Meg was nearby she nearly reached for her hand bell, then stopped herself with a chuckle. How easy it was to become spoiled, she thought drowsily. As if she could not undress herself now that she had an abigail!

Free of her gown, she crawled into bed and shut her eyes determinedly, hearing Meg's quiet movements in the next room as she fussed with Aimee's gowns. Before drifting off, a small, involuntary smile touched her mouth. She wondered what Lord Lucan would say if he knew he was perfectly correct. She didn't even own a corset.

It was nearly six o'clock when she awoke. Meg must have come into the room while she slept, for her mauve dinner dress was laid out neatly across the chair. As this thought went through her head, a soft scratch upon the door heralded her abigail's arrival.

"Ah, you're awake," said Meg, setting down the jug of hot water for the wash basin. "I stepped in before but thought 'twas a shame to wake you when you was sleepin' so peaceful like." She moved about the room, chattering happily as she did her duties. "Miss Aimee has been fillin' my ear for the past hour with tales about this Mr. Charles Perth. I was struck all of a heap when she told me he was a-going to be one of them viscounts someday! Oh my stars, I cried! And ain't she going to make a grand viscountess! Some of them ladyships keep their noses so high in the air, I say 'tis a refreshin' change to meet someone who ain't too high and mighty to gibble-gabble with someone below her station!"

Attending with only half an ear, Diana rubbed her eyes. "Yes, well, the gentleman in question knows next to nothing about my sister, so perhaps she shouldn't count her chickens this soon," she said absently. "Is there time for you to fetch me up a cup of tea?"

This Meg was more than happy to do, since it would afford her a chance to converse with Felix the footman, whom she privately considered more interesting than ten

71

viscounts or even a royal duke.

Left alone, Diana pulled off her chemise, and made good and thorough use of the hot water. She had not taken a close look at her body in the mirror in a long time, but from the moment she'd returned to London, Diana had been struck with an inexplicable urge to do so. Now, as if a magnet pulled her to the looking glass, she felt compelled to take critical stock of her own proportions.

Dispassionately, she knew she ought to be thankful. Her high, pink-tipped breasts were shapely and full, yet not so full as to present a problem when it came to the high-waisted styles of the day. Her sparse eating habits had kept her stomach enviably flat, while her gently rounded hips and buttocks curved smoothly into slim, supple thighs. For a time, when she was married to Edmund, she had hated the sight of her own body, for that was the only thing about her that had interested her lascivious husband. He had told her in one of his more magnanimous moments that she was as luscious a morsel as he had ever set eyes on—as though she were a succulent round of beef to be consumed! *Luscious!* She had despised that particular word ever since.

Her lips twisting in bitterness, Diana suddenly wondered whether Lord Lucan also thought of her as a luscious morsel. Or, to use a more acceptable term, did he find her desirable? For one unsettling instant she pictured herself with him, before the hot color flooded her cheeks. Appalled at the unintentional direction her thoughts had taken, Diana spun away from the glass and snatched up the clean chemise Meg had laid out for her. Pulling it roughly over her head, she castigated herself. What in heaven's name possessed her to think such a thing, and about *him*, of all people? She had long ago decided that *that* sort of thing was not for her. It was disgusting and degrading, and any decent woman avoided it at all cost. Thank the dear Lord she was a widow, and would never have to go through it again! A woman would have to be insane to seek out such an experience voluntarily, she told herself angrily. Yet, part of her had always argued against this logic, for why was it that so many women did?

She dashed an impatient hand into the air, unwilling to explore this very reasonable objection. What was more to the point was that she must never lower her guard, never lose sight of her own, very personal reason for not encouraging any gentleman's attentions. And it would be all too easy to do this, she feared, for the truth was she had always liked the company of men, preferring their sensible conversation to the uneducated, insipid prattling of her own sex. It was just that she could not always fathom their way of thinking.

As for flirtation, she could never claim to be a match for a man like Lord Lucan. He was obviously very skilled at the art of dalliance, for had he not already vanquished her anger twice with his whimsical charm? And in two short days, no less! He was very dangerous, she decided. His admiring glances and clever compliments were designed to feed her vanity and lull her into submission. And as for his assertion that he regarded her as a virtuous woman—poppycock! She would stake the few jewels she owned on the expectation that the Earl of Lucan would, sooner or later, be making her a dishonorable proposal.

And then there was Sir Henry. Diana frowned, surprised that he had not entered her mind in over twenty-four hours. She was neither so vain nor so cynical that she believed every gentleman who smiled at her was similarly bent upon offering her insult. Surely there were some men whose intentions were honorable, and surely Sir Henry Neyle was one of these?

Even after all this time, she could not help but think of the baronet as an exceptional man. Though she had not consciously yearned for him over the years, it had not come as a complete surprise to her that her heart still beat a little faster when he was near. At eighteen, she had held him in girlish fascination, had, in fact, pictured herself in his arms all too often. Why, she could not recall one instance of his ever doing anything even remotely forward or disrespectful. His eyes were always laughing and gentle, never bold or penetrating, like Lord Lucan's.

These ponderings began to lead her up the old, half-forgotten path. *If* Sir Henry were to look her way once more, and *if* he were to make her a declaration—? Disgusted with herself, Diana made an exasperated sound. What foolishness! She could not, *would* not, consider remarriage, not even with Sir Henry.

However, there was a small voice inside her which taunted: *Oh, yes, you would, you weak, little hypocrite. With Sir Henry Neyle, you would indeed.*

Meg's bustling appearance effectively brought Diana's broodings to a halt. "Here's your tea, ma'am," she announced, her cheeks still flushed with the satisfaction of knowing Felix's eyes had followed her up the stairs. "Hot and black just the way you like it," she continued. "Miss Aimee's already dressed and ready to go." The abigail set the cup and saucer on the small table next to Diana. "You'd best let me help you into your gown so I can get started on your hair. Did you get rested?"

"Yes, thank you." Diana reached gratefully for the dainty china teacup. Perhaps a few swallows of strong tea would dispel the nonsensical notions from her head.

Half an hour later, Meg was putting the finishing touches on Diana's hair when Aimee put her head inside the door. "Aren't you ready yet?" she inquired anxiously. "The carriage Aunt Serena sent for us has arrived." Casting an admiring glance at her sister, she added, with mock remorse, "Oh, you look simply divine in that color! Now I *know* I haven't a prayer's chance with Charles. I may as well stay home and knit stockings with— Oh, all right, all right. Don't glare so, Diana. I'm only funning. I'll run and bid Tildy good night. Do hurry, now!"

Diana's abigail gave a giggle as Aimee ducked out of sight. "She sure is anxious to see her cousin, ain't she, ma'am? I just hope she remembers what I told her. Miss Aimee, I said, mind you don't let the gentleman see how taken you are with him. Cool and mysterious, that's what the gents like. Nothing catches a man's fancy like a bit of challenge, no matter what his age or rank!"

Diana's brows shot up. "You told her that?"

Meg nodded, her garrulous affirmative including several more worldly remarks of similar nature.

The young widow's eyes closed for a moment. "It may be true," she remarked, half to herself, "but how my dear sister will choose to interpret 'cool and mysterious' remains to be seen. Oh, I cannot *wait* for this evening to be over!"

Contrary to what the dowager believed, the Honorable Charles Perth was neither spineless, nor easily intimidated. Yes, as a child he had gone in terror of his grandmother, but that fear had long since ceased to exist. Since both his parents resided in the country, it fell to him to see to his grandmother, whose dragonlike personality did not match her frail constitution. He considered it his duty to try to keep her happy, and if it pleased her to think she could bully him, why, it was all one to him. He was loath to admit it, of course, but he did bear some affection for the old woman, though she had never done anything very much to deserve it. After all, she *had* locked him in a closet once, something he had never quite forgotten. So it was with a certain understandable caution that he approached his grandmother when she summoned him to her side.

He knew he had been invited to her house for a definite purpose. Like many unmarried men, Charles had developed a sort of sixth sense which alerted him to danger of the matchmaking kind, and tonight's dinner party had, for some obscure reason, aroused his suspicions. However, he considered it fruitless to think of turning down the querulous old woman's invitation, for, like many females, his grandmother could be relentless in her persistence, as well as extremely cunning. At the age of nine-and-twenty, he could only wonder that, thus far, he had been spared any attempts to settle his future. Perhaps, he reflected darkly, she had only been biding her time.

The problem was, he had no intention of allowing his grandmother to choose him a wife. An eloquent shudder ran over his tall, angular frame at the thought. It was his usual wont to avoid the dowager's wearying displays of temper by simply letting her have her way, but a fellow had to draw the line somewhere, dash it! Unfortunately, he knew that when he began to drag his feet, some particularly abrasive fireworks were going to go off.

Which cousin his grandmother might wish him to wed he was unsure, but he suspected it was his cousin Aimee. After all, when Cousin Diana had been to town six years before, the dowager had made no effort to throw the pair of them together. Almost, he wished she had, for perhaps he might have been there to save her from that blackguard, Edmund Verney. A chivalrous man, Charles had been aghast at his cousin's predicament, and had his grandmother requested it, might have married the poor girl himself, simply out of compassion. However, such a solution had never been suggested, for he'd been in Newmarket on the fatal night, and by the time he'd returned, Diana's betrothal was already a *fait accompli*.

Being also a reasonable man, Charles refused to form a prejudice against Cousin Aimee before he met her. After all, he told himself, it was hardly her fault if his grandmother had decided to play matchmaker. Come to think of it, he'd seen the chit at the family reunion three years before, hadn't he? Without much success, he attempted to summon up some recollection of her appearance, but all he could remember was that she had dark hair and was rather plump. Of course, there was a chance she had improved, for wasn't Diana well above average? Well, all he could do at the moment was hope for the best.

By many, Arlington Street was considered to be an extremely agreeable avenue in which to reside, for not only did its graceful thoroughfare run parallel with St. James's Street, it lay directly adjacent to Green Park. It was not, perhaps, as awe inspiring as a Grosvenor Square address, but it was more pleasant and more convenient. Its residents were blessed with their very own entrance to the pretty little meadow; those fortunate enough to dwell on its west side were afforded a delightful, pastoral aspect from their windows. Indeed, Arlington Street appeared to offer one all the advantages of the country within easy distance of the countless diversions that only the Mayfair area could provide.

The street was said to be well inhabited, for many persons of the first rank and consequence chose to live here. Historically, its list of illustrious residents had included such names as the great Lord Nelson and Mr. Charles Fox, as well as a vast number of dukes, marquises, earls, and other members of the aristocracy, particularly those in ministerial positions. Diana's great aunt, the dowager Lady Torrington, resided in number five, a large house which held the distinction of being once owned by Sir Robert Walpole, and subsequently, by his witty and well-known son, Horace.

The dowager's home was in its way a showplace, for it boasted, among other things, a particularly elegant mahogany staircase, a superb collection of paintings including two by Sir Joshua Reynolds, and a magnificent gold and blue Axminster carpet woven especially for the drawing room. It was an impressive house, and as always, Diana was touched with a sense of wonder as she followed the dignified footman up the sweeping stairway to the first floor, her gloved hand lightly grazing that exquisite rail with its finely carved, barley-sugar balusters. Intoning their names in suitably stentorian accents, the tall, peruked servant stepped aside, allowing the two sisters to move past him into the drawing room.

Seated in the center of a blue velvet Sheraton couch, Great-aunt Serena dominated the scene in a gown of flowing purple. With brief surprise, Diana realized that Cousin Charles was not the only other guest, for an elderly, rather rotund gentleman was in the process of rising to his feet. To that gentleman's left stood Charles, elegant in a coat of dark blue superfine, cream-colored pantaloons, and a neckcloth whose intricate folds proclaimed it the work of a master.

From the manner in which the dowager introduced the older gentleman, Diana deduced that Lord Hervey's friendship with Great-aunt Serena had strengthened since last she was in town. His stays creaking noticeably, the old peer executed a portly bow, and beamed benevolently at the two sisters.

"'Pon my word, Serena," he remarked, "of *course* I remember your niece! Couldn't forget a pretty face like that! Evening, my dear. And this is Miss Farington. How-de-do, young lady."

While Diana smiled and shook hands with his lordship, she was conscious that Aimee's greeting to Lord Hervey sounded, at least to her ears, a trifle distracted. One quick look was enough to supply the reason. Aimee's blue-eyed gaze had encountered Charles's, and to Diana, it was clear that something more than a mere courtesy glance had been exchanged.

Nudging her blushing young sister gently, Diana said, "It's lovely to see you again, Charles. I trust I find you well?"

Recovering from her daze, Aimee added her greeting. "Hello, Charles," she said softly.

Charles's smile, as he replied, held a slightly bemused quality, and Diana could not help noticing how his green eyes kept shifting back to Aimee. It seemed the lavender gown had done the trick, she thought in amusement.

"Now then," interrupted Great-aunt Serena with a thin cackle, "we can all be comfortable. Charles, go and pour out some sherry for your cousins, will you? And there's madeira there, as well as brandy if you want it. Thurstan will take the madeira."

Charles readily performed this task, for it offered him the chance to move to a position where he could inspect Aimee without her knowledge. While he was no callow youth to be riveted to the floor by a mere pretty face, to say that he was pleasantly surprised would be to understate the matter. Could he possibly be this lucky? he found himself thinking.

By *Jove*, she *had* blossomed, he marveled, as the red liquid splashed into delicate crystal goblets. Covertly, his eyes drank in every entrancing detail. Such a dainty figure! Such angelic features! Her heart-shaped face was just as sweet as anyone could wish, and as for those melting blue eyes—! They seemed to Charles to hold everything he had ever yearned for in their sparkling depths. However, Charles was unquestionably a gentleman, and had far too much delicacy of principle to embarrass a gently bred girl by making sheep's eyes at her. And so, after gratifying Aimee with those first few looks, he made sure not to glance at her again, at least not more than any other person in the room.

Disappointed, Aimee waited in vain for Charles's sea-green eyes to seek hers once more. Minutes passed. She darted yet another look at him, but he appeared wholly engrossed by Lord Hervey's lengthy dissertation on the trials and tribulations of persons afflicted with gout. How they had arrived at the topic she had no notion, for she had paid heed to no one but Charles since she stepped into the room. And Charles had not spoken since Lord Hervey began to talk, some five or six minutes before. Even Aunt Serena looked absorbed, for she kept nodding, the single ostrich feather adorning her turban bobbing up and down with fascinating regularity.

Frustrated, Aimee cudgeled her brain. What could she do to make him look at her again? What was it Meg had told her? Cool and mysterious, that was it! The advice had a sound, sensible ring to it, but how on earth did one go about looking mysterious? The best she could do, she finally decided, was to stay with what she already knew.

It seemed like ages before she was able to catch Charles's eye again, and then she quickly seized the opportunity to send him the sirenic smile she had practiced in her mirror. Once she was sure he had noticed, she added, for good measure, the single eyelash bat which had seemed so effective on Sir Henry.

Charles blinked. What the deuce was the girl up to? In his opinion, virtuous young ladies ought *not* to bat their eyelashes at gentlemen in that precise way, and certainly not in such an inviting manner. To be sure, he did not wish to marry a flirt, for in his experience such females harbored some vain urge to continually add to their list of conquests. That might be good enough for some men, but not for Charles Perth!

However, a second later he decided he must have imagined the whole thing, for Aimee's eyes had dropped demurely to her lap, where her hands lay modestly folded. No, he assured himself, such a fair creature as Miss Aimee Farington could not be anything but perfect. He would ask her to go driving tomorrow.

It was but a few, short minutes later that Diana began to realize the dowager was expecting another guest. Of course she ought to have known, for Aunt Serena had always been a stickler for social conventions, and was unlikely to sit down to dinner with an uneven number of covers. Moreover, the missing guest would need to be a gentleman, so that the same number of representatives from each sex might be maintained. Now, who else would her aunt invite? Diana wondered. She soon had her answer, for not five minutes later the door to the drawing room was flung grandly open and the latecomer's name announced.

As the gasp escaped Diana's lips, she shot an accusing look at her aunt. How dared Aunt Serena pull such a sly trick! No doubt this was what Aimee had been concealing from her!

The young widow's bosom rose and fell, heaving with the unbearable indignation of being forced into what she considered an untenable position by her meddling, matchmaking, unscrupulous relative. How could the Earl of Lucan have had the *audacity* to come here tonight? Oh, how could Aunt Serena *do* this to her!

Chapter Five

Undisturbed by Diana's outrage, Aunt Serena beckoned to the earl. "Well, come in, come in!" she told him imperiously. "Diana, Aimee, you both know his lordship. For pity's sake, Diana, don't just sit there gaping like a henwit. The man doesn't have two heads, does he?"

Diana's rigid stare could not have more clearly conveyed her belief that Lord Lucan was encroaching where he had no business. However, if her perturbation had been less, she might have taken the trouble to notice the almost imperceptible check in his stride at his moment of entry. As it happened, the earl had believed himself a last-minute addition to a sizable dinner party, an impression shamelessly given him by the wording in the Dowager's invitation. However, save for the presence of Lord Hervey, he instead found himself in the midst of a small family gathering—moreover a family he scarcely knew! Only his good breeding saved him from appearing as disconcerted as he actually was. And by the look on Diana's face, he was not the only one who had been duped.

Though he maintained his outward impassivity far better than Diana, he was nearly as angry as she. If the dowager viscountess thought she had done him a favor, by God, she was wrong! Not only had she placed him in an awkward position, but there could be little doubt that whatever progress he had made with Diana was in danger of being negated. But he could hardly expect otherwise, could he? It would be illogical as well as unreasonable to think Diana would welcome the very interference he resented. He would simply have to repair the damage—somehow.

He soon began to realize the challenge he had in store, for the lady was making a studied effort to ignore him, and he could not catch her eye. Eventually, however, he saw her sneak a peep in his direction, an action which filled him with a relief so great it ousted his vexation. She was simply playing obstinate! Well, let her, he decided in amusement. It was far more stimulating this way, after all. He had never liked things to be too easy, and why should wooing the lady of his choice be any different?

The conversation of the evening did not begin to prosper until the weather, the fading state of the old queen's health, and Princess Charlotte's pregnancy had all been perfunctorily discussed. The Prince Regent's latest extravagances were discreetly passed over, as were the shocking antics of his despised wife, Caroline of Brunswick, who had taken up residence in Italy with an Italian adventurer named Pergami. The red-faced, hard-drinking Princess of Wales had become such a source of embarrassment to her country that to introduce her into polite conversation was not considered particularly nice, especially by the highest sticklers.

By this time, they were seated in Aunt Serena's dining room, a large salon brilliantly lit by candelabra, as well as the great crystal chandelier suspended just above the center of the rosewood dining table. Rich damask curtains hung at its windows, fine paintings adorned its satin-covered walls, while at one end, a fire crackled in a marble fireplace, providing the diners with an ample amount of warmth.

Although Diana would not for the world have admitted that anything about Lord Lucan interested her in the least, her ears automatically pricked up when Cousin Charles asked him about his country estate. Curiously, she listened to the earl's description of his holdings in Cornwall, its location but a bare mile inland from the great granite cliffs edging the turbulent, often savage, Cornish sea. With a few swift words, he sketched for them an image of that faraway part of England where, he assured them, superstition still ran rampant and the past could seem more real than the present.

Intrigued in spite of herself, Diana studied the earl's face. "It sounds as though you miss the place," she said, careful to keep her voice neutral. It was the first time she had addressed him directly.

He answered her gravely. "I do, Mrs. Verney. When I am not there, I miss it very much."

"Then I wonder you do not stay there," she countered, wondering if she merely imagined that gleam of mockery in his eye.

The earl's broad shoulders lifted in a slight shrug. "Like all good things, I appreciate Cornwall more when I have been away from it for a while," he said smoothly. "And I like to see for myself what is happening here in the hub of our country. Many Cornishmen think the pixies are of greater concern than any of England's more tangible problems."

"Pixies!" snorted the dowager, pushing her food around her plate. "What poppycock!" She obviously felt that the subject had been adequately discussed, for she steered it into another, quite unrelated channel.

"Speaking of poppycock, would you believe that Thurstan"—she gave Lord Hervey a fond look—"wants to see me decked out in jewels? A woman of my age! Preposterous, ain't it?"

"What jewels?" asked Aimee with interest.

Aunt Serena looked smug. "I mean the Charles II tiara, of course. The fool man thinks I ought to wear the ugly thing!"

"But why do you not, Auntie? I have never even seen the Torrington diamond."

"Because it's too damned ostentatious to wear," snapped the dowager. "And don't get any ideas into your head, missy, because you ain't going to wear it either."

"It'd look wonderful on you," said Lord Hervey loyally. "You wore it when you were young."

"That was different! I was beautiful then," she grumbled, casting her elderly crony a frowning look. "But I won't be bamboozled into making a spectacle of myself now. Aimee, how was your shopping expedition? I suppose you spent enough to ruin me."

"Oh, we had the grandest time shopping, Aunt Serena! But we could not decide about one thing. Shall I truly be needing a riding habit?"

"Of course you will, silly girl," responded the old woman severely. "Oh, you mean, am I really going to buy you a horse, is that it? Didn't do it last time Diana was here, did I? Can't recall why. Silly of me. Well!" Her voice altered. "Charles?"

Fork paused midair, Cousin Charles fixed her with a wary look. "Yes, Grandmama?"

The dowager's voice was piercing. "Your driving skills may be lamentable but I cannot deny you have an eye for a horse. I should like you to procure a suitable mount for your cousin Aimee."

Charles's fork went down. Horses were serious business, and the assessing look he shot his young cousin held none of its former bemusement. "I could, of course," he said bluntly, "but without knowing how well she can ride—"

"I ride very well!" put in Aimee with an indignant look.

He sent her a charming smile. "Yes, of course you do."

His fingers ruffled through his auburn hair. "But, ah, how well?" he added.

Aimee smiled back. "Extremely well. Perhaps you would like me to prove it to you?" she suggested with pert hopefulness.

Those blue eyes, like two bits of night sky, were too much for Charles to resist. "Ahem. Yes, perhaps that might be a good notion." He saw his grandmother's sudden grin. "Makes sense, after all," he explained lamely. "Can't buy a lady a horse without knowing what sort of cattle would suit her."

"But what about Diana?" queried Aimee, unwittingly providing the dowager with her opening.

To Diana's horror, Aunt Serena's small, glinting eyes fell on the earl. "Rumor has it, Lucan, that when it comes to horseflesh, you ain't one to be taken in by mere show. Got a sharp eye for quality, they say." She gave one of her thin cackles. "Perhaps you would be good enough to oblige an old woman and find a horse for Diana."

Diana's fork clattered to her plate. "Aunt Serena!" she objected, in a strangled voice.

"Ah . . . naturally, I would be delighted to be of assistance to your niece," said the earl, his annoyance with the dowager returning. "But perhaps Mrs. Verney would prefer her cousin to purchase her mount?" he suggested, searching for a route out of the quagmire.

The dowager cut short Diana's sputters. "Oh, stop your fussing, girl! Four eyes are better than two! They can go looking together! We ladies don't wish to be bothered with the rubbishy details of the business."

With a slight cough, Charles came to the earl's rescue. "Shall we take a look-in at Tatt's tomorrow?" he offered. "It ain't a sale day, of course, but it don't hurt to see what's available."

Angered by the way in which her needs were being attended to without her consent, Diana said tightly, "Is it

86

too much to hope that I might have some say in the matter? It might save his lordship a great deal of trouble if he were acquainted with what would suit *me!*"

"By all means," put in the earl, beginning to appreciate the humor in the situation.

Diana's eyes flashed. "First of all, I will *not* ride a horse whose tail has been docked—"

"Very wise," he agreed.

"Because it is a cruel practice," she continued, ignoring him, "of which I heartily disapprove. And secondly, I refuse to be put upon a slug of any sort. I require a horse with spirit." She raised her chin at the earl. "I trust you can recognize spirit when you see it, my lord?" she added in a sweet tone.

The earl could no longer conceal his amusement. "Aye," he said softly, his gray eyes alight with laughter, "I recognize it, Mrs. Verney."

Once the ladies left the gentlemen to their port, conversation between the three men remained desultory until Lord Hervey excused himself and wandered vaguely out of the room. The dowager had most expressly desired him to do so, and so the obliging little man made his way down the corridor to the music room, where he settled himself in a comfortable wing chair and eased his gouty foot upon a stool.

Left alone with the earl, Charles Perth cleared his throat. "S'pose I ought to apologize for my grandmother," he remarked, gazing absently into his glass. "I'm afraid there's nothing anyone can do once the old girl gets the bit between her teeth. Hope you understand."

"Actually," remarked the earl, fingering the stem of his goblet, "I'm beginning to find her rather entertaining."

"Are you?" Charles leaned back in his chair and stared thoughtfully at the other man. "You might not think so if you had to deal with her all the time. Got you here tonight by some trick, I'll wager."

Although he did not mention the deceptive invitation, the earl's silence gave Charles his answer. "I confess I was surprised," he said finally. "I cannot claim more than a slight acquaintance with the Dowager Lady Torrington, so I suppose I assumed there would be quite a number of other guests." He did not add that he had hoped that Diana had requested that he be invited. That had clearly not been the case.

"Well," said Charles comfortably, "between the two of us, we ought to be able to see that the girls have decent mounts. I wonder if Miss Farington rides as well as she claims."

"It appears that you are destined to find out."

"It does, doesn't it?" A tiny smile twisted the corners of Charles's mouth, and a few seconds went by before he gathered his thoughts to focus on another matter. Leaning forward to direct a frank look at the older man, he said carefully, "Y'know, I'm devilish glad to see my cousin Diana back in town. She's a fine girl."

The earl scrutinized Charles. "Indeed," he agreed imperturbably.

"A dashed fine girl," repeated Charles with emphasis. "Don't know what my grandmother has in mind, but, dash it, I s'pose it's my responsibility to keep an eye on her. Female relative and all."

The earl's left eyebrow shot up, and Charles shifted a little in his chair. "Ahem. Yes, well, perhaps you're thinking I ought to have done a better job of it the last time she was here."

"You were not the girl's chaperon," Lord Lucan pointed out, very kindly exonerating him. "It would hardly be fair to hold you in account."

"Uh, yes, but a fellow still feels he should have done something more." His fingers ruffled through his hair, effectively completing its disarray.

Charles found himself being examined by a pair of keen gray eyes. "You would have been what? About four-and-twenty or thereabouts?" inquired the earl, his tone casual. "Just the age where it would have been natural for you to have fallen under the spell of a lovely young girl like your cousin. I imagine her marriage must have dealt you quite a blow."

Charles straightened, recognizing that, as far as probing was concerned, the tables had just been effectively turned. "What? No, no, beg your pardon, Lucan, but don't misunderstand. I mean, Diana's a capital girl, and all that, but I never—" His eyes filled with dawning comprehension. "I think what you want to know is if we'll be stepping on each other's toes in Jermyn Street. Is that it?"

Whatever the earl was thinking, his face did not betray him. He said only, "I prefer to know who my rivals are."

Pleased that he had not been forced to ask the earl point-blank about his intentions toward his cousin, Charles reached to refill both their glasses.

"Like that, is it? Thought so. Well, I wish you luck, Lucan, but bearing in mind those black looks Diana keeps throwing you, I'd lay odds against your chances of success."

The earl sipped pensively at his port. "Yes, well, tonight would certainly suggest that conclusion," he murmured.

Slowly, the amusement vanished from Charles's expression. "I may as well warn you, if you mean to court my cousin, you'll be seeing more and more of my grandmother's meddling. She's enough to provoke a saint—which I ain't!"

"Perhaps someone ought to have taken a crop to her

backside when she was young," offered the earl dryly. "I wonder what she was like at, for instance, Miss Aimee Farington's age. Very like, I should imagine."

Taking instant exception to this ludicrous comparison, Charles opened his mouth to say, "Oh, come now, Lucan," when he suddenly recalled Aimee's coquettish smile and fluttering eyelashes. His mouth closed abruptly and he stared at the earl. "Good God. I wonder if that look she gave me was really meant to be . . ." His voice faded.

Lord Lucan favored Mr. Perth with a commiserating look. "I saw it. She's going to lead you a devil of a dance, you know."

And so, when Lord Hervey reentered the room a short while later, it was to discover that the conversation between the two men had lapsed into meditative silence. Indeed, each man wore such a remote look upon his face that Lord Hervey could not help wondering if Serena had been mistaken. What could her grandson and the earl possibly have had to discuss privately, after all?

The portly little man shook his head in perplexity, and muttered the word, "Females!" under his breath. This short utterance, rather to his surprise, brought both men's heads swiveling in his direction.

"Just so," agreed the earl in an ironic tone.

Charles nodded gloomily.

In the drawing room, Diana was attempting to explain to the dowager just why she was so excessively agitated.

"But it was positively insupportable of you, Aunt Serena!" she was saying in acute frustration. "To encourage the man in this way is ridiculous, and I utterly refuse to allow it to continue! Aimee," she accused, "*you* knew he would be here tonight! Whatever possessed you to be a party to this?"

"Balderdash," grunted the dowager, rapping her cane sharply on the floor. "I merely wanted to test the man. Handles himself well, don't he? Far better than you do, missy! Lord, girl, I thought you was going to disgrace me by succumbing to a fit of the vapors!" she added in disgust.

Eyes flashing, Diana warned, "It would have served you right, and I may do so yet! And, I promise you, Aunt Serena, if you ever do this to me again, I shall do more than that! I shall . . . I shall go into strong convulsions and take to my bed for a week!"

"Don't be a fool, Diana," said the dowager repressively. "It don't at all become you. I quite fail to understand how you can kick up such a dust over the matter. I can think of a score of women who'd trade half the teeth in their heads to be in your position, you featherbrained girl! Don't you realize that Geoffrey Trevelyan is a marital prize of the first order? You ought to be thanking me for inviting him, instead of flying off into a pelter! No doubt you'd have fallen on my neck with joy if I'd invited that Neyle popinjay!"

"Sir Henry Neyle is not a popinjay!" corrected Diana with considerable heat. "And I should not have desired you to have invited him either! It would have been just as bad—no, worse!"

"Aye," snapped the dowager. "Worse, because the man hasn't any breeding to speak of!"

"You know, Diana," said Aimee suddenly, "poor Lord Lucan did offer to let Charles buy your horse. I think he felt very awkward about it, and I think you are being most unfair. None of this is his fault, you know."

The truth of this struck Diana with blinding force. And with this came the realization that she was behaving with such ingratitude that she had completely forgotten his chivalrous action in the Park. And even though he'd had an ulterior motive for acting as he had, still, she *was*

91

being unfair.

Ashamed of herself, Diana bit her lip in chagrin. "Yes, Aimee, you are quite right. I should know better than to place the blame at the wrong door."

So it was that when the three gentlemen joined the ladies a few minutes later, Diana determinedly sought the earl's eyes and sent him a swift, embarrassed smile. His response, a slow, sensual curve of his mouth, told her she was forgiven but it also contained a message. His pursuit of her would continue, it said, as clearly as if he'd stated the words aloud.

The latter half of the evening passed more felicitously than the first, and when Diana tumbled into her bed much later that night, the only conclusion she was able to reach about the state of her emotions was that they were in hopeless disorder. In fact, never before in her life could she recall being so torn between the clearly logical and the obviously imprudent. For she was prepared to concede—in the darkness of her own room and only to herself—that there was something about Lord Lucan that made him impossible to dislike. Even while she had been angry with him, a tiny inner voice had whispered confidently that it would pass, and that he would forgive her display of temper. Goodness, she had not indulged in such irrational behavior in years! Where was this so-called composure for which she was known?

Rolling to her side, Diana punched at her pillow in frustration. Well, so what if she did like the Earl of Lucan? It would be senseless, even foolhardy, to encourage the abominable man. However, perhaps if she stood firm it might be possible simply to be his friend. Yes, that was a thought. She would rather like to be his friend. But was that at all likely? Would a man like Geoffrey Trevelyan be satisfied with mere friendship?

*   *   *

The earl did not go directly home after the dowager's dinner party. He went instead to the house of a fashionable, rather dashing widow who was neither so young as Diana, nor so weighted down by social or moral convention. Knowing this, Diana might have leaped to the conclusion that Mrs. Clement was his lordship's mistress, but she would have been wrong. If the earl had, once or twice, accepted the lady's invitation to spend the night, it would be rather unfair to fault him for this. After all, he had the same needs as any other man, and the truth was, he liked Mrs. Clement very well. And the lady could be very persuasive.

Cynthia Clement was renowned for her late night parties. Her rooms during these sparkling little affairs were often a trifle thin of the company of ladies, but the numbers of gentlemen who flocked to that small house in Cork Street invariably made up for it. For although Mrs. Clement was only moderately pretty, among the gentlemen, at least, she was very much admired. She had an informed mind, a lively and generous disposition, and above all, she possessed the infinite good sense to be very, very discreet.

Relinquishing his hat and cloak at the door, the earl mounted the stairs to the first floor salon, where the din of voices told him the majority of her guests were gathered. He paused at the threshold, surveying those within with a faint smile on his lips. Spying him immediately from the far side of the room, Mrs. Clement excused herself from the gentlemen who surrounded her and approached him with a wide smile and outstretched hands.

"Why, Geoffrey, I had quite given you up! You naughty boy, wherever have you been?"

Her light tone assured him she did not expect an answer. "Good evening, Cynthia. How lovely you look," he said courteously, raising her delicate hand to his lips.

93

Her pleased expression displayed uneven teeth. "What fustian! I look perfectly dreadful, as you well know, but never mind that. Do you care to play faro? There's a game begun almost an hour ago in my dining room. Lord Ivor is holding the bank, and Mr. Pennistone was just trying to persuade me to join them."

His lordship's idle glance swept the room. "Faro?" he said absently. "No, I don't think so. Not tonight."

Though he was unaware of it, the earl was a favorite with Mrs. Clement. His elusiveness attracted and intrigued her, while their few encounters had left her astonished at his ability to give as much pleasure as he took. She had frequently wished that some of the other gentlemen were as patient and as sensitive to her needs. However, she was too wise and too lazy to chase him, and too content with her lot to dwell upon what she knew was not to be.

She therefore sighed, and said, without petulance, "There now, I might have expected you to be difficult. You've come for some purpose, I'll wager, and I don't suppose it's to see me."

He glanced down at her, a quirk in his smile. "Of course I came to see you, Cynthia. You and one other, that is."

"So frank," she murmured, her dark eyes peeping up at him from under darker lashes.

"You prefer me that way, remember?" he reminded her.

"I do, indeed." She tapped his arm with her fan. "I'll leave you on your own, then. Will you be staying long?" This time, it was as close as she would come to a bolder invitation.

He did not misunderstand. "No," he said gently. "Not long."

*　　*　　*

"Your bet, sir?" prompted Lord Ivor in an impassive voice.

Sir Henry Neyle hesitated. Faro, he decided sourly, was rapidly becoming a dead bore. He glanced around the room as if in search of inspiration, and instead beheld the Earl of Lucan framed in Mrs. Clement's narrow doorway. Wasting no time, he quickly seized this as a face-saving excuse to leave the game.

"What, you here, Geoff?" he called out jovially. "Stay a minute and I'll join you, old boy. So sorry, Ivor, but I must be on the toddle." Coolly, he scratched out his vowels, then nodded farewell to the group of men huddled round the widow's dining table.

"So what brings you here?" he inquired, ambling over to join the earl.

Lord Lucan shrugged indifferently. "The same as you, I suppose." He turned and made his way back to one of the emptier rooms, where a pair of armchairs near the fire had been recently vacated.

"How were you doing?" he asked, settling himself into the closer of the two.

"Oh, well—" Sir Henry waved one pale hand languidly as he sank into the second chair. "Truth to tell, I was losing, and losing don't agree with me overmuch. It does tend to alleviate the tedium of the moment, however."

The earl yawned. "I could suffer a little tedium over the thrill of gaming away my blunt. You're going to be dodging the duns if you're not careful, Harry."

Sir Henry lost some of his languor. "I know, dammit. I expect it's time to start looking about me for an heiress I could stomach in my bed. A depressing thought, since heiresses tend to resemble their horses—at least in facial structure. Last year's crop was the sorriest lot I ever saw in my life."

Without emotion, Lord Lucan watched the other man

withdraw a small enamel snuffbox from his pocket. "Have you been to see Mrs. Verney?" he said abruptly, coming to the point of his visit.

A trace of mockery glinted in Sir Henry's pale blue eyes. "Certainly. I'm as interested in the enchanting Diana as you are, old boy. Any objection?" he added, his tone holding a challenge.

For a long moment, the earl made no answer. "Actually, yes," he said frankly. "I won't have her offered insult, Harry."

The baronet's fair brows rose haughtily. "Oh, really?" he drawled. "You don't credit me with much finesse, do you? I suppose you're still hoping to wed the wench. A pity she's not an heiress, or I'd give you a run for your money. I'd win, too, for it's you, old boy, who lacks finesse." A new gleam entered his eye. "How bloody provoking that no one knows where that aunt of hers is leaving her fortune. The old girl's so full of juice one might be tempted to give her a little . . . squeeze . . . just to see what dribbles out." He flipped open his snuffbox with one thumb and helped himself to a generous pinch.

The earl's gray eyes raked the other man's face. "I trust that was a joke, Harry. You would not hurt an old woman."

"Hurt her? You mean physically?" Sir Henry looked genuinely shocked. "Good Lord, man, do I look like a murderer?" He shuddered eloquently. "Come, come, Geoff, old boy. Can't you recognize a jest when you hear one? 'Twas but a flash of wit, nothing more."

"Very witty," remarked the earl dryly. As if unable to bear the other man's presence any longer, he rose to his feet. "I'll bid you good night, then."

"Of course, Geoff, old boy," the baronet murmured, as he watched his friend depart. "But then, there's more than one way to squeeze an orange, now isn't there?"

*   *   *

96

Lord Lucan's thick black brows were drawn sharply together as he made his way along the streets of Mayfair toward his town house in Bruton Street. Absorbed in thought, he paid no heed to the late-night chill or the tendrils of thick gray fog swirling about his heels.

Sir Henry Neyle, he was musing, was not exactly his bosom friend, but until now they had seemed to find each other's company tolerably amusing. Until now, thought the earl, his scowl deepening. Now he was no longer amused.

It was rapidly becoming plain to him that the bonds of friendship did not stretch as far as he had thought. Sir Henry quite clearly subscribed to the precept that all was fair in love, except that to the earl's way of thinking, there was very little of the loverlike in the intent to offer a virtuous lady like Diana Verney a slip on the shoulder. Even were it offered with the greatest finesse in the world, Lord Lucan was sure that Diana would consider such an offer an insult. And he could not help but agree.

Of course, there were women who, far from being offended by such an offer, would consider themselves flattered, and they were not necessarily women of low birth, either. But Lord Lucan was confident that his beautiful Diana was not one of these. Moreover, since he strongly suspected that her marriage to Edmund Verney had been unpleasant, he preferred that she be spared any further distress. Why he should feel so strongly about this all of a sudden, he did not pause to analyze. But just the thought of that scoundrel Verney being married to Diana brought the earl's fingers bunching into hard fists. He'd been barely acquainted with the man, but he'd known enough *of* him to be disgusted by the stories he'd heard. And he damned well did not want Harry causing her more pain!

As he had quite truthfully told Diana, he had admired her for a very long time. Could it really be six years since he had first seen her? He could recall as if it were yesterday exactly how she had looked when he'd first clapped eyes upon her, how her golden hair had been piled high atop her head, how her demure white gown had clung so tantalizingly to her figure. A small corsage of pink roses had been pinned at her breast, he remembered.

A mere minute of conversation with her had been enough to assure him that the proud tilt to her chin sprang, not from a sense of her own consequence, but from courage, a feisty, stubborn kind of courage that demanded she conceal her own nervousness. He had thought her beautiful, of course, and wildly desirable, and that, combined with the spirit she'd clearly possessed, had been enough to make him want her, a wanting that had never quite gone away.

With a tired sigh, the earl breathed in the cold night air, his hands thrust deep in the pockets of his coat. Even yesterday in the Park, he thought, hadn't she shown courage? Even when her pale, strained features had betrayed her inner apprehension, she had held her head high. And after his assistance with the Lady Edgerton business she had rallied gamely, not faltering once throughout the remainder of the drive.

The major mistake of his life, he reflected, was allowing his father to arrange his first marriage. He had not expected love, nor had he looked for it or even desired it, particularly. However, he had wanted companionship, hoped for children, and expected faithfulness . . . and his wife had given him none of these things. Despite all this, he did not feel bitter, since he doubted whether Laurette had been any happier than he. And since she had been dead now for nearly two years, he had had ample time to come to terms with his feelings. He knew he did not want to spend the rest of his life alone, and therefore it was logical that he remarry.

A pity he had gotten off on the wrong foot with Diana that first day. He realized now that he ought not to have studied her so openly, but he'd been unable to prevent himself from doing so. His nature had always been direct—too direct for some. Briefly, he wondered if his elevated station in life had encouraged him to be this way. No, he decided, that was gammon. He would have been the same had he been born in a haycock and raised in the meanest circumstances.

Dammit, if only he had been free to woo her the first time around! Since Laurette's death, he'd been making more of these periodic visits to London, hoping Diana would eventually come back. As she finally had.

Well, he would win her now, he told himself, his jaw set in a stubborn line. And it would have to be soon. If she accepted an offer from him, Sir Henry would never have the chance to make his dishonorable offer, and she would never need know of the intended insult. It was, he reasoned, a most satisfactory solution to the problem.

And so, though some inner voice was urging him to go very slowly in his courtship, another part of him was equally determined to move swiftly. After all, there was no doubt in his mind that he was the right man for Diana.

All he had to do was convince her of that.

Chapter Six

The next few days were unseasonably warm and bright with sunshine. For Diana, they were days of unalloyed pleasure, for no dark event occurred to mar their early spring glory or make her regret her decision to come to London.

On the first morning after Aunt Serena's dinner party, she, Aimee, and Miss Tilden set out for the nearest lending library. There, they encountered a number of people, mostly ladies who were known to Diana. Most of the women greeted her with a mixture of surprise and kindness, which in turn surprised Diana, for she had been prepared for much less in the way of welcome. She was even more gratified when three of these ladies proceeded to pay her a call the following day, and in return, Diana began making her own morning visits, dutifully introducing her young sister to various members of the *ton*. Best of all, she managed to avoid Lady Edgerton completely, which she could not deny was a factor in the success of these hours.

Cousin Charles called upon them twice, which cast Aimee into such raptures that Diana was forced, out of a sense of duty, to remind her young sister that there was really nothing remarkable in their own cousin paying them a visit. She did not, of course, wish to be deliberately unkind but she firmly believed that Aimee needed to be brought to a sense of reality about the situation. After all, there was no guarantee that Charles was looking to marry and she did not want Aimee to be hurt. Whether her warning was sown upon fertile ground, however, was uncertain.

The second time Cousin Charles came to call he brought Lord Lucan with him. They had been looking at horses together earlier in the day, and it seemed to Diana that the two men were getting along amazingly well. Upon this occasion, she welcomed Lord Lucan's company, it giving her sister a chance to converse with Charles without their cousin feeling obliged to give Diana equal time. And since the earl said nothing too provoking, she was able to enjoy the time she spent in talking with him without reservation. Indeed, they had more than once exchanged amused looks at some of Aimee and Charles's discourse, which they could not help but overhear.

Aimee had worn a pout after each of Charles's visits. "He is so very proper, Diana," she complained. "I thought he would pay me compliments and flirt with me. Eliza told me that is what the London gentlemen are wont to do."

Diana regarded her sister earnestly. "It is greatly to his credit that he does not," she protested. "And hardly surprising either, considering you are chaperoned. I can think of no reason why Eliza Fingleshaw should be held as an expert on these matters. Anyway, I don't believe Cousin Charles is the sort of gentlemen who, er, flirts."

"But, Diana," said Aimee, disappointed. "I can't quite believe that."

"And why not?" inquired Diana, threading her needle. She was mending a torn flounce on Aimee's gown.

"Well," said Aimee, mulling her answer over with

some care, "I know it will sound shockingly vain, but I . . . I cannot help but think he admires me, Diana. I can't explain it, but . . . it's in his eyes, you see. I daresay you don't know what I mean," she added naively.

"Actually," remarked Diana, recollecting a similar expression in the earl's gray eyes, "I believe I do. But Aimee, what you probably see is his . . . attraction to you physically. It does not mean he is in love with you. *That* is completely different. It is very important that you understand that. Nor is love necessarily accompanied by a desire to flirt."

Aimee looked crestfallen. "Well, then, how will I know if he is in love with me?"

"I expect he will show it in other ways," replied Diana, quite firmly.

By prior arrangement, Cousin Charles brought round a perky little brown mare two mornings later for Aimee to try. Diana had no reservations about allowing Aimee to go, for their cousin was not only a complete gentleman, but a bruising rider, as well. He ought, she reasoned, to be able to curb any desire on Aimee's part to display her riding prowess to an excessive degree. At least Diana placed her reliance on his being able to do so.

Aimee's eyes widened with pleasure at her first glimpse of the horse. "Oh, Charles, what a beautiful creature!" she cried, in the most natural fashion she had yet used with him. "Is she truly for me?" Her glowing gaze was riveted on the mare, so that she missed his amused expression.

"Well, the truth is she ain't exactly ours yet," he answered, shoving his hands in his pockets. "Belongs to a fellow named Montague. Friend of mine, y'see. He agreed to let me borrow Pansy so you could try out her paces. Dashed silly name, but we can always change it. If she's right for you, then I'll make him an offer."

"Oh, I'm sure she'll be perfect," replied Aimee caressingly, more to the horse than to her handsome cousin. Her hands reached out to stroke the mare's satiny neck. "Won't you, Pansy? What a little beauty you are!" she whispered.

Thinking to himself that the term fit the girl better than the horse, Charles watched his cousin indulgently. After all, he had gone to a dashed lot of trouble to persuade Monty to consider parting with Pansy, so he was pleased to see that Aimee apparently appreciated his efforts on her behalf. Since at the moment, at least, Pansy had drawn the whole of her attention, he turned aside to deliver a message to Diana.

"Lord Lucan is fetching a horse around for you to try, Diana. Sent his apology for the short notice, and asked me to tell you . . . ah, I mean *ask* you to . . . ah . . . be ready." As Diana's face stiffened, her cousin's voice grew hesitant. "Ought to be here soon. Hope it ain't a problem . . ." Charles dwindled into uneasy silence.

Although Diana did not immediately reply, the glint of wrath in her brown-gold eyes would have been evident to anyone. Be ready! So now, *now*, she was supposed to make herself ready at the earl's least command! Dictatorial, arrogant man! Forcing herself to respond as evenly as possible, she retorted, "All right, Charles. I'll go and change into my habit, then. Thank you for telling me."

Diana walked briskly into the house, wondering crossly what sort of a horse he would attempt to foist upon her. Since this would be the first time she had ever ridden in London, the earl could know nothing of her abilities in the saddle. And since she had not deigned to defend those abilities, as Aimee had done, she found it difficult to believe he would take her at her word and bring her a worthy mount. If he did not, she thought mutinously, she would soon show him how wrong he had been not to listen to her! It was irksome enough to feel she had to prove herself capable of handling the beast before it was purchased!

Still stewing, Diana paced back and forth the length of her bedchamber. He ought to have called and let her know. He ought to have asked if she were free. At the very least, he could have sent her a note! She had nearly made up her mind to deny him admittance when Miss Tilden peered hesitantly into her room.

"Diana, dear, do you have any idea where I put my— Why, whatever is the matter?"

"That man!" ground out Diana, halting her steps. "That horrid man has *dared* to send me messages through my own cousin. He dares to tell me to be ready for him when he arrives at some unspecified time which is probably soon! Can you credit such arrogance, Tildy? He deserves to be punished!"

Miss Tilden looked perplexed. "What horrid man are you speaking of, my dear? Do we know any horrid men? I cannot conceive who—"

"Lord Lucan!" interrupted Diana fiercely. "He is bringing me a horse and I am supposed to make myself ready for him."

Miss Tilden blinked. "Well, in that case, perhaps you ought to begin putting on your habit, my dear."

Diana stared at her companion. "Tildy! Do you seriously expect me to do this man's bidding? Simply drop everything and jump to obey?"

Miss Tilden cast a quick glance around the bedchamber. "But what is it that you must drop?" she inquired, in reasonable bewilderment. "I thought you said you had no plans for the morning."

Diana waved an impatient hand. "I do not! But what is that to the point? I *might* have had other plans! He could not have known!"

"But do you?" continued Miss Tilden, with what Diana considered exasperating persistance.

Frustrated, Diana resumed her pacing. "No! That is—no! But, do you not see? Here is a man who . . . a philanderer, Tildy, who—"

"A philanderer?" repeated Miss Tilden in bafflement. "Are you sure, Diana?"

"Positive," asserted Diana fervently. "He has *flirted* with me, Tildy. He had dared to—*ooh!* I cannot speak of it."

Miss Tilden looked askance. "Well," she declared, with an air of disapproval, "if he has flirted with you, Diana, you must have nothing more to do with him! We cannot allow him into the house again! You are not to go riding with him. You must tell her ladyship that—"

"No, Tildy, no!" protested Diana, oddly unwilling to go to such extremes. "You do not understand. He is not that bad! He is not like Edmund, for heaven's sake. It is just that he is so . . . so . . . irritating. So *infuriating!*"

Miss Tilden's bombazine-covered chest rose and fell in a slightly reproachful sigh. "I cannot make heads or tails out of what you are saying, Diana. Are you or are you not going riding with this man?"

Her eyes focused somewhere in the distance, Diana suddenly smiled. "Oh, I daresay I shall, Tildy. But not, I fear, today. I have suddenly recalled several letters that I must write. If his lordship wishes for company, I shall suggest that he ride with his groom!"

Miss Tilden looked dubious. "Goodness, Diana," she quavered. "I do hope you know what you're doing . . ."

In preparation for the impending confrontation, Diana changed into her most becoming morning gown, and was on the point of descending to the first floor when sounds from below told her the earl had arrived. Unable to resist stealing a look out the window of her bedchamber, Diana tiptoed back into her room and peered downward. Below her in the street stood his lordship's groom holding the reins of a large bay gelding and a smaller, rather unprepossessing gray mare. Obviously, the bay belonged to his lordship, so the mare must be for her. Well, the animal did not look like a *complete* slug, she mused, but of course one could tell very little without closer examination. As with people, a horse's appearance could be misleading.

As she entered the drawing room, Diana could not help noticing that Lord Lucan looked far more at home in his riding coat and breeches than he had in formal evening clothes. Somehow, the very casualness of the attire accentuated his masculinity, reminding her of the underlying reason for his presence. This man, she told herself warningly, was only here because he wanted her to become his mistress. It would not do to forget that fact.

Ignoring her greeting, the earl took a step forward, then seemed to check himself. "My dear Mrs. Verney, did you not receive my message?" he asked, rather abruptly.

"What message was that, my lord?" inquired Diana in an innocent tone.

His eyes passed over her gown. "Your cousin was to ask you to be ready for riding. You look quite enchanting, my dear, but I must ask you to put on your habit as quickly as possible. I've brought you a horse I think you will like."

Diana yawned delicately. "My dear Lord Lucan, I fear you can have no conception of how busy I am. I cannot possibly go riding this morning. I am sure I have at least a dozen things to do. Of course, had you made your request—dare I call it a request?—in a less peremptory style, perhaps I could have rearranged my schedule."

"Ah, I see," he murmured, a hint of lazy humor entering his voice. "This is a display of claws. Well, then, what are they?"

Diana stared at him. "What are what?"

"What must you do that is so important?"

Taken aback, Diana answered, "Why, for one thing, I have letters to write—"

"Write them later," he advised. "The horses are waiting and the weather is perfect."

Diana bristled. "Has anyone ever told you that you are insufferable?"

"Yes, you!" he replied with a chuckle. "Now, be a good girl and go put on your habit—" He paused, then added, in a disarmingly humble voice, "please."

She eyed him for a long moment, then saw the faint quiver at the corner of his mouth. "Oh, you are odious!" she exclaimed. "I would send you about your business, my lord, except for the fact that—" She stopped.

"Yes?" prompted the earl, an unholy glint in his eye.

"—that it would not be fair to the horse!" she finished, with something of a snap.

The earl was left kicking up his heels in the drawing room for a mere fifteen minutes, for Diana, once deciding to relent, was not about to waste time dallying when she could be enjoying her favorite form of exercise. Her crop tucked beneath one arm, she soon returned, and even went so far as to bestow a genuine smile upon the earl.

"Well, shall we go?" she inquired. "I should not like to keep this spirited animal you have brought me prancing in the street."

The provocative words slipped out automatically, for this verbal sparring with him was becoming a habit. And not only that, she realized suddenly, it was actually exhilarating to speak thus. But how foolish she was to allow the mere bantering of words to excite her, she thought in embarrassment.

As if trying to read her thoughts, the earl cast her a slightly quizzical look as he gestured toward the door.

"After you," he said.

Once outside, Diana approached the mare critically. It was certainly not the showiest horse in the world, but that did not matter in the least. What concerned the young widow was the mare's quality, and with this in mind, she began circling the horse, assessing every detail of the animal's physique.

She was interrupted by the earl's amused voice. "I assure you, my dear, she's quite healthy. No spavins, cataracts, corns, or dropsy. Her teeth are good, her hocks are not enlarged, and no respiratory disease has yet settled in her lungs. Nor does she bite, kick, or bolt, as far as I have been able to determine."

Ignoring his bantering tone, Diana replied fairly, "Indeed, in appearance, at least, she seems satisfactory. And her tail has not been docked, thank goodness. What is her name?"

He made a wry face. "Ophelia. Someone apparently had a liking for Shakespeare. I trust that neither of you will end your days floating down the Thames, however."

Diana smiled involuntarily as Ophelia tossed her head and shifted her feet, as if to suggest her disdain for such a notion. "There, now, we won't allow that to happen," she told the mare. Reaching into her pocket, Diana withdrew a small lump of sugar. "Here, Ophelia," she offered, her voice soft and coaxing. "I've brought you a treat."

As the mare's nose nuzzled gently into Diana's hand, the earl took the opportunity to study the woman he intended to marry. She appeared absurdly young to him at that moment, as if the six intervening years had never been, and she was no more than a young girl of eighteen or nineteen, an innocent in a world of sophisticates. Her face, he observed, was clear of the tiny lines which many women her age already wore about their eyes and brow. Not only that, but she still retained that indefinable air of purity he'd noticed long ago, well before she had entered into that travesty of a marriage. How this could be was a bit of an enigma to him. In fact, there was a good deal about Diana that he failed to understand, but he was becoming more and more determined to do so.

About to comment upon the mare's friendliness, Diana glanced up, catching her breath as she encountered the earl's speculative gaze. There was that expression in his eyes again. It burned her, that look, and filled her with . . . something. Confusion? Fear? No, not fear, but an uneasy, shaky sort of feeling that brought a weakness to her knees.

"My lord?" she inquired, summoning a reproving tone. "Is there, perhaps, a spot on my nose to make you stare so?" It would never do to let him know how strange he made her feel.

He answered immediately, breaking the spell with some easy reply as he offered her a hand up onto Ophelia's back. What he actually said Diana would have been hard put to repeat, for her thoughts were in such a whirl that she barely attended. That smile of his was dangerous, she reflected a little nervously. Good gracious, it was nearly enough to wipe away her suspicions, nay, her *knowledge* of his true intentions! Such a state of affairs must not be allowed to continue! But what on earth was she going to do about it?

It may or may not have been this episode that brought both riders to a state of somber reflection, but whatever the case, they reached the Park without much conversation passing between them. It was still early enough that the dew sparkled wet upon the grass, and as they urged their mounts to a brisker pace, a small flock of starlings rose up from some nearby sanctum, objecting shrilly to their presence. Of either Aimee or Charles, there was no sign.

109

"Come," said the earl, turning to Diana. "Let's give these horses some exercise. Brutus is longing for a chance to stretch his legs, and at a guess, I would say that Ophelia shares his sentiments."

Diana's eye brightened at the opportunity to display her horsemanship. As they eased the horses into a canter, she discovered that Ophelia, far from being a slug, was just about the sweetest-goer she had ever been privileged to ride. The mare responded instantly to her rider's directives, her silken mouth sensitive to the slightest movement of the reins. She was fast, too, and Diana, delighted by Ophelia's unexpected fleetness, narrowed her eyes against the wind and gave herself over to the enjoyment of the ride.

When at last they slowed, the earl turned to observe her reaction. "Well?" he inquired, one dark brow rising. "What do you think of her?"

"I think that I owe you an apology," Diana told him ruefully. "I honestly did not think much of your choice until now."

"Ah," said the earl in satisfaction.

"She is a perfect lady," she continued, reaching down to pat Ophelia's glossy back, "yet with enough spirit and passion in her to satisfy the most particular rider. I should very much like to own this graceful, splendid animal."

The earl maneuvered his gelding nearer to Diana. "A perfect lady for a perfect lady," he stated simply. "Each with more than her share of spirit . . . and passion."

Diana flushed a little. "My lord, please. You must not say such things."

Lord Lucan regarded her intently. "Why not? There's no one but you to hear me. Come, let's neaten you up a trifle." He startled her by reaching casually to tuck back a golden curl that had escaped from its confining coil. As he did so, his thumb brushed her cheek—on purpose,

Diana was convinced—causing her to involuntarily tighten her grip upon the reins. To her embarrassment, the mare's obedient sidling brought the two horses even closer, so that the side of her leg pressed against the earl's top boot.

"I think Ophelia has developed a liking for Brutus," remarked the earl in a lazy voice. "How very convenient."

Hastily urging her mount into a walk, Diana searched for an appropriate response. Finally she said, in a faint but dignified voice, "You have not yet indicated, my lord, whether I passed muster."

Following beside her, the earl's brows lifted, and a trace of laughter crept into his voice. "Passed muster, my sweet? Once again you are confusing me. As charmingly as ever, of course."

She threw him a resentful look. "I refer to my ability in the saddle, of course. Are you satisfied that I can stay on a horse without falling off? Will you purchase Ophelia for me?"

To her discomfiture, he laughed. "My dear Diana, I fear you are laboring under a misapprehension. Ophelia is yours. I've already paid for her."

Diana stared at him, torn between amazement and an unseemly urge to scratch the smile from his face. "I have not given you leave to make free with my name, my lord," she pointed out, seizing upon the inconsequential with icy determination.

"Not yet," he swiftly conceded. "An omission we shall have to rectify."

"And I was under the impression that my aunt was to pay for the horse!" she pursued, eyeing him with suspicion.

"Oh, I promise you I'll send her the bill. Good God, did you really think I would put you on trial? I shouldn't dare, you know." He had the temerity to grin at her.

"Oh?" she said, glaring back.

"I've already had a taste of your temper," he reminded her, by way of explanation. He chuckled again, a deep sound that was curiously infectious. "In any case, I never for a moment doubted your ability to ride well."

Diana was puzzled. "But my cousin merely borrowed the horse he brought for Aimee!"

"Ah, but that was different," said Lord Lucan enigmatically.

"And why is that?"

He decided to be blunt. "Because your sister is a regular minx, and will say anything to impress your cousin. If I were he, I wouldn't believe half of what comes out of her mouth."

"That's not true!" cried Diana, defending her sister hotly. "How can you say that? You don't even know my sister! And Aimee happens to be an extremely competent horsewoman!"

"Is she?" he said, with detached interest. "Well, good for her, then. But I still think she's bound for trouble. If you want my advice, you'll keep a tight hold on her bridle while she's in town."

Diana's lips tightened. "I really don't recall asking your advice," she countered. At his amused look, she added bitterly, "I suppose the next thing you'll say is that trouble runs in the family!"

The words slipped out before she could stop them. Horrified at the inadvertent reference to her own scandalous past, Diana averted her eyes, wondering what answer he could possibly make. Perhaps he was so shocked he would merely pretend he had not heard. *Dear Lord, that would be worse than anything else*, she thought, though she had not an inkling of a notion why that should be so.

His eyes compassionate, the earl said deliberately, "No, I wouldn't say that." When she did not respond, he sighed, and said, as gently as possible, "Diana, look at me. My poor girl, I would never say such a thing to you! What makes you think that I would?"

At length, Diana turned helpless eyes upon him. "I'm sorry," she said inadequately.

He reached out to clasp her hand. "Don't be sorry. Say anything you like to me, but don't apologize. It's the best way to deal with my sort. That's what I've been trying to show you. That we can bypass all the polite, conventional, empty"—he hesitated, searching for a suitable word—"*palaver* that most of humanity seems to indulge in. The poppycock, as your aunt would say. The inanities. I'm no great hand at that kind of thing, as you probably noticed."

"I noticed," said Diana, swallowing hard as she pulled her hand from his warm grasp.

"Besides," he added, "you didn't ask for what happened to you. That's the difference between you and your sister."

"Oh, but I did," she muttered, too softly for him to hear.

At the far end of the Park, Aimee was fast approaching the conclusion that Cousin Charles was not as easygoing as he seemed. The uncompromising set of his mouth told her that she had done something wrong, but why, she wondered, did he not say anything? Good gracious, his very bearing was condemnatory, she noted in distress. She must end this silence.

"Charles, are you . . . are you angry with me?" Aimee cleared her throat nervously and fixed him with an imploring gaze. "Please speak to me."

Thawing only slightly at the entreaty in her voice, Charles turned his head to send her a look of acute male exasperation. "Dash it, Aimee, you just don't *do* things

113

like that in Hyde Park! Neck-or-nothing riding is for the *country!* Don't you know that?"

"Oh," said Aimee, much abashed. "No, I didn't."

"What the devil made you take off like that, anyway?" asked Charles with a frown.

A lump began to form in Aimee's throat. "But I thought that . . . well, when you said there was nothing grander than allowing a horse its head I thought you meant . . . oh dear! I am so sorry, Charles. I see I made a mistake."

Once begun, Cousin Charles seemed intent on giving her a complete trimming. "You're dashed lucky no one saw you!" he grumbled, ignoring her apology. "No one but a pair of servants, that is, and a handful of nursery brats and governesses!"

Reaching out, he snapped his fingers under her pert little nose. "If they had, I'd have given *that* for your chances of getting into Almack's!" he told her brutally. "And what's more, word would soon have gotten around that Aimee Farington is a hoyden and a romp! What a pretty hobble that would have been, eh? Is that what you want? To set the London tongues wagging about your exploits?"

A single teardrop trembled in the corner of Aimee's eyes. "Please don't be angry with me, Charles. I won't do it again."

"And if that weren't bad enough," continued Charles irately, "you had to go and ride through the pond! Not around the pond, mind you, but *through* it!"

"I only did it to make the little boy laugh. He looked so sad, sitting there with his broken toy boat. I do hope his papa fixes it for him!"

Charles gave her a pained look. "Well, he laughed all right! So did all the other brats within a hundred yards of us! And who would not, to see such a spectacle?"

Unchecked, the teardrop slid down Aimee's pale

cheek. "Was I truly so very bad?" she whispered.

"Bad!" snorted Charles. He was about to add several more choice words upon her want of conduct, when he noticed the tear. "Oh, Lord," he relented with a groan. "For God's sake, now, don't cry, Aimee! I didn't mean to rip up at you." Realizing how heartless he must have sounded, Charles strove to make amends. "Hang it, if we'd been in the country, I wouldn't have objected in the least! You're a Trojan in the saddle, Aimee! Got a dashed fine seat, as a matter of fact. Who taught you to ride?"

Aimee brightened a little at the compliment. "My papa. He was once an excellent horseman, but he doesn't ride much any more. He had a fall a few years ago, and finds it uncomfortable."

"Well," said Charles matter-of-factly, "he knew what he was about, that much is obvious. I'll have to have a talk with Diana, though. We can't have you making these kinds of mistakes."

"No," agreed Aimee, her face once more downcast. This was not going at all the way she had planned, she reflected unhappily. She had meant to make a favorable impression upon Charles, not provoke him into lecturing her like a child!

As for Charles, his opinion of his cousin had, in the last half-hour, undergone a rapid and thorough transformation. His sanguine conviction that such an angel could not be less than perfect had fled faster than Pansy across the grassy fields of Hyde Park. Granted, she was a regular out-and-outer in the saddle, but a delicately nurtured, gently bred girl hardly out of the schoolroom ought not to behave in such a hoydenish fashion!

Lucan had been right, Charles sighed inwardly. Cousin Aimee would likely prove as difficult to handle as his grandmother. Did he really want to leg-shackle himself to a girl like this? Lord only knew what sort of a dance she would lead him on next! He was going to have to give this some serious reconsideration.

When Aimee's escapade came to Diana's ears, her first reaction was one of reproach. However, it very quickly dawned upon her that her sister was still smarting from Cousin Charles's strictures, and for her to add her own admonishments would be superfluous. Notwithstanding this, she did point out, as gently as possible, something she was sure their cousin's delicacy would forbid him to do.

"You see, dearest," she explained, compunction filling her brown-gold eyes, "because of what happened to me, you must take even greater care of your reputation. I cannot overstress this. There are those who would be only too glad to dredge up an old scandal. They would compare the two of us, you see. They would say that the Farington girls are all the same, that we are bold and ill-bred, and that no decent man would consider allying himself to one of us. And the damage could even extend to Elizabeth and Dorothy and Louisa."

Aimee stared incredulously. "But that is so unfair!" she cried out. "All I did was allow Pansy to gallop! And the pond was hardly a pond at all. Scarcely deep enough to wade in!"

Diana nodded. "Yes, well, it does seem unfair. I told you things were different in London. You must learn to conform, at least on the surface. Enough to fool people. I don't believe Cousin Charles would like you to become a complete pattern-card of propriety. How dull!" she added, with an encouraging smile.

Aimee scowled. "I am beginning to think Charles is a bit of a prig," she retorted. "He will not flirt with me, but he is only too ready to give me a rake-down when I make a mistake!"

"If you give it some thought," said Diana patiently, "I

think you will see that his actions can only commend him. He is trying to protect you from—"

"From myself!" flashed Aimee, springing to her feet. "Oh, I understand perfectly!" And with a tiny sob, she ran from the room, leaving Diana to stare after her in distress.

It was not the most propitious moment to receive a caller. Nevertheless, when Sir Henry Neyle was ushered into the drawing room less than a minute later, Diana was able to force away her frown and to greet him with a semblance of a smile.

It had been nearly a week since she had seen him, and she realized with some surprise that she had devoted very little thought to him in the interim. However, his presence served to reawaken her awareness of his existence. What a contrast he was to Lord Lucan, she found herself thinking. How incredibly handsome he was, so tall and slim, with so classic a profile and hair more golden than her own. She could only wonder why such an Adonis had never married, when he could surely have had his pick among the eligible young ladies.

"I am so very glad to find you at home," said Sir Henry, lifting her hand and pressing it to his lips. With a boyish smile, he went on, "I was moping around this afternoon, feeling quite ridiculously bored, and then I said to myself, Harry, old boy, why don't you just pay a visit on the charming Mrs. Verney? *She'll* cheer you up! And here I am!"

Diana's smile warmed in automatic response to his charm. "Well, I cannot promise to cheer you up but I shall certainly try. May I offer you some sherry?"

"Well . . ." His eyes sparkled with mischief. "What I'd truly like is a glass of brandy. Does that shock you?"

"Not at all," she answered, calmly ringing for Lawrence.

The brandy was soon delivered, and Sir Henry, glass in

117

hand, followed her across the room, and flustered her by easing his chair a little closer to her own. "Do I make you nervous?" he asked, watching her face.

"Nervous?" echoed Diana. "No. No, of course not."

"Good. I should dislike that to be so. I want us to be comfortable together." He crossed one elegantly clad leg over the other, and sent her another enchanting smile. "So, pray enlighten me, Mrs. Verney. I am dying to know the answer to the mystery."

"I beg your pardon?" said Diana in perplexity.

With a sip of his drink, Sir Henry appeared to be studying the tassel on his gleaming Hessians. "To put it simply, why the long rustication? Did you dislike London as much as that?" He sounded diverted by the possibility.

Diana gave a small laugh. "Of course not. I merely stayed in Wiltshire to be near my family. It is very pleasant there."

His raised eyebrow connoted disbelief. "Indeed? But *not* dreadfully exciting, I'll wager." He took another swallow of the brandy, savoring the fiery liquid as it ran down his throat.

"No," she admitted, feeling defensive. "But I was not looking for excitement, Sir Henry. I had just lost a husband, you may recall," she added, seeking refuge in this excuse.

He smiled. "Ah, yes. How could I have been so stupid as to forget? Allow me to extend my condolences, Mrs. Verney, though I realize, of course, that they're a trifle late."

"Thank you," she murmured, wishing she could come up with a more witty, more sociable reply.

Suddenly, the baronet leaned forward and regarded her intently. "I never forgot you, you know."

"Oh?" All at once, Diana felt breathless. "How . . . how kind of you, Sir Henry."

"Not kind," he informed her dryly. "The truth of the

matter is that it would be hard for me to forget a woman as beautiful as yourself."

Diana could only gaze at him in wonder. Had this divinely handsome man just told her she was beautiful?

"You won't run away again, will you?" he asked, setting down his glass abruptly. "Because I do want us to become more closely acquainted. That would make me so very happy."

Diana's heart began to beat faster. "It would make me happy, too," she answered shyly.

Slowly, the corners of the baronet's mouth lifted. "Good," he said, very softly. "You see? I knew you would cheer me up."

Chapter Seven

On the whole, the days preceding Aunt Serena's ball passed a trifle too quickly for Diana's peace of mind, and on the morning of that event, she was not yet mentally prepared for it. After all, the ball's purpose was to launch her beloved sister into the world of the London *ton*, the world that Diana had for so long chosen to eschew. Recognizing, however, that it was far too late for retreat, the young widow resolutely thrust aside her worries. It was perfectly natural, she chided herself, to feel a bit apprehensive, but it would not do to let her imagination run wild. Aimee would be fine, and as for herself, well, she was not about to cry craven now!

The ball, Diana knew, would trigger an onslaught of invitations to every sort of social function, making it necessary for them to plan each day with almost military precision. Indeed, she thought wryly, there were those who treated the London Season as seriously as one of Wellington's campaigns—the enemy, of course, being all unmarried gentlemen of rank and fortune.

To be honest, Diana supposed she was no better than the rest, for she was as anxious as any matchmaking mama for her sister to marry—though not just any gentleman would do, of course. It was still far too early to ascertain whether Cousin Charles would prove a contender for her sister's hand, but Diana could not deny that she would hail such an occurrence with relief. Aimee, she had decided, needed a husband whose steadying influence would counterbalance her volatility, and she rather thought that Cousin Charles might be that man. Without doubt, however, the sensible course was to encourage Aimee to keep an open mind, and this was what Diana had been attempting to do for the past few days. There would be many other young men as eligible as Cousin Charles, as she had dutifully pointed out to her pugnacious sister.

Beyond all this, there were other concerns preying on Diana's mind, not the least of which was her own future. Just lately, she had been unnerved to discover that what she had so wholeheartedly believed she wanted—to remain a widow—no longer seemed as enticing. Her doubts on the subject needed to be resolved, and when was she going to have a chance to reflect upon it? After tonight's ball, she would be lucky to have enough time to sleep, much less think!

Oh, if only her emotions would not keep flip-flopping! On some days, she would find herself believing that her only hope of happiness lay in remaining a widow, yet on others, she would discover that the notion of remarriage (if she did not dwell overmuch upon its implications) was almost appealing. This latter way of thinking occurred more when she was feeling lonely or tired or when Aimee's bright but ceaseless chatter reverberated in her ears. Widowhood seemed more attractive at night, when memories of Edmund's pawing sent shivers of revulsion up her spine.

Sir Henry Neyle, she decided, was largely responsible for this soul-searching, for his remarks of the other day had seemed to indicate that he was considering making her an offer. Diana did not know what answer she would make—that was one of the things she had yet to decide—but still, how very gratifying it was! There was so much to admire abut Sir Henry, she reflected. He was strikingly handsome, his conversation was light and witty, and it was reassuringly obvious that he cherished no dark, ulterior purpose in seeking her out. Furthermore, in his company she could feel more like the self-possessed, sophisticated woman she longed to be, a woman who was not thrown out of countenance by an overbold look or a mocking remark. And he did not stand so close to her that he affected her ability to breathe properly, as another certain gentleman was discourteous enough to do.

But she must not start thinking of *him*. Instead, Diana determinedly turned her attention to the ball gown she had chosen to wear for the evening. It was new and made of Italian crepe, its unusual color, according to the dressmaker, being the exact same shade of turquoise blue as the Aegean Sea. What would Sir Henry say when he saw her in it, she wondered? Picturing the scenario, her eagerness for the coming evening began to quicken. Sir Henry's divinely blue eyes would shine with admiration, and he would lift her hand to his lips, and murmur something perfectly delightful, something like—

"Diana!" A sharp rapping sound put an end to her reverie. "Are you there? Can I come in?" Aimee opened the door enough to poke her head inside the bedchamber.

"Of course," said Diana in resignation. "I was just about to come down." Observing Aimee's odd expression, she added, more curiously, "What is it?"

Instead of perching on the bed as she usually did, Aimee drifted across the room to gaze broodingly out the window. "I wanted to talk to you, that's all," she replied, her back to Diana. After a pause, she threw over her shoulder. "Do you think it is going to rain?"

"I hope not. But in case it does, I think we should do as Aunt Serena wants and take our evening clothes over to

Arlington Street. We can get ready over there just as easily, and Meg can come with us . . . Tildy, too, if she likes."

Aimee nodded absently. "You know," she said, "I've been thinking about what you said." She swung around suddenly. "About Charles, I mean."

"Oh?"

Wandering over to the dressing table, she began to finger the various articles on its surface. "I don't always listen to you, Diana, but this time I am wondering if perhaps you are right. Why should I marry Charles? Why should I wed someone who is going to do nothing but find fault with me?"

"Now, Aimee, I never said—"

"It would make far more sense to marry someone who adores me, someone who will worship the very ground I walk on. Someone rich, of course, and divinely handsome. Someone who will never tell me what to do, or, more importantly, what *not* to do!"

Diana eyed her sister. "I really don't think that—"

"Someone," continued Aimee relentlessly, "who will love me so much that if I even *look* at another man he will be jealous enough to blow his brains out!"

"Oh, dear." Diana sank helplessly into the nearest chair. "I fear you would not care for that, my dear, if you would but consider—"

Aimee's lip curled. "Naturally," she went on, "I should not desire him to go through with it. But would it not be wonderful to be so loved, so adored, so *venerated?*"

"It might sound pleasant, of course, but do you not think such devotion might become a bit wearying?"

Aimee put down the brush she had been holding and gave her sister a puzzled look. "Wearying?"

Diana searched for a better word. "Tedious, then. Or even oppressive. And only think how difficult it would be to feel deserving of such adoration!"

123

Ignoring the latter part of this speech, Aimee frowned. "Do you mean it might be boring? I hadn't thought of that."

"Perhaps you should," Diana advised, as gently as possible. "Marriage is not something to be treated lightly, my dear. It can be of very long duration."

Aimee's nose wrinkled. "But I can't always resolve these things just by thinking them out. For me, it works best if I can, well, try it first, to see for myself."

"Well, you cannot do that with marriage!" objected Diana, somewhat sharply.

Aimee gave her a surprised look. "I know that. I just meant that if I were to find a gentleman who *adored* me, I could better judge whether I liked it or not."

"Yes, but—" Diana began.

"I shall have to give this some more thought. Goodness, Diana, you have helped me excessively. Thank you so much!"

And before Diana could say anything more, Aimee flitted from the room.

Aunt Serena cockily prophesied a successful evening all around.

"People flock to my parties," she boasted to Diana, a short while before the preball dinner was due to commence, "because my house is large enough to accommodate 'em all in comfort, and because I put out more than an adequate number of chairs." Her beady eyes silently appraised Diana's gown as she rambled, "And I serve decent refreshments—no paltry skimping there, I'll have you know! Good wine and good food, that's the ticket! Parties ain't the place to pinch pennies, Diana. Remember it, and you'll never want for guests."

"I'll commit it to memory," promised Diana in a mechanical tone.

124

Why must Aunt Serena prate on about this now, she wondered? Surely her aunt must know there was no question of Diana giving any but the smallest, quietest parties—unless, of course, she remarried, thereby acquiring a home with sufficient space to . . . oh, drat Aunt Serena for harping upon the subject, anyway, thought Diana moodily. This was not the time to begin thinking about *that* subject.

Silence reigned for a short time while under the watchful eye of the dowager, Diana's abigail deftly arranged her mistress's golden tresses. When Meg had given a final pat to her work, she tactfully withdrew, leaving Diana alone with the dowager viscountess. Diana's features were set in a cool, pale mask as she turned to exchange stares with her aunt.

Scowling, Aunt Serena broke the silence, no longer circumventing the point she wished to make. "Your presence is a drawing card, too, Diana. Some members of the *ton* will be here just to have a look at you, to see if there's anything to gossip about. And they'll be wondering how little Aimee will conduct herself." *That* ought to bring the girl to life, thought the dowager grimly.

"It doesn't help me at all for you to say that, Aunt Serena," Diana replied, a trifle jerkily.

In response, the dowager's tone sharpened. "It's best if you know the truth! You may think you're up to snuff, but you ain't! You live with your head in some plaguey dream cloud half the time, girl." For emphasis, her cane thudded upon the wooden floor. "Watch yourself tonight! Get rid of that Friday-face and try to act natural. And for God's sake don't disappear anywhere. We don't want to start any talk."

Diana looked stubborn. "The point is taken," she retorted flatly. "Now, if you don't mind, Aunt Serena, I'd rather not discuss it any more."

Yielding to the steel in her niece's voice, Aunt Serena inclined her head. "Very well, Diana. As long as you bear it in mind. I've already warned Aimee, and I'm done warning you—my constitution won't bear any more scandals!"

There were to be thirty guests for dinner. Initially, Aunt Serena had dug in her heels at Diana's request that Sir Henry Neyle be included, but later, to her niece's surprise, she had suddenly capitulated. The truth was, the dowager had decided that more, rather than less, exposure to the baronet's scintillating charm might provide an effective cure for what she considered Diana's corkbrained infatuation with the man. With this new strategy in mind, she seated them together, while cunningly placing the Earl of Lucan within the young widow's view, next to a singularly ravishing (but married) young countess, who had been invited for this sole purpose. On Diana's other side, she put Lord Bathurst, Edmund's uncle.

Unfortunately for the dowager's plan, Sir Henry was on his best behavior this evening. As it happened, competition over a woman invariably heightened his desire to possess her, but in Diana's case, intuition also warned him he was treading on thin ice. Thus challenged, he remained confident but cautious, for even though Diana did not exactly fit his image of a dashing young widow on the lookout for a cicisbeo, Sir Henry could not conceive of a woman who would be unswayed by his powers to charm. He had, in short, made up his mind to play what he felt was a winning hand with a little additional caution.

As delighted as she was to find Sir Henry beside her at dinner, a quarter of the way through the meal Diana had still not been able to exchange more than a few polite words with him. This was due to Lord Bathurst, who was one of those not-so-rare human beings who loved the sound of his own voice, and, who, being very much aware of his own consequence, held the belief that Diana must be equally impressed.

Outwardly, Diana had been lending her late husband's uncle a polite ear, but inwardly she was chafing at his long-windedness. Would the man never stop talking? His lordship had never seemed quite so tiresome as he did at this moment.

". . . lament that I was absent when you arrived in London," he droned in Diana's ear. "My physician felt it advisable that I should drink the waters, y'know. Dreadful time of year to visit Bath. Dreadful! Waste of time, too, for it didn't do me a whit of good, and so I shall tell him, the old squeeze-crab! Every time I listen to that charlatan . . ."

Reaching for her wine, Diana sensed Sir Henry watching her, as he had been doing through much of the dinner. She shifted restively, not daring to look his way too often. Out of nowhere, she recalled her abigail's advice to Aimee. *Don't let the gent see how taken you are with him* . . . Well, that hardly made sense, did it? For how else would a gentleman know how a lady felt about him?

". . . have every right to expect your husband's nearest relation to be on hand to advise you," wheezed Lord Bathurst, patting her hand in a fatherly way. "Naturally you are confused and in need of counsel, for females, in general, are not equipped to make difficult decisions without the guidance of a male . . ."

Between mouthfuls, his lordship prosed on with boorish relentlessness, bringing Diana to the limit of her patience. Finally tossing caution to the four winds, Diana flashed Sir Henry a quick smile, and was elated to discover that she was still the object of his blue-eyed and rather pensive gaze. For Diana, it was a heady experience to have one of the most handsome men in London sitting next to her with his eyes pinned to her face.

". . . cannot entirely approve your decision to live on your own," rattled Lord Bathurst, growing, if possible, more pompous by the minute. "Had I been consulted, I should have advised against a step which might, for an older woman, be considered acceptable, but for a woman who is only just past the first blush of youth . . ."

As his lordship buzzed on, rather like a bee in a particularly fragrant flower, Diana nodded automatically and allowed her thoughts to roam. Although she was not at all sure she wished to remarry, still, how very agreeable it was to have a suitor—for such was she beginning to regard Sir Henry—who made her feel so safe. The emotions he kindled were temperate rather than fiery, and far easier to deal with than those disturbing, turbulent feelings Lord Lucan aroused in her breast.

It was really most unlike Aunt Serena to be so accommodating as to put Sir Henry next to her at dinner. Or had she known that Lord Bathurst would monopolize her so completely that she would have practically no chance to converse with Sir Henry? And whatever had possessed her aunt to place Lord Lucan next to the Countess of Uxbridge? She could not even understand why Aunt Serena would have invited her at all, for the woman looked out of place in this respectable lot of people.

As Lord Bathurst paused to drink, she took the opportunity to study Lady Uxbridge. Honestly, the woman was almost too beautiful, she noted in vague disapproval. With all that glossy, auburn hair and those heavy-lidded green eyes it was small wonder she managed to keep a bevy of gentlemen swarming around her everywhere she went.

128

Covertly, Diana watched Lord Lucan to see how he was reacting to all that allure. He was smiling at something Lady Uxbridge was saying, she observed with a flicker of annoyance. No doubt his reply would be as outrageous and flirtatious as those he fed to herself! For some indefinable reason this notion made her angry, and turning back to Lord Bathurst with a jerk of her head, Diana proceeded to bestow upon that gentleman such a brilliant smile that he decided that he must be even wittier than he had realized.

The truth of the matter was that Lord Lucan was not at all eager to converse with Lady Uxbridge, and would have been far better pleased with some other choice of dinner partner. Despite her seductive eyes and voluptuous figure, Lady Uxbridge did not attract him in the least. Be they ever so beautiful and high-born and discreet, he disliked women who foisted their more than half a dozen illegitimate offspring upon their long-suffering husbands. In particular, he decided he disliked this lady's perfume, a heavy musk, which seemed to have gotten into his food.

So far they had spoken only of trivialities, but as this was going through his mind, she leaned toward him, her scent wafting over his plate more potently than ever. "Such an insipid set of people," she drawled, her rich voice at so low a pitch that only he could hear. "I swear Lady Torrington has assembled in this one room some of the dullest folk in London—save you and I, of course, and perhaps the charming Sir Henry. It makes one wonder why one came, does it not?"

Out of courtesy, he smiled. "If respectability is insipid, madam, then perhaps you are right. Lady Torrington is a high stickler. I doubt you will find many scandals brewing here."

Any irony in his tone was lost on Lady Uxbridge, who generously offered him a fuller view of her bosom. "You

129

and I could always brew one ourselves," she murmured with a suggestive side glance that might have floored a less experienced man. "I just *love* a nice little scandal," she added, licking her lips.

His sardonic reply was intended to squelch that little idea before it took further root in her mind. "We could," he said smoothly. "But then, I hesitate to tread where so many others have trod before. It seems a trifle . . . redundant. Don't you agree?"

This was the exchange that Diana witnessed, but by averting her gaze she missed Lady Uxbridge's furious expression. Diana knew only a sharp stab of unexpected misery as she beamed determinedly at Lord Bathurst. One need not be very much up to snuff, she reflected, a shade bitterly, to discern that Lord Lucan was very much a ladies' man.

Both Aunt Serena and Cousin Charles considered it entirely proper that he lead Aimee out for the first set of country dances. Aimee, certainly, considered it her due. However, she was piqued to discover that Charles felt it unsuitable for him to claim her hand more than once in the same evening. Completely forgetting her own assertion that her cousin was dull, she redoubled her efforts to attract his interest.

"Lady Jersey has given me permission to waltz, Charles," she told him very sweetly and very pointedly, as they waited for the musicians to begin.

Charles noticed her frown. "Oh? Well, that's good, ain't it?"

"Yes, of course it's good," she snapped.

He stared at her in puzzlement. "Then why the gloomy face?"

"Why, what can you possibly mean, Charles?" replied Aimee, her tone brittle. Racking her brain, she wondered how she could possibly make her meaning any clearer. Surely Charles could not be so stupid that he was unable to take a hint.

The dance began, and there was little opportunity to talk until it ended. As he escorted her back to the dowager's side, Aimee managed to hiss into his ear, "I have *one* unclaimed waltz, Charles."

He halted abruptly, and her hopes soared. "Let me see your dance card," he instructed.

Eagerly, Aimee handed it over, but Charles's next words left her nearly speechless. "You ain't got a dance with Lord Lucan, have you? Dash it, that must have been an oversight on his part. I'll just go drop a hint in his ear."

Aimee stared at him in outrage. "Charles," she said finally, "don't *you* want to waltz with me?"

He gave her a genuinely rueful look. "Can't do that, Aimee. Might cause talk. Once is enough."

"But you are my *cousin!*" she squeaked, her hand flying to her mouth as if to control her own voice. "No one would question your right to a second dance."

Charles cleared his throat uncomfortably. "Yes, well, we have to be careful. Reputation is everything, y'know. At least with this set of people it is." He did not add that people might assume that more than mere cousinly affection existed between them—and he was not ready to admit that there was.

Her heart filled with hurt and rage, Aimee spun away from him with a stifled sob. She would teach Charles a lesson, she thought. By the end of the evening, he would be very sorry he had not taken that dance.

Some hours later, however, all was not going according to plan. True, Aimee never lacked either partners or compliments, but none of this seemed to make her feel any better. She had just sent her current partner off to fetch her a glass of punch when she caught sight of

Diana, who was bearing down upon her for the very purpose of having a little talk with her high-spirited young sister.

"Diana," said Aimee in a strained voice, before her elder sister could speak, "who is that girl dancing with Charles?"

Diana turned to look. "I believe her name is Drusilla Low," she said tautly. "She is about your age, Aimee, and seems pleasant. Perhaps you might become friends."

Toying with her fan, Aimee wrinkled her nose in distaste. "I doubt it," she said, her tone as short as Diana's. "Have you noticed how our cousin dances with all the plainest girls? What do you think of that?"

"I think it is very kind of him," replied Diana. She drew closer to her sister and added in an undervoice, "And I also think your own behavior this evening has been most unwise."

"Unwise?" Aimee gave a tinkling little laugh. "What have I done? Certainly I have not danced *twice* with any man—as this Drusilla Low has done. Have you noticed that she is quite the plainest girl in the room?"

Diana rubbed her forehead, where a throbbing ache was starting to grow. "I had not given it much thought, Aimee. Why are you saying this? It is unlike you to be so unkind."

Aimee's cheeks pinkened with indignation. "Because it is *my* ball, and Charles is *my* cousin, and he has danced with that Low girl *twice*, Diana! And only once with me!"

With a sigh, Diana strove to keep her voice calm. "I strongly urge you to forget Drusilla Low and start thinking of Aimee Farington. Have you forgotten everything I told you? You promised to behave!"

"I *am* behaving! I am very popular, haven't you noticed? I told you I would be good at flirting! I have been putting your theory to the test, and so far I can assure you that being put upon a pedestal is far from dull!"

132

At that moment, Diana's hand itched to slap her sister's face. "You promised not to do that!" she accused.

Feigning innocence, Aimee arched her brows. "Did I? I don't recall. I do know that I am a grand success, Diana. Every one of my dance partners has begged to be allowed to call upon me tomorrow. All but one, that is, and it isn't very hard to guess who, is it?"

Hearing the pain in her sister's voice, Diana's anger fell away. She longed to comfort Aimee, but could only reach out to touch her arm in sympathy. "I am sorry, Aimee," she said quietly. "But you cannot expect Charles to follow you around like a lap dog! He is a grown man of nine-and-twenty, and has, I daresay, a great deal of experience with women. He will not fall for these tricks. Be patient and try not to behave like . . . like a—"

"Like a child!" Aimee's voice was rising and her breath was coming in short gasps. "You think it is childish of me to want him to like me, don't you?"

Diana sighed. "Aimee, please. I'm sure he does like you. But he is not going to make a fool of himself in front of—Oh, I didn't mean— Aimee, come back!"

But her sister had taken affront, and was already stalking back to Aunt Serena. A few minutes later, as she chatted with a young woman of her acquaintance, Diana observed that Aimee's next dance partner was Lord Lucan, and that the musicians were striking up a waltz. Her heart sank. If *he* let loose his charm on her impressionable young sister, there could be no telling what damage might be done. Prepared for the worst, Diana excused herself, and, locating a chair near her aunt, promptly collapsed into it. To her annoyance, Aunt Serena seemed to be paying scant heed to the girl she was supposed to be chaperoning. She could overhear most of what the dowager was saying, and it appeared that her aunt was exchanging a series of grievances with Lord Hervey, the follies of modern youth figuring chiefly

133

among her complaints. Wondering uneasily whether either Aimee or herself had inspired this conversation, Diana tried not to listen, tried to watch her sister and Lord Lucan without appearing to, tried to forget the throbbing pain in her head, and tried not to be glad that the earl had not sought out Lady Uxbridge once during the entire evening. She also tried not to think about her own dance with Lord Lucan, which was soon to come, or to wonder why Sir Henry had not signed her dance card at all.

To Aimee's chagrin, Lord Lucan did not present the appearance of a man who was enthralled by the charms of his partner. Her fluttering eyelashes won no response from him, no more than did the archly vivacious remarks that the other gentlemen had seemed to find so amusing. Suddenly recalling her resolve to find a husband for Diana, Aimee was assailed with a flash of guilt. She had lately become so involved in her own problems, she had nearly forgotten poor Diana. She must be brave, she decided, and put aside her troubles. She must push forward with her original plan.

Brightening a little, Aimee studied the earl's lean, rather swarthy face. Well! The place to start was obviously here. She might be naive, but she knew that this man was interested in her sister in a way that he quite obviously was not in herself. And was that not a telling sign of a good prospective husband? After all, she reasoned, if he was truly in love with Diana, of course he should *not* be wanting to flirt with anyone else!

In a manner which lacked her previous coyness, she remarked, "I suppose you would not frown so if I were Diana." Rather to her surprise, it was actually a relief to speak in her own natural voice. Flirting was much harder work than she expected!

Surprised by the about-face in his partner's behavior, Lord Lucan assessed her with suspicion. "Your sister would give me no reason to frown," he said dryly.

Aimee flushed. "Meaning you do not care for my behavior, I suppose."

"I think," he said, studying her, "that if you continue as you are, you'll soon be out of your depth. To tempt providence, Miss Farington, can be foolhardy."

Aimee pouted. "Now you sound like Charles. You older men are all the same, I think. Lecture and scold, scold and lecture! It's all I hear, even from Diana."

The earl's hard mouth relaxed into a surprisingly sympathetic smile. "When one is seventeen, the whole world can seem an adversary. I remember quite clearly how it was."

Taken aback, Aimee regarded him silently, as if seeing him for the first time. Suddenly, without knowing why, she said, "Lord Lucan, do you think nine-and-twenty is too great an age to wed with seventeen?"

The waltz was about to end, and as the music drew to a close, the earl took this opportunity to form a careful reply. "Age is less important than circumstances," he said finally. "It is something to consider, but there are no magic formulas, Miss Farington. There are enough limits in life without that."

"Oh." Aimee looked thoughtful. "Yes, I suppose that is true."

"Is everything all right?" inquired Diana, seizing the first opportunity available to speak to Aimee after the earl had left. "I hope Lord Lucan did not say anything he should not. I watched you but I could not tell for sure."

Aimee gave a rippling laugh. "Everything is fine. His lordship did not flirt with me, if that is what you mean. In fact, he is very sober, like Charles, only even worse, I think. He behaves like an uncle. But he gave me some advice which I found most sensible, so the dance was

135

not a waste."

"Really? What advice did he give you?" Diana looked a little amazed.

Aimee shrugged. "Oh, something about not tempting providence, or some such thing. He thinks that age is not as important as love, Diana. He thinks Charles is not too old for me."

Diana's brows rose. "He said that?"

"Well, not exactly, but words to that effect." Aimee appeared more cheerful than she had in days. "I cannot talk anymore, Diana. The cotillion is next, Aunt Serena is waving at me, and that young man at her elbow is waiting for me. Do stop worrying, Diana. You'll give yourself the headache!" she added, and hurried away.

As she stared after her sister, an amused voice said, "My dear Mrs. Verney, are you worrying again?"

Diana jumped. As usual, he was standing too close, so that she could almost feel the warmth of his body across the small space which separated them. And how was it possible, she asked herself wildly, that one's heart could hammer so violently against one's ribs? For the love of heaven, why did he make her so nervous?

Lord Lucan's eyes slid over her with masculine approval. "What?" he teased. "Don't tell me you've nothing to say to me. No rake-downs? No scolds? I thought I'd be due for a tongue-lashing or two by this time."

Diana forced a light laugh. "You make me sound like such a harpy, my lord. Am I truly so difficult?"

The curl of his mouth signified his amusement, but he said only, "Don't be ridiculous, Diana. Come, let us walk upon the balcony. I'm devilish hot in this coat, and I'm tired of trotting around the room in time to music. There are several things I do well, but dancing really isn't one of them. That gown, by the way, is delightful. You are the fairest maiden at the ball, my dear."

"Except that I'm no maiden," she murmured, then

blushed at her own boldness. Even to herself she could not have explained why she felt compelled to point this out.

Surprised, the earl's eyes narrowed a little. "No," he agreed, a trifle shortly. "A poor choice of words, perhaps. Let us not refine upon it."

They made their way through the press of people to the double doors which led onto the long stone balcony stretching the length of the back of the house. To Diana, it was as if she were in a dream in which she was moving toward the inevitable. The doors stood open to let in the flow of evening coolness, and pools of light lit the center of the area, leaving the far recesses of the balcony shrouded in darkness. They were not the only couple who had stepped out that evening for a breath of air, but for the moment they were alone.

He turned her around with firm hands, but when she had braced herself to repel his embrace, his hand went instead to her chin, raising it so that she was forced to gaze directly into his eyes.

"You are so beautiful," he said huskily. "Diana the goddess, the eternal virgin. Maiden or not, that is how I view you."

In a sudden panic, she pushed his hand away, but his eyes still held her captive. "You must not say such things, my lord. I wish you would not."

"Why?" he asked in a caressing voice. "Tell me why, Diana."

He was too close; she could not think. "You must know why," she stammered.

"No, I don't." He was studying her intently. "You are not indifferent to me. In fact, I think you like me very well indeed."

"Yes, I do, but please," she implored, "you must say no more. There is no purpose in . . . in this. Oh, you will ruin everything!"

He turned her words around. "On the contrary, there is a purpose. I am a man who always has a purpose in mind, Diana." Gazing at her steadily, he tried to tease her out of her somber mood. "Don't you want to learn about the things I do well, my sweet?"

"I don't think so." She shook her head, a sharp jerk of absolute denial.

Suddenly, he knew he could not wait, that he had never meant to wait, that he had brought her to the balcony to ask her to be his wife. When she knew he wooed her in earnest, she would not be so reluctant.

"You know what I want, don't you?" he murmured, approaching the subject cautiously. "You know it's right, don't you, Diana? Sweet, sweet Diana." He reached for her hands, pulling her closer. "I want you, Diana, in every sense of the word. I want you to be my—"

"No!" Incredibly, she found the words to stop him, and she poured them out in a rush he could not interrupt. "Don't say anything more, I beg you! It's not right, at least not for me! You don't know me at all. Please, please believe me when I say that I have no wish for a . . . a warmer relationship with you or any other man."

Realizing how cold she sounded, she added pleadingly, "But I would very much like to be your friend. Just your friend." She moistened her lips. "I *am* fond of you— Geoffrey. Do you think that might be possible? Can we not just be friends?"

He was staring at her, his disappointment acute and unmistakable, even in the darkness. "You like me," he repeated slowly. "But not well enough to consider— Dammit, I don't believe it, Diana! I'll swear you feel what I feel!" His hands reached out to seize her, to kiss her against her will, but once more, miraculously, cruelly, she said the only thing that could have stopped him.

"Please, Geoffrey, don't treat me the way Edmund

did." There was a thread of naked misery in her voice. "Please be kind to me. Be my friend."

He had to force himself to remember she meant no insult. "Confound it, Diana, don't compare me to *him*."

"I'm sorry," she faltered. "I didn't mean to—" There was so much more she should have said, but then there were voices and laughter as two other couples, talking loudly, stepped out onto the balcony. "Let's go back in," she urged. "Aunt Serena will be furious if anyone has noticed I am out here with you."

Cursing himself for his own impatience, the earl scowled. "We are going to discuss this some more," he said flatly.

Diana laid her hand on his arm. *"No!* I've told you I want to be your friend. That's as much as I'm willing to give, my lord. And that is quite, quite final."

Chapter Eight

Lord Lucan sighed inwardly. He was leaning against the wall at yet another interminable ball, watching (with manifest indifference) yet another set of dancers—or was it the same confounded set?—wheel about the room. As always, he was at pains to disguise his true purpose, for the last thing he wanted was to give the gossip-tabbies something to sink their teeth into—which would happen if they realized he was only here to keep a proprietary eye on Diana.

She went past him at that moment in the arms of a retired captain of a Hussar regiment, a brash young man at least five years younger than himself. With a short sigh, the earl folded his arms across his chest, reflecting that it was foolish to be jealous of the man. To his knowledge, Diana never danced with any gentleman twice, and never gave the least indication that she favored one man over another. And from the looks on the faces of some of her partners, it was his conjecture that she could well have had her pick of the lot.

To be honest, if she had demonstrated partiality toward anyone, he would have to say it was himself. At least, in the two weeks that had passed since he had made the incredibly stupid blunder of speaking too soon, she had twice allowed him to drive her in the park, as well as accompanying him there on horseback a number of mornings. She had obviously been quite serious about wishing to be his friend, he thought wryly. One evening, too, he and Charles had escorted her to the theater, along with that madcap sister of hers and the dowager viscountess. Had it not been for the appearance of Sir Henry Neyle during one of the scene breaks, the evening would have been one of the most pleasant he had ever spent.

The earl's mouth hardened at the memory. Unless he was misreading the situation, Diana was far too impressed by Sir Henry. It had rankled him that the entire time Harry was in their box she had behaved unnaturally, as if she considered the baronet's visit some great, extraordinary honor. Of course, he mused, there was no real cause for alarm, since he could not imagine Diana consenting to become Sir Henry's mistress. What worried him was that the baronet might toy with her affections, for he was beginning to realize that Diana was a very vulnerable woman, and he did not want her to be hurt.

If only he had not been so bacon-brained as to offer her marriage before she was ready! Like the merest whipster, he had rushed his fences, attempting to build upon a relationship whose foundations were incomplete. He should have given her time to realize that she wanted him as much as he wanted her, instead of being so damned impatient! Now he could only cling to the hope that if he waited long enough, there might come a time when he would dare to broach the subject again. Certainly he did not intend to give up, for without doubt, platonic friendship with Diana would eventually become a torture in itself.

"My, my, what deep, dark thoughts must be taking shape in that head of yours!" murmured a teasing voice

141

at his side.

The earl glanced down, surprised that he had not observed Mrs. Clement's approach. "Hello, Cynthia." Suddenly glad of her company, he smiled affably, and pushed away from the wall. "Come. Let's find a more comfortable place in which to talk. How have you been?"

"Oh, horribly lonely," she complained, a spark of mischief lurking in her brown eyes. As his dark brows shot up, she added, "No, no, I am only funning, Geoffrey. You know me. I am never lacking for companionship—only money." The faint sigh which accompanied these last two words hinted at desperate struggles with creditors and tradesmen's bills.

He led Mrs. Clement to a nearby couch within an alcove, saying, in the forthright fashion which Diana found so disconcerting, "What, have you no protector at the moment to keep you in funds?"

Mrs. Clement's color heightened at his plain speaking. "I have several very dear friends," she said, hedging the question, "each of whom would help me if he could but—" She shrugged her white shoulders philosophically. "What can I say? I am not the only one with problems these days."

"I see." His gaze inscrutable, the earl fingered his quizzing glass. "How much do you need?"

She leaned forward eagerly. "Not a great deal. Five hundred or so would see me through to the end of the month." She saw his eyes drop to the expensive-looking jewels about her throat. "Glass," she confessed, with brief embarrassment. "I sold the original long ago."

"You know, Cynthia, if you would stop wasting the ready on all these parties—"

"I know, I know." She waved a hand at him. "But my parties are what make me fashionable, Geoffrey. And I have never been able to economize. I've never really needed to, although eventually I suppose—" She broke

142

off with a smile. "What a bore I have become. Let us speak of something more cheerful."

He ignored this. "I will give you five hundred for friendship's sake. But only once."

The addendum brought a pinkness into Mrs. Clement's cheeks. "Naturally," she responded with dignity. "And I shall pay you back when . . . when I can."

He shook his head. "Consider it a gift," he ordered. "And in return, you can do something for me."

"Of course, Geoffrey. Anything at all."

"Really? Well, this is fairly simple." His keen eyes swept the room, then paused. "Do you see that woman directly across from us, the one in blue? Her name is Diana Verney."

"Edmund Verney's widow? Yes, I see her."

"I want you to keep an eye on her for me. You attend many of the same social events, I'm sure. In a sense, I want some assistance in guarding her."

Mrs. Clement's gaze grew speculative. "From any particular gentleman?" she inquired offhandedly. "Or all of them?"

There was a rough edge to his voice. "Only the ones who don't know how to behave themselves. I especially want to know whether she sees much of Henry Neyle. This is between you and me only, you understand."

"Of course," she murmured, giving him a reproachful yet curious look from under her lashes. "Is she the one you wanted to marry?"

"What?"

"You told me once, in one of your more, shall we say, loquacious moods, that the only woman you desired to be your wife was unavailable. And with Edmund Verney gone . . ."

Unable to recall making any such confidence, the earl regarded her quizzically. "Foxed, was I?" he inquired. "That must have been quite a while ago. And I suppose we were alone?"

She smiled slightly. "Yes, we were alone." Being a woman, she could not resist asking, rather wistfully, "Do you love her?"

"Love?" he repeated. His lips twisting wryly. "A word so often misapplied, so much abused. What does it mean, Cynthia? No, don't try to answer," he added. "The poets bend their minds to that task, and even they don't shed much light." He sat forward, prepared to rise. "Do not forget . . . this conversation was strictly between ourselves. And now, my dear lady, should you care to dance?"

"I should be delighted, my lord," replied Mrs. Clement, placing her hand in his.

Across the room, Diana had thanked her partner and rejoined Aunt Serena, who, perhaps because Lord Hervey was late in joining them, was behaving more querulously than usual.

"Diana," she grumbled, "I am uncomfortable. This idiotish chair is constructed all wrong for old bones like mine. Why Lucretia Corewood cannot put out something better than this for her guests is beyond me. She married above her station, which probably has a great deal to do with it. I told you we should have gone to the Rillingtons' soiree instead."

"Aimee wanted to come here, not I," Diana pointed out, a little dryly. Her own feet hurt but there was nowhere else to sit at the moment. With a sigh, she said, "Aunt Serena, would you like to go home? I am sure once Lord Hervey arrives he will be happy to take you—"

"No, no," interrupted her aunt curtly. "It's early yet. Where's that sister of yours?"

"I don't know." Diana glanced around. "She was with Charles a few minutes ago."

Aunt Serena lost interest. "Well, if the chit is with Charles she's safe enough. *He* knows where to draw the

144

line, though some of 'em certainly don't! Have you spoken to her lately about her behavior? I thought I caught her doing the eyelash bit again with Captain Peterson. I swear the girl takes after me," she added cryptically.

Diana was startled. "You? Good God, don't tell me you used to—Aunt Serena, you never did!"

"Not after I was married," said the old lady coolly. "But when I was seventeen, by gad, they were lined up for miles outside my door. Went to my head a trifle, it did."

Somehow, Diana could not quite envision Great-aunt Serena fluttering her eyelashes and smiling coyly at some young man in . . . well, he would have been wearing a periwig, wouldn't he?

"Well, I must say," she remarked rather accusingly, "I think your behavior has been quite hypocritical. When I think of some of the things you have said to me concerning the need for propriety—"

"Poppycock!" said the dowager with a sniff. "I never got myself into a situation I couldn't handle, that's the difference between you and me! We were wiser in those days, I daresay. Knew enough not to trust a man. Never let 'em know it, either. Flattery! That's what they like. Men are as vain as peacocks about some things . . . like their virility. Worse than women, some of 'em. Like that Sir Henry of yours."

Such comments as this never failed to irritate Diana. "Sir Henry is not vain," she said defensively. "I cannot imagine what he could have done to make you dislike him so."

Aunt Serena made a disgusted sound. "I don't dislike him. I don't even know him! Don't want to know him either! My eyes tell me the man's a loose fish and that's enough for me." The dowager ignored her niece's expression. "Now, who's that dancing with Lucan?" she went on. "Oh, the Clement woman. Now, there's an example for you not to follow."

Her curiosity roused, Diana turned to look at the couple. In animated conversation, they might as well have been alone for all the notice they were giving those around them. "Who is she?" she asked.

A certain hollowness in her tone caused the dowager to give Diana a sharp look. "She's a widow like yourself," she said brutally. "A prime example of a woman who lives by her wits. Her wastrel of a husband died about ten years ago and, being a typical spendthrift, left her stranded with a mountain of debt. But she survived, paid 'em off, and can still put her foot into many respectable Mayfair homes. Many," she added with emphasis. "But not all."

"What do you mean?" faltered Diana, who had been noting how intimately the earl was smiling down at Mrs. Clement.

"I mean, Diana, that she sold herself for money. Oh, don't look so horrified—women do it all the time! It ain't their fault most often."

"But . . . but she is here—"

The dowager snorted a laugh. "Of course she's here. Egad, I never realized you was so naive, Diana. These so-called gentlemen with their polished manners and noble lineages . . . do you think they all sleep with their wives? Or live celibate lives if they've none?"

"I can't say I've given the matter much thought," replied Diana tartly.

"Maybe you should! Y'see, as far as society is concerned, it don't much matter what you do, as long as you don't get caught. The Clement woman's discreet, and that's why she's still accepted into all but the most select circles. Discretion is what counts, missy."

Such a life sounded very depressing to Diana. "Then how do *you* know about it?" she countered.

Aunt Serena sighed. "I ain't dead yet, Diana. I keep my

146

ear to the ground. But I can't tell you the particulars. If she and your Lord Lucan are more than friends, that's their business. I do know the Duke of Wellington was besotted by the Clement woman some years back, but that's ancient history. *Now* it's the Wilson sisters."

Caught between dismay and a certain fascination with the topic, Diana found herself asking, "Who are they?"

"Courtesans, Diana . . . demi-reps, if you like. Whatever you choose to call 'em, it amounts to the same. You've seen 'em driving in the Park, though 'tis possible not to know it, for they dress as finely as you and I. In any case, they need not concern you, as long as you understand and accept that they exist. I thought you knew all that seeing that Edmund—"

"Yes, yes," struck in Diana rapidly, "but I thought it was only he who . . . who went to such women."

The dowager rolled her eyes. "Lord have mercy! Well, never mind this now, the music is ending. Do you have a partner for the next set?"

Diana consulted her card. "Why, yes," she said, brightening. "Sir Henry."

"Lord have mercy!" repeated the dowager, more sourly.

Aimee's ratafia in his hand, Charles Perth stared at the empty chair before him, then rapidly scanned the faces in the nearby crowd. Dash the girl, where had she gone? Five minutes ago he had deposited her in this very chair and made it clear that she was to stay there while he procured her drink. He gazed around, starting forward as he spied a dark-haired girl about Aimee's height. But it was not she, he saw, as soon as she turned her head.

Racking his brain, he tried to remember what color she had been wearing. Pink, wasn't it? And a dashed fetching shade it had been, he thought inconsequently. It had made her little face look so enchanting, he had known he would be unable to concentrate on his dance steps, and had suggested that they sit out the set and partake of refreshment instead.

Could she have left the ball room? Perhaps she had only gone to the ladies' retiring room to freshen up? As this notion took root in his mind, Charles's frown began to fade. Yes, that was it very likely—though why she could not have mentioned it to him before, he could not conceive. He felt dashed silly standing around holding a glass of ratafia, vile beverage that it was. Why the ladies insisted upon drinking it he could never understand, for it was disgustingly sweet, and nearly as spirituous as a good glass of wine! Brandy, now, that's what women ought to drink!

Making a mental note to encourage Aimee to imbibe something more palatable, Charles dumped the ratafia into the base of a tall fern which had the misfortune to be placed nearby.

Quitting the ballroom, he glanced up and down the adjacent corridor. Several ladies and gentlemen stood about, exchanging conversation and gossip, but of Aimee there was no sign. He traversed the length of the passageway, passing by the room reserved exclusively for the ladies from which emanated a variety of female voices. He paused, but did not recognize Aimee's voice, though his sharp ears identified two or three others of his acquaintance. Where the devil *was* she? he wondered, his brow puckering. He had just begun to retrace his steps, thinking he ought to go and discover whether Diana knew anything, when he heard what sounded like an agitated giggle.

Pure instinct told him it came from Aimee, and he swung around, his green eyes alert. At first, he saw nothing. Then he noticed what looked to be a small alcove at the end of the hall, extending around the corner

148

beyond the casement window overlooking the back of the house. A window seat followed the wall into the recess.

Gritting his teeth, Charles bore down upon this hideaway with savage exasperation. What game was the little minx up to this time?

It never occurred to him that she was not alone, and the sight which met his startled gaze so enraged him that his reaction was considerably more unrestrained than he would later care to remember. In fact, he so far forgot himself that he exclaimed, "What the deuce—!" a phrase he normally would not have used in front of a gently bred lady.

Aimee was sitting next to Captain Peterson, who, when Charles invaded the alcove, had just succeeded in capturing one of her dainty hands and was pressing it to his rather full lips—despite her attempts to prevent him.

"Just *what* is going on here?" demanded Charles, fixing the captain with a freezing stare. "Unhand my cousin, sir!" he added, his voice vibrant with indignation.

Looking chagrined, Captain Peterson jumped to his feet. "Er . . . hallo, Perth. We were just . . . ah . . . I mean the young lady and I were only . . ." His quick grin won no response from Charles. "I mean, there's no point in raising a dust about this, is there, eh? Miss Farington and I were only conversing. No harm done, eh?"

"Conversing," responded Charles in a curt tone, "can be done in the ballroom. We will detain you no longer, sir. Miss Farington accepts your apologies."

Favoring Aimee with a short bow, Captain Peterson cast Charles a sullen look and made his departure.

"Insolent fellow," muttered Charles under his breath. Then he scowled at Aimee, unaware that his next words quite spoiled the whole scene for his cousin, who until this point had been regarding him as something of a Galahad.

"Dash it, what were you at, to come in here with that fellow? You've no sense at all, have you? Bird-witted chit!" He ignored the stiffening in Aimee's expression. "Peterson ain't someone you should trust, dash it! Why, the fellow's a born rascal if I ever saw one!"

Aimee's blue eyes took on an angry sparkle. "Nonsense, Charles. How dare you speak so to me! I think it is very high-handed of you when I am sure this is none of your business! I don't have to listen to you, you know!" she added.

The two cousins glared at each other, each feeling shabbily treated by the other.

"What do you mean, you don't have to listen to me?" echoed Charles irately. "Ain't I your only male relative here in town?"

"That doesn't give you the right to tell me what to do!"

"Dashed if it don't! It gives me a share in the responsibility to see that you don't ruin yourself with your own headstrong behavior!"

Aimee stamped her foot. "Well, I do not intend to do that, Charles. You are making a great piece of work over nothing! Do you know what I think?" she threw out. "I think you are jealous!"

Charles snorted. "Of Peterson? Not likely! The fellow's got drooping shoulders. Has to pad his coats to get a decent fit!"

Aimee gaped at him. "Well, of all the things to say!"

Almost to himself, he remarked, "And to think that when I first saw you I thought . . ."

"You thought what?" demanded Aimee.

"Never mind," he told her in a voice of grim warning. "I sent Peterson off with a flea in his ear, and I'll deal the same way with any other fellow who tries to take liberties with you. Dash it, Aimee, what possessed you to let him hold your hand? What if someone other than me had come upon the pair of you?"

She would not tell him she had planned it so, that she had meant to stay in the corridor and had not known of the existence of the alcove until they were inside. She would not tell him that he was supposed to be jealous.

"Captain Peterson was merely complimenting me on the shape of my hands," she retorted, not without pride. "I have very nice hands, Charles, though I am sure you have never taken the trouble to notice."

"A likely story," scoffed Charles. "What a flighty chit you are, to fall for such a rubbishy excuse to manhandle you."

"Flighty, am I?" she gasped. "Well, you are starchy, that's what you are. Starchy and priggish! I pity the poor female who becomes your wife, Charles Perth, because she will be bored to death, do you hear me? Bored to death!"

"Well, it dashed well won't be you!" he told her crushingly. "I'd as lief marry a Billingsgate fishwife as a spoiled brat who won't listen to reason!"

"*Ooh!*" said Aimee furiously. "I hate you, Charles!" And gathering her skirts, she rushed past him back down the hallway into the ballroom, leaving her cousin staring after her in fury.

To Diana's relief, Lord Hervey soon arrived to take his usual place at Aunt Serena's side. Thus, by the time Sir Henry Neyle came up to claim Diana for the waltz, Aunt Serena and her elderly crony were deep in conversation, which was all that saved Sir Henry from the dowager's vitriolic tongue.

Unaware of his narrow escape, Sir Henry guided her suavely through the press of people. "How very charming you look this evening, my dear. I see you received my small offering."

Diana glanced down at the fragrant little corsage of

151

violets pinned to her gown. "Yes, and I thank you for them," she said with a smile. "It was very thoughtful of you to think of sending me flowers."

"I think about you a great deal," he murmured significantly. "Do you care to rest some more, or shall we dance?"

"Really, Sir Henry," she responded, relaxed enough in his company to be able to joke a little, "you cannot seriously believe that hovering over Great-aunt Serena is *restful?* By all means, let us waltz."

Diana by now had the opportunity to dance that most risqué of dances, the waltz, with a variety of gentlemen, and had formed the opinion that Sir Henry Neyle was the most graceful of them all. He was in every way perfect, she reflected. In looks, charm, grace, and address, he was surely every woman's dream. He was tall, his entire form was as exquisitely sculpted as a Greek statue—and he was unmarried. Each time she was with him she had become increasingly aware of the envious looks cast her by other women. How would it feel, she wondered, to be married to such a man as this? That would be turning the tables, wouldn't it? She would be an object of envy, instead of the butt of painful, wicked gossip. It was not the first time this notion had drifted through her thoughts, but it had never before seemed quite so alluring.

"You dance divinely," he complimented her as they turned about the floor. "I have been looking forward to this moment all evening."

"You, Sir Henry, are becoming a sad flatterer," she retorted, trying not to betray how much his words pleased her.

"Only since you came to town, I promise you," he replied, allowing his lips to twitch just enough to take the absurdity out of the statement.

She laughed, as he had planned she should. "I might

have come sooner had I known the reception I would get. You really must stop this, Sir Henry, else my head will be so swollen none of my bonnets will fit." Her eyes twinkled at him. "And since I cannot afford to buy any more for a while, that would place me in a predicament. I would have to stay at home."

Sharing the joke, his lips curved in amusement. "And what a great shame that would be," he agreed, giving her hand a light press. "You win, then, my fetching little widow. I'll pay you no more compliments tonight." Over the top of her head, his eyes moved restlessly. "Lord Hervey seems very devoted to your aunt," he said casually.

Diana nodded. "Oh, yes, I believe he is."

"Too devoted, perhaps," he suggested.

"Why, what can you mean?" Diana shot an involuntary glance at Lord Hervey. "I am sure he does her a great deal of good. She is lonely for those of her own generation."

Sir Henry cleared his throat. "Yes, well, lonely old women with more money than they know what to do with frequently attract . . . devoted admirers."

Diana looked shocked. "Oh, no, Sir Henry, Lord Hervey is not like that. I am persuaded his attachment to my aunt is most sincere."

"Oh? I must bow to your judgment then, for I do not know the man. I have heard, however, that he is none too plump in the pocket. If I were heir—or heiress—to a vast fortune, I would not care to see it usurped by someone else."

Diana hesitated before answering. "I am convinced Lord Hervey is innocent of such villainous motives," she replied, her answer even more direct than he had hoped. "I've no idea where Aunt Serena will leave her fortune, for she is impossible to predict. It will not be to me, at any rate, for I am too often in her black books." She

153

smiled. "Anyway, she will probably outlive us all."

"A pity," he said softly. "Ah, well. You and I, my dear, shall not regard it, shall we?"

"Of course not." She smiled again, wondering at his meaning.

"I'd like to visit you tomorrow, if I may." Suddenly, the pressure of his hand brought them an inch or two closer. "I think you know why."

"T-tomorrow?" She nearly stepped on his foot.

His eyelids seemed to droop as he gazed down at her. "This is not the place for private conversation. As a mature woman, I'm sure you understand me."

Diana's heart leaped in her chest. He was going to make her an offer! Feeling as though the room was too warm, as if she were being suffocated by a situation in which she had no control, she somehow managed to stammer out, "Certainly, Sir Henry. I mean . . . why do you not come at two o'clock? I think I can arrange to see you . . . alone."

The last strains of the music drew to a close and Sir Henry gave her a formal bow. "Until tomorrow," he murmured.

Twelve hours later, Diana paced the floor of her bedchamber, fraught with indecision and self-doubt. Was she out of her mind? Was she really considering accepting Sir Henry's offer? Her hands clenched in nervous anticipation, she tried to review the facts as calmly as possibly. First of all, Sir Henry was, in essence, the physical embodiment of the man of her dreams, and though she was wise enough to realize this was not a reason to marry him, still, it could not help but weigh in his favor. Secondly, she had to admit that life as a widow might eventually become wearisome, even lonely. Not that she did not enjoy Tildy's company, but just lately there was an odd discontent building within her, along with a new yearning, a *need* to take more from life, to feel complete in a way she had never experienced. It was most unsettling.

For some obscure reason, learning of Mrs. Clement had cast a damper over her spirits. Diana was finding it impossible not to dwell upon what her own life might have been like had she chosen to accept Lord Lucan's dishonorable proposal. Not that she would ever have seriously considered becoming the earl's mistress, but still, it did make one pause to consider the negative aspects of being without a husband. A woman alone had a great handicap, for the world she lived in was a man's world, built by and for the convenience of the male sex. At best, a respectable woman coped with rules and conventions designed to limit every aspect of her existence, at worst . . . at worst, she might be forced to compromise her own values—as Mrs. Clement must have done.

Who knew what trials the poor woman had been forced to suffer before she made her fatal decision? No longer horrified, Diana resolved not to pass judgment on Mrs. Clement, but she was also going to make very sure she did not emulate her. Determinedly forcing Mrs. Clement from her mind, she resolved to concentrate on her own problems.

As usual, she was interrupted. "Diana!" called Aimee through the door. "I . . . I'd like to talk to you, if I may."

Diana sighed. She could not very well put Aimee off, for her sister was obviously unhappy, and had been moping about the house all morning. Apparently, she had decided it was time to confide.

"I suppose you've noticed I've been a bit melancholy," floundered Aimee, upon entering. "I could not talk about it before, but I want to tell you that . . . that there is no question of my . . . my marrying Charles."

Her voice quivered as she spoke.

Wrapping an arm around Aimee's drooping shoulders, Diana drew her sister forward to sit upon the bed. "Tell me what happened."

In a forlorn little voice, Aimee related the details of the previous night's quarrel. "And then I told him I hated him, Diana. Of course I do not, but he was being so horrid that I had to say *something*. And now I feel so utterly wretched, I don't know how I shall go on living!"

Hiding her dismay, Diana searched for something positive to say. "Don't cry, dearest. Everything will work out." Since this did not seem to do the trick, she went on, "I'll tell you what I think. I have always thought Cousin Charles would make you an excellent husband, but I also believed the disparity in your ages might be too great. And then, observing him that first night, I had the distinct impression that he was, well, quite bowled over by you. And I began to wonder if I was wrong." At Aimee's involuntary squeak, she held up her hand. "But Charles is a man who believes in propriety, Aimee. He does not want a wife who flirts with every man she meets."

Aimee sniffed tearfully. "He called me a spoiled brat."

Diana sighed. "Well, you are a little spoiled, perhaps, but never a brat. You just need to grow up a bit more. That's why I hoped you would wait another year before coming to London." She patted her sister's hand consolingly. "Cheer up. You may very well have succeeded in making him jealous. From what you tell me, he must have been extremely upset to have reacted as he did."

"That's so, isn't it?" Rubbing her reddened nose, Aimee's piquant features took on a hopeful expression. "I didn't think of that before."

"You look tired. Why don't you rest for a while?"

Aimee rose obediently. "Yes, I think I will. I did not

get much sleep last night." She had almost reached the door when she turned around. "Oh, Diana?"

"Yes?"

"Remember I told you how I wanted to be adored? And how I might try to make some gentleman worship me so I could find out if I liked it?"

Diana nodded.

"Well," said Aimee tremulously, "I decided that wouldn't be very nice. I mean, it seems a rather silly reason to make someone else suffer, doesn't it?"

"Yes, I think it does," returned Diana gravely.

"So I shan't do it," said Aimee, and closed the door quietly behind her.

After some debate, Diana decided not to tell Miss Tilden about Sir Henry's impending visit. It was becoming Miss Tilden's daily habit to rest in her room after luncheon, and it seemed better not to give her news that might disturb her sleep. There was always the chance that her elderly companion might feel it her duty to stay and act as chaperon, which was really quite unnecessary. After all, she had promised Sir Henry that she would receive him alone, and alone she meant to be!

Two o'clock came, and as Sir Henry was ushered into the drawing room, Diana was struck anew by his elegance. The studied disorder of his golden locks became him, as did his coat of dark blue cloth, which fit his upper torso as if it had been sewn together as he stood in it.

In his leisurely fashion, he moved toward her, saying, with an engaging smile, "I am most punctual today, am I not? As we get to know each other better, you will find that I am frequently forgetting my engagements. But this is hardly one I could forget, is it?" He had taken possession of her hand as he spoke, and now raised and pressed it to his lips, rather lingeringly.

157

When he did not release her, Diana began to blush. "Sir Henry," she reproved, "you really must not—!"

He laughed softly, and reached for her other hand. "No, *really*, Diana! Do not tell me you are prudish, for that I refuse to believe. However, at this stage, I admit a show of reluctance is not unpleasant." His lazy eyes explored her face, then dropped to survey the rest of her. "What a beautiful creature you are, my dear," he added appreciatively.

"Sir Henry, you promised me last night you would stop saying these absurd things," she reminded him, very conscious of the warmth of his hands against hers.

In response, he pulled her closer. "My friends call me Harry. Do you think you could call me that?"

"I think," said Diana awkwardly, "that we had better sit down. Would you care for some refreshment?"

With a slight shrug, he set her free. "Very well. To please you, Diana, I am willing to play this hand however you wish. Some brandy would sit very well with me, if you have it."

Afterward, when the drink was in his hand and they were seated together, at his insistence, on the couch, he said, "Forgive me for proceeding with such haste, my dear. It did not occur to me that you would wish it otherwise."

Relieved that he understood, Diana said, "It is not in my nature, Sir—I mean, Henry, to rush into these things."

His eyes gleamed. "You are wiser, perhaps, than I, for I have been wanting this since I first saw you in Jermyn Street a month past."

"Oh?" she said, a little startled.

"But in the interim, I've grown quite fond of you," he explained. "And affection makes an alliance so much more enjoyable, does it not?"

The word *alliance* reassured her, for Diana had begun

158

to feel a trifle uneasy about his meaning. "Oh, yes," she agreed fervently. "Mutual affection is everything. Else I could not consider—" She stopped just short of saying "marriage," for he had not yet said that word, and she feared he might think her overeager. "I am fond of you, also," she said instead.

At this, he moved closer, so that there was scarcely an inch between them. "That pleases me more than you can know," he whispered, instinct warning him to honey his words. "In fact, it makes me quite the happiest man in London, Diana. I want to become the most important person in your life. When we're together, I want it to be the most wonderful event of our lives. Tell me you want that, too, Diana."

This was it, then—her first real offer of marriage. There was no magic, no fireworks, only a curious feeling of detachment, as if she were not a participant in the scene. Yet it was what she had been waiting for, what she had come to the conclusion was best for her in the long run.

"I want that, too," she heard herself say, and tried to force herself to believe it. Of course she *must* believe it. Hadn't she spent most of the morning convincing herself that marriage with Sir Henry Neyle was the best, the most logical course? That there were more reasons to say "yes" than "no"?

His expression turned triumphant. "Marvelous," he breathed, expelling air from his lungs as if he had been holding it inside. Then his right arm was about her shoulders, and he was pulling her against his chest. "Come closer, love, and give me a kiss to seal the bargain," he coaxed, his voice soft and urgent.

It was not an unreasonable request. Mutely, Diana closed her eyes, feeling his lips covering hers, growing more demanding, forcing her mouth open . . . Oh, God, oh God! It felt so much like Edmund kissing her, that, repulsed, Diana's eyes popped open and she struggled to push him away.

"Is something wrong?" inquired Sir Henry, looking quite surprised.

Diana suppressed a shudder. "I . . . I'm sorry. I do not care at all for the taste of brandy," she stumbled, improvising rapidly. "It's nothing to do with you, Sir . . . I mean, Henry . . . *Harry!* Do not be insulted, please. It is merely the taste. I find it quite . . . repugnant."

He sighed slightly, and drew away. "Very few women care for brandy," he agreed. "I should have thought of that. Sorry, love. Next time will be better, I promise." His eyes narrowed thoughtfully, he rose to his feet. "I will give some thought to the arrangements."

As soon as he was gone, Diana flew upstairs and threw herself onto her bed, burying her face in her hands. What was the matter with her? Here was the most handsome, the most elegant man she had ever met in her life, and she was as repelled by his kisses as she had been by Edmund's horrid embraces! What was *wrong* with her? There had to be something wrong with her, something that made her different. Otherwise, how did other women *do* it?

It had been a mistake to consider marriage, she now realized. But, my God, what a scandal it would be if she cried off! He would tell people, it would get about before she could put a stop to it . . . what was she to do? Aunt Serena would kill her if she caused another scandal!

Slowly, Diana sat up and forced herself to think rationally. She could write him a note, explaining that she had changed her mind and could not marry him. Yes of course, Felix could deliver the note within the hour.

Her brow knit anxiously as she searched for flaws to her plan. She did not know where he lived. Had he ever mentioned it? But, no, that was a minor detail. Her footman could easily discover Sir Henry's direction. The important thing was to think of a plausible excuse, for she could not very well tell him the truth. She could not say she found his kisses revolting!

It was then that she heard it. A low, soft moan followed by a feeble thump, as of a foot scraping against wood. It was so out of place it pierced right through Diana's distress, forcing her head to jerk up, cocked at an angle to listen. Had she imagined it?

"Diana . . ." It was the merest whisper of a cry but it was enough to banish Sir Henry completely from her mind. Leaping up, Diana was across the narrow hall in three steps. Her heart in her throat, she flung open her companion's door, and for a bare instant, froze.

Miss Tilden lay crumpled upon the floor like a rag doll thrown by a child.

Chapter Nine

"Tildy!" she gasped. "Oh, my God, what happened?"

Her heart in her throat, Diana rushed forward, going down on her knees beside the elderly little woman. "How long have you been like this? Where are you hurt?"

Miss Tilden's complexion had a gray cast. "My ankle, Diana," she whispered, her face contorted in pain. "My foot . . . I think my foot must have been asleep and I . . . twisted my ankle . . . and fell. . . ."

Diana stared in shock as Miss Tilden went suddenly limp. Tildy had obviously fainted, and as for her ankle, it was probably sprained or broken. Either way, she thought grimly, they would need a physician at once.

Later, the events of that afternoon would blur in her memory and she would hardly recall ringing for Meg or the dreadful minutes that passed while her abigail rushed to find Felix, her footman. What would stay clearly in her mind were Miss Tilden's heartrending groans and the gratitude she felt toward Felix, who lifted Miss Tilden and set her back upon her bed as tenderly as if she were a baby.

Then came the long wait, while her footman set out to track down Dr. Hatfield, Great-aunt Serena's physician. It seemed like forever to Diana, but it actually took Felix little more than an hour to locate the doctor. This highly distinguished member of the medical profession was to be found, not at his home or at the bedside of some other ailing patient, but at a nearby coffeehouse where, his manservant woodenly informed Felix, he had taken his niece to enjoy that popular beverage. Familiar with the establishment to which he was directed, Felix quickly ran his quarry to earth. Why it was that the good doctor's plump arm was wrapped around his niece's waist, or why that young lady was giving her so-called uncle a flirtatious slap on the thigh, Felix neither knew nor cared. What mattered was that the doctor accompany him back to Jermyn Street with dispatch. Bearing this in mind, Diana's stalwart footman did not hesitate to make clear that the injured lady was a Dear Friend of the Dowager Lady Torrington's niece. Whether or not this nudge was necessary he would never know, for Dr. Hatfield surged instantly to his feet, prepared to depart despite the pouting objections of the young lady.

Dr. Hatfield's diagnosis was that Miss Tilden's ankle was only sprained, and that it was a minor miracle she had not broken her hip when she fell. Cook had managed to obtain ice while Felix was gone, but even so, the poor lady's ankle turned blue-black and continued to swell even after the ice was applied.

The doctor left, and such practical tasks as assisting Miss Tilden into her nightdress fell to Diana and Meg, as Aimee could only hover and talk, rather like an anxious butterfly. Shooing her sister away with impatience, Diana stayed by the elderly woman's side until her even breathing assured the young widow that she slept. Tildy had been in obvious pain, and had finally consented to take a spoonful of the laudanum which Dr. Hatfield had prescribed.

To pass the time while she was waiting for Miss Tilden to fall asleep, Diana had mentally composed her note to

163

Sir Henry, changing it over and over until she was satisfied. Worry and stress were beginning to take their toll on her energy, but as she had eaten little else that day, her appetite was as yet undiminished. Happily, she had also had time to recollect that Sir Henry was much too noble a gentleman to speak to anyone of their engagement before the news was inserted in the papers. Her equanimity thus restored, she descended to the dining room to eat her dinner.

Diana would have been aghast had she known that Sir Henry possessed few of the scruples for which she gave him credit, and was at that very moment preparing to brag of his victory to the one person his boasting would most enrage. He was a member of several men's clubs, but on this particular evening he had decided to drop in at White's, which he knew to be a favorite haunt of the Earl of Lucan's.

The earl was sitting in a large wing chair reading a newspaper when Sir Henry strolled languidly into the room.

"Why, hullo, Geoff, old boy," he said in his mocking way. "Mind if I join you? One's own company can get devilish boring after a while."

The earl lowered his paper, his gaze aloof. "Can it?" he said. Perceiving the other man's smug expression, he cast it aside altogether, adding with an air of resignation, "So what have you been at, Harry? You look as pleased with yourself as a cat in a pot of cream."

"Do I?" responded the baronet, pulling over the nearest chair. "Well, I've good reason to, old boy." He paused, searching the earl's impassive face. "I've beaten you, Geoff," he announced, a flash of exultation seeping into his voice. "I've vanquished the citadel." His long fingers toyed restlessly with his quizzing glass and the fobs which hung from his waist.

164

Lord Lucan betrayed no visible sign of alarm. "And which citadel is that?" he inquired, sardonically indifferent. "Your interests jump about so, Harry, I cannot keep them straight."

A smirk crawled over Sir Henry's face. "I speak of the beauteous Diana, of course. She whose face and figure we have both been coveting—for our disparate purposes. I thought you'd like to know who won."

His steel gray eyes pinned to the other man's face, the earl said, very levelly, "You had better explain what you mean by that, Harry. Exactly."

Enjoying himself, Sir Henry withdrew his snuffbox from his pocket. "Why, I intend to," he replied, "but first . . ." Prolonging his moment of triumph, he took a generous pinch of snuff and placed it on the back of his right hand. Lifting it close to one beautiful nostril, he said, "I paid a visit on our fair widow today," and inhaled deeply.

"And?" prompted the earl, his displeasure thinly veiled.

Sir Henry's mouth drew up in distaste. "Have you tried this mixture? It's the same sort Alvanley's been using, but I'm not sure I like it."

"Stop trifling with me, Harry, and get to the point."

With a careless shrug, Sir Henry snapped shut the hinged top of the snuffbox. "It's quite simple, old boy. You aspired to be the lady's husband, while I, on the other hand, cherished the desire to enjoy her favors outside the confining bonds of matrimony. And she has selected me."

If Sir Henry was expecting a violent reaction, he was doomed to disappointment. The earl's thick black brows drew sharply together, but he said only, "Gammon, Harry. You must be cast-away if you believe that—or if you think I'll believe it."

For an instant, irritation flickered in the baronet's eyes. "You think so?" His short laugh held a jeering note. "Well, you are free to believe what you will. However, not four hours ago, the incomparable Diana granted me an interview—alone—wherein I made my intentions plain. The fact is, old boy, that Diana has most charmingly consented to become my mistress. Sweet as nectar she was, when I kissed her," he taunted.

The earl was unprepared for the sharp, sickening pain which pierced his chest. "Harry," he said, after the briefest of pauses, "you are either foxed or lying." Somehow he spoke normally, controlling his urge to knock the other man senseless.

Sir Henry rose to his feet, all traces of good humor evaporating. "You may go and ask the lady if you like," he retorted angrily. "And then you may come back and offer your apology. I do not care to be called a liar."

The earl stood, too, and his voice was curt. "If you aren't lying, then you must have misunderstood her—or she you! Devil take the woman! Ten to one she thought you meant marriage! She is not the woman to accept a carte blanche from anyone, least of all you, my fine buck."

Sir Henry stared at him in consternation. "That's pitching it too strong," he objected, his lips twisted in a sneer. "I tell you I never once said the word *marriage!* No woman her age could be so naive!"

Lord Lucan's expression froze the other man's blood. "This woman could," he said icily. "And if you breathe so much as a syllable of this to anyone, Harry, and I mean *anyone*, I'll break every bone in your body, do you hear me?"

Sir Henry retreated by two steps, knowing the earl was well equipped to carry out his threat. "You go see her," he muttered. "You'll see I'm right."

"I intend to," returned the earl grimly. "Right now."

*   *   *

166

After a quiet dinner with Aimee, Diana excused herself and made her way down to the study. She had meant to write the note to Sir Henry immediately, but overwhelmed with fatigue, she simply sank into the desk chair and buried her face in her hands. This constant round of late nights was debilitating, for a lifetime habit of early rising made it difficult to make up her sleep in the morning. And then, of course, last night she had lain awake for hours thinking of Sir Henry.

Diana rubbed at her temples, reflecting upon the number of mistakes she had made in her life. Perhaps remaining so long in Wiltshire had been yet another mistake, for if her existence there had been pleasant, it had also been dull. Here in London, life was not always as pleasant or as insular, but at long last she was beginning to feel really *alive*, to feel like a living, breathing woman who was more than just a hollow shell, void of all emotion. It stimulated her, this new life. There were problems to be faced and dealt with, decisions to be made, the responsibility of managing a household and servants and Aimee; in short, a more normal life for a healthy young woman of four-and-twenty years. And yet, wasn't there even more than this? Was not the most normal life of all that of wife and mother?

A wave of depression slammed her with this thought, drenching her with its implications. As much as she disliked the more intimate aspects of marriage, she was well aware that without the act of love, she would never hold a child of her own in her arms. Could this be part of what she had been longing for of late? And if so, would crying off from her engagement with Sir Henry be still another terrible mistake?

In the frustration of indecision, Diana's fingers dragged through her hair, loosening its fastenings so that the thick golden mass fell about her shoulders. Absently, she reached to remove the remainder of the pins, shaking

167

her head so that her tresses tumbled to their full length just short of her waist. What *was* it she truly longed for, she wondered, her fingers mechanically arranging the pins into a neat pile on the desk. Was it possible to know? Oh, why was it all so complicated?

Absorbed in introspection, Diana did not pay immediate heed to the commotion at the front door or hear the low voice of the earl demanding her whereabouts. It was not until his steady footsteps sounded in the hall outside the study that her head snapped up and her senses spiraled into alertness.

Framed in the doorway, the earl's expression was nearly as black as his hair. "Ah, here you are," he said, with a silky sort of brusqueness to his tone that she had never heard. "I want to have a word with you, if I may." Diana looked at him in astonishment. "Oh? And what right do you have to barge into my home without so much as a by-your-leave?"

Favoring her with another dark look, he stepped inside, shutting the door firmly behind him. "The right of someone who has your best interests at heart," he shot back. In three strides he was across the room and leaning over the narrow desk, his face thrust near hers. "I just spoke to Sir Henry Neyle a while ago," he informed her, his chilly gray eyes boring into hers.

"Oh, really!" Resenting his air of interrogation, Diana drew back indignantly, her chair bumping the wall. "And that should interest me, I suppose?"

"It should," the earl answered, keeping a tight rein on his temper. Straightening to his full height, he began to circle the desk. "I would have thought you'd want to take better care of your reputation," he said suavely, narrowing the gap between them with a purposeful step.

She leaped to her feet. "I have not the least notion what you mean," she retorted, backing away with a wary look. "Have you perchance been drinking?"

Shoving the chair aside, the earl took another step. "Believe me, I considered doing just that," he told her, a hard line to his mouth. "Instead, I came to tell you not to be a little fool. What in Satan's name goes on in that beautiful head of yours, Diana? Is your infatuation with Harry Neyle so strong you are willing to ruin yourself?"

Unable to fathom his meaning, Diana glowered up at him. "I don't know what you're talking about! How *dare* you speak to me like this? You are the most disagreeable, overbearing man I ever—"

His fist crashed down so hard upon the desk that the hairpins scattered. "Shut up, Diana, and listen to me," he thundered. "Are you aware that you accepted a carte blanche this afternoon?"

"*What?*" she gasped, her jaw dropping. "A c-carte blanche? I did no such thing! How dare you make such a . . . a *vile* accusation!" Something in his silence rocked her confidence, but she added, in dignified tones, "Not that it is any business of yours, but Sir Henry did me the honor to ask me to be his wife this afternoon, and I—"

"Damnation!" The harshly uttered word was enough to end her protest. "I thought it might be something like this. My foolish and very naive little widow, don't you recognize an improper proposal when you receive one?" Reaching out, he captured her hands in his, and drew her closer to trap them against his chest. "I just finished listening to Harry brag of his triumph and it was enough to turn my stomach. Good God, Diana, the man has been looking upon you as fair game ever since you arrived!"

Slowly, the color drained from Diana's face. "But . . . but he *asked* me . . ." she insisted, with desperate obstinacy. "You must be wrong."

"What exactly did he say?"

Her eyes fluttered shut in an effort to remember. "He spoke of an alliance between us. We talked of the importance of mutual affection . . ."

169

Sensing her bewilderments, the earl tried to be gentle. "Did he ever say the word *marriage?*"

Diana's eyes flew open, bewilderments in their brown-gold depths. "Not . . . not precisely."

He sighed. "Then I beg you will forgive my sharpness, Diana. There existed that slight chance that you actually understood. . . . It made me furious to think you might have knowingly accepted him. There are other kinds of alliances beside those bound by sacred vows, my poor innocent."

Despite the kindness of his tone, Diana's humiliation was crushing. "Naturally, I know that," she flared, snatching her hands away from his. "It simply never occurred to me that Sir Henry would . . . oh, I could *murder* him!" Her bosom heaved, and a familiar lump of misery burgeoned in her throat. How she hated being made to look the fool!

"Even so," she cried suddenly, "I don't know why you should be so vexed when you tried to offer me the same!"

If she had slapped him in the face, the earl could not have been more dumbfounded. "*I beg your pardon?*" he said incredulously.

Diana eyed him uneasily. "You meant to offer me a . . . a carte blanche, did you not? Before I stopped you, that is?"

In an odd tone, Lord Lucan repeated, "You thought I was asking you to be my *mistress?*"

"Are you . . . are you saying you were not?" she faltered, a curious weakness creeping into her knees.

"Hell's teeth, no!" he exploded, so loudly that she jumped. "I was *trying* to make an honorable offer, dammit! But you could not consider anything of a warmer nature—or at least that was the excuse you gave!" His eyes glinting with fury, he muttered, "Tried, sentenced and condemned, by God, for a crime I didn't commit! For the love of heaven, Diana, I could wring your pretty neck!"

Stunned to the core, Diana gazed up at him with stricken eyes. "I'm sorry, my lord . . . Geoffrey . . . what can I say? You gave me no reason to suppose . . . I mean, I simply assumed—"

"Well, you assumed wrong!" he snapped. "And I gave you *every* reason to suppose! I told you right from the start that I regarded you as a virtuous woman, but you just took it into that obstinate head that I was a womanizing scoundrel, despite anything I said or did!"

"Well, I had evidence!" she flashed, hurt by his derision. "Why, that very first day you threw me a kiss! If that is not a sure sign of a . . . a . . ."

"Profligate?" he suggested sarcastically.

"It is not," she returned with a glare, "the usual behavior of a gentleman."

Controlling his rage, the earl forced himself to alter his tone. "Perhaps not," he conceded. "I told you before, Diana, I don't live my life by other people's rules."

"You are fortunate! Being a peer—and a wealthy one, at that—you can afford to flout convention!"

"Yes, to a degree I can," he agreed. "And you could, too, if you married me. Rich countesses can set their own rules."

"Like Lady Uxbridge?" she said, without thinking.

"What the devil has she got to do with this?"

"Oh, nothing! I just thought perhaps . . ." Diana broke off, biting her lip.

"Thought *what?*"

"I wondered if you and she had been . . . close. And Mrs. Clement, too. It has not escaped my notice, my lord, that the ladies seem to find you vastly entertaining." Somehow, she could not keep the accusing note from her voice.

He stared, then disconcerted her by looking genuinely amused. "Well, I suppose it's a good sign that you noticed," he said, reaching once more for her hands. "No, Diana, I have never found Lady Uxbridge even remotely appealing. And Cynthia Clement is no more than a friend."

Diana knew she was blushing. "I . . . I see. Then, I am sorry, my lord. I have misjudged you all along and you did not deserve it."

"No, by God, I didn't!" he said feelingly.

With lowered eyes, she added, "You must find me very stupid. I . . . my experience with men is not very great, I fear. It is my only excuse."

Before she realized what he intended, his arms had gone around her waist, encircling her loosely. His mouth was inches from her ear. "You're not stupid, Diana," he said softly. "Never think that about yourself, my darling. You're just woefully green." After another moment, he said, "Are you going to marry me?"

"I don't know," she whispered in confusion. "I'm just so tired, too tired to think sensibly." She did not add that his nearness was making it virtually impossible to think at all.

She was having the same effect on him. "Do you have any idea how beautiful you look?" There was a warm, seductive quality to his voice, a husky resonance which told of an unspoken need. "With your hair flowing down your back like a . . . like a river of golden honey?" His quickened breathing warned her what was coming next.

"Please." It was so faint a protest it deserved to be ignored.

"Please what? Don't try to tell me not to kiss you, Diana. You know it's too late for that."

Despite these words, for the space of several seconds he gave her a chance to deny him. Then his mouth slowly lowered to cover hers, exploring the sweet softness of her lips with his own. Wisely, he concentrated on making it a gentle kiss, curbing his ardor in the hope that restraint would find its own reward.

Too weary to fight him, too full of the knowledge of her

own blunders and stupid prejudices, Diana stood meekly in the earl's arms. Men needed this sort of thing, she told herself with a sort of muddled logic. And after misjudging him so dreadfully, perhaps she owed him this? At least this once? If she could only bear it, if she could only conceal her distaste, then perhaps she would stop feeling so horribly guilty and foolish and confused.

How many seconds did it take for her to realize that there was no distaste to conceal, no disgust to bear? Edmund's kiss had always made her flesh creep, Sir Henry's had made her ill, but Geoffrey Trevelyan's kiss was actually . . . why, it was actually pleasant! Marveling at the firm tenderness of his mouth, Diana parted her lips, daring to experiment with something she had feared she would always loathe.

Encouraged, the earl's arms tightened, crushing her against his body so she would know how much she aroused him. With less caution, his hands slid down the length of her back, caressing her warm body through the thin fabric of her gown. It was when he reached the curve of her hip that Diana experienced the first real stab of desire she had ever known.

Merciful heaven, what is happening? Diana's eyes had been closed, but now they burst open, full of unbound panic. She would never quite remember how she managed to tear her mouth from his, but suddenly they were apart, each of them panting and violently unhappy.

"No more . . . no more, please!" Surrendering to her own cowardly fear of the unknown, Diana choked the words out as if they were her last, her voice raw with pent-up emotion.

"What is it, Diana? What's wrong?" Though he said it very carefully, the earl's frustration was more than evident.

"I'm not . . . I'm just not ready for this." How lame and clumsy the words sounded, even in her own ears.

173

"Please forgive me," she whispered.

"Did you love Harry, then?" he asked flatly. "Is that what this is all about?"

Turning the question over in her mind, Diana was amazed by her own answer. "No, I didn't love him at all." Her eyes reached out to him imploringly. "But please try to understand. This afternoon I thought I was affianced to him and now you tell me I'm not. It's a bit of a shock, you know. And now, too, I must correct this odious situation before there is a scandal. Not to mention that poor Tildy sprained her ankle this afternoon, which really was dreadfully upsetting." Her hand swept across her brow. "And I am tired. My head is spinning with problems right now, and . . . and I can deal with no more."

"I see." The earl's face was inscrutable. "I am sorry to hear of Miss Tilden's accident." He hesitated. "And my offer of marriage? Will you consider it?"

It took Diana several seconds to form a reply. "My first marriage was terribly unhappy . . . I daresay you have guessed as much." Her voice was so low he had to bend his head to hear. "When I came to London, I believed I could never marry again. I'm still not sure I can. It seems like such a great risk to take—"

"Much of life is a risk," he interrupted.

She nodded wearily. "Oh, yes. But there are other considerations which . . . which I cannot explain. All I can say is that I would need time to think it over."

"You were willing enough to risk it for Harry," he pointed out in a dry tone.

"Yes, well, I have not told you the whole," she said awkwardly. "I know it sounds terribly capricious of me, but I was intending to cry off. After he left this afternoon, I realized I could not go through with it for . . . for various reasons."

The confession reheated the ashes of the earl's

174

patience. "Then it would obviously be unfeeling of me to press you for an answer this night," he responded. "If you will but agree to consider my offer, then I will be content."

She hesitated. "Yes, my lord, I can agree to consider your offer, but I cannot promise—"

"Of course you cannot," he said quickly. "I simply ask that you think it over. Later, when you are not so tired and overset."

Diana could do nothing but agree, for after wronging him so dreadfully, there could be no disputing that she owed him a fair, well-considered answer. Before taking his leave, Lord Lucan made Diana promise to take no action regarding Sir Henry, assuring her that he would deal with the baronet himself. Again, she was too tired to argue when he made it sound so logical. And from the hard look in his eye, there could be no question but that the Earl of Lucan was perfectly capable of dealing with any trouble Sir Henry Neyle might choose to cause.

Notwithstanding that it was the first night in nearly a week that Diana slept late, the moment she awoke, the flood of memories brought her to instant alertness. Recalling how she had nearly stepped headlong into the very kind of scandal she wished to avoid, Diana wondered how she was ever to trust her own instincts again. What could have fooled her into thinking Sir Henry so safe? Could it have been because he had never really touched her emotions at all?

Lord Lucan had called it an infatuation. That might have been true when she was eighteen, but this time around, she doubted it had been even that. To be strictly honest, had it ever been more than the simple wish to be the envy of those who had hurt her with their gossip? Or had she needed to prove to herself that, in her new maturity, she could succeed where before she had failed? Perhaps she had even had a subconscious desire to turn back time, to start from where she had left off before the night of Edmund's attack. With a regretful sigh, Diana came to the lowering conclusion that whatever the reason, she had behaved like a complete ninnyhammer.

But how could she have been so blind about Lord Lucan? Since the first day she had driven out with him, Diana had recognized his attractiveness, but that had only made him seem more dangerous. Until now. Now she no longer found him at all threatening. Odd, how easily she was able to summon his image when already Sir Henry's angelic countenance was faded and blurred. With new honesty, Diana acknowledged that the earl was a far more attractive, dynamic, *exciting* man than Sir Henry.

What was it that Aunt Serena said? *Sir Henry was as pretty as a girl*, that was it. Viewing them through new eyes, Diana was inclined to agree. The earl possessed an indefinable air of masculinity, a presence that outweighed and would probably outlast Sir Henry's fairness of face. Lord Lucan's features did not look like they had been chiseled from marble, but rather as though they were hewn from granite—as strong and firm as his touch. Such thoughts brought back memories of his kiss, and of the powerful sensations which had seemed to originate in the nether regions of her body.

Unfortunately, however, the sensations were now gone and therefore could not be subjected to reexamination. Had it actually been pleasure she felt? Or had it merely been part of her panic? Replaying the scene in her mind, Diana did not realize that the inner mirror in which she now saw the event was growing more and more distorted. Had she really felt anything at all? Perhaps she had only *wanted* to feel something so badly that her body had fooled her! Was that possible?

MORE PASSION AND ADVENTURE AWAIT... YOUR TRIP TO A BIG ADVENTUROUS WORLD BEGINS WHEN YOU ACCEPT YOUR FIRST 4 NOVELS ABSOLUTELY *FREE* (AN $18.00 VALUE)

Accept your Free gift and start to experience more of the passion and adventure you like in a historical romance novel. Each Zebra novel is filled with proud men, spirited women and tempestuous love that you'll remember long after you turn the last page.

Zebra Historical Romances are the finest novels of their kind. They are written by authors who really know how to weave tales of romance and adventure in the historical settings you love. You'll feel like you've actually gone back in time with the thrilling stories that each Zebra novel offers.

GET YOUR FREE GIFT WITH THE START OF YOUR HOME SUBSCRIPTION

Our readers tell us that these books sell out very fast in book stores and often they miss the newest titles. So Zebra has made arrangements for you to receive the four newest novels published each month.

You'll be guaranteed that you'll never miss a title, and home delivery is so convenient. And to show you just how easy it is to get Zebra Historical Romances, we'll send you your first 4 books absolutely FREE! Our gift to you just for trying our home subscription service.

BIG SAVINGS AND FREE HOME DELIVERY

Each month, you'll receive the four newest titles as soon as they are published. You'll probably receive them even before the bookstores do. What's more, you may preview these exciting novels free for 10 days. If you like them as much as we think you will, just pay the low preferred subscriber's price of just $3.75 each. *You'll save $3.00 each month off the publisher's price.* AND, your savings are even greater because there are never any shipping, handling or other hidden charges—FREE Home Delivery. Of course you can return any shipment within 10 days for full credit, no questions asked. There is no minimum number of books you must buy.

4 FREE BOOKS

TO GET YOUR 4 FREE BOOKS WORTH $18.00 — MAIL IN THE FREE BOOK CERTIFICATE T O D A Y

Fill in the Free Book Certificate below, and we'll send your FREE BOOKS to you as soon as we receive it.

If the certificate is missing below, write to: Zebra Home Subscription Service, Inc., P.O. Box 5214, 120 Brighton Road, Clifton, New Jersey 07015-5214.

FREE BOOK CERTIFICATE

4 FREE BOOKS

ZEBRA HOME SUBSCRIPTION SERVICE, INC.

YES! Please start my subscription to Zebra Historical Romances and send me my first 4 books absolutely FREE. I understand that each month I may preview four new Zebra Historical Romances free for 10 days. If I'm not satisfied with them, I may return the four books within 10 days and owe nothing. Otherwise, I will pay the low preferred subscriber's price of just $3.75 each; a total of $15.00, *a savings off the publisher's price of $3.00.* I may return any shipment and I may cancel this subscription at any time. There is no obligation to buy any shipment and there are no shipping, handling or other hidden charges. Regardless of what I decide, the four free books are mine to keep.

NAME

ADDRESS _____ APT _____

CITY _____ STATE _____ ZIP _____

TELEPHONE
( )

SIGNATURE _____ (if under 18, parent or guardian must sign)

Terms, offer and prices subject to change without notice. Subscription subject to acceptance by Zebra Books. Zebra Books reserves the right to reject any order or cancel any subscription.   019102

GET
FOUR
FREE
BOOKS

(AN $18.00 VALUE)

ZEBRA HOME SUBSCRIPTION
SERVICE, INC.
P.O. Box 5214
120 BRIGHTON ROAD
CLIFTON, NEW JERSEY 07015-5214

Engulfed in self-doubt, Diana forced the matter from her mind, and consequently remembered Miss Tilden and her injury. Honestly! Here she was lounging in bed, when Tildy should have been her first and primary concern. Meg had stayed with her during the night, of course, but still! Hastily snatching up her dressing gown, Diana was in the process of disentangling its sleeves when she crossed the threshold of her companion's room.

She found, however, that all had gone well in her absence. Assisted by Meg, Miss Tilden had already finished most of her breakfast and was halfway through her morning chocolate. Aimee was there, too, and had been entertaining Miss Tilden with an edited version of her London triumphs.

Tildy insisted that she was feeling better. "I daresay I shall be up and about in a trice!" she remarked. "The important thing is that I can still knit, for I have several more skeins of yarn to use up."

However, Diana's keen eyes took in the elderly woman's pallor. "Well, that may be, my dear Tildy, but today you must stay in bed. And I intend to remain home today to take care of you."

"Oh, but you will miss your outing!" objected Tildy in dismay.

With a start, Diana realized she had forgotten all about their plans for the day. "Ah, but you forget," she soothed, "I have seen Madame Tussaud's wax figures before. It is not so great a treat for me as you may imagine."

"Charles has been there several times," inserted Aimee with a nod. "He says that after you've seen them once, the whole thing becomes devilish flat . . . *sadly* flat, I mean," she corrected, with a quick glance at Miss Tilden. "But I still want to see for myself. I wrote him a note this morning to remind him, just in case he forgot our outing or . . . or changed his mind. It was a very polite, genteel sort of note, Diana, just to show that I have forgiven him."

"Forgiven him for what?" inquired Miss Tilden, stifling a yawn.

"Oh, he and I have been at loggerheads on one or two occasions," replied Aimee, rather airily. "But all that is going to change! Today, he is going to see me at my very best. I shall become the model of propriety and decorum he wishes. My eyes will stay modestly cast upon the ground, my remarks limited to the most circumspect observations. I shall shriek in horror at the gruesome displays of the victims from the French Revolution. I will clutch at his sleeve to show him that my sensibilities are simply too overset by it all. I have it all worked out perfectly!"

"That sounds a bit extreme," said Diana dryly.

Aimee shrugged. "Perhaps. But that is how a good many of these London girls behave, after all. And some of them are already betrothed! I have been watching them, you see, and although it seems nonsensical to me, it does seem to be what the gentlemen like."

"The best thing you could do is behave like the nice, normal girl you are," advised Diana tartly, "and forget all this play-acting! How is Charles to learn to care for you if you persist in changing personalities? Just be yourself, Aimee," she pleaded.

Aimee regarded her dubiously. "It may come to that in the end," she said with a sigh. "But I find it hard to believe that the real me could interest Cousin Charles."

"Fiddle!" Diana was about to turn to Miss Tilden for support when she saw Meg put a finger to her lips.

"She's gone off to sleep," explained the abigail softly. "I gave her another dose of laudanum with her food, for her ankle's painin' her some, though she won't admit it."

"Good," approved Diana, as they tiptoed from the

178

room. "Sleep is the best thing for her right now."

"I expect she'll sleep for most of the day, ma'am," offered Meg. "I don't mind sitting with her, if you'd rather go."

Diana glanced at Aimee. "I'd really prefer to stay here, if you think you will be all right. I've already told Tildy I'd be here, and besides, I need a chance to rest and . . . think."

"Don't worry about me," said Aimee with a sunny smile. "I shall be on my best behavior. Nothing can possibly go wrong."

Charles scanned Aimee's note three times before he made up his mind. Was she truly no longer angry? Or was this some childish trick?

He had been in a quandary about the outing, not knowing whether she would still be expecting to go. He had been furious the previous evening—even to the point of tossing off a few brandies before he went to sleep—but this morning, depression had replaced all the anger. Though she was not strictly beautiful, he considered his cousin Aimee the most engaging girl he had ever met. If only she were not so dashed unconformable! The woman of his dreams had always been lovely, circumspect, gentle . . . and, of course, devoted to no one but himself! She was not a wild, impulsive, flighty romp of a girl who flirted with other men. Oh, the deuce! Ruffling his hair, he wondered what he should do.

Should he court his cousin? He was reasonably sure it would please Aunt Serena, but for once, he did not give a damn whether it did or not. He tried to envision himself married to Aimee, and suddenly began to chuckle. It would not be the peaceful union for which he longed, that much was certain!

He glanced again at her note. She would be waiting, it informed him. Moreover, she had apologized very prettily for her indiscreet behavior, and assured him that he would have no further cause to be ashamed of her. Ashamed? Had he been ashamed of his cousin?

No, by Jove, he hadn't! The emotions which assailed him were nothing to do with shame. It had been jealousy, pure and simple . . . and hurt, too, when it came right down to it. Hurt that Captain Peterson's attractions had been able to lure her away from him so easily. He'd thought she'd been delighted at the opportunity to sit out the set with him. And then she had been gone!

Charles scratched at his head in uncertainty. Females, he reflected, did tend to do unaccountable things, so how could he expect little Aimee to be any different? Ah well. With any luck, today's outing would help him make this extremely difficult decision.

Chapter Ten

After flitting around the drawing room for a number of minutes, Aimee forced herself to sit, resisting the urge to fly to the window each time the rumble of carriage wheels reached her ears. She was wearing a new and very flattering gown of ice blue, but it was not doing as much to bolster her confidence as she'd hoped. Despite her brave words to Diana, she was feeling very nervous about seeing Charles, as evidenced by the restless fluttering of her hands and the strange churning in her stomach. She knew she had treated her cousin badly, and was firmly resolved to make it up to him. But would Charles forgive her? Had the apology in her note been enough? Would he come? If *only* he would come, Aimee prayed silently, she would be as meek and biddable as he wished.

For what seemed like the hundredth time, she glanced at the clock upon the mantelshelf. He was clearly going to be late, she thought. The only alternative brought back her nervousness; her stomach tightened into knots and her imagination leaped into action. He was not going to come. He had read her note, but instead of forgiving her, he had crumpled it, tossing it over his shoulder with a contemptuous curl to his lip.

Filled with foreboding, Aimee began to envision the

subsequent scene. She would go away forever, and only then would Charles realize that the only woman he could ever love had vanished from his life. She would waste away to an early death and when it was too late he would come (haunted with regret) to lay roses (preferably red ones) on her grave. Of course he would soon die of a broken heart and someone—perhaps Diana—would suggest that they be buried together. . . .

So affected was Aimee by this melancholy scene that huge tears welled in her blue eyes. She groped for her handkerchief, and sobbed into it with an abandon which would have been the envy of many an actress. The storm was of short duration, however, for an instant later, her cousin's familiar footsteps sounded on the stairs. With a muffled gasp, she dabbed frantically at one eye and then the other, blew her little nose and stuffed the sodden handkerchief under the cushion of the chair. By the time Charles entered the room, Aimee had managed to snatch up a book from a nearby table, reclaim her chair, and have the book open in her lap.

If her greeting held only a fraction of its usual vivacity, Charles gave no sign that he noticed. She gazed at him in trepidation, but to her astonishment, instead of hurling aspersions or indeed, displaying any sign of ill humor, he caught up her hands in a light squeeze, something he had never done before.

His first words surprised her even more. "You're looking as fine as fivepence this morning," he said, clearing his throat. As it happened, he had rehearsed this remark very carefully on the way over, but as Aimee's reddened nose and woebegone expression could hardly escape his attention, he abandoned the rest of his speech and said instead, a shade awkwardly, "I say, you haven't been crying, have you? Are you not feeling quite the thing?"

"No, no, I am perfectly well," she responded, then

blurted out, "Oh, I am so glad you came! I was afraid you might have . . . forgotten or even that you might still be . . . be angry about last night."

Charles's mouth curved in a lopsided smile. "Who me? No, no, I ain't one to stew for days, the way some do. Don't fret about it, kitten. I've forgotten it already." He hesitated, his expression turning doubtful. "But are you sure *you* ain't still miffed? I was dashed hard on you, I know. I can't think what made me say such brutish things."

His admission made her feel doubly ashamed. "No, you were quite justified, Charles," she protested. "It was my fault entirely. I ought to have known better than to allow Captain Peterson to . . . to . . ."

"Well, it won't happen again." he said gruffly. "You'll know better next time."

"I hope so." Deciding that this was as good a time as any to seem submissive, Aimee hung her head and said, "I *know* that as my only male relative here in town, I really must let you advise me. Being a mere female, I simply do not have the least notion how to go on. If only I were a man!" she sighed, raising ingenuous eyes to his.

This was doing it much too brown, and Charles gave her a suspicious look. Wondering if she could possibly be in earnest, he retorted, "Now, Aimee, there ain't nothing wrong with being a female. Why, it's a dashed fine thing to be! I mean, where would we all be without females? Nowhere, that's where!"

Aimee's nose wrinkled in perplexity. "Nowhere? Oh, you mean because we can make babies?"

"Well, I suppose that's what I meant," he answered, looking disconcerted. "Dash it, how did we get on to this? We'd better go!" he said, taking her by the arm.

Babies, however, had always been of great interest to Aimee. "But Charles," she argued, as he propelled her toward the door, "we cannot make babies on our own, you know. Men are as—"

"Now, Aimee!" cut in her cousin hastily. "This really ain't the time to discuss this!"

She eyed him anxiously. "Oh, very well. I did not mean to make you angry."

"I'm not angry!" he insisted, sounding exasperated.

"Then why are you raising your voice? I'm not deaf!"

Charles strove to remain calm. "It's just that it ain't the kind of thing you ought to discuss with a man," he explained. "Delicate subject, and all that."

Aimee looked quite shocked. "Well, I know that! I wouldn't dream of talking of such things with anyone but you, Charles. But, you *are* my cousin, after all." She gave him a trusting smile, and tucked her hand under his arm. "You are different from all the other gentlemen . . . so much *nicer*—though you do lecture a shade too much! But I *do* feel safe with you, and I did *not* with Captain Peterson. In fact, I did not like him at all," she confided, "and I was *so* relieved when you rescued me! I could not help thinking you were just like Lochinvar!"

"Who?" said Charles blankly.

"Goodness, haven't you read *Marmion* yet? Lochinvar is a gallant knight who rescues fair Ellen from her dastardly bridegroom. You really must read it, Charles, it is so romantic! He rides all alone, and never stops, not even to eat! He just rides and rides—until he reaches a river that no one can ford, and then he swims across—"

"Sounds like a dashed noodlebrain to me," put in Charles with only mild interest. "Why didn't he just offer for her himself? Seems a lot more logical."

"Oh, but he did!" she explained. "But her father refused to consider his suit. So he stole her away, right in the middle of a ball!"

Charles's face was eloquent of skepticism. "Sounds like the poor fellow was touched in the upper works!" he declared. "Anyway, you're talking a pack of nonsense, Aimee! *I* didn't steal you from any bridegroom. Wouldn't do that," he added, thinking it over. "Bad *ton!*"

"If you say so, Charles," said Aimee in disappointment.

"We'd better go," said her pragmatic cousin, whose definition of romance did not include having to swim rivers or do without his dinner. "My coachman don't like me to keep the horses waiting."

All the way to Madame Tussaud's, Aimee behaved with a flawless decorum which her cousin found unconvincing but restful. Madame Tussaud was soon to leave Blackheath to resume her tour of the country, and the newspapers had urged anyone who had not yet viewed her famous wax figures to do so before it was too late. Charles, no great admirer of wax figures, had nonetheless offered himself as escort when he'd discovered that Aimee wished to go.

"I can't say I'm wild about seeing 'em again," he remarked, giving her a hand out of the carriage. "But I don't mind it if it pleases you. As long as you don't take it into your head to drag me to the British museum!" he added, somewhat obscurely.

Within, there was a surprising crush of people, for the recent announcement—coming as it had at the onset of the Season—had brought out the curious in droves. Glancing around at some of the other visitors, Aimee grew stiff with annoyance. A little ahead, and not five feet to their right was that odious girl who had danced twice with Charles at *her* come-out ball!

Drusilla Low was clinging to the arm of a gentleman named Mr. Peacham. As it happened, Mr. Peacham was one of Aimee's most ardent admirers, and between this and the fact that Drusilla Low had obviously—as Aimee privately phrased it—*set her cap* for Charles, there would be little chance, she was sure, of avoiding them. Nevertheless, she attempted to point Charles in the opposite direction.

"Dash it, Aimee, don't push," objected Charles.

"You're going the wrong way."

"Oh," she replied, gritting her teeth as Charles steered the exact course she wished to avoid.

Naturally, since Mr. Peacham was extemely tall, his somewhat protuberant brown eyes noticed them at once. "Why, if it isn't Miss Farington!" he cried in delight. "Of all the wonderful coincidences!"

To Aimee's chagrin, they became a foursome within minutes. She was unsure just how this came to pass, but blamed it entirely on Miss Low, who was—as the seething Miss Farington later told her sister—nothing but a cunning little jade when it came down to it. (For what other reason could Miss Low have had for addressing the majority of her remarks to Cousin Charles, as if Mr. Peacham and herself were but two more of Madame Tussaud's wax figures?)

She would have enjoyed herself so much more had she been able to have Charles to herself, Aimee thought bitterly. Of course, it would have been the simplest thing to make them feel unwelcome, but Aimee's breeding forbade such a course. A proper young lady would allow no vestige of her resentment to show, she reflected with resignation. And was she not determined to show Charles that she was not a spoiled brat? Well, she would prove it! With this in mind, Aimee pinned a rather fixed smile to her lips and directed it at the other couple.

Actually, Miss Low was not as plain as Aimee previously thought. Her aura of plainness arose from her sallow complexion and the unfortunate fact that none of the pastel colors she favored suited her in the least. However, her features were regular and her eyes a fine shade of blue. She had a pretty laugh, but used it too frequently, as if everything either gentleman said was uncommonly amusing. She also had the unfortunate habit of appending any of Aimee's remarks with her own, which very soon began to take its toll upon Miss Farington's nerves.

When Aimee, regarding the figure of the great Horatio Nelson, remarked to Charles, "He is so lifelike!" Miss Low chimed in with, "Oh, yes, indeed! He looks as if he could step right off the pedestal, does he not, Mr. Perth?"

When they paused to examine the wise, benevolent features of Benjamin Franklin, Aimee said, "I wonder what it is like to live in America?" Miss Low immediately tacked on, "I have always felt it would be the most fascinating place to visit, don't you agree, Mr. Perth?"

At this, Aimee put up her chin and said, "I daresay it must be shockingly primitive there! What do you think, Charles?"

But Miss Low jumped in with, "Oh, yes! I should be far too frightened to go! A woman is better off remaining in the country in which she was born, don't you agree, Mr. Perth?"

"But I should very much like to meet an Indian!" said Aimee defiantly. "Wouldn't you, Charles?"

Miss Low shivered, and for the first time advanced her own opinion. "I am very sure Indians are quite horrible," she stated, but spoiled it all by adding, "Don't you agree, Mr. Perth?"

At this point, Mr. Peacham, who was obviously a proponent of accuracy, enthusiastically inserted, "Actually, in places like Philadelphia and Boston, I believe there is no danger at all. I am told that these towns are considerably less provincial than we English believe, and that no Indians reside anywhere near them."

No doubt Miss Low would have renewed her protestations in America's favor had not Charles suggested they move on, as there was a group of people pressing them from behind. Even as he spoke, he caught the eye of

187

a large fat woman who was glaring at them.

"Oh, yes, *do* let us move on," urged Miss Low in agreement.

A short while later, as they paused before the figure of Voltaire, Charles put up his quizzing glass, ostensibly to better examine the great man's erudite features. Miss Low sighed, and expressed the wish that she were better acquainted with his work.

"Common sense is not so common," quoted Aimee in a sedate voice.

Miss Low's eyes narrowed suspiciously, Mr. Peacham looked impressed, and Charles said, "Eh?" in rather a startled voice.

Aimee tipped her head toward Voltaire. "He said it," she explained, looking pleased with herself. She was not about to tell them it was her father's favorite remark. Let them think she read Voltaire!

Miss Low made a quick recovery. "Why, how clever you are, Miss Farington!" she affirmed, with a warm smile for Charles. "Of all things, I do so admire an educated female do not you, Mr. Perth?"

Aimee's sharp eye saw Charles's lip quiver, but he said only, "Oh, aye!" in a tone of such cordiality that she stared at him. He was actually enjoying himself! she realized incredulously. How *could* he, when she was feeling so utterly miserable? Could he actually be flattered by Miss Low's fawning effusions?

It only grew worse. Charles began to make jocular observations about each of the figures, to which Miss Low would say, "Oh, Mr. Perth! You are so droll!" until Aimee longed to box both their ears. Mr. Peacham seemed oblivious, and continued favoring them all with more historical tidbits, to which, out of common civility, Aimee was forced to respond, "How interesting!" or "Indeed!" because Miss Low had ceased to pay him any heed

188

at all.

Quite suddenly the room was too crowded, too warm. "Charles, does it not seem rather warm in here?" she murmured, staring fixedly at the waxy face of a young Queen Elizabeth. "There are too many people in here. It makes it difficult to breathe properly."

"It *is* warm," concurred Miss Low at once. "Perhaps you should sit down, Miss Farington. I would be happy to stay with you," she offered with sugary solicitude.

Charles frowned. "Are you all right?" he inquired, glancing down at her in concern.

"I—I think so. I do not want to sit down," replied Aimee irritably. "I want to see the rest of the exhibit!"

"Quite natural," agreed Mr. Peacham, bobbing his head. "It would be a severe disappointment to miss anything."

To Aimee's surprise, Charles gripped her arm a little more tightly from thence on. They soon entered the next room, which held the most grisly (and therefore the most popular) of the exhibits, the Chamber of Horrors.

It was this room which housed the ghastly replicas of the victims of France's guillotine, modeled by poor Madame Tussaud under gruesome circumstances. The French government, explained Mr. Peacham, had forced Madame to model the severed heads brought to her, no doubt many of whom had been known to her personally—including the ill-fated king and queen. Ironically, the murderers themselves eventually lost their heads, and these were also on display: Fouquier–Tinville, Hébert, Robespierre, and the murdered Marat lying in his bath.

What glimpse she got of them made Aimee feel nauseous. Recalling how she had bragged to Diana of how she would shriek with horror at the sight, she could only wonder at her own simplicity. It truly was a chamber of horrors, she reflected, feeling her head begin to throb. The problem was that her imagination was so very vivid.

"Charles," she whispered, tugging his sleeve. "I do not think I want to see any more. I'm afraid I don't feel very well after all. I am so cold all of a sudden . . ."

With what speed and efficiency Charles whisked her out of the museum she could only afterwards marvel. She did not, of course, realize how pale she had become, nor how distasteful Charles had begun to find their two companions. She was a little dizzy, and exceedingly grateful for the support of her cousin's arm as they exited the building. She never would remember just how Charles located his coach, but manage it he did, and with astonishing efficiency.

Once inside, out of all possible view, Aimee closed her eyes and leaned against Charles. Though her cheeks felt hot, she was shaking with chills that seemed to have taken over her small body. She did not even realize that his arm had gone around her or that her face was pressed against his waistcoat.

"Charles," she murmured, after a moment. "I think I should warn you that I might be sick."

She could feel his body shift. "Lord, Aimee, are you sure?"

"No." Her voice was very faint. "I shall try . . . very hard not to be . . . but if I am, you won't despise me . . . will you?"

Charles gazed rather wonderingly down at the soft black curls brushing his chin. "Where do you females get your crackbrained notions?" he said soothingly. "M'father says my mother is the same way. Always taking some odd notion into her head and clinging to it like a dashed limpet."

Aimee clutched suddenly at his waistcoat, and Charles braced himself. "No, I'm all right," she assured him, drawing an uneven breath. "You did not mind leaving

Miss Low, did you?"

"Of course not, kitten." His voice was queerly strangled.

"Charles?" she whispered, after a few more minutes. "This is the second time you have rescued me, you know."

Beneath her cheek, Charles's chest shook just a trifle. "Oh, is that what I'm doing?" he inquired, absently stroking her midnight curls.

"Oh, yes. For I should have disgraced myself utterly had you not been there."

"Just like that queer fellow with the odd name," he joked.

"Yes, just like Lochinvar," she whispered into his coat.

Shortly thereafter, they arrived back at Jermyn Street, and Charles, after explaining the situation to Diana, proved himself equal to the task of carrying his damsel in distress up two flights of stairs to her room. Even had she wanted to object—which she did not—Aimee was still feeling far too unwell to walk. Charles laid her gently down upon her bed, and after expressing his willingness to do anything in his power to help, promptly removed himself from the premises.

"Oh, Diana, I'm so sorry," moaned Aimee, as her sister helped her into her nightdress.

"Hush, now. I'm afraid you have a fever, my dear," Diana stated, touching her sister's brow. "You will have to stay in bed, at least for a day or two," she went on, tucking in the sheets. "But I have some news to cheer you up. A letter from Eliza arrived a short while ago."

"Oh, good," said Aimee, her voice whisper soft. "I'll wait and read it a bit later, I think."

As it transpired, Aimee was ill for more than a week.

and between nursing her and taking care of Miss Tilden, Diana was kept exhaustingly busy. Meg was a great help, of course, but theirs was a small household, and her abigail had many other chores to do. Moreover, Meg was equally fatigued, so that out of pure kindness, Diana insisted she take her afternoon off, as usual.

The house seemed filled with flowers, for a host of Aimee's admirers appeared to have discovered she was ill. The most prized of these arrangements were the ones from Charles, which took the place of honor at the side of Aimee's bed, but there were many others besides. Lord Lucan had sent flowers, also, but these were for Miss Tilden, which pleased Diana so much that she immediately sat down to write him a note of thanks.

Encouraged by the warmth of her letter, the earl presented himself at Jermyn Street the afternoon Meg was out. He had called twice before, but upon both occasions Diana had been tending to Aimee, and had come downstairs for only a few minutes to speak to him. This time, however, Chance favored him, for both patients were asleep and Diana had a few spare minutes on her hands. She was sitting alone, idly flipping through the first pages of a novel when he arrived.

She put it down at once, and had she not looked so exhausted and pale, the smile she bestowed upon the earl would have made him feel quite jubilant. However, since he was very worried that she, too, might succumb to influenza, he only frowned.

"You are not taking care of yourself, Diana," he said, in his blunt way. "You look positively hagged."

There was a time when such a remark would have kindled her temper, but Diana was so glad to see him she only laughed.

"Why, thank you, my lord," she said affably. "How pleasant it is to know that I may always count on you to deliver a pretty compliment!"

He smiled a little. "Yes, I've a way with words, don't I? Seriously, though, aren't you getting any rest at all? You don't look it."

"Not a great deal," she admitted. "But I assure you I don't regret it. Aimee is much better today, and is hoping to be up and about by the end of the week. And if only—" she broke off suddenly. "But let us sit down! What an uncivil hostess I am become!"

He waited for her to sit, then pulled a second chair close to her side. "If only what, Diana?" he inquired, reaching for her hand. "Is the little minx causing you more difficulty?"

His touch made her feel oddly revived. "You must not call her that," she reproached. "She has been feeling so miserable and has scarcely complained at all! No, the problem has nothing to do with Aimee. It is simply that her closest friend, Eliza Fingleshaw, is coming to town sometime next week and, well, I am not at all pleased. I'm afraid Eliza has the worst possible influence upon my sister."

The earl's brows shot up. "Oh? Then why do you not forbid the friendship?"

Diana laughed lightly. "Aimee is my sister, not my daughter, Lord Lucan. Moreover, the Fingleshaws are my parents' neighbors, and would undoubtedly take instant umbrage were I to suggest that their darling Eliza is of a sadly unsteady character—which she is!"

"Nonsense," he said impatiently. "If the girl encourages your sister to behave wildly, it is your duty—or that of your parents—to put a stop to it!"

"Yes, you are right, I know," she agreed. "But Aimee is so delighted, you see. And it is the only thing that has been able to cheer her up—save the knowledge that Charles has called a number of times to see how she goes on! I'm afraid *his* opinion is the only one that really counts with Aimee."

"Then ask him to use his influence," the earl advised. "Good God, Diana, you don't need to carry the whole burden yourself! What about your great-aunt? Why don't you speak to her about it?"

"I would, if I thought it would do any good. But it seems that Aimee and Aunt Serena have been getting along quite famously, and I should so hate to spoil that! You won't repeat this, I know, but according to Aunt Serena, she and Aimee are remarkably similar in character! I could scarcely credit it, when she told me!"

Lord Lucan looked unsurprised. "I can credit it," he said dryly. "They are both shockingly spoiled, mollycoddled by their relatives, their every whim catered to—"

"Surely I do not do that!" Diana exclaimed. "Oh, you are roasting me again—are you not? I am too tired to be sure."

"Let me take you for a drive," he urged. "The fresh air will do you good. How long has it been since you were out of the house? Days, I should guess."

"Thank you, I should very much like to," she replied casting a wistful glance toward the window, "but I have given Meg the afternoon off, and there is no other female in the house to attend to the patients. Tildy cannot put her full weight on her foot yet, so—oh, *pray* do not scowl so!" she said, impulsively squeezing his hand. "I promise I am not just inventing excuses."

His gray eyes probed her face. "Tomorrow then. Don't say no, Diana. I won't accept a refusal."

She could not help smiling at his domineering tone. "You are a shocking bully, my lord," she scolded. "I should refuse, if only to give you the set-down you deserve!"

"I only want to take care of you," he pointed out, in a tone that made her color up.

Diana's eyes dropped, then rose. "To own the truth,"

she confessed, "there is nothing in the world I would rather do than drive out with you."

"Good!" The earl had been clasping her hand all this time, and he chose this moment to raise it to his lips. "By the way, you may be interested to know that your 'betrothal' is now at an official end. I spoke to the gentleman in question, and he has promised not to trouble you again."

Involuntarily, Diana's fingers tightened in his. "How can I ever thank you?" she asked, her voice full of emotion. "I have worried and worried that perhaps I should have spoken to him myself, but—"

"Indeed, had it been an honorable offer, I daresay you would be right," he cut in. "But in such a case as this, I hardly think we need observe the niceties. Do not worry so much, Diana."

Her sigh was faint but discernable. "I do worry a great deal," she admitted. "It's in my nature, I think. But life is far from simple."

However, the earl was bent upon making life as simple as possible for Diana, and when he left her house a short while later, he paid a visit on Great-aunt Serena. The Dowager Viscountess of Torrington kept him kicking up his heels a mere twenty minutes before she deigned to put in an appearance, an interval which Diana could have told him was remarkably short for the old lady. He could not regard it so, however, and although he bore with good grace the intervening minutes while her servants fussed about arranging her cushions, footstool, and shawl, his patience had nearly run out by the time she dismissed them.

Comfortable at last, she turned her attention to her visitor. "Well, well!" she cackled, peering at him with interest. "Ain't this a surprise! Sit down—no, not there!

Over here where I can see you!" She watched as he obeyed, then went on, "Now, what brings you to see an old woman like me? Or need I ask?" she added archly.

The earl's bow had been courteous enough, but he was not about to beat around the bush. "Madam, I have just paid a call upon your niece," he told her brusquely. "Are you aware that she is on the verge of collapse?"

"How should I be aware of it?" returned the old lady curtly. "I ain't been there in over a week. And I don't plan to go, either, not while there's any risk of contracting an infectious ailment! My nieces are young. They can handle it—I can't!"

"I have no quarrel with that," he said impatiently, "but has it occurred to you, ma'am, to send an envoy to inquire how they are? Diana is looking burnt to the socket from the strain of playing nursemaid. In short, ma'am, she is in need of assistance."

"I see," said the dowager, after a pause. "And you came here to tell me of my negligence. Well, believe it or not, impudent young jackanapes, I received a note from Diana not two days ago assuring me she was perfectly well and in need of nothing! So what do you have to say to that, eh?"

"I say that if you know Diana as well as I, you must also know that would be her response. She is foolishly obstinate about some things, and likes her independence. But good God, ma'am! All you need do is send over one or two of your maidservants to give her some assistance! She has only the one to help her, and it is obviously not enough."

"And what business is it of yours?" inquired the dowager with sarcasm. "You seem to be mighty interested in things that don't concern you!"

Controlling his temper, he said, "Anything to do with Diana concerns me."

"Then why the devil don't you make her an offer?"

196

she said sharply.

"Dammit, I have!" he fired back.

The dowager's tongue clicked in dismay. "Oh, good God, do you mean to say the fool girl rejected you?"

The earl shrugged. "Not yet. To be honest, at the moment, I doubt that Diana is in a fit mental state to consider a proposal of marriage. Perhaps if she had some relief from her nursing duties, she could begin to consider it. But that is not my motive, Lady Torrington, so do not think it. I merely want to see Diana restored to her usual blooming health."

"Well, I ain't at all sure I have any maidservants to spare," snapped the dowager petulantly. "I don't waste good money on servants I don't need!"

The earl's lip curled. "In that case, ma'am," he said in a hard voice, "I will take up no more of your time."

"Oh, sit down, sit down," she barked. "Don't take everything I say so damned literally. Mayhap I could spare one of my girls. I'll have to give it some thought."

The earl bowed, but remained standing. "Thank you, ma'am. I am confident you will make a wise decision."

Aunt Serena took rather approving stock of the earl's solid six-foot frame. "In a hurry to leave, are you?" she complained. "Well, I can understand it. Why would you want to talk to an old bore like me? In my day I used to be what they call a diamond of the first water, but I daresay you won't believe it. Ha! Well, beauty don't last, does it? So make sure it's more than Diana's beauty that you want, my fine lad!"

"Have no fear of that," he said truthfully. "And whether you believe it or not, ma'am, I don't find you at all boring. You can be a most diverting woman—when you choose to be." To prove this, he sat back down, prepared to keep her company for a while.

"Toad-eater!" said the dowager viscountess, regarding him with sour pleasure. "You're as bad as Thurstan, then. Worse, actually, for there's some excuse for him! *He* remembers what I looked like when I was in my prime!" She paused. "I was acquainted with your grandfather, the fourth earl," she said abruptly. "Knew him well, in fact. You've something of a look of him. He was a devil of a rake, y'know."

"Indeed," said the earl, rather ruefully. "Well, it don't run in the family, ma'am, in case that's what you're wondering. My oats were sown long ago."

"Good," nodded Aunt Serena. "Diana don't need another one of those on her hands. Keep your chin up, boy. You've my blessing in this matter."

Chapter Eleven

When a fresh-faced young maidservant presented herself at Jermyn Street the following morning, Diana received her with some puzzlement. The girl, Mary by name, brought with her a note—as caustically worded as one might expect in a note from Aunt Serena—but as the dowager made no reference to the earl's visit, Diana was at a loss as to why she should have sent the girl at all. However, since she was ready to admit that they needed another woman in the house, it was with alacrity that she accepted the use of Mary's services. Mary's presence enabled Diana to get in a well-deserved rest, and by the time the earl arrived later that afternoon, she was looking and feeling better than she had in days.

She related the incident to the earl as they set out. "I cannot quite imagine Aunt Serena thinking of it on her own," she confided, as his well-sprung curricle carried them along the Mayfair streets. "It is most odd, don't you think?"

"Very odd," he said imperturbably. "She would have done better to have thought of it sooner, but it was good of her all the same."

Diana looked at him closely. "Actually, it crossed my mind that it is more the sort of thing you would do. But that is silly of me, isn't it?"

"Very silly," he agreed. "What a fine day it has turned out to be. That cloud formation ahead of us looks almost like some sort of running animal. A stag, perhaps? What do you think?"

"You are not trying to change the subject by any chance, are you, my lord?" she inquired in a suspicious voice.

"I?" Lord Lucan shot her a lazy look. "Since when have I ever been anything but direct with you?"

"To my knowledge, never!" she admitted. "But then, you have never seemed the sort of man to see fanciful creatures in the clouds, either!"

"No?" He sighed audibly. "Dear me, I suppose I have not. What a pity."

She eyed him for a few seconds, then decided to try a more straightforward approach. "I would rather that you do not play games with me, my lord. Why do you not simply admit it?"

"Admit what, my dear Mrs. Verney?" The earl's expression was as devoid of guilt as a small child's.

"Admit to sending the maidservant," she said with a touch of impatience. "Or should I say, of coercing my aunt into sending her!"

He appeared to debate his answer. "Coerced is a strong word, Diana," he replied at last. "I prefer 'suggested.' It has a nicer ring to it."

"Then it *is* you I have to thank." The words were not what he expected and he gave her a sharp look. "It was such a practical solution," she went on, unconscious of his scrutiny, "I was almost sure you must be behind it. I'm afraid it never occured to me to ask my aunt for assistance, though now I see that it would have been the sensible thing to have done."

They were nearing the entrance to the Park, which was congested with vehicles, and the earl sent his pair the signal to slow. As he maneuvered them unerringly into line, he remarked, a shade casually, "I had a notion that you would be up in arms at my presuming to interfere."

"Well," she said, thinking this over with a puckered brow, "I suppose a few weeks ago I would have been very much put out by it. But how ungrateful I would be to resent what was so sorely needed and was meant to be a kindness! It means a great deal to me that you took the trouble. We have become very close friends, I think."

"Yes, haven't we?" he concurred, rather tonelessly. Silence reigned as he navigated the curricle through the entrance gate to the Park. They were a little way along the carriage way when he said, "But I hope you do not forget that we might be a great deal closer."

Diana examined her fingertips as if she had never seen them before. "No," she answered, a note of constraint entering her voice. "I have not forgotten your offer, Lord Lucan. I know that is what you are hinting. But things have been so . . . so busy lately that I have been unable to come to any decision." As if her words were somehow hurtful, she added quickly, "I am greatly honored by your offer, Lord Lucan. I think I forgot to tell you that before."

"Yes, well, I was worried about that," he said flippantly, but could have kicked himself when he saw the way her hands jerked in her lap. "Forgive me, Diana. That was a shabby thing to say. I'm afraid I have no excuse."

She shook her head slowly. "Not so, my lord. You have every excuse in the world. I am treating you quite outrageously, I know, by not . . . not giving you an answer." She swallowed hard. "You cannot know how badly I feel about it. I must try your patience very much."

"On the contrary, I am pleased that you are willing to treat my offer as the serious matter it is. It was not lightly made, I assure you."

"I know." Her voice was unusually subdued. "And I shall give it very serious thought. I promise."

"I can ask no more than that," he replied evenly.

They were both unaware that several carriages behind, the eyes of a certain lady were upon them. Accompanied by her current lover, who also happened to be her distant cousin, Lady Uxbridge had also chosen that afternoon to take the air. Her motive, however, was somewhat different from Diana's, for she went to the Park because it was fashionable to be seen there, and because it usually provided her with some trifling new piece of gossip. During the fashionable hour, the congregation of carriages frequently came to a complete standstill, affording one the opportunity to converse with whomever happened to be at hand.

"It's a bit like the game of roulette, isn't it?" she murmured to her companion, a fair-haired youth at least fifteen years her junior. "Think of it! Why, one might meet anyone—even one's own spouse. That would be a novelty, wouldn't it? I do not think I've set eyes on poor Uxbridge in over a week." Her full lips slid into a satisfied smile. "Not that it matters when I have you, David, dear."

Knowing she did not require an answer, her companion smiled his beautiful smile and said nothing. He was simply an ornament on this occasion, a youthful foil for the countess's ripened perfection.

Lady Uxbridge was in a good humor this afternoon, and even as her brooding gaze rested upon the Earl of Lucan, her sunny mood did not completely recede. It had been so long since a man had rejected her so rudely that she could hardly believe it had happened. He really ought to be punished, she mused. Then her curious gaze shifted to the golden-haired woman beside him. So he persisted in playing escort to Edmund Verney's widow, did he? Her heavy lids drooped as she considered that interesting fact.

When the countess's coachman was forced to halt their progress a few minutes later, she was still deep in thought, and had she not looked up quite by chance, might have missed her opportunity to speak with Sir Henry Neyle. His knowing eyes were upon her, and since the baronet's peculiar brand of charisma had always appealed to her, she sent him her most tantalizing smile.

He doffed his beaver at once. "Good day, Lady Uxbridge. How very well you are looking, ma'am."

"And you, Sir Henry," she drawled in her languorous manner. "Always so gallant, so polished. I make no doubt you hold half the female hearts of London in your grasp."

He bowed. "You flatter me, ma'am." His eyes shifted to the face of her companion, and he cocked an inquiring eyebrow. "Dear me, let me guess," he said cordially. "*Not* the worthy Lord Uxbridge, and certainly not one of your own charming progeny."

She looked amused. "Certainly not. My children are far too young to live in London." She waved a white hand. "This is David. He is very shy."

Sir Henry reached for his quizzing glass. "Really?" he said, examing the youth in polite disbelief. "Are lapdogs shy?"

The countess's full lips curved. "You are very naughty, Sir Henry. You will hurt David's feelings. David and I enjoy a pleasant, cousinly friendship, don't we, darling?"

"Heavens, can it talk, too?" inquired Sir Henry with ruthless humor. "My dear Lady Uxbridge, with all due respect to your pretty companion, I implore you to do me the honor of joining me in my curricle. Send David home to play with his rattles."

She'd been hoping for the invitation, and did not care how it was couched. "Why, what a splendid notion," she replied. "I believe I shall do just that. David won't mind, will you, David?" She naturally did not add that she would pay him well not to mind in the least.

The transfer was soon made, and Lady Uxbridge settled herself contentedly beside Sir Henry. Each was anticipating a very pleasant interlude, and since both parties were well-seasoned in amatory matters, a great deal of ground was covered in a very short time.

"Now, why," pondered Sir Henry, not ten minutes later, "have we never done this before? I own I cannot think of a reason."

"Can you not? I can." The countess's side glance was replete with meaning. "I have seen how the suave Sir Henry amuses himself with the ladies. One might conjecture he has had his hands full enough."

Sir Henry's teeth flashed. "You flatter me, ma'am. But one does one's poor best."

"But how splendid," she murmured. "I so admire a man who tries to do his best. It makes me want to know that man better."

"For you, ma'am," he said gallantly, "I would strive to new heights of endeavor. Though I warn you I am no child, like your David. But experience yields other benefits."

"You interest me profoundly," she replied, rolling the words off her tongue in a way that made her meaning obvious.

His eyes dropped to the ripe swell of her breasts. "May I say, my dear lady, that your sentiments are entirely reciprocated?"

More by accident than design, Lady Uxbridge's gaze fell once more upon the Earl of Lucan, whose curricle was no longer so far in the distance. Almost without thinking, she said, "You used to be much more in his company."

"Who?" With difficulty, the baronet tore his eyes from her bosom, where the taut contours of her nipples were remarkably visible. "Oh," he said, following her gaze. "Now, that, dear lady, is quite another story. Hardly of interest to us, is it?"

In many ways, Lady Uxbridge was very intelligent. "Ah," she said, with a brittle smile. "There has been a rivalry between you. For the golden-haired lady in the earl's carriage, perhaps?"

Sir Henry looked vaguely disgruntled. "Aye. 'Tis still a sore point with me, I confess."

The countess looked thoughtful. "I know exactly what you mean, darling." She shrugged, somehow making the movement into a sensuous wriggle. "Never mind," she said softly. "A man like you needs a woman of passion and imagination . . . a woman like me."

Sir Henry's own imagination was well at work. "Where can we go?" he muttered. "Where, Sophia? And when?"

"Patience," she warned. "We go nowhere right now. Discretion, darling. Above all, remember discretion . . ."

Even after she returned home, a glow of cheerfulness enveloped Diana, and her feet were light as she mounted the stairs to her room. The outing in the Park had done her a great deal of good, and except for those few, uncomfortable seconds when the subject of matrimony had been raised, the earl had kept the conversation diverted from all but the lightest topics. How easily he could make her laugh, she thought with amazement. All things considered, she had seldom enjoyed herself as thoroughly as she had this day. She had even told him about her love of sewing and designing clothes, which was not something she told just anyone. And he had been genuinely interested!

Tossing her gloves and bonnet onto her bed, Diana hastened to take a dutiful peek at her patients. However, since they were both occupied—Aimee with the latest Gothic romance and Miss Tilden with a new pair of stockings—she left them in peace and withdrew once more to her bedchamber. She had a hazy notion that she might catch a quick nap before dinner, but unfortunately both mind and body refused to allow her this respite. It was impossible to relax, or indeed to do anything but stare out the window while her mind reviewed every minute of her drive with the earl with disturbing accuracy.

It was true that he had made her laugh, but in retrospect, she could see that his desire to possess her was as powerful as ever. It was in his gestures and his voice, in every syllable he uttered, in the warmth of his smile, in every expression that crossed his face—and it was in his eyes.

With absent steps, Diana went to the chair beside the window and sank into it, a long, ragged sigh escaping her lips. What *was* she going tell him? No matter what he said, it was wrong to keep putting him off like this. Of course, she had been very busy, and he had been excessively understanding about that, but common sense warned her that any man would grow tired of waiting.

He would make her a good husband.

The thought came winging out of nowhere, and with it came a wild longing to become his wife, a yearning to leap headlong into an alliance which offered, not only security, but a reasonable hope of happiness and tranquillity. It was a tempting proposal, but she suddenly realized that as tempting as it was, whether or not he would make her a good husband was no longer the primary issue.

Would she make him a good wife?

Oddly, this had become the crux of the matter, the concern which kept her from jumping at the chance to wed a man who was becoming more dear to her with every passing hour. It was difficult to pinpoint exactly when this shift in priorities had occured. How many days had it been since she'd acknowledged her own susceptibility to his charm? How long since she'd begun to let down—cautiously—some of her defensive barriers? Today, for instance, she'd realized that when his gray eyes smiled into hers she could smile back—spontaneously, naturally, and without a trace of a blush. When had that happened? And though she was still absurdly conscious of both his physical presence and his forceful personality, she no longer felt threatened by it. So why, oh, *why* did she suddenly feel so blue?

Tired of sitting, Diana abandoned her chair and began to pace, as if movement would help her make sense of the senseless, of the tangles and contradictions of her turbulent emotions.

First, despite all the progress she had made, the notion of marrying Lord Lucan still made her uneasy, even apprehensive. *Why?* His kiss had been pleasant, hadn't it? And even though she was convinced that those other, strange sensations had been a product of her imagination, at least she was certain his embrace had not been disagreeable. So why didn't her dread of intimacy simply abate?

She paused to scowl at her reflection in the cheval glass, as if it were somehow responsible for her quandary. Well, kisses were one thing, she mused, staring into her own troubled eyes. But the earl was going to want more than kisses. Intuition warned her that Geoffrey Trevelyan was not a man who would settle for anything less than a complete surrender. And he deserved nothing less.

Her mouth drooped at the thought. Yes, Geoffrey *deserved* a wife who was willing to surrender herself to him, body and soul. What he did not deserve was a wife who would try to foist him off as she had done with Edmund—though, to be honest, she doubted she could do it. Those gray eyes of his might smile at her, but they were also keen enough to see through any prevarication or excuse. What possible chance was there of fooling him? What possible chance was there of making him believe she desired his lovemaking?

On the other hand, assuming there was a chance of duping him, should she do it? Was it better to lie to him or to tell him the truth? Long, soul-searching seconds ticked away while Diana thrashed through the pros and cons of the question. Without doubt, the truth would hurt him, she reflected, but what good was a marriage based on lies? When it came down to it, neither choice was acceptable. She refused to hurt him and she couldn't lie to him. And, anyway, she reasoned despondently, even if she told him the truth, there was little likelihood that he would be able to accept it or understand it.

Which left her with a bleak third alternative. If she did not marry him, she would have to do neither. They could just go on as they were, and he would never need to know that there was anything wrong with her. Perhaps, if she were positive that he loved her, she would be brave enough to chance it. But he had never said a word about love.

By the morning of the following day, Aimee had finished the last of the romance novels she had borrowed from the circulating library just prior to her illness.

"Diana," she said, arriving at the breakfast table with a stack of volumes, "do you think you could return these and get me some more? Are you going anywhere near the lending library today?"

"Well, I wasn't planning on it, but there is no reason why I could not," replied Diana with a smile. "Mary can stay with you and Tildy, and Meg can come with me."

"Oh, good! Otherwise it is too tedious just sitting

around with nothing to do. If only I weren't so tired," she sighed, "I could go with you."

"Give yourself another day or two," Diana advised. "You are much stronger, I know, but not quite strong enough for that."

Aimee nodded glumly. "Oh, and Diana, if Charles happens to visit while you are out, may I receive him?"

"I see no reason why not. Did he say he would come?"

"No, but I am hoping he will. He has been quite attentive lately. Have you noticed?"

Diana reached for a slice of toast. "Indeed I have, and I am very glad. You had better make me a list of the books you have already read, by the way, so I do not borrow the same ones again."

"Yes, I'll do that right after breakfast. Thank you, Lawrence," she added, accepting her morning chocolate from the butler's hand. Her nose wrinkled as she surveyed the various dishes that Cook had prepared for them. "Oh dear. I still do not have much appetite. None of this looks at all appealing."

"But you must eat something, my dear. You have grown sadly frail these past few days."

Aimee gazed pensively down at her slim arms and tiny, delicate wrists. "I had a notion it was an improvement," she replied. "I thought it gave me a sort of ethereal look, like a heroine in a romance."

Diana shook her head. "Ethereal, no. Sickly, yes." Observing her sister's mulish look, she said hastily, "Do not forget, the sooner you recover your strength, the sooner you can begin attending parties again. And Charles does not want you to lose more weight. He told me he thought you were far too thin," she finished smoothly.

It was a masterful touch, and so near the truth it hardly signified. "Did he really say that?" Aimee asked, as eagerly as if it had been a compliment.

"Yes," Diana affirmed, "that was his meaning, though he did not state it quite like that. He is very concerned about you."

"Well!" chattered Aimee, excitedly reaching for the plate of eggs. "I had better eat, then! I think it is a good sign, don't you, Diana? After all, if he noticed I was thinner, that means he was *looking* at me! And if he is *concerned* about me that must mean he *cares* for me—at least a little. Don't you think so, Diana?"

Diana concealed a smile as her sister proceeded to heap her plate high with food. "Yes, Aimee. I think you may be right."

Colburn's circulating library offered its subscribers a widely diversified assortment of books. It had a congenial atmosphere, and for little more than four pounds per year, its patrons were afforded the considerable convenience of borrowing their books rather than purchasing them for a great deal more at Hatchard's.

Diana had always enjoyed coming here, and would have been quite content to spend the entire morning browsing among Mr. Colburn's well-stocked shelves. As it was, she spent some twenty minutes thumbing through one or other of the books until a pair of giggling young females disrupted her concentration. Reminded of Aimee, Diana replaced the book she had been skimming and returned to the section of the library where there was an abundance of lurid-sounding Gothic romances. Unfortunately, all the copies of the one book Aimee had particularly requested—*Glenarvon*—seemed to be absent, though she was able to find three other titles which looked to be just Aimee's cup of tea (including Mrs. Radcliffe's *Mysteries of Udolpho*).

She gathered these, along with the sole novel she had selected for herself—Jane Austen's *Emma*—and carried them up to the front counter. To her profound dismay, she arrived there at the very moment that Lady Edgerton entered the shop. She had seen the woman on one or two occasions, but this was the first time they were to be in such close quarters together.

Quickly averting her gaze, Diana took a deep breath and addressed the clerk behind the counter. "Do you have any more copies of *Glenarvon?*" she inquired.

The clerk, a sad-faced, little brown mouse of a man, peered at her over the rim of his glasses. "'Tis a popular book, ma'am," he responded in lugubrious accents. "Everyone wants to read it. I doubt there's a copy anywhere in here—unless someone returned one this morning, that is. Would you like me to look?"

"Please do." Diana inclined her head.

Lady Edgerton was standing directly behind her, and she could feel the woman's hard gray eyes boring into her back. With tautening nerves, Diana strained to recapture the insouciant attitude the earl had helped her achieve that first day in Hyde Park. To her surprise, the strategy worked better than she expected. The memory of Geoffrey Trevelyan's scandalous remarks regarding Lady Edgerton and her corset brought a resurgence of, not only her confidence, but the amusement she had felt about it afterward. Silent laughter welled inside her, sending an unbridled flash of pure daring coursing through her veins. Why should she be intimidated by this pitiable busybody? Why should she shrink from facing her, as though she had some reason to be ashamed? Abruptly, Diana made the decision to greet Lady Edgerton, if only to show that she cared not a straw for the woman's malicious gossip. Chin proudly aloft, she turned her head.

"Good day, Lady Edgerton." Diana's gaze was unwavering, her tone cool but meticulously polite.

At first, Lady Edgerton merely stared back. Then, in

the abrasive voice Diana remembered only too well, the woman who had once made life so difficult for her answered, "Good day," and allowed her lips to purse into a factitious smile.

Diana smiled pleasantly. "Such a long time it has been since we met. You do not seem to have changed at all," she went on, exulting inwardly as two bright spots of color entered Lady Edgerton's fleshy cheeks.

"Indeed," responded Lady Edgerton, looking as if she had just swallowed something extremely sour. Her eyes roved jealously over Diana's face and figure. "Neither do you," she added shortly.

"On the contrary, I have changed a great deal," said Diana seriously. "One cannot marry and lose a husband and remain unaffected. Some sort of adjustment is necessary. And as you have reason to know, my suffering was even greater than most." She watched with detachment as ugly crimson and purple streaks mottled Lady Edgerton's complexion. "But since then," she explained, "I have learned that there are ways to deal with unpleasantness—and those who derive pleasure from it."

Lady Edgerton's mouth fell open, then snapped shut tightly. "Indeed," she hissed, through shut teeth.

Knowing she had the upper hand, Diana was contemplating her next remark when the clerk returned.

"I'm very sorry, ma'am," he informed Diana, shaking his head gloomily. "No copies of *Glenarvon* have been returned. I feared as much."

For the first time, Diana noticed that Lady Edgerton held a book tucked under her arm. At the clerk's remark, she whipped it out and thrust it under the poor man's nose.

"Here is your *Glenarvon*," she spat, waving it wildly. "Here, take it, take it! It's disgraceful what they will publish these days. Caroline Lamb ought to be ashamed of herself!" She glared at Diana, the tip of her tongue snaking out to moisten her pale lips. "Ashamed!" she repeated with sudden relish. "No doubt Mrs. Verney will enjoy it." Then, like an indignant duck, she pointed her quivering nose at the ceiling and waddled out of the library.

The door slammed shut, and Diana and the clerk exchanged looks. "Is it truly that bad?" she asked him in amazement. "What can possibly be in it that is so objectionable?"

Looking doleful, the little man scratched his head. "Well, I don't rightly know, ma'am. I haven't read it myself. They say Lady Caroline put a lot of real people in it, which I reckon has got some 'em a bit riled." For the first time, the corners of his lips twitched. "Who knows? Maybe she saw herself in it," he said dryly.

Diana left the library with a proud spring in her step. She had actually done it! She had faced Lady Edgerton, spoken with her, and come out of it feeling reasonably victorious. And what was more, that spiteful insinuation at the end had not bothered her one jot. Not one jot! In fact, it had rolled off her as easily as if it had been no more than the commonest civility. She could not wait to tell Geoffrey!

Civility. Polite Society placed such importance upon civility, yet Diana had just discovered what a wealth of meaning might be conveyed within its boundries. It was quite possible to deal with people like Lady Edgerton in a firm, nonoffensive way. No doubt it was an art which required practice—but she had done it!

For perhaps the first time, Diana realized how much she had despised herself for being weak, for caring about the gossip, for allowing a woman like Lady Edgerton to make her feel uneasy. From now on, she mused, she would be strong and self-assertive. She would not run away from life, but would take it by the horns, give back measure for measure . . .

"If you please, ma'am," panted Meg, from five feet behind. "I can't keep up with you. I've got this bunion on my toe and it's started a-paining me again."

Diana slowed at once. "Why didn't you tell me, Meg?" she asked. "I could have brought Mary instead."

Meg shook her head. "I don't mind," she said bravely.

"Nonsense, of course you must mind. We shall hire a hack to take us home. And when Dr. Hatfield visits us later, I shall be sure he looks at your toe."

As she glanced up and down the street in search of a hired hack, a familiar voice floated through the air, raising goose pimples on her flesh.

"My dear Sophia, you look simply marvelous! No really, you *do*, my dear. It's the most flattering bonnet you could have purchased."

Not ten feet away, Sir Henry Neyle and the Countess of Uxbridge stepped out of a millinery shop. Diana's new-found confidence was about to undergo its first test.

Chapter Twelve

There was no time to walk away, no place to hide. And no *reason* to hide, she reminded herself fiercely. Braced with resolve, Diana's shoulders squared and her face took on an aspect of aloof determination. She would deal with this situation as effectively as the last.

By this time, Sir Henry had seen her. "Well, well," he drawled, his seemingly ever-present smile curling his lips. "My dear Sophia, just see who is here. It is Mrs. Verney, my love. What a delicious situation! I simply *must* introduce you to each other."

Later, Diana would wonder if she'd made a mistake. But such was her animosity toward the smirking blond demigod before her that she acted on pure instinct.

She forgot civility. She forgot everything but the one lesson Aunt Serena had taught her the year of her come-out: the correct way to administer *the cut*.

If there was such a thing as a correct way to be rude, Aunt Serena had explained it in detail. The *cut direct* was for the most obnoxious. It meant crossing to the other side of the street, or going especially out of one's way to avoid the obnoxious person. The *cut indirect* was slightly less rude. Done correctly, one simply looked another way, as if one did not observe the obnoxious person in question. The *cut sublime* was a variation. One glanced up to admire the rooftops, or a handsome balcony or whatever else was about, so that the obnoxious person was outside the perimeter of one's vision. The *cut infernal* was the opposite. One stared at one's feet or the cobbles or pretended to search for a coin one had dropped.

Diana's cut was more than direct. She simply gazed right through Sir Henry as if he did not exist, allowing her eyes to sweep the surrounding area once, in a rather bored fashion. She then turned and strolled away in the opposite direction, while the astonished baronet stared after her in inarticulate fury.

He had good reason for that fury. Several amused onlookers had witnessed the scene, and some had tittered quite openly. Such episodes as this, he knew, had a way of becoming widely known. To his increased annoyance, even Lady Uxbridge was smiling.

"Poor darling," she purred, touching his arm. "She does not seem to wish for your acquaintance, does she?"

"Or yours," he muttered, his suaveness deserting him. "Bitch," he added, under his breath.

To which woman he referred was unclear, but Lady Uxbridge did not even blink. "Come, Henry," she murmured, with a shade less sympathy. "You make a fool of yourself by standing here like this, pouting like a lovesick school boy. The little slut is not worth it, believe me."

Reluctantly, Sir Henry pulled his gaze back to the lady he was escorting, his manner almost surly. "Come on, then," he growled. "I need to purchase some snuff."

She smiled complacently, knowing he needed more than snuff. They had had no chance to be together the previous day, for she had needed time to make arrangements, and to dispose of David. Though her young cousin was a fine stallion, in the final analysis he was too like a blank page for her taste. Sir Henry possessed far more in the way of wit and sophistication—which one appreciated a trifle more when one had been without it for a while. Yet, in his own way, he too was a beautiful, sulky little boy.

Poor Henry had suffered a blow to his pride, but Lady Uxbridge did not for a moment doubt her ability to make him forget the whey-faced widow with the golden hair. When it came to men and their needs, Lady Uxbridge considered herself unsurpassed in knowledge. And she was going to make certain that Henry found this out very soon.

"How is your foot?" Diana asked Meg, once they were far away from Sir Henry. "I am so very sorry to have done that to you, but I'm afraid it could not be helped."

"It's . . . it's not too bad," gasped the abigail. "Goodness, ma'am, you certainly have a heap of hurry-scurry in you today."

"Er, yes, I suppose I do," Diana replied contritely. "But no more, I promise." Her eyes swept back to the street. "We shall find a hack—oh! Better yet . . ." She took two quick steps toward the busy thoroughfare and waved her hand.

Without doubt it was Aunt Serena's coach. Diana recognized it from the Torrington crest on the side panel as well as the brawny coachman on top. But surely, Aunt Serena would not be out so early? The dowager viscountess almost never ventured out of her house before three in the afternoon.

The coachman also recognized Diana, and brought the coach to a halt. "Morning, ma'am." He touched his top hat respectfully.

Diana smiled up at the man. "Good morning, John. Is my aunt within?"

"Nay, 'tis 'is lordship," replied the coachman with a

wink. "Do ye be needin' a ride, ma'am?"

Before Diana could reply, Lord Hervey stuck his head out the window. "Oh, it is you, my dear," he said brightly. "I thought I heard your voice. 'Pon my word, what luck! Tell John where you wish to go, and we shall take you there at once. And in the meantime, p'haps you can give me some advice."

Once inside, Diana sank into the squabs with a grateful sigh, while Lord Hervey beamed at her from the other seat.

"And how is that pretty little sister of yours feeling? Did she receive my flowers? Serena told me she had the influenza, and that you, Mrs. Verney, were on the brink of collapse."

Diana raised her brows. "The brink of collapse? Where can she have—oh, Lord Lucan must have told her that. It is a slight exaggeration, my lord." She smiled. "And, yes, Aimee received the flowers, thank you. Her health is much improved, and we are hoping she will be able to resume some of her activities quite soon."

"Good, good." Lord Hervey's double chin wagged with enthusiasm. "Serena said she sent one of her girls to help out. Now isn't that just like Serena? Your aunt's a generous woman, y'know. And regal! I always tell her she should have been a queen. Could have run the country better than . . . ahem. Well! It don't do to criticize our sovereign, of course. God save the king, and all that."

Diana repressed a smile. "Yes, Aunt Serena is very much the *grande dame*."

"Aye, she is that," he agreed. He stared pensively out the window for a few seconds then looked back at Diana. "Her birthday's coming soon, y'know. That's what I wanted to talk to you about."

"Oh?"

His head bobbed. "Wanted to do something special for

218

her, y'see. Throw a surprise party—something of the sort."

"That is very kind of you, Lord Hervey, but I am not completely sure that is a good idea. Surprises make her feel enfeebled, and are bad for her heart—or is it her digestion? I cannot quite recall."

"That won't do, then." Lord Hervey's chin sunk to his chest. "Well, let's see what you think of my other notion. I'd like to have the Torrington diamond reset for her. Thought it would look well in a necklace instead of a tiara. Serena pretends she don't like that diamond but that's just a lot of twaddle!" His voice dropped to a confiding whisper. "Ever notice your aunt has a little vain streak?" He nodded indulgently. "The truth is, she hasn't worn that tiara since her hair turned gray! So I thought, why not put the Torrington diamond in a necklace? A thing like that ought to be worn once in a while," he added simply. "No sense in owning it otherwise."

Diana sighed. "Lord Hervey, I really wish I could advise you, but I just do not know what to say. You will simply have to put it to Aunt Serena. If she likes the notion, I think it would be splendid. No one has seen the Torrington diamond in years."

Childlike pleasure spread over Lord Hervey's pudgy countenance. "Aye, I'll do that, I think. A woman like your aunt ought to wear a necklace fit for a queen."

With much the same amount of delight, Aimee's blue eyes lit when Diana presented her with the library books. "Oh, good!" she exclaimed, examining the titles intently. "And you were able to obtain *Glenarvon*! I'll read that one first."

Diana's gazed musingly down at her sister. "I'm not at all sure I should let you," she said half-seriously. "Whatever it's about, it seems to have set a great number

219

of people in a bustle. I have it from no less a personage than Lady Edgerton that it is quite shocking."

Aimee looked up quickly. "Lady Edgerton! Oh, Diana, was she there?"

"Yes, indeed." said Diana calmly. "And I even spoke with her."

"Goodness, Diana, why? Whatever did you say to her? Was she polite? And were you?"

"Well, I was, but she was barely so. And the reason my dear, was mostly to prove to myself that I could do it. Never mind her. Did Charles visit while I was gone?"

"Alas, no," said Aimee, sighing wistfully. "It has been very boring while you were gone. I sat with Tildy while she finished another pair of stockings, but then she wanted to take a nap, so I've just been lying here thinking."

Diana surveyed her with interest. "Oh? About anything in particular?"

Aimee eased herself into a more upright position. "As a matter of fact—yes. I've been thinking about you."

"Oh? What about me?" For some reason, Diana was disconcerted.

"I've been wondering," said Aimee, rather timidly, "about you and Lord Lucan. I've been wondering if perhaps you ought to marry him, Diana. I know it is none of my business," she went on, rushing her words as if she feared interruption, "but I have seen such a difference in you lately. You seem so much more animated. And it is all because of him, is it not?"

Diana walked to the window, her back to her sister. "What makes you say that?" she said in an odd tone.

"I say it because it is the only possible answer. Just because I am young, Diana, does not mean I am blind. I told Mama before I left home that I would find you a husband. I haven't done much of a job of it, I'm afraid, but I think perhaps you found him by yourself."

There was a long, heavy silence before Diana swung

around. "Well, you are wrong," she stated dully. "I do not need a husband. I am happy the way I am." Sensing her sister's disbelief, she added, almost angrily, "For God's sake, Aimee, I have been through all that once! I've *earned* my independence. I'd be a fool to relinquish it!"

"But, Diana," faltered the younger girl, "doesn't every woman need a man? Isn't that the natural order of things? And anyway, if husbands are so . . . so horrid, why are you anxious for me to have one?"

Diana came close, and took firm hold of her sister's hand. "You are mistaken. I was never anxious for you to have a husband at your age, Aimee. But, sooner or later, the world we live in dictates that young girls marry. What other choice do we have? Men deem us inferior creatures whose mental powers cannot possibly be as great as theirs. We are considered unworthy of a good education, and those few of us who manage to live by what wits we possess are scorned, or considered outré. Why, even those of our own sex take this stand. Look at Hannah More, who says that young women should keep silent, so as not to *usurp the authority of men!*" Realizing that the faint furrow on Aimee's brow had deepened considerably, Diana paused. "Well, just listen to me," she said, more lightly. "I daresay I am as much a hypocrite as any. However, few men are monsters, and if I seem anxious it is only because I want you to marry a kind man, a man like Cousin Charles, who will treat you gently and with consideration."

"But, Diana," said Aimee, her eyes troubled, "don't you think Lord Lucan a kind man? Don't you believe he would treat you well?"

Diana sat back, and her eyes grew distant and faintly moist. "Yes," she whispered. "He is an extraordinarily kind man."

"Then, why not marry him, Diana? Hasn't he asked you?"

'Yes, he has asked."

"Then, *why?*"

Diana struggled to answer. "Because . . . because . . . oh, it's so complicated, I scarcely know myself! No, that's not true. You see, part of it is that I love him." Her head was bowed so that she missed her sister's incredulous look. "Yes, I think that's it. I've loved him for a long time now, but I'm afraid it is not enough."

"I don't understand."

Diana rubbed her temples wearily. "No, I don't expect you to understand. I don't want you to understand."

"Well, that's all right. After all, it's not for me to understand," replied Aimee, with unaccustomed logic. "But don't you think Lord Lucan will want to understand? It doesn't seem fair not to have a reason you can explain, Diana."

"No." Diana chewed her lower lip reflectively. "No, it doesn't, does it?"

Tossing aside his shirt, Sir Henry eyed the elaborate Chinese screen with impatience. "Aren't you ready yet?" he called out.

"Patience, darling . . ." Lady Uxbridge's throaty voice drifted low and sultry from behind the screen.

They were in someone else's house, someone he did not even know, but who, according to Sophia, owed her this favor. It scarcely mattered. He did not give a damn where they went, as long as he could put an end to the ache in his loins. He had reached the point where he neither knew nor cared whether it was Sophia or Diana his body craved. He only knew that Lady Uxbridge would serve the purpose adequately enough.

"Henry."

He glanced up, and in an instant all thoughts of Diana trundled from his head. What she wore was so transparent it could scarcely be called a gown, and what was under it was altogether spectacular. As experienced as he was, as many women that he had seen in their most natural state, he did not think he had ever seen her match.

"Sophia," he whispered, taking a jerky step forward. She held out her arms. "Come to me, darling."

Her emerald eyes were assessing his physique with a frankness which equaled his, and when he seized her, her hands were just as eager.

"What a beautiful man you are," she remarked, her head cocked to the side. With a teasing laugh, she tried to plant a kiss on his nose, but he forestalled her attempt with his mouth.

"On second thought," she murmured, after his long, hard kiss, "I think I should call you a boy." An irresistible, spoiled little boy," she added, her voice languorous. "And I know just what little boys like."

"Then show me," he mumbled, his lips roving her throat. "Show me, Sophia."

She drew back a bit, toying with him still. "Polite little boys say 'please'," she said playfully.

His nibbling kisses dropping ever lower, he responded, with more of his characteristic mockery. "But I . . . was never . . . a polite . . . little boy."

After partaking of a small nuncheon, Diana went upstairs to keep Miss Tilden company, and was just in time to witness the completion of the two hundredth pair of woolen stockings.

"I am becoming a trifle tired of making stockings," Tildy confessed, putting her needles down with relief. "I think I will make scarves for a few weeks instead. But I must find a way to get these stockings to the Foundling Hospital right away. Not that it is cold, of course, but the children do need them eventually. We may as well send them along while we are right here in London."

Once Miss Tilden switched projects, Diana knew she would fret until all of the first had reached its intended beneficiaries. She therefore said, without hesitation, "I will take them there myself, Tildy. Perhaps even this afternoon, for I have nothing else to do today."

"It is too good of you, my dear," quavered the elderly woman, pressing her hand gratefully. "I do so hate to ask you, but you see, I always think of the children when I am making them, and how pleased they will be to receive something new." She sighed wistfully. "I wish I could go myself, but my ankle is still much too weak."

"But healing very nicely, according to Dr. Hatfield," said Diana bracingly. She leaned forward to kiss Tildy's soft, wrinkled cheek. "I shall have Mary pack up the stockings directly. But before I go anywhere, why do we not sit here and have a nice coze, and perhaps play a hand or two of piquet?"

At much the same time, the earl was scanning through some documents relating to his estate in Cornwall. At least he was *trying* to scan them, but unfortunately he had done so three times already and absorbed next to nothing in the process. How could he read when, instead of words, he saw Diana's lovely, vivid face? How could he focus upon anything but her radiant smile and sparkling eyes?

No woman had ever had such an effect upon his ability to concentrate. On the whole, he had no particular objection to being thus distracted (indeed, it was extremely pleasant) but he wanted to understand the rationale behind it. Was it possible that he had actually fallen in *love*? The earl's lips twisted in sudden self-mockery. Was a logical man like himself going to admit that such an emotion existed?

Casting aside his papers, the earl leaned back, linking his fingers behind his head. Love was such a difficult concept, he reflected. It was impossible to define, which was why he had always been so skeptical about it. In his salad days, he had fancied himself in love a hundred times, but in the end each of his loves had drifted away and he had never cared. Would he care if Diana went away? If he was never to see her again? Astonishingly, the very notion flooded him with such an ache that his eyes screwed shut with the pain. Well, that gave him his answer, said a taunting voice in his mind.

But would it last?

He spent a number of minutes pondering the question, but concluded that it was something that only time could decide. And it was really quite irrelevant, he thought, with unconscious arrogance. He had made up his mind that she was the woman he wanted for his wife, and that was final.

If only *she* would make up *her* mind! He had told himself over and over that she would accept him, that she *must* accept him, that there was no reason why she should not accept him. And when she did, he thought suddenly, he knew exactly what he was going to do—down to the last, intimate detail . . .

Damn! He shifted uncomfortably, aware that he ought to cut off this particular daydream before he had cause to regret it. Night and day he'd been dreaming of Diana, and unfortunately, his heated imagination was getting too good. But, sweet Jesus, he wanted her badly. He wanted to hold her in his arms and make love to her, kiss those sweek pink lips and chase away all her fears. He longed to assure her that whatever she wanted for the rest of her life would be hers, for he would make sure that she got it. Instinct told him that if he could only put his arms around her, he could convince her to accept him. But for

225

some inexplicable reason he wanted her to say 'yes' without his using the force of their physical attraction as persuasion.

Just lately he'd begun to feel confident that she would soon come to the only reasonable conclusion. She must realize that a strong rapport existed between them, and it was obvious she was attracted to him. Since he was a man, the earl reasoned with masculine logic. Thus he could not think of a single reason why Diana should not accept him. So why the devil was she taking so long to decide?

Puzzled, he stared reflectively off into space. Confound it, he wished he understood. Was it her freedom she feared losing? Or was it something else? Was it something about him? Without realizing it, his fingers began to crumple the thin sheet of paper beneath his hand. He glanced down, then smoothed it mechanically and heaved a long, exasperated sigh. Well, there was obviously no use in trying to read any more documents today. His secretary would not be happy with him, but his secretary could go to the devil.

He would go and see Diana, and hope to God that this would be the day she would accept him and put him out of his misery. For after all was said and done, nothing could possibly be worse than this wretched, damnable waiting.

"Do you wish to play again?" Diana glanced at Miss Tilden as she gathered up the cards, deftly reducing them to a neat pile within seconds. Her long, graceful fingers automatically began to reshuffle the stack.

Regarding her former charge fondly, Miss Tilden leaned back against the pile of feather pillows which served as necessary prop to her frail body. "You are so clever with cards, my dear," she remarked. "I am no match for you, am I?"

"Certainly you are," replied Diana, still shuffling, "when you concentrate. But perhaps you are too tired to play again?"

"I am a little tired," the elderly woman admitted. "I'm getting old, I suppose." She semed to hesitate, and Diana shot her an inquiring look. "I hope I'm not too much of a burden to you," she said suddenly. "I worry about that, you know."

"A burden?" Diana was genuinely amazed. "Wherever did you get such a foolish notion? Tildy, I *love* you. You could never be a burden to me."

"You are such an angel," said Miss Tilden, much moved. "All your family is dear to me, but you, Diana, have always held a special place in my heart. You are like the daughter I never had. But I do wish I could see you looking happier."

Diana gave a little laugh. "But Tildy, I *am* happy. I have never been happier in my life than I am right now."

Miss Tilden shook her head. "Not so," she said wisely. "You are not satisfied with your life, Diana. And that is understandable. You need more than the company of an old woman like me, or even your sister, bless her heart. You need a husband and children of your own."

Diana sighed. "Perhaps I should tell you that Aimee and I had this same discussion a short while ago." She paused, choosing her words with care. "Well, I will tell you what I told her. I do not think that marriage agrees with me. I have not told you this, but Lord Lucan has asked me to marry him, and I have given his offer a great deal of very serious consideration. To be honest, if I were to marry he would be the only man I could consider." Her mouth turned down sadly. "But I have come to the conclusion that . . . that it would be best if I do not accept."

Miss Tilden's eyes were not as sharp as they had once been, but they saw more than one might suspect. "I see.

227

Have you told him yet?"

"No."

"And when do you plan to do it?" she prodded gently.

"I don't know." Diana shrugged.

Miss Tilden frowned. "Do you plan to reconsider your answer, or is it absolutely final?"

"I don't know," Diana repeated. Her fingers were suddenly clumsy, and the deck of cards flew from her hand to spread over the counterpane. She quickly gathered them up, and smiled the bright, false smile which Tildy found so disturbing. "Let's not discuss it anymore, shall we? If you are tired, I will send Mary to fetch your drink, and then, my dear Tildy, I plan to take those stockings straight to the Foundling Hospital where they belong."

"Very well, my dear," replied Tildy submissively. There was nothing she could do, after all. And when Diana bent to kiss her brow and tuck in the sheets, Miss Tilden did her very best to smile. Even though her heart was very heavy.

Diana descended the stairs intending to send Felix to fetch one of Aunt Serena's carriages, but the earl's arrival made this unnecessary. Her pulse leaped the instant she saw him, but rather than dwell upon the possible reasons for this, she put it down as simple cowardice. She absolutely dreaded having to tell him she was not going to be his wife.

"You are going out?" he asked, observing her carriage dress, and the large valise near the door.

She cleared her throat. "Yes, but I am in no hurry. I can visit with you for a short while before I leave."

Perhaps she should tell him now . . .

As usual, he had taken her hand, and was standing far closer than a gentleman ought. "Where are you going?" he asked sharply. "You are not leaving town, are you?"

She smiled slightly. "Goodness, no. The valise is full of

Tildy's stockings. I am off to the Foundling Hospital to deliver them."

He looked incredibly relieved. "Then, you must allow me to take you there," was his prompt response. "My curricle is just outside."

Diana wavered. "Thank you, my lord. It is very kind of you," she said finally, knowing she was being a coward. She would put the dreaded interview off until later, when the stockings were delivered. In the meantime, she would try to gather the requisite courage.

As soon as they were underway, she told him about her encounter with Lady Edgerton, which seemed a safe enough topic. She'd been certain he would find the story humorous, but he surprised her by saying, quite seriously, "Be careful how you deal with her sort, Diana. That woman can be quite vindictive when aroused to it." She was silent for so long he glanced down at her curiously. "Come, tell me what's wrong."

He didn't miss much, she thought. She'd been staring straight ahead at nothing in particular, but her thoughts had traveled far back in time . . .

"I was only remembering what happened six years ago. Foolish of me, I suppose. To look back on a painful part of one's life can do no good."

"If looking back serves a useful purpose, there's nothing wrong with it," he countered, guiding the horses around an apple cart. "Sometimes one gains enough in wisdom and understanding to justify it."

Diana sighed. "I suppose you are right." Seeking to change the subject, she said casually, "I saw Sir Henry today."

The earl's head swiveled. "And?"

"And I cut him. Quite publicly." She waited for his reaction, her eyes in her lap.

He said nothing for so long she glanced up, and saw that his lips were tightly compressed. "Was I wrong to do

229

so?" she said anxiously. "He was about to address me, and he was with that odious Lady Uxbridge." When his face darkened with anger, her voice filled with the need for reassurance. "Are you angry with me, Geoffrey? It all happened so fast I did not have time to consider." Her use of his name was an unconscious slip.

"No, of course I'm not angry with you, Diana," he said curtly. "Nor am I sorry you did it. What infuriates me is that the blackguard spoke to you at all. He swore upon his honor he would not."

"Well, I doubt he will do so again," she said hopefully. "I did not dare to look back, but I would think he'd be quite angry with me now. I daresay he will no longer wish for my acquaintance."

The earl's eyes glinted a little. "Yes, I'm sure he was quite put out. But to be certain he does not forget himself again, I will pay him another visit."

Something in his tone made her eyes fly to his face. "You will not do anything absurd, will you?"

"Absurd? Such as what?" he inquired, amused despite the anger burning inside him.

"Oh, I mean hit him, or . . . or call him out," she explained.

He shrugged. "I'll do whatever is necessary. Are you concerned for his safety?"

She stared at him. "*His* safety! Good God, I don't care a jot about his safety. It is *your* safety which concerns me, my lord. Sir Henry is obviously a man without honor. I shudder to think what he is capable of doing. I—I simply do not want you to be hurt on my account."

"My dear Mrs. Verney," said the earl, his spirits considerably lightened. "I am touched. Fear not for my safety, ma'am. I am fully capable of taking care of myself. Has no one ever told you that boxing is one of my pastimes?"

"No, of course not!" she retorted. "Why would

230

anyone tell me such a thing?"

"Well, it is," he replied. "It's something I do rather well, in fact."

"Then that explains why you're so—" Realizing what she had nearly said, Diana blushed to the roots of her hair.

His black brows shot up. "So what, Diana?"

"Oh, I . . . never mind."

How appallingly inelegant it would have been to comment upon his muscular physique! It would make him think she had studied him in a most unladylike fashion—which to her shock she realized was the truth. . . .

Of course, he guessed what she had meant to say. "Dear Diana, you are so very sweet," he said, quite tenderly. "So very respectable."

She made no answer, for his words were like a hot knife twisting inside her. She was not sweet at all, she thought in despair. He would not think so highly of her later, nor would he speak so gently. Not after she had turned down his offer of marriage.

Chapter Thirteen

"Would you care to stay for tea, my lord?"

For the first time in over two hours, Diana's voice was hesitant, even a little shy. While delivering stockings to the Foundling Hospital, she had been perfectly in control, and the ride back to Jermyn Street had been companionable and peaceful. Somehow she had managed to steer clear of any topic even remotely connected with marriage, and had even managed to keep her private thoughts on other paths. Yet now, as she stood beside the earl upon the front steps of her house, she suddenly longed to be done with it. It was time to tell him.

Something told her he knew it, too. Whether it was the flicker of his eyes or that instant of stillness about his stance she did not know, but whatever the case she was certain he knew it. She also had no doubt that he was anticipating her acceptance.

"I'd like that very much," he answered, gazing down at her with a pensive air. With a jerk of his chin, he instructed his groom to continue on to the mews. "Providing, of course, that you offer me something to eat," he added, in a joking tone.

"Naturally," she replied with dignity. "I need no reminder, Lord Lucan. I am as hungry as you are."

232

Her reproachful look made him laugh, and as they stepped into the house, he placed a proprietary hand at her waist. He did not ordinarily touch her thus, but he was obviously in high and very confident spirits and Diana found she could say nothing. Indeed, the knowledge that she was about to dash those spirits weighed heavily upon her, although it did not quite account for the bewildering tingle which went racing through every nerve in her body at very much the same instant.

Once inside, Diana composed her features and forced what she hoped was a note of cheerfulness into her voice. "Goodness, delivering those stockings took much longer than I expected! Aimee and Tildy are sure to have eaten already so I shall not ask them to join us. Aimee, in any case, is probably engrossed in *Glenarvon* and would not wish to be disturbed." She untied the ribands of her bonnet and laid it carefully upon the pier table at her elbow. "Lawrence, pray send up the tea tray immediately. And some of those delicious cakes which Cook made just this morning. It is well past tea time and his lordship is famished."

"Yes, as it happens, I am," remarked the earl, his hard mouth slanting ruefully as he handed the butler his hat. He followed her toward the stairs, saying, "You allow your sister to read books like that?" He sounded mildly surprised.

"Books like what?" she inquired over her shoulder.

"Books that are written out of spite, meant to stir up trouble rather than to instruct or entertain. It's not even well written," he added, as they reached the first floor.

"Have you read it?"

He shook his head. "Not word for word. I wouldn't waste my time on it." He saw her inquiring expression. "My dear Diana, it's the sort of story that will only encourage your sister to engage in foolish histrionics. Its

233

characters are so clearly cast from life they are completely recognizable. Lord Byron is the hero—if one can call such a dastard a hero—and Caro Lamb is the heroine. And Lady Caroline's representation of her mother-in-law, Lady Melbourne, is purely malicious. She has set the seal on her own social disgrace by airing her grievances so openly."

"Oh." Diana mulled this over, then said in a placating tone, "Well, I cannot actually forbid Aimee to read it, but I will drop a hint in her ear. Better yet, I will ask Charles to do so." She took a seat and patted the chair next to her invitingly.

Lord Lucan strode forward, a glint in his eye. "An excellent notion but for the fact that she will very likely be done with it by then," he agreed. He sat as if he were in his own home, stretching his long legs out in front of him.

Despite her apprehension, Diana could not prevent her lips from twitching. "Well!" she said, her manner more relaxed. "I believe that is what you sporting gentlemen call a *'flush hit'*? Or am I mistaken?"

He grinned. "Are we sparring again? I meant only to offer a little friendly advice."

"And I should hardly be so uncivil as to ignore it," she said, more seriously. "But I still contend that your opinion of my sister is too severe. Reading is merely a diversion for her, my lord. She does not pattern her life around such melodramas."

He shrugged. "If you say so. It is none of my affair, after all."

Normally, she would have made a point to agree with him, which would have set off another whole round of such banter. However, there were more important matters on Diana's mind, and until Lawrence arrived with the tea tray and the necessary accouterments for their repast, she scarcely knew what conversation passed between them. As soon as the butler left, she noticed that the earl sat straighter, and there was an air of expectancy about him which brought a tightness crawling into the pit of her stomach. How on earth was she going to do this?

As calmly as possible, Diana poured the steaming tea into two dainty china cups. "Is this one of your sugar days, my lord? Or will you drink your tea black?"

"Sugar, by all means," he replied lightly. "I'm in a festive mood."

The tension felt like tiny needles pricking at her skin. With a curious kind of detachment, Diana noticed that her hands were quite steady as she passed over the teacup. How very strange that was. And how ludicrously fragile the cup looked in the earl's hand.

Although there was no longer any reason to put off the inevitable, she heard herself say, "Do try a cake, my lord. They are very good."

Inwardly, she castigated herself, scorning her own cowardice, despising her weakness. It was stupid and cruel to keep procrastinating merely because the interview was bound to be painful. Had she not decided to be strong? Yet a part of her knew this was not quite fair, for it was not fear which made her hesitate, but a reluctance to hurt the man she loved.

She sat stiffly, unable to do more than study the earl over the rim of her teacup. How, she wondered, could she ever have thought him unattractive? Loving him as she now did, she believed him superior in every way, and this included physical appearance. Indeed, she mused, how could she ever have thought to resist a man so compellingly masculine? Especially when the entire force of that masculinity was centered so flatteringly upon herself?

His dynamic presence filled the room, dwarfing everything in it. It had always been so, she reflected even that first day he had visited her, and even six years before that. At age eighteen, she had been in awe of him, mistaking his blunt, forthright manner as something threatening or formidable. However, at four-and-twenty, she had been unable to preserve this attitude, despite all efforts to the contrary. Looking back, she could now admit that not once since her arrival in London had she ever been truly angry with him. In fact, every one of their encounters had been impossibly exciting, and her so-called anger had been but a willful self-delusion, an excuse to engage in verbal sparring matches that acted like a tonic upon her frozen emotions.

She must tell him. But could she possibly hope to make him accept her decision when it was not what he wanted? She doubted he would give up easily. He was a man who met life boldly and confronted every challenge head-on. Could she convince him that—this time—the conservative approach was best? She had to try. She had to do what she believed was right, though it made her feel as treacherous as Judas. Taking a deep breath, Diana set down her teacup and cleared her throat.

"Geoffrey—"

Her use of his name was inadvertent and probably unwise, for it brought an intensity to his eyes that made her nerves jump. She stumbled over her next words.

"I—I know you will not mind if I call you Geoffrey . . ." *Dear God, why did she have to sound so foolish, so gauche, so young?* Diana flushed, and made her voice firm. "I've been thinking about your offer."

"And?" The earl set down his cup and leaned forward, his eyes locked on her face.

She moistened her lips. "This is very difficult for me to say, but I'm afraid I . . . I cannot marry you. I thank you for your offer but my answer must be . . . no."

What poise she possessed caved in with a crash. Lord Lucan's expression barely altered, yet the room was all at once a void, full of nothing but stark, rigid silence. The afternoon grew colder, the shadows longer, and a chill wrapped itself around Diana's heart.

A handful of seconds slipped by before he spoke. "Well, that was short and sweet," he remarked, with unnatural flippancy. "Is that it? Shall I go now?" His disappointment was so tangible she could feel it.

Stricken with guilt and remorse, Diana stretched out a hand, but he pointedly ignored the gesture, and her hand dropped limply back into her lap. Her face was very pale.

"Please listen, Geoffrey," she begged. "It's important to me that you understand." His mouth was tight and uncompromising, but she went on, imploringly, "Whatever you may think, this has not been an easy decision for me to make. If you think I do not care for you, you are wrong. Quite the contrary, I care for you very deeply— too deeply to marry you."

He frowned, but his mouth lost some of its pinched, icy look. "I think that you had better explain that," he said carefully.

"I am trying to!" Unable to stay still, Diana stood and walked to the window, her arms wrapped under her breasts in an unconsciously shielding gesture. Now that she faced him, she realized that she would have to tell him the whole truth, that there could be no half-measures or cowardly evasions. Feeling his gaze on her back, she swung around, endeavoring to put into words what she had been unable to tell Aimee.

"You see, my first marriage was a disaster in every sense of the word. I've told you that, I think. Edmund cared less than nothing for me, and to be frank, I felt the same for him." Her voice wavered a little, but she controlled it and looked him straight in the eye. "I am no innocent girl, Geoffrey. I was Edmund's wife in the fullest sense, and I know what is involved."

The earl stared at her, baffled. "Naturally, I assumed as much," he replied, a note of harshness in his voice.

"But what the devil does that have to do with us?"

Sensing his frustration, Diana's eyes clouded with anguish. "Geoffrey, what I am trying to tell you is that I found that particular part of marriage excessively distasteful. Edmund knew it and went to other women for his pleasure—with my blessing, I am ashamed to say."

Those piercing gray eyes were riveted to her face, unrelenting and keen, demanding an explanation that she hardly knew how to supply. He was making this horribly difficult for her.

She swallowed hard. "You see, it is because I . . . I love you that I cannot marry you. I owe you a great deal, I know. These weeks with you . . . have brought me out of my cocoon. Because of you, I have felt so *alive* and . . . and *whole* . . . and for a while I really thought it might work. But it's not enough. I love you with all my heart, Geoffrey, but marriage is not for me. I . . . I could not suffer through . . . all *that* again. Not even for you. And eventually you would despise me for it. And if you went to someone else, I could not bear to live."

Lithe as a panther, the earl was out of his chair. "Diana," he said stubbornly, "at the risk of sounding like an utter coxcomb, I think you might find the experience different with me. Edmund Verney was the lowest kind of vermin, my dear. I doubt he tried overmuch to please you." He had planted himself directly in front of her and was scowling fiercely.

A fleeting smile touched her lips. "Edmund never did anything to please me," she agreed, reaching up to trace the line of his jaw with her finger. "But, Geoffrey, I have decided I cannot take that chance. I cannot, in all conscience, accept your offer because I know I would make you miserable. It is for your own good."

He closed the remaining gap between them, his hands clamping around her wrists with unconscious force. "Dammit, Diana, I am miserable now!" he retorted, his

238

fingers tightening as if he longed to shake her. "Forget your damned scruples and marry me! Give me a chance to prove I can make you happy! I think what you are saying is complete rubbish, but if in truth you find that you cannot stomach me, why then I'll—I'll leave you alone. I swear it."

His grip on her wrists was too tight, but she ignored the pain, for it was nothing in comparison to the wrenching agony in her heart. Perilously near tears, her voice quivered.

"A little while ago you told me I was sweet, but it is you, Geoffrey, who are sweet. Sweet and hopelessly unrealistic. It would never work, my dear, don't you see? Were I to deny you, sooner or later you would go to another, and though I would try to understand, I fear my love for you would suffer as a result. I know many men have mistresses, but I could not just look the other way. I would want to kill her, whoever she was. Don't you think that would be an odious marriage? Do you see that I am right?" Now that she was finally telling him, the words came tumbling from her mouth. "Why risk it, Geoffrey? If we do not marry, we can remain friends which is far better, for we will not lose each other. It is a good compromise. Please, please, try to see that I am right."

Hearing the obstinancy behind the plea, he stared at her in despair, racking his brain for some magical words to make her see things his way. Out of nowhere, his own advice came back to haunt him. *There are no magic formulas* . . .

"This is not logical, Diana," he said inadequately.

"But it *is* logical," she objected. "Think about it, my dear. If we can remain friends—"

"Dammit, Diana, I don't want you as my friend!" he exploded. "I want you for my wife. I want you in my bed so I can make love to you as often as possible, preferably every day for the rest of my natural life. I want you to bear my children, Diana. I want sons who look like me and daughters who look like you with topaz eyes and glorious golden hair. I want to be able to—"

"You seem to want a great deal!" she interrupted, with new coolness. "And I do not think you are even *trying* to understand! I have spent *hours* agonizing over what is best for both of us. But it seems that you only consider what is best for you!"

"Not true!" he retorted, stung. "I know what you need better than you do, my girl. What you need is to be kissed and bedded by someone who knows what he's doing! And you need someone to paddle some sense into you so that you'll stop torturing yourself—and me, I might add— with these harebrained, foolish flights of fancy—"

"Flights of fancy!" she echoed, in sudden, vibrant fury. Something inside her snapped at the phrase. "If you think for one moment," she blazed, "that Edmund Verney's crude, animalistic embraces were merely some flight of fancy, or some . . . some figment of my imagination, then pray allow me to correct you. My husband hurt me, Geoffrey Trevelyan! On my wedding night he left me with nothing. Not my virginity, not my pride, not my self-respect, and certainly not with any expectation of future happiness." She laughed, and the laugh was laced with bitterness. "No, let me correct myself. He did leave me one thing. Pain. A great deal of it, in fact. I vowed long ago never to repeat that experience—at least not voluntarily. So, my lord, unless you are prepared to force me against my will—"

The injustice of the suggestion cut him to the quick. "Don't be ridiculous," he rasped, finally giving her that shake. "Dammit, Diana, you're not listening to me! If you think I would treat you anything like that cur treated you, then you're out of your senses!"

"Oh, really! You're a man, aren't you?" she cried, too near hysteria to consider the wisdom of her words.

The earl's face whitened with rage. "Why, how clever of you to notice!" he said sarcastically. "Since the game is up, I shan't scruple to give in to my bestial instincts. We men are all the same, you know. When all is said and done, there is little to choose between us."

As he spoke he jerked Diana against him, his expression more savage than she had ever seen it. Before she could do more than stare up at him, his mouth was seizing hers, his lips cleaving hungrily while his thrusting tongue forced its way forward. It was an aggressive kiss, yet it did not inflict pain, and it evolved so quickly into one of passion and sensuality that Diana's senses skittered and spun. It was a kiss that might have won the day if he had not gone a step farther and slid his hand between them to caress her soft, quivering breasts.

But Diana was not yet ready for this. Dazed to the point of numbness, she recoiled from his touch, pushing against his chest with the whole of her strength. Then the earl, failing to comprehend his mistake, compounded his error by trying to renew the embrace, but this only made Diana struggle more. Ugly memories of Edmund erupted in her mind, and for a moment she forgot who it was that held her, forgot that she loved him, and acted on pure instinct. Recalling something she had once done to Edmund, she raised her knee, aiming for the earl's groin.

The earl's quick reflexes came to his aid, enabling him to turn just enough so that she barely grazed his thigh. However, though he tried to catch her, the force of her attempted kick put Diana off balance, and she tumbled to the floor.

For an instant, he stood over her like a conqueror, his legs spread wide, his fists planted firmly on his lean hips. But as she stared dully back, it was as though a curtain had been ripped away, and for the first time he really saw the dark torment behind the brown-gold eyes. He had sensed that there were things she preferred not to discuss, things which had to do with her unhappy marriage, but now he was truly beginning to understand. Wishing it were possible to murder Edmund Verney all over again, he dropped to his knees beside her.

"Forgive me, Diana!" He said it twice more, gathering her into his arms with a tenderness so at odds with his previous behavior that Diana simply accepted it and clung to him, sobbing into the white material of his shirt.

"God, I'm sorry, love," he murmured, over and over in her ear. "I'll never do that again to you, darling, I swear upon everything I hold sacred. I'll never hurt you again, Diana. Please stop crying, darling."

"But you didn't hurt me," she gasped, fighting for composure. "And I know you're not like Edmund. I don't know what made me say that."

"No, I promise you I'm not," he said, kissing the top of her head. "So it hardly makes sense to assume that going to bed with me will be unpleasant, does it?" he inquired. He pushed her hair back out of her face, stroking the soft golden curls which had escaped confinement. "I did not think I was that unappealing to you."

"You don't understand. It's not you," she insisted, her voice husky with emotion. "It's—it's me, Geoffrey. I didn't want you to know, actually. I'm horribly embarrassed to tell you, but there's . . . there's something wrong with me."

"Nonsense," he replied. "What could be wrong?"

"I don't know," she almost wailed. "But there is something different about me. I'm just not like other women."

He gazed at her in tender bewilderment. "I'll vouch for that," he said, his lips twisting. "You're far more beautiful, muddled, and maddening than any other woman I've ever known!"

"Don't tease me," she begged, and amazed him by pressing her lips to his hand. "Let's forgive each other

242

and forget this ever happened. I don't want to brangle with you."

"Nor I with you," he agreed, helping her to her feet. "You've said you care for me—well, I care for you, too. A very great deal, in fact." His hands cupped her face, and for a long moment he stared into her tear-soaked eyes. "You *must* marry me, Diana," he urged. "There's nothing wrong with you. Let me prove it to you."

It would be so easy to give in, but having come this far, Diana was determined to stand firm. After all the soul-searching, after all the procrastination and vacillation, she had done what she had to do. As difficult as it had been, she had finally told him, and now it was evident that she would have to be strong for them both.

"No, Geoffrey," she said bravely, ignoring the leaden ache in her chest. "I refuse to do something that will only cause us both more pain."

His clenched jaw was set in an obstinate line. "You know I'm not going to give up, Diana. You think about it some more, won't you, darling? Promise me you'll think about it some more."

Uncertain whether such a promise would be more cruel than kind, Diana hesitated, but before she could answer, there were footsteps on the stairs.

"Forgive me for interrupting, madam," said Lawrence a moment later. "But you have visitors."

"Visitors?" Diana repeated blankly. "Who can be calling at this hour?"

His fastidious fingers held a small calling card by its corner. "A Mrs. and Miss Fingleshaw, madam. I took the liberty of putting them in the morning room. They appeared to know you."

Slowly, Diana sank into the chair behind her, her gaze fixed on the butler. "First Lady Edgerton, then Sir Henry, and now, *now* Eliza Fingleshaw," she said faintly. "What could possibly happen next?"

Chapter Fourteen

In the end, Diana was obliged to invite Eliza and her mama to stay for dinner, for they showed no disposition to keep their visit short. They had arrived in London only that afternoon, having bounced around for the better part of the day in Mr. Fingleshaw's rumbling old traveling coach.

"It is dreadfully antiquated," complained Eliza, a tall, angular girl with sandy hair and pale bluish-gray eyes. "But as many times as we have mentioned it to Papa, he refuses to spend the money on a new one."

"My husband has the most tiresome notions," stated her mother with a trill. "Only fancy! He did not want me to bring my darling Eliza up to London to visit her bosom friend, the *confidante* of her entire childhood!" Her chair creaked as she made impatient gestures. "Can you conceive of anything more nonsensical? As if we should be infringing somehow upon dear little Aimee's Season— which I know we could not possibly do."

Eliza giggled, and looked at Aimee. "I have *so* much to tell you, but I shall wait until I have you all to myself. Mama says I can invite you over just as soon as we are settled. Of course, I am not officially *out*, but Mama says there are still a number of things I can do. It will be such capital fun!"

"Perhaps I should warn you that Aimee has been ill," interposed Diana firmly, "and may not be quite ready for all the activities you are planning."

Mrs. Fingleshaw's alarmed gaze shifted between the two sisters. "Ill? I do trust it was nothing serious? I noticed she looked thinner, but I put it down to the unaccustomed strain of town life."

Diana folded her hands. "Well, she is much better now, ma'am. But, yes, it was fairly serious for a spell."

Eliza turned to Aimee. "Have you had a great many offers?" she asked, bouncing a little. "I cannot wait to hear about all those suitors you mentioned in your letters! Who was that scowling gentlemen who left just after we arrived? I saw him through the morning room window, you know. He is not one of your suitors, is he, Aimee? I thought he looked quite frightening, and not at all handsome."

"Goodness, no, Eliza," scoffed Aimee, with a swift, sidelong glance at her sister. "Lord Lucan is too old for me. He is Diana's friend."

"Lord Lucan?" repeated Mrs. Fingleshaw in an impressed voice. "My dear Diana, do not tell me that a peer of the realm has chosen to honor you with his attentions?" Her eyes goggled as she strained forward in her seat.

"Not at all," lied Diana. "Lord Lucan *is* a friend, but nothing more than that."

Despite this assertion, an arch smile sprang to Mrs. Fingleshaw's lips. "Silly goose! You need not keep secrets from me, my dear. Think how long your mama and I have been acquainted! I am perfectly aware that she and your papa yearn to see you happily established and that you are a dutiful, sensible girl. It would be the most natural thing in the world for you to look about for a husband while you are here. There is not the least

245

occasion for you to pretend otherwise."

Concealing her annoyance, Diana kept her reply courteous. "Indeed, ma'am, I think you do not understand. I have no wish to remarry. And my parents want only what is best for me."

But Mrs. Fingleshaw was obviously unconvinced, for she waved a waggish finger, and said, "Now, now, my dear. I shall say no more. No one will ever be able to say that I, Eudora J. Fingleshaw, do not know how to keep a secret!"

They soon went in to dinner, where the conversation quickly turned to the subject of Aimee's success and the host of delights in store for Eliza.

"Freddy has told me all about Vauxhall Gardens," Eliza announced, rather breezily. "Perhaps he will be able to take us there himself, for he is right here in London. In fact, though Mama did not tell you, that is the main reason for our being here. He has been sent down from Oxford for the rest of the term."

"What, again?" said Diana involuntarily.

For the first time, Mrs. Fingleshaw appeared a trifle discomposed. "Yes, is it not the most tiresome thing? My son seems to have gotten in with the wildest set of young men. They are constantly getting him into one scrape or another. I don't scruple to tell you that Mr. Fingleshaw is enraged, but I think it preposterous to believe that our Freddy has anything to do with these shocking schemes they hatch. He was always such a good boy." She sighed, abandoned her obstinate defense of her son, and dabbed her mouth with her napkin. "Mr. Fingleshaw has bidden me to bring him home," she added glumly.

Diana remembered Freddy Fingleshaw as having been a very nasty little boy, but tactfully refrained from making reference to the multitudinous troubles he had caused during his more youthful years. Instead, she suggested that they repair to the drawing room for coffee.

"I fear I cannot ask you to stay much longer," she said pointedly, "as Aimee needs her rest. I am hoping she will be herself again in a very short time."

"May she visit me tomorrow?" asked Eliza hopefully. "We can just sit in my room and talk. She can even lie on my bed if she wishes."

Diana hesitated, but was unable to think of a reason to refuse. "I don't see why not," she said finally. "It sounds like a perfect arrangement. I think Aimee is ready to begin making some short outings."

Aimee and Eliza exchanged eager glances. "Oh, good!" they said, so nearly in unison that they both went into a fit of the giggles.

"Oh, Eliza! I am so glad you have come!" cried Aimee, reaching impulsively for her friend's hand. Then they both laughed again in a giddy, girlish way that set Diana's teeth on edge.

Thanks to Eliza Fingleshaw, she reflected gloomily, Aimee's behavior was already backsliding.

That night, Diana was too tired to do more than fall instantly asleep, but a loud crack of thunder awoke her sometime near morning. Still drowsy, she lay for a while listening to the hard, steady beat of rain, but instead of drifting off again her mind grew gradually alert. She thought of her childhood, and of the carefree existence she had led until Edmund entered her life. She thought of her wedding night, and of the many long, lonely nights she had lived through since then. She recalled how she had locked her door against Edmund, and why it had been necessary to do so. And she thought about Geoffrey Trevelyan.

Every fiber in her body ached to be with him. How wonderful it would be, she thought, to have him sleeping next to her, to hear the reassuring sound of his breathing in the dark. She could imagine how blissfully safe she would feel knowing that he was right there within the reach of her hand. It had been a long time since she had felt that kind of security, security derived from the knowledge that there was someone strong to lean on—someone who cared. She was honest enough to acknowledge, however, that the strange, restless ache inside her was a great deal more complicated than a simple need for protection.

She had to admit that what he said made sense. How could intimacy with him be anything like intimacy with Edmund? Geoffrey would be caring and considerate; he would never try to hurt her—at least not intentionally. Many years before, her mother had told her that it was a woman's duty just to lie still and let her husband do what men were intended to do. That it was all that was required of her, that it was what a good and dutiful wife did. It had sounded depressing at the time, and it sounded just as depressing now. Why, oh *why* could women not enjoy it? At least just a little?

But perhaps they did. She wished she knew another woman with whom she could discuss the matter. Aunt Serena was out of the question, and as for Mama, the subject had obviously made her extremely uncomfortable. Rolling to her side, Diana pulled the blanket up to her chin and gazed rather sadly into the blackness. If only she had a close friend, someone with whom she could discuss things of a private nature, perhaps she might understand a little more about it. But there was only one person in her life who came anywhere near to fitting this description. And that was Geoffrey himself.

The following morning, Cousin Charles came by to inquire whether Aimee was fit enough for a drive in the Park. Though the ground was still wet, the rain had cleared the air and the sun was peeping over the tops of the houses in a most determined fashion. Diana's gray mood began to lift as she observed Charles's attentiveness to her sister. Under her approving eye, he handed Aimee into his carriage as tenderly as if she were a china doll, and tucked a blanket over her knees with the most painstaking regard for her comfort.

At least things were going well in that quarter, she reflected. Cousin Charles would surely be making her sister a declaration quite soon—at least, as long as Eliza Fingleshaw did not put a spoke in the wheel.

Diana reentered her house with a sigh, and decided that it was time to pay a visit on Aunt Serena. She had not done so since before Aimee had taken ill, and though this could hardly be said to be her fault, she could not banish the feeling that she had been derelict in her duty toward her aunt.

Apparently, Aunt Serena shared that opinion. "Well, well!" she remarked, as disagreeably as ever. "Fancy you taking the trouble to come all the way to Arlington Street only to see me. What cataclysmic event can have prompted this, I wonder?"

Preserving her calm, Diana dropped a quick kiss on her aunt's cheek and sat down. "No, I'm afraid we have had no cataclysms today, Aunt Serena. Is your stomach troubling you again? Is that why you're so peevish?"

The dowager eyed her with disfavor. "Impertinent girl," she grumbled. "I don't know why I can't get any respect out of you. Your sister's just as bad."

"Now that is unfair and you know it. Would you prefer that we bow and scrape? I thought you disliked that sort of thing."

The dowager's cane thumped the floor. "Hang it, girl. I do! For land's sake, now, don't go looking smug just because I agreed with you. How's little Aimee? Why didn't she come with you?"

Diana sat back and adjusted her skirts. "Cousin Charles has taken her for a drive. She is much better, but still a trifle weak. I am planning to bring her to see you as soon as I can."

Aunt Serena's chin drooped thoughtfully. "See that you do. I like the chit. She knows what she wants and has the spunk to try to get it. Behaves a bit silly, of course, but she'll grow wiser with time."

"I certainly hope so," agreed Diana, a shade dryly.

The dowager shot her a look. "You've got spunk, too, Diana. But you've got to learn to take what you want from life, and stop namby-pambying around. It puts me completely out of patience with you."

Diana's mouth hardened. "Oh, does it?" she said coolly. "Well, I am sorry to hear it, for I plan to continue namby-pambying my own way through my own life, Aunt Serena. Perhaps I should inform you that my chief concern at this time is Aimee. I want to see her married to someone who will be kind to her. And I am hoping very much that someone will be your grandson."

"Hang it, of course she's going to wed Charles," replied the dowager, glaring impatiently. "If she wants him, she'll have him. The boy hasn't a prayer's chance of escaping. What you should be concerned about is yourself, birdwitted girl! Are you going to marry Lord Lucan or not?"

Diana returned the glare. "And just what makes you think he's asked me?"

"Hang it, I *know* he's asked you. He told me so himself!"

"Well, he should not have!" snapped her niece, keeping her temper with difficulty. "And, no, I am not going to marry him!"

Once more, the dowager's cane thumped. "Confound it, girl, why the devil not? Haven't you the wit to see the man's in love with you?"

250

For a time Diana did not reply. Then she said, more quietly, "I know he cares for me, Aunt Serena. Whether he loves me or not is another thing entirely." She shifted restlessly, her hands massaging her knees through the thin muslin. "But after much thought, I have decided that I do not wish to marry him."

The dowager looked disgusted. "Pah! Of course you do, addlepated girl. Where on earth have your wits gone? Why, any sensible woman would want to marry a man like that. I'd marry him myself if I was forty years younger!"

"Oh, would you?" said Diana stiffly. "Simply because he is wealthy and bears a title, I suppose."

"There is that, of course," nodded Aunt Serena. Then she leered, and began jabbing the air with her finger. "That and the fact that he's put together damned nicely! Most of these high-born young whippersnappers mincing around London wouldn't strip to half such advantage. Manly, that's the word for him. A discriminating woman learns to appreciate such things."

Though she knew she ought to be shocked, Diana amazed herself by laughing. "For pity's sake, Aunt Serena," she begged, "*do* keep your voice down. The servants are likely to hear!"

Paying no heed to the suggestion. the dowager scratched her nose reflectively. "What's more, it's my guess he'll know what he's doing between the sheets. Well, at his age, he should, but that ain't always the case," she added inconsequently. "At any rate, he ain't a philanderer, which is a strong point in his favor. He told me he's sown his share of oats, but that he's done with all that. He's ready to settle down now."

Diana sat back and stared at her aunt. "Well! You and he are certainly on intimate terms," she remarked, rather crossly.

Aunt Serena preened. "Yes, I always had the knack for

getting a man to talk. Some women are born with it, others just ain't!"

Abruptly, Diana decided it was time to change the subject. "Has Lord Hervey spoken with you about your birthday?" she asked.

"My birthday? Oh, you mean that business about resetting the Torrington diamond?" Aunt Serena cackled. "Imagine Thurstan thinking of such a thing. The man's completely besotted with me. He even took a house on Bennet Street just to be near me!"

Diana sighed inwardly. "Yes, he seems very devoted. So you think it's a good notion?"

"Lord, no!" scoffed the dowager, smiling fondly. "What do I want with another necklace? I told him the diamond belongs in the tiara. It was a gift from Charles II, for land's sake. One doesn't chop up an heirloom like that!"

"I thought you might feel like that. But he seemed so delighted with the notion I was reluctant to say so."

Aunt Serena stared off into space for a few seconds. "He keeps asking me to marry him," she said suddenly. "But I keep turning him down."

Diana was surprised. "Oh? Why?"

She received a sharp look for her pains. "I don't need a reason, missy. When you reach my age, you can be as peculiar as you choose. It'll be your prerogative, but right now its's mine."

With a sigh, Diana studied the old woman's face, her gaze softening as she took in the fine, aristocratic bones beneath the wrinkled flesh. "You are a little, ah, unconventional," she admitted. "But as often as you annoy, confuse, and bewilder me, there are times when I really don't think I would have you any other way. It seems very strange," she added musingly.

Great-aunt Serena grinned. "Ha! Thank God there's

some sense in you, Diana. There's hope for you yet!"

For the next few days, Aimee divided her time fairly evenly between Eliza Fingleshaw and Cousin Charles. She and Eliza spent the bulk of their time gossiping and giggling—concerning what, not even Diana cared to guess. One might arguably claim that the healthy glow in Aimee's cheeks owed its restoration to Eliza's visit, but in her elder sister's opinion, it was merely the natural consequence of fresh air, increased activity, and improved appetite. These, in turn, were all linked to Charles and his efforts on her young sister's behalf, for Aimee's mornings were almost exclusively taken up by her handsome cousin.

Unfortunately, Aimee's recent and rather engaging display of good judgement had all but vanished. She no longer seemed to think before she spoke, and to Diana, what came out of her sister's mouth seemed more foolish than ever. The day that Cousin Charles escorted Aimee and Eliza for a walk in Green Park was not, as it later proved, the culmination, yet at the time, it crowned what was clearly becoming a threat to Aimee's future hopes. Diana was never to know exactly what occurred, but the look of stoicism on Charles's face when they returned might have been laughable had it not seemed so ominous. Ominous, too, was the speed with which he made his departure, so that when, an instant later, Eliza went into one of her fits of insane giggling, Diana rounded on her guest with a most uncharacteristic snap.

She soon left the room, for she could not quite care for the bold way Eliza returned her gaze, or the manner in which her pale eyes glinted back. And knowing that Miss Fingleshaw was fundamentally just as much a mischief-maker as her brother, Diana could not help feeling uneasy. She reassured herself, however, with the reminder that Eliza's mother intended to leave London by the end of the week, and so was able to push the matter from her mind. She might not have done so had she been privileged to hear the ensuing conversation.

"Aimee," whispered Eliza, when Diana's footsteps had faded away, "it's all set with Freddy. All we must do is smuggle your evening clothes out of the house. You had better give them to me today, so your sister does not become suspicious."

Aimee nodded slowly, "Yes, but, Eliza, I'm not at all sure I shouldn't simply tell Diana what we are planning. To own the truth, I would feel a great deal better if I had her consent."

"Absolutely not!" hissed Eliza. "You must do nothing of the sort. She would only spoil everything! Anyway, you do not need her permission. She is only your sister, not your guardian."

When Aimee frowned, Miss Fingleshaw's voice turned coaxing. "Oh, do not be so provoking. It will be such fun! Freddy is bringing some of his Oxford friends, so we will have a surfeit of male protection. Nothing can possibly go wrong, and your sister need never know anything about it."

Aimee's blue eyes held a troubled look. "Yes, but I keep thinking that . . . that Charles would not like it," she said.

"Oh, pooh," said Eliza, scorning this sentiment. "Who cares what he thinks? That cousin of yours is not nearly as remarkable as you led me to believe. He is positively stodgy, Aimee. I cannot see you married to someone like that. You need to meet a more exciting man, a man who knows how to flirt!"

"Charles is not stodgy!" objected Aimee indignantly. "At least, he is a little, but in a rather endearing way. You

254

will like him more when you are better acquainted."

"Perhaps," conceded the other, "but does he ever flirt with you? Ever?"

"Well," said Aimee weakly, "not exactly. But he did take me home when I thought I was going to be sick . . ."

Eliza began to laugh. "Oh, Aimee," she gasped, clutching her side, "you cannot know how ridiculous that sounds."

Aimee eyed her bosom companion ruefully. "I suppose it does. You know, Eliza," she said sadly, "I think I have changed."

Within Castle Tavern, at Holborn, Charles Perth and Lord Lucan were drowning their disparate sorrows in a glass of daffy. Charles was feeling very much put out, and in consequence, had imbibed more than his usual amount of the sporting gentleman's favorite drink, known in certain circles as Blue Ruin, and in the Daffy Club simply as daffy.

"Y'know," he said moodily, "I ain't at all certain I ought to get married. Females are a deuced lot of trouble when it comes down to it."

"True, but they also offer certain undeniable compensations," replied the earl, as sympathetically as possible. His mood was not much better than Charles's, but the other man obviously needed to talk.

Raising a shoulder, Charles rapped the table with his knuckles and stared into his glass. "She's been thick as thieves with that Fingleshaw hussy ever since the cursed girl arrived. All I hear these days is 'Eliza says this' and 'Eliza says that'!" he groaned. "Frankly I'm fed to the teeth with Eliza, and I don't give a brass farthing what she says or thinks! You'd think she was a damned oracle or something! If it were up to me, by God, I'd send her to

Jericho and never bring her back!"

The earl raised a dark brow. "Well, then, why don't you?"

Charles glanced up. "What d'you mean?"

"I mean," said his companion patiently, "that according to her sister, your opinion carries great weight with Miss Farington. I think she would listen to you if you tried to, er, suggest such a course."

Charles shook his head. "Diana told me something of the sort, too. Thought she must be thinking of somebody else. Aimee never listens to a word I say. At least, I don't see a sign of it." He sat up straighter and cocked an inquiring and slightly befuddled eye at the earl. "What about you? Going to pop the question soon?"

The earl's lips twisted bitterly. "If memory serves, I've offered for Diana three times already. And I feel like I've done nothing but knock my head against the stable door."

Charles shot him a commiserating look. "In love with her, eh?"

For a few seconds, the earl said nothing. "She suits me," was all he finally got out. He was not sure he could talk about his problems, at least not without a little more daffy in his system.

Under normal circumstances, Charles might have held his counsel, but he had already had enough gin to make him feel expansive. "She more than suits you, I'd say," he said shrewdly. "I thought you was looking devilish out of sorts lately. Knew another fellow who had just that look. Sick with love, he was. Married the girl in the end. She made a new man of him."

"Sick with love?" repeated the earl derisively. "He sounds like a damned milquetoast."

Charles hooted. "Jack Brinvilliers? Not on your life, my friend. Ever hear of the Marquis of Vale? Course you have. He had the devil of a reputation until last year. Then he fell in love and, well, that was that. He didn't come up to town this Season because Amanda's increasing," he went on, gesturing vaguely. "Won't leave her side. Expecting an heir in June."

The earl drained his glass, eying the other man in rather somber silence. "Do you really believe in love?" he said suddenly.

Charles's glass stopped en route to his mouth. "Hang it, man, of course I do!" he said in surprise. "Don't you?"

"I mean a love that never dies," the earl explained. "A love that . . . that *nourishes* without destroying. A love that doesn't burn itself out with the spending of passion." His gray eyes seemed lit from within, as if illumed by the intensity of his emotions.

Charles fortified himself with another swig of daffy before replying. "I do," he said, wiping his lips. "Can't say I ever thought about it quite like that, though. I ain't got much of a way with words. But I know I love Aimee Farington, and I know that love ain't going to disappear tomorrow, or next year, or ten years after that."

"Then you are fortunate," the earl told him with a frown.

Charles refilled both their glasses. "Why?" he asked. "You think your love for my cousin Diana ain't going to last?"

His companion stared at the floor. "No. No, actually I'm beginning to believe it will."

Charles's brows shot up. "Well, then? What's the problem?"

"Well, for one thing, it leaves me feeling too damned open!" The earl sounded unsettled. "I may be a blunt, logical man, but I'm considerate, too, I think. But Charles, I've never in my life worried about a woman's feelings like this! I've never worried about what other people might do to hurt her, or what kind of pain she's suffered in the past. I don't mean to say I'm usually callous about such things, but—"

"—but you never cared about anybody as much as you care about Diana," Charles finished with a grin. "Aye, you're showing all the signs of it, my friend." He took a few swallows of daffy, and added, reflectively, "I s'pose it's because you've more than just yourself to worry about now. You feel protective, but you also feel a bit . . . a bit opened up. That's the word you used, ain't it? *Open.*" He shrugged. "Not much you can do about it. It comes with the territory."

Having lost complete track of how much gin he'd consumed, the earl prepared to toss off some more. "Well, here's to love," he said, raising his glass. "The most disconcerting emotion around! Though since she won't have me I don't know what the devil good it's going to do me!" he added in frustration. "And that's the second part of the problem!"

Charles sucked on his lower lip, trying to think of some sensible advice. "Stop askin' her," he said suddenly. "Give her a chance to get worried."

The earl grimaced. "You don't know Diana. She'd be delighted. She'd think I'd finally come to my senses. She'd think I wanted to be her *friend!* Her *platonic* friend," he added, with a meaningful belch.

Charles shook his head sympathetically. "You've got a problem," he admitted. "I've got a problem, too. Eliza Fingleshaw's my problem. It's ain't as bad as your problem, but it's a problem." He scratched his head. "Y'know, I always thought I would marry a docile girl . . . someone quiet and submissive . . ." He stopped and puffed out his cheeks, looking thoughtful.

The earl decided to be helpful. "Docility can be deceptive," he pointed out. "Boring, too."

"Boring," repeated Charles, refilling their glasses. "No, Aimee ain't boring." He took another swig of gin and rolled it around his mouth. "By George, I'll do it!" he said with an air of decision. "I'll offer for her! Just as soon as the Fingleshaw girl leaves town, that is," he added with a wink.

"Coward!" mocked the earl. "Does Eliza the Oracle frighten you as much as that?"

"Aye!" Charles grinned drunkenly. "She's worse than my grandmother!"

Chapter Fifteen

"Damn him."

Sir Henry grimaced as he fingered his jaw, and forgot, for once, to admire himself in the mirror. There were lines of discontent about his mouth and eyes, but these were cast into the shade by a large and singularly resplendent greenish gray bruise. Still, it could have been worse, he supposed—considering the solidity of Lord Lucan's fist. The old boy could have broken his jaw if he chose.

"Why didn't you hit him back?"

The baronet's reverie broke, and he swung around. "Really, Sophia," he answered wryly, "physical violence has never been my forte. It's such a shocking waste of effort, my dear. I don't hold with it at all." He dusted his fingers on the front of his dressing gown, a fastidious gesture which was becoming a habit.

"Nevertheless, it is monstrous that he should treat you so," she exclaimed, crossing to his side. "And all because you spoke to the whey-faced widow!"

"Whey-faced? Diana Verney?" Sir Henry's brows rose quizzically.

Sophia Uxbridge tossed her thick red mane from her face. "I think her so. Do you disagree?"

He sensed a challenge in her voice, and responded accordingly. "I could never disagree with you, love. You hold me in the palm of your hand." He saw her quick smile and recollected her appreciation for a double entendre. "And I always rise to the occasion," he whispered, with his most engaging grin.

The lady's smile widened, but then she noticed the wince that accompanied his grin. "But, darling, *something* must be done," she insisted, studying the bruise. "You cannot simply accept his insult."

He shrugged. "What can I do?"

"Has it never occurred to you that words can be more vicious than any weapon?"

His expression became a little meditative. "Now that you mention it, love, yes, it occurred to me when I was a sniveling brat of five or so—but I won't relate the reasons for my enlightenment. It's *so* boring to talk about the past." There was a puckering about his mouth, but it faded quickly. "Suffice it to say that I have kept my tongue sharply honed since then."

"Then let us use our tongues, Henry darling. You say he wants to wed this woman, well? Then let us cast a little doubt upon the lady's reputation. A little gossip can do a great deal of harm—if one desires to be thought respectable."

Sir Henry hesitated, then his voice turned faintly malicious. "Why not?" he said, reaching out to pull her against him. "The little bitch deserves it. But I think I'll leave the details in your very capable hands."

The countess's capable hands slipped through the opening in his dressing gown. "You please me so much more than David," she whispered. "Touch me."

Sir Henry's angelic blue eyes darkened. "As always, Sophia, you find me perfectly willing to oblige . . ."

*   *   *

261

"Do you have everything?" Diana regarded her sister anxiously. "And are you *quite* certain you feel well enough to do this?"

Not quite daring to meet her sister's eyes, Aimee glanced idly around her bedchamber. "I feel fine, and yes, I think I have everything. My night dress, toothbrush and tooth powder, hair brushes, clean clothes for the morning . . . what else is there?"

"And you won't stay up too late or do anything foolish?"

Aimee gave a light laugh. "Goodness, Diana, you really must stop worrying. Spending one night under Eliza's roof will not send me into a decline, you know!"

Diana sighed. "I know. It's just that you are still so thin, and between the two of us, Eliza's mother is *not* as reliable as I would like."

"You forget that I am seventeen, not seven," said Aimee firmly. "Even Mama does not worry as much as you."

Holding fast to the knowledge that Eliza would soon be gone, Diana forced a smile. "Very well. I shan't say another word."

"Oh, I just remembered." Aimee pulled open the drawer next to her bed and pulled out a book. "I promised Eliza I would lend her my copy of *Glenarvon*."

"What did you think of it? Did you like it?" asked Diana curiously.

Aimee's nose wrinkled. "Not really. I don't know why exactly, but in a way it seemed rather silly." Her expression turned prosaic. "But I daresay Eliza will love it. It is just her sort of thing."

"I see. Well, you are probably right about that."

"Aunt Serena says Lady Caroline Lamb is nothing but a nasty little hussy," stated Aimee. "She says people who purposely cause horrid scandals should be banished to the Antipodes—though I daresay she did not mean it."

She sighed. "Personally, I think Charles is far nicer than Lord Byron. Not as romantic, perhaps, but, well, *nicer!*"

"Then you do still wish to marry Charles?" asked Diana bluntly.

"Well, of course, I do!" Aimee sounded startled. "How can you even ask?"

Diana hesitated. "Be careful, then. I do not think he likes Eliza. You wouldn't want to . . . to drive him away."

"Drive him away? What do you mean?"

"Well . . . if and when a gentlemen contemplates marriage, I am sure he likes to receive, oh, a great deal of notice . . . or attention, if you prefer, from the object of his affections." At Aimee's bewildered stare, Diana went on hastily, "Naturally, I am no authority on the male sex—God knows my experience is limited—but one cannot help making certain observations about gentlemen in general. They are a bit like children, I think—at least many of them," she amended. "I am concerned that if you devote too much time to Eliza, Cousin Charles might feel, well, slighted. Just lately, I thought he looked a trifle put out, so to speak."

To Diana's surprise, her sister nodded. "Yes, I thought so, too," she said. "I said something about it to Eliza, but she only laughed. Almost, Diana, I felt a little angry with her at that moment." She frowned at the memory, then said, with brooding hesitancy, "Diana, do you think there is any chance that Eliza could be jealous of me?"

Grateful that the possibility had finally occurred to Aimee, Diana replied, "As a matter of fact, I think it quite likely. I hope you know that I have no wish to spoil your friendship, but neither would I like to see Eliza spoil your future expectations."

"Oh," said Aimee, thinking this over. "No, neither would I." She sighed suddenly. "I told Eliza I had changed, and I really think I have, for there are some things about her that I no longer like. I really think I'll be glad when she leaves." Then she smiled cheerfully. "In any case, one more day and she will be packing to go home, and then, Diana, I will be sure to devote myself *entirely* to Charles. I intend to make it indisputably clear that I am the perfect wife for him."

Though Diana still felt a twinge of foreboding, she made the firm decision to dismiss it. Obviously, Aimee was not so taken in by Eliza as she had thought, while her own tendency to worry was working overtime. Beneath her silliness, Aimee appeared to possess an intrinsic streak of plain common sense that would, in all likelihood, see her safely through these early stages of adulthood. Perhaps, she reflected, Aimee *was* a little like Aunt Serena, after all.

"My God, Eliza! What have you done to my dress?"

Garbed only in her stockings and chemise, Aimee stared in dismay at the neckline of the evening gown which they had smuggled out of the house the previous day.

Eliza smirked. "I knew you'd be surprised. I worked on it 'till midnight last night. What an improvement, eh?"

"An improvement?" Rushing to the mirror, Aimee held the rich blue fabric up to her thin frame. "Diana would kill me if I wore this in public!" she wailed. "Oh, Eliza, why did you do it?"

Eliza pulled a gruesome face. "Pooh! Who cares about Diana? I did you a favor, ninny. I thought you wanted to have some fun."

"I did." Aimee eyed the other girl doubtfully, then her eyes dropped to the dress. "I wonder how it will look," she said, fascinated by the notion.

"Well, there's only one way to find out, isn't there?"

Aimee pulled the dress over her head and twitched it

264

into place. The neckline was nearly two inches lower than it had been before, highlighting the shadowy cleft between her young breasts. Several seconds elapsed while she stared at herself in bemusement. "If Charles saw me in this," she said candidly, "he would be quite, quite shocked. I cannot even think what he would say."

Eliza rolled her pale eyes. "Then he must be the stodgiest man alive! Haven't I told you time and again that gentlemen adore seeing a little glimpse of bosom? I heard Freddy and his friends talking about it one time, and you should have heard the things they were saying." She giggled. "It makes them feel queer all over, and the most peculiar thing happens to a certain part of their anatomy. Of course, they must have been foxed, for I heard them say—"

"Eliza!" cut in Aimee, rather apprehensively. "They will not be foxed tonight, will they? Because I really cannot even consider going if—"

"Rubbish!" Eliza was contemptuous. "You want to see Vauxhall, don't you? Freddy says it is the most vastly exciting place in London! And the fireworks, Aimee— you know you've always wanted to see them! Think how much more fun it will be without stuffy Diana and stodgy Charles along to spoil the fun." Her words must have amused her for she began another round of giggles.

Aimee eyed the other girl as if she were some rare zoological specimen. "But what on earth will your Mama say? She will think me shockingly fast!"

Eliza's sharp shoulders rose and fell. "Oh, Mama is not nearly so nice about these things as you imagine. And it is not as though *I* were wearing it, you know. She will probably think it all the crack, especially if you tell her your stuffy sister bought it for you. Everyone knows she has been a model of propriety since her marriage."

Aimee's sapphire eyes glinted with wrath. "It would be better for our friendship," she said stiffly, "if you refrain from making any more personal remarks about my sister and cousin. Otherwise, Eliza, I am going to become very angry."

Eliza's startled look quickly faded to amusement. "Oh, very well," she said grudgingly. "But do let's finish getting ready. Freddy and his friends will be here soon!"

While Aimee's conscience continued to prick her, Diana was sitting at home, plowing determinedly through the final pages of *Emma*. For a while, she had played piquet with Tildy, but the elderly woman tired easily, and had soon gone off to sleep. Once or twice, the sound of a rumbling carriage reached her ears, but otherwise the house was quiet. The servants were in the kitchen, and though their voices occasionally drifted up to the first floor, they did not penetrate inside the drawing room.

The clock struck ten just as she finished the last chapter, and she put the book aside, stretching the cramped muscles of her arms and legs. Odd, how greatly her evenings contrasted with those first, hectic days in London. Aimee's illness had caused her to miss nearly three weeks of the Season, and one by one, her many beaux had drifted away to hover around other, more available girls. Two or three of the most devoted still came to call, and occasionally sent flowers, but of these none seemed at all suited to be Aimee's husband. Perhaps Cousin Charles's frequent presence had been noted and deemed significant, for the stir her sister had created had quietly dwindled to nearly nothing. So it was that Charles remained the only possible candidate for Aimee's husband. Not, Diana reminded herself, that it was at all necessary for Aimee to be married at so young an age. But that would mean more London Seasons, and who would play the chaperon if not herself? Certainly not Mama, for she would never leave Papa for so long, and Papa hated to travel because of his back. Aunt Serena continued to harbor the fantasy that she could do it, although Diana had rarely seen her leave her chair at any ball or reception that they attended. And since Lord Hervey was always monopolizing her ear, the dowager viscountess scarcely noticed what Aimee was doing at all!

Shoving aside her sister's concerns for the moment, Diana absently traced one of the stripes in the sofa's fabric. She had blocked the earl from her mind all evening, but now she allowed herself the luxury of wondering where he was and what he was doing. She was feeling very lonely. She was often lonely these days, but just now it was worse than usual, a dull, heavy weight in the center of her chest. And it was useless to pretend ignorance of the reason. Earlier in the evening, she had paced the floor in a caged fashion, trying unsuccessfully to erase the suspicion that she was the biggest fool who ever lived.

Well, now that she had played cards with Tildy, finished her library book and had a glass of wine, there seemed to be nothing else to do—nothing to prevent her from going over it again. Of course, she *could* go and write to Mama, but her frame of mind was so dreary that she feared it would show in her letter. No, she had better finish hashing it out now, so that—hopefully—when she retired for the night, she might be granted a peaceful, dreamless sleep.

Diana's lip curled a little. That was the worst time, wasn't it? Those occasional nights when she could not fall asleep, and was forced by some inner demon to relive every mistake she had ever made. The truth was, for the past six years she had cherished a very poor opinion of herself, and her behavior of late had done nothing to improve it. It had not always been so, of course. The carefree days of childhood had been unfettered by guilt, and if her father had been more interested in his books than in any of his offspring, she could not recall it greatly troubling her. Her mother, too, had always been sweet and loving, and Miss Tilden had been yet another blessing.

No, it was in the later years when it began, for she had never stopped blaming herself for Edmund. She had never quite banished the belief that she deserved what she got, that it was her rightful punishment for that foolhardy, hopelessly indiscreet venture up those stairs. That belief lay buried, but alive and ever-present, a skeleton in her own personal closet of memories.

Oh, her emotions were so muddled! Lord Lucan had thrown her life into a havoc, just when she had begun to sort it into some semblance of order. Yet she was glad, yes *glad,* he had done so, she thought fiercely. To know him was an honor, to love him, a privilege. That he wished to marry her was beyond wonderful, beyond anything she could ever hope to express in mere words. She could delude herself no longer. With every shred of her being, she wanted, yearned, and *ached* to be his wife.

Her lower lip tucked between her teeth, Diana tried to sort it out a little more logically. He had asked that she reconsider her refusal. Well, what if she did just that? With sinking spirits, Diana realized that her conscience would demand she confess her secret. And if she did, would he still want her? He believed her modest and respectable, even virginal. But what would he think if she told him that six years ago she had crept up those stairs like a thief, intending to eavesdrop shamelessly on Sir Henry and his partner? He had disparaged Aimee's inconstant behavior, but even Aimee had done nothing as bold and brazen as that! How highly would he think of her then?

Diana shifted restlessly. If only she could be sure that he loved her. He had said he cared for her, but she could not believe it was the same thing. True love was more than caring—it was all-encompassing, inviolable, uplifting. It was both elemental and spiritual, disordered pulses and unquestioning trust. It was a connecting of eyes, a yearning to drink in every feature of the loved one's face, a contentment in his presence. Love was forgiving anything, even what one could not understand. It was *not* the same as caring, she thought broodingly. One could care for a pet, for God's sake.

Since their last meeting, she had come to believe that if he truly loved her, she would be able to tolerate his caresses. She might never truly enjoy them, but would that matter? The children she would doubtless bear would more than compensate for the discomfort. He had spoken of sons and daughters as if he wanted them as desperately as she. How easily she could envision them—gray-eyed sons with black hair, perhaps daughters who resembled herself. She longed for them almost as much as she longed for him.

Jumping to her feet, Diana went and poured herself another glass of sherry. She almost never drank spirituous beverages when alone, but tonight it seemed to calm her nerves. All she had to do, she told herself staunchly, was tell him she had had a change of heart. Phrased like that, it sounded as easy as adding a column of numbers. And after that, she could confess her disgraceful conduct, and await his response.

As she sipped her drink and contemplated this course she heard the faint ringing of a bell. Curious, she listened intently. Who could be calling at this hour? Had Aimee changed her mind and decided to return home?

A minute later, her butler's measured footsteps sounded on the stairs. "A dispatch for you, madam," he revealed, placing a small, white envelope in her hand. His normally wooden countenance looked mildly disapproving.

It was from Aimee, and judging from the near-

269

illegibility of the hand, it had obviously been written in considerable haste.

Dear Diana, it read, *I am writing to tell you that I have gone with Eliza to Vauxhall Gardens. I am sorry now that I deceived you, but I truly did believe that Eliza's Mama meant to go, and that everything would be Perfectly Respectable. Eliza did not want me to write to you, but my conscience dictates that I make a clean breast of it. Freddy and three of his friends are to escort us, so I daresay everything will be just fine. I did not lie to you about feeling well, so do not worry about me! As long as you know where I am, then I think I will be able to enjoy myself.*

Scrawled across the bottom was, *Your loving sister, Aimee.*

"Oh, no!" moaned Diana, scanning the note twice through. "Oh, Aimee, Aimee, how *could* you?" Then the set of her mouth began to harden. "Drat those odious Fingleshaws," she muttered, wadding the note into a tight ball. "This is positively the last straw!"

She threw it into the fire and reached angrily for the bell cord.

Meanwhile, Aimee was finding herself in a far less enviable position than she had anticipated. Freddy Fingleshaw had been ogling her for most of the evening, while his three friends, wild young bloods wholly unsuited to be their escorts, proved themselves so lost to propriety that they, in turn, ogled almost every female who passed, one even going so far as to chase one straw-haired damsel across the lawn.

They had located a vacant supper box easily enough, but the four gentlemen (if such they could be called) had ordered a great quantity of rack punch, and seemed bent on consuming it all in the first hour. To Aimee's further distress, Eliza appeared to be on far too friendly terms with one of Freddy's friends, a young man called Boxy, who flirted with them both and sat with his arm around Eliza's waist. For the hundredth time that hour, Aimee wondered how Eliza had inveigled her into coming. She had known it was wrong, and indeed had been much inclined to refuse simply because she had not yet recovered all of her strength. Though she had felt well enough when they departed the house, fatigue was beginning to creep into her muscles, and she began to wish she could lie down.

As she watched Eliza whisper into Boxy's ear, she realized what little affection she retained for her friend. She would never have believed Eliza could behave so vulgarly. Recalling how Diana had always disapproved of Eliza, she decided her sister's opinion had been warranted. Somehow or other Eliza had changed, transformed from the fun-loving, rather mischievous compatriot of childhood into an ill-bred creature she scarcely knew. Moreover, it seemed strange to Aimee that Mrs. Fingleshaw had permitted the excursion when she was not able to come along. If Eliza's mother had the headache, Aimee reasoned, then they ought to have stayed home. It was unfortunate, however, that these revelations had not occurred to her an hour sooner.

"I say," said Freddy Fingleshaw, quite suddenly, "let's go for a bit of a stroll, Aimee. I'll show you some more of the Gardens."

Dismayed, Aimee glanced at Eliza's brother, taking in the sharp-featured face with its wispy blond eyebrows and reddish eyelids. "No, thank you, Freddy," she answered, as politely as she was able. "I'd really rather not."

Freddy puffed out his cheeks, his shortsighted gaze flicking over her insolently. "Why not? Not afraid of me, are you? Known me all your life, haven't you?" He took a another swig of punch and wiped his lips, staring at her in a challenging manner.

Eliza tittered. "Oh, why don't you go with him?" she urged playfully. "He only wants to kiss you, you know."

A certain hauteur crept into Aimee's voice. "Nonsense, Eliza. Freddy and I are like brother and sister to one another."

"Now *that's* moonshine," protested Freddy, leering a little. "You're far too pretty to be a Fingleshaw! Fact is, you look hellish fine in that gown." His head turned. "Don't she, Boxy? Bang up to the nines, eh? Eliza never looked half so good in her life, I'll swear. All the Fingleshaw females are deuced chicken-breasted," he added, eyeing the soft swell of Aimee's bared bosom with lewd appreciation.

Eliza stuck out her tongue, but Aimee favored him with a reproving look. "Well, this is really too bad of you, Freddy!" she said with dignity. "I think you must be foxed, for I have never heard you speak so discourteously before."

"Not foxed yet," he replied, laughing unpleasantly. A nasty gleam entered his eye. "What's the matter with you, anyway? You're hellish high in the instep tonight. P'haps we ain't good enough for you now that some fancy honourable is waving his handkerchief in your face?"

Goaded by this disparaging reference to Charles, Aimee snapped, "Well, at least my cousin treats me with respect, which is a great deal more than I can say for you! I would not go walking with you if you were the last man in London, Freddy Fingleshaw, for I do not trust you at all! Nor you, Eliza, for it is obvious that you betrayed what you knew was to be kept in strict confidence!" She rose to her feet and glared at them mulishly. "I am excessively sorry I came, and I would very much like to go home!"

This announcement was greeted with general mirth.

"Oh, come *on*, Aimee," said Eliza, rather mockingly. "Don't put yourself into such a taking! Freddy didn't mean anything did you, Freddy?"

"I want to go home," repeated Aimee stubbornly.

"Well, who is going to take you home? You won't go with Freddy, will you? Do be reasonable, Aimee!"

Freddy, who was far closer to being foxed than he was willing to admit, looked sullen. "I say, Aimee, I don't think I like your manner very much." He came round the table and seized her by the arm. "If I want to take you for a walk, then by God, you are going for a walk!"

"Oh, no, I'm not!" Aimee drew back her foot and kicked him hard in the shin—twice.

Freddy let go with an undignified howl. "Why you little she-devil!" he exclaimed, rubbing his leg. "Now where the devil are you going?"

Aimee had darted away, and was bolting over the grass with gazellelike speed. She had an excellent sense of direction, and was already calculating the exact location of the Garden's entrance when by pure chance she caught sight of a familiar face. Filled with relief, she changed course at once, for Freddy was now hot in pursuit, and she was already starting to get a stitch in her side.

"Oh, Sir Henry!" she gasped, hurling herself at the baronet. "Thank God you are here! Can you help me, please? I am being followed!" She clutched at his arm, hardly noticing that his companion—a very beautiful lady—was inspecting her with cold green eyes.

Sir Henry Neyle could not conceal his astonishment. "Why, it's . . . Miss Farington, isn't it?" His hooded blue eyes had just taken in her disheveled appearance when Freddy arrived.

"Who the devil are you?" demanded Eliza's brother, before being lanced to the quick by Sir Henry's cool stare. Freddy goggled wordlessly as the baronet lifted his quizzing glass and surveyed him with clear contempt.

"I *do* beg your pardon," replied Sir Henry, sounding bored, "but is it possible I know you? Miss Farington, I hope you will not tell me you are acquainted with this gentleman?"

"I am, indeed!" shot back Aimee wrathfully. "And he is no gentleman!"

Sir Henry's shoulders shook slightly. "But, my dear girl, I thought you craved excitement?" he murmured.

She glanced at him in surprise, then remembering, blushed. "Not that sort of excitement," she said tartly. "Now, *do* go away, Freddy! You look quite nonsensical standing there with your mouth open." She tucked her small hand under Sir Henry's arm. "*This* gentleman will take care of me," she added innocently.

A trifle startled, Sir Henry exchanged a meaningful look with Lady Uxbridge. "This, my dear, is Mrs. Verney's little sister. Pretty, isn't she? But, of course you have met. You were at Miss Farington's come-out ball . . . *and* dinner."

As Freddy stalked away, Aimee eyed Lady Uxbridge with interest. "Oh, yes. I remember. You sat next to Lord Lucan and flirted with him quite shockingly. I was watching you, you know, to observe how it was done."

Lady Uxbridge looked taken aback. "How what was done?"

"Flirting," explained Aimee. "I wanted to see how you went about it. You looked to be just the sort of lady who would know."

As the countess's eyes narrowed, Sir Henry quickly intervened. "Come, Sophia, let us enlighten the young lady on a few of the finer points. Her education has been sadly neglected."

Aimee frowned. "Oh, but I want to go home. You see, I am still a little weak from being ill. I should not have come here tonight at all. If Diana knew what was intended, she would never have—"

"Your sister does not know you are here?"

Aimee looked embarrassed. "Well, actually she does, but—oh, it is too complicated to explain! Please, could you just escort me to the entrance and summon a hackney to take me home?"

His blue eyes gazed down into hers rather pensively. Then he bowed. "I shall be happy to oblige you, Aimee, love—after a bit." He covered her hand with his own. "But first, let us talk a little while. If you are weary, little one, I will gladly find you a place to sit."

Suddenly, Lady Uxbridge gave a shrug. "Go with him, my dear," she urged. "I promise you will find him good company. *I* always do!"

Aimee hesitated. "But . . . will you not come with us?"

The countess looked amused. "Goodness, why would you want me along? I shall find some diversion or other to keep me entertained. Henry, shall we meet, say, in an hour?"

He bowed. "I will meet you right here, Sophia." Then he turned his attention to Aimee, projecting the full force of his charm. "And now, little Aimee, I intend to provide you with some of that excitement you crave . . ."

Chapter Sixteen

With supreme effort, Diana thrust her fury aside and reviewed the situation from a sensible standpoint. It was very likely, she decided, that Aimee really was as safe as she claimed; nevertheless, inaction was completely out of the question. Aimee's note had intimated that Mrs. Fingleshaw was not to accompany them, a circumstance which in itself was enough to rekindle the angry glitter in Diana's eyes. She had always thought the woman's sense of responsibility was lacking, but such laxity as this surpassed everything! No, there was no help for it. She would have to go to Vauxhall herself, retrieve her sister, and while she was at it, give the Fingleshaw offspring a raking-down they would long remember! However, Vauxhall Gardens was a huge place, and at night it was unwise to venture there alone. She therefore made up her mind to take her burly footman along for protection.

She would have preferred Lord Lucan as escort, but there were several excellent reasons for not seeking him out. For one thing, locating him would be sure to entail a delay, and for another, there existed a distinct possibility that wherever he was, Cousin Charles would be with him. And if their cousin got just one whiff of this, there was no saying but what it might destroy whatever desire he might still have to offer her sister marriage. No, it was best to deal with this herself, and hope to God that the whole situation could be kept as secret as possible. At any rate, fetching her sister home should be simple enough with Felix along.

However, as they approached Vauxhall Gardens, Diana began to feel less sanguine about the matter. Illogical as it was, she had the oddest presentiment that Aimee was in trouble, which sharpened her sense of urgency.

"Stay close to me," she instructed Felix, as she paid their entrance fee, "and if you see anyone who looks even remotely like my sister, for goodness sake, tell me! Thank God it is not a gala night, for the crowds would have been horrendous."

"Yes, ma'am!" replied her footman, his enthusiasm ill concealed. Game for a fight, he flexed his large hands hopefully. Any rascal who had the bloody nerve to bother his mistress would be in for a regular set-to!

As they traversed the gravel-lined walkways, Diana paid scant heed to the twinkling Chinese lanterns hanging in the stately elms, or the fragrant flowers, or the songs of the nightingales in the distance. She ignored the openly admiring glances cast her way by pleasure-seeking bloods on the strut for an available female, but such looks increased her unease. Her nerves on the stretch, she strained her eyes every time she saw a young girl with dark hair or heard a high-pitched giggle or shriek. But it was never Aimee.

Eventually, she and Felix headed for the supper boxes with the hope that the Fingleshaws might still be dining. There were more than a hundred of them, and she found it distinctly embarrassing to have to peer into each box— particularly because of the ribald remarks this elicited from some of the occupants. Nevertheless she did so, for her determination to locate her sister was increasing steadily. She was thankful she had taken the precaution to bring Felix, for without doubt she would have been accosted many times over but for his presence. Because she felt so safe, however, all Diana's attention was focused to the fore—and so she never noticed that at one point a silent figure slipped quietly from one of the supper boxes to trail behind them like a shadow.

In the end, Diana heard Eliza Fingleshaw before she saw her, for Eliza's voice was loud and her abrasive laughter carried on the breeze.

"There they are," she told her footman with a grim gesture.

"Don't you worry, ma'am" he replied. "We'll whisk Miss Aimee 'ome in a pair o' winks!"

Diana was within ten feet of the Fingleshaw's box when she realized that Aimee was not in it. Indeed, the scene which met her eyes was so much worse than she had bargained that she stopped dead and stared in disbelief. A young man with a slurred expression had his arm curled around Eliza's waist, while Freddy and two others had acquired a pair of garish-looking females of dubious reputation. None of them took any notice of Diana.

Her first, ruling emotion was utter fury. Fixing her eyes on the sandy-haired blond, Diana's voice rang out clear and cold with contempt. "All right, Eliza, where is my sister?"

Eliza Fingleshaw looked up, and her pale eyes widened. "Oh, my God," was her sole response, "I told Aimee not to write that wretched note!"

Diana's features were icily stern. "I asked you where Aimee is, Eliza, and I expect an answer—now!"

To her consternation, Eliza only shrugged. "I've no notion at all." She pointed an accusing finger at Freddy. "My clodpole of a brother chased her away, then was poor-spirited enough to surrender her to someone else. It was only a little while ago, so . . ." She shrugged again, drifting into awkward silence.

Diana transferred her gaze to Freddy Fingleshaw. "Do you mean to tell me," she exclaimed, "that you *left* my seventeen-year-old sister in the clutches of a perfect stranger? And that none of the rest of you had the common decency to be concerned? Who the *devil* is she with?"

Freddy looked uncomfortable. "Hang it, *I* don't know. She wouldn't come back with me. Doesn't like me. Anyway, he wasn't a stranger. Said she knew him, or some such thing."

Diana's temper flared. "Both of you ought to be thoroughly ashamed!" she said scathingly. "Have you *no* sense of propriety? You conduct yourselves as though you were raised in a brothel! Eliza, you may consider yourself no longer welcome in my house. I am completely disgusted with you. You may be sure I intend to tell your mama about this—and do not think I will omit to mention it to your papa, either!" She turned, addressing her footman in a decisive tone. "Felix, you must locate Lord Lucan and beg him to come at once. I do not know where you may find him, but try his house first, then my cousin's and then White's. After that, I leave it up to you. Why do you hesitate? Go! And hurry!"

She whirled to face the others. "And now, Freddy, you and I are going to search for Aimee. You will give me the protection of your escort, for it is the very least you can do after your disgraceful behavior. Perhaps I may then tell your papa that you did something useful."

Her threat apparently struck home, for Freddy Fingleshaw scrambled to his feet. "Oh, very well," he muttered, casting her a look of dislike. "Where do you want to look?"

"I believe you can best answer that. Where would *you*

279

take a young lady in this place?"

Freddy cocked his head, and exchanged significant looks with his companions. "Depends," he said rudely, "on my intentions."

"Assume they were dishonorable!" she said with a snap.

"Well, I suppose it would have to be the Dark Walk, then. One likes one's privacy, y'know." Freddy affected a knowing sneer.

Someone guffawed, but Diana merely held out her hand. "Come on, then," she said curtly. "And do not forget for one instant that I am depending on you for my safety. If you *dare* to abandon me, you will never cease to regret it!"

Unfortunately, it soon became evident that Freddy was more inebriated than he had first appeared. He was able to walk and talk, but his gait was rather lurching, and his interest in rescuing Aimee appeared meager, at best.

"Honestly, Freddy," cried Diana, when he stumbled and nearly fell, "you are worse than useless! How much have you had to drink?"

"Not foxed yet," he mumbled. "Only slightly disguised. Feel a bit queasy, though. Like to sit down."

"Well, you cannot sit down," she told him severely. "We must keep looking for Aimee."

"Aimee?" His tone was vague and rather pettish. "Pretty little filly, ain't she? Only wanted to kiss her, y'know. Don't know why she ran away."

"Oh, just be quiet, Freddy!" she snapped.

On this path there were no Chinese lamps to guide them, and what light there was filtered down to them from the moon, which was nearly full. Diana kept her ears attuned for any sound that might reveal Aimee's whereabouts, and continued to hush Freddy whenever he tried to speak. There were a profusion of leafy alcoves along the Dark Walk, and from the muffled giggles, scuffling sounds, and occasional shrieks, it was obvious that many of them were occupied. Again and again, she called out her sister's name, but each time she was disappointed.

They had nearly reached the end of the walk when first a small figure and then a larger one materialized some twenty feet ahead of them. Could it be Aimee? Some sixth sense told her it was, but then the man spoke, and for an astonished instant, Diana checked her steps.

"Now, now, love," drawled a familiar voice, "I really must protest. We both know there were no snakes in there. First, spiders, then bats, and now, snakes. Egad, what other excuse can you invent, I wonder?" A soft laugh sent chills down Diana's spine. "You promised me a kiss if I listened to your story, and having done so, my dove, it is time for you to pay the forfeit. You babble *quite* charmingly, but Scheherazade you're not. Don't struggle so. I don't want to hurt you."

"But you have not heard the most diverting part of the story yet! And there *was* a snake! It went right over my foot!"

It *was* Aimee!

The hysterical edge to her sister's voice brought Diana surging forward. "Let go of my sister, Henry!" she cried out.

"What the devil—!" Sir Henry's head jerked around, and Aimee wrenched herself from his grasp.

"Oh, Diana, thank God you have come!" A tiny sob escaped her lips as she stumbled into Diana's arms. "I am so very tired, and Sir Henry had been most disobliging and ungallant! Please, please, take me home, Diana, and make him go away."

The light was far too dim to discern Sir Henry's expression, but the sardonic silkiness in his voice warned

281

Diana that he was very angry.

"So," he purred, "the fair widow has come to rescue her little sister. Almost, Diana, my admiration is roused. And you appear to be unescorted, my pet. Do you think that is wise?"

Diana lifted her chin and peered at him through the evening shadows. "Of course I am escorted," she replied. "Freddy, come here this instant and show yourself!"

There was no response, and she turned around. To her acute dismay, Freddy lay slumped upon the ground and from the faint, whiffling sound emitting from his mouth, he was obviously fast asleep.

"Oh, Freddy!" she said despairingly. "I should have known better than to trust you!"

Sir Henry had taken the opportunity to move, and his hands closed on her wrists with unexpected strength. "I cannot quite decide which one of you is more delectable," he mocked. "Your sister is a mouth-watering little morsel, but you, Diana, are indisputably an entree. Would that I could sample you both at once," he added crudely. "'A titillating notion, don't you think?"

"Let me go!" She struggled, but he twisted her arm behind her, at the same time reaching for Aimee. "Go into the arbor," he directed the younger girl, giving her a push. "Go, or I'll break your sister's arm. Move!"

"Let her go, Harry."

This time, everyone jumped. Diana did not recognize the woman's voice, but it was plain that Sir Henry did.

"Why, good evening, Cynthia," he remarked, after a stunned moment. "Did you think this was a party? I hate to be rude, but it is not, you know. Do go away, love. I am otherwise engaged."

Cynthia Clement did not move. "Perhaps it is too dark for you to see I have a pistol in my hand. Release Mrs.

282

Verney at once or I will be forced to shoot you."

Sir Henry snorted a laugh. "Or Mrs. Verney," he countered, gripping Diana tightly. "Or yourself, or some other passing fool. What the devil are you about, Cynthia? What is Diana Verney to you?"

"That is none of your affair," she answered. "And there is nothing to prevent me from walking so close to you that I see precisely where to aim. Give up, Harry. This is not the sort of game you like to play. The odds are too much in my favor."

Diana heard her cock the pistol, and realized in horror that the woman was not bluffing. So, apparently, did Sir Henry for he let loose of her arm and thrust her at Mrs. Clement.

"Oh, very well," he said, making a clucking noise with his tongue. "I wouldn't *really* have broken her arm, you know. Egad, no. *How* distasteful." With disconcerting aplomb, he strolled past them and melted into the darkness.

Diana turned to Mrs. Clement. "Thank you," she said, a shade hesitantly. "But . . . why? We do not even know each other."

"Perhaps we should leave talking for later," advised their rescuer. "Right now, I believe your sister requires assistance. Take her left arm and I shall take the right. It leaves my pistol hand free," she added dryly.

The three women made their way to the end of the Dark Walk and out into the wider lane at the end. Once more, Chinese lanterns twinkled, and Mrs. Clement tucked the tiny, silver-chased pistol back into her reticule.

"I always carry a pistol when I go out at night," she said calmly. "On occasion, it has saved me considerable distress and inconvenience."

Wondering which term she would apply to their

encounter with Sir Henry, Diana gave her a curious look. "I see. Well, we are both extremely grateful for your assistance, but I do not understand how it comes about that you were there to help us. Almost as if you appeared on cue."

Cynthia Clement smiled at the phrase. "Almost," she agreed. "Let us just say that I am acquainted with Lord Lucan. I knew he would want you to come to no harm, so I took what I felt were the appropriate steps."

Diana could not help stiffening a little. "Oh?" she said, her tone very casual. "You are closely acquainted with his lordship, then?"

"Not in the way that you are thinking, my dear. He is no more than a friend." She glanced around. "Oh, good, there is a place for your sister to sit down."

Recalling that this woman was noted for her discretion, Diana felt it wisest not to pursue the matter. Instead, she assisted Aimee to the bench, saying, "As it happens, I have sent my footman to convey a message to Lord Lucan. I am hoping he will come and . . . and take us home."

Though Diana did not know it, she sounded a little uncertain. What if Felix was unable to locate him? They might be forced to wait a long time, and Aimee's face was white with exhaustion. Ought she to wait?

"A wise move," approved Mrs. Clement with a nod. "He should be here soon then."

Diana eyed her with half-jealous fascination. That another woman should be so certain about what Geoffrey would or would not do aroused a mixture of emotions in her breast. Had Mrs. Clement been his mistress? She was not pretty, but she had an interesting face, with a pair of expressive, dark eyes which looked as though they had seen a great deal.

"How can you be so sure?" Diana asked at last. "That

is, if you are only a little acquainted with him . . ."

Mrs. Clement touched her arm. "My dear, one cannot spend ten minutes in his lordship's company without knowing him for a gentleman one could rely upon in a crisis. What a pity you did not bring him with you tonight. That other young man was quite worthless."

"Freddy Fingleshaw," sighed Diana. "Yes, perhaps I should have gone straight to Geoffrey, but . . ." As if he were there already, Diana glanced around hopefully.

With characteristic tact, Mrs. Clement switched her attention to Aimee. "Do you feel well enough to begin walking toward the entrance? It would make it simpler for Lord Lucan to intercept us."

Aimee nodded, and rose to her feet. "Thank you," she said. "My knees are not nearly so shaky as before. Keeping Sir Henry at bay was the most wearying thing I have ever done, you see. I have never talked so much in my life."

Mrs. Clement's brows rose. "If you succeeded in holding him off, you must be very clever indeed. Harry can be a most persistent gentleman . . . when he is not feeling indolent, that is."

"Oh!" Aimee digested this for a moment. "Do you know him then?"

"Oh, yes. Everyone knows Sir Henry." Mrs. Clement's voice was light, but Diana read volumes into her reply.

They were halfway along the Grand Walk when Diana spied the earl. She knew a wild longing to run into his arms, but could hardly succumb to the impulse in such a public place. Still, a wellspring of happiness flooded her heart, so that her chest felt ready to burst with the mere joy of seeing him. In a matter of seconds, however, it became obvious her delight was not shared.

"What the deuce is going on?" rasped the earl. "Your

285

footman said you were in trouble." His eyes shifted. "What's the trouble, Cynthia?"

Diana was taken aback by the roughness in his voice, but when he turned and addressed Mrs. Clement before she could even speak, her mouth dropped open with sheer outrage. The fact that he made free use of the widow's Christian name only exacerbated the situation.

"Thanks to Mrs. Clement," Diana put in acidly, "there is no trouble now. I do not wish to go into detail at the moment, but Aimee has had a bad experience and I require some assistance in getting her home. I had meant to ask you to help us, Lord Lucan, but perhaps it is too great a thing to ask!"

Ignoring her sarcasm, the earl's eyes flicked over Aimee, taking in the lowered neckline of her gown. "What the devil has she done now?"

His arrogant assumption that whatever occurred had been Aimee's fault infuriated Diana. "She has done nothing!" she countered, with an angry look. "What an insufferable thing to say!"

The muscles of his jaw tautened. "So I'm an insufferable man," he flung back. "Cynthia, perhaps you would care to enlighten me?"

However, once again Mrs. Clement proved herself the soul of tact. "Forgive me, my lord, but it is not my story to tell. I know you will see to the ladies, so if you will excuse me, I will go. A friend of mine is waiting for me."

As she started to walk away, Diana said quickly, "Oh, but I have yet to thank you properly! Do call on me tomorrow, so we may become better acquainted."

Mrs. Clement looked back, but her eyes went past Diana to the earl. Then slowly, as if she had received some signal, her head shook with regret. "I'm sorry, my dear. I do not think that I can do that."

Perplexed, Diana watched the widow hurry away, then her attention returned to Aimee. "Please, Geoffrey," she urged, concern for her sister cleansing the anger from her voice, "Aimee is exhausted. Please help me to get her home."

Though the set of his mouth was still rather grim, the earl's reply was far more civil. "Of course. My coach is at the entrance. Do you wish me to carry you?" he asked Aimee in a neutral tone.

Aimee's laugh had a listless quality. "Gracious, no. If we do not go too fast, I . . . I can manage. Charles did not come with you, did he?" she asked fearfully.

"No." Lord Lucan gave her a curious look. "No, I'm sorry, he did not."

"Oh, thank goodness! Please do not tell him about any of this!" she begged. "Promise me you will not tell him!"

"Very well. I promise," he said, soothing her agitation as best he could. "Now, come along, Miss Farington."

They reached the carriage in a short time, and Diana let out a sigh of relief as they settled back against the cushions. She held her sister against her, and within a few minutes, Aimee's eyelids had drooped shut. She was fast asleep.

"What happened?" said the earl. He spoke in the quiet authoritative voice of a man who expected the complete truth.

Diana shrugged. "Except that the whole episode is due to Eliza Fingleshaw—and her odious brother, Freddy— I'm not actually sure." Oddly reluctant to mention Sir Henry's involvement in the scene, she said, "She ran away from Freddy only to be waylaid by . . . by another gentlemen who compelled her to accompany him to the Dark Walk. Fortunately, I arrived before things were . . . out of hand."

She knew the earl's penetrating eyes rested on her

face, for the gas-lit street lamps cast a margin of illumination through the coach's windows. Weird, elongated shadows slid along the inner panels, then repeated as each lamp along the avenue was succeeded by the next. He still had not spoken, and, unnerved by his silence, Diana went on in haste. "What I cannot understand is why Mrs. Clement felt obliged to rescue us. I hope you mean to explain that to me."

"What do you mean 'rescue *us*'? What happened, Diana?"

Inwardly, she cursed the unconscious slip. "Oh, it was merely this, ah, man threatened me also—just for a moment. Naturally, there was no real danger. Then your friend Mrs. Clement arrived, so conveniently, and frightened him away with her pistol."

She could almost see the curl of his lip. "A man threatens you in such a place, and you say there was no real danger? I can't believe you're really that naive, Diana. Why don't you tell me the truth?"

"And why don't you?" she countered.

"What the devil is that supposed to mean?"

"It means that I would like to know just how close you really are to Cynthia Clement. You told me before you were only friends, but something she said made me wonder. Was she your . . . your *mistress?* And did you set her to spy on me?" Diana's heart thumped painfully as she waited for him to answer.

She heard him sigh. "To bed a woman once or twice doesn't make her your mistress. For God's sake, Diana, why does it matter so much? It's in the past."

"I don't know," she whispered. "Perhaps it doesn't matter at all. But I wanted to know." She noticed he had not answered the second part of her question.

Another few minutes passed in silence and the coach slowed to a halt in front of Diana's house. "Shall I stay a little while?" he asked, when they stood outside the coach. A unmistakable flame of longing burned in his eyes. "We could . . . talk."

She did want him to stay. Tonight, more than ever, Diana yearned for his company, a yearning so powerful she came near to being vanquished. But she had yet to cope with Aimee, and was herself too tired to parry the questions she knew he would ask. And when Geoffrey learned the truth, he was bound to be furious. She knew he would condemn her decision to rely upon Freddy for protector—which admittedly had been an error in judgement—and although she was grateful to Mrs. Clement for her timely rescue, the woman had unfortunately made Diana more conscious than ever of her own deficiencies. Cynthia Clement had succeeded where Diana had failed, and quite frankly, it rankled just a little.

Yet, Diana's eyes were hungry as she gazed up at the earl. "You'd better go," she said finally. "After all, it must be nearly midnight. But . . . thank you for coming when I needed you, Geoffrey. You are so good to me."

He gave her a rather ironical bow. "Yes, well, that's what friends are for, isn't it?" he replied flippantly.

Aimee slept until noon the following day, but other than that, she appeared to have suffered no ill effects from her ordeal. She confessed the entire tale to Diana, and promised with wholehearted fervency to renounce her friendship with Eliza Fingleshaw. It was necessary to give Miss Tilden a slightly edited version of Aimee's adventures, since she was naturally surprised to find her home, but other than that, the two sisters both agreed to put the entire adventure behind them.

Diana had every intention of paying a visit on Mrs. Findleshaw that afternoon, so that when Aimee suggested that she and Mary take a quiet stroll in Green Park—which was, after all, within yards of Aunt Serena's—she gave her immediate approval to the scheme. When Aimee grew tired, she could return to the dowager's house until Diana came to fetch her in the carriage.

The interview with Mrs. Fingleshaw went far better than Diana expected. Mrs. Fingleshaw professed herself quite horrified about the entire episode, and even went so far as to declare that when her son had sufficiently recovered from the consequences of his excesses, he would make his apology in person. Diana coolly assured her that this was unnecessary, and though both Eliza and Freddy were obviously in store for a rare dressing-down from their parent, it was clear that in the future, the Fingleshaws and the Faringtons would be seeing considerably less of each other.

As she had half-known she would do, Diana decided to pay a call on Mrs. Clement next. She had discovered her direction some weeks before, during the first stages of her fascination with the woman, and now that she had an excuse, the temptation to visit the woman was irresistible. When she was ushered into Mrs. Clement's drawing room—which was as tiny as her own—she could not help being amazed by the lavish touches amid the general shabbiness. Mrs. Clement evidently had a taste for luxury which did not match her income.

"Ah, yes, I thought you might come," said the widow from the doorway. Gliding into the room with a fluid grace, she shook Diana's hand and invited her rather gravely to sit. They did not immediately speak, but studied each other overtly, a weighing-up process made necessary by their interest in the same man.

"I have seen you from a distance," stated Mrs. Clement musingly, "but up close, in the light of day, I can more fully appreciate your beauty. I understand what it is he finds so attractive."

There was no need to ask who "he" was.

Diana cleared her throat. "I came to thank you once more—and to discover your true motives for assisting us."

Mrs. Clement smiled. "You are suspicious of me. That's understandable, of course. But, in truth, it is much as I told you last night. Lord Lucan had expressed to me his concern for your welfare, and I merely sought to do what I thought he would wish. He is a good friend, and a good man."

"That is all he is to you? You do not love him?" Diana's fingers were tightly laced together in her lap.

The widow gave her a considering look. "I have always had a soft spot in my heart for Geoffrey. I shan't lie to you about that. And yes, we spent some time together—briefly—a few months after his wife died."

"You were lovers, you mean," said Diana curtly.

Mrs. Clement looked amused. "You desire frankness, then? Yes, Mrs. Verney, on less than a handful of occasions we were lovers. But love had very little to do with it, my dear. And I tell you that only because you are in love with him yourself. You have a need to know."

Diana nodded. "It's true," she replied pensively. "You do understand."

"I wonder if you realize how much I envy you. You're fortunate I have not a vindictive temperament."

"Why should you envy me? You appear to have everything you need, and your freedom besides."

"On the contrary, I have almost nothing," countered the widow. "I am constantly in debt, and the various gentlemen with whom I share my time are only generous when the mood moves them. There is no security in such an existence, Mrs. Verney, which is why I have decided to remarry. I am glad you came today. I wanted to tell you

291

about this myself."

Slow dread crept over Diana. "Remarry?" she echoed sharply. "Who?"

"Lord Bathurst, your late husband's uncle, has made me an honorable offer," replied the other, with dignity.

Diana's mouth gaped open. *"Lord Bathurst?"* she repeated incredulously. "But ... but he is the most top-lofty, pompous man alive! ... although very worthy, of course," she added, guiltily recalling the man's kindness to herself. "But he is much, much older than you, surely!"

The widow's shoulders lifted. "Yes, he is dreadfully pompous and tedious, but even the dullest man needs a woman," she said prosaically. "I appeal to him, you see, because I remind him of some long lost love of his youth. It's an amusing situation, actually. You see, I believed he was offering me a carte blanche ... and it was only after I accepted him that I discovered it was a proposal of marriage!" She said it almost merrily. "You cannot imagine my surprise! But I grew accustomed to the notion almost at once, for I'm sure you are aware that he is a wealthy man. I thought it best to explain all this to you, for it will put us more or less in the same family. I shall be sort of an aunt to you, I suppose—at least until you remarry, of course."

Diana looked a little bemused. "And do you ... I mean, is it possible that you *love* him?"

Mrs. Clement laughed, a pleasant, musical sound that nevertheless held a dash of bitterness. "Forgive my amusement, Mrs. Verney. It has been a long time since I was asked such a question." Slowly, her smile faded to seriousness. "No, I do not love him. Nor does he love me, though at the moment he believes he does. I intend to provide him with an heir, however, which should go a long way toward binding us together."

A tiny frown furrowed Diana's brow, and she moistened her lips, daring to ask the question foremost in her mind. "But . . . without love . . . do you not find the whole notion . . . rather distasteful?"

Mrs. Clement regarded her shrewdly. "Distasteful? You are speaking of the marriage bed, I collect. What an odd conversation we are having!" Observing the flame of color in Diana's cheeks, she said, "No, don't apologize— I am not offended, I promise! We have something very basic in common, don't we? You feel it, too—I know you do."

In the brief period of assessment which followed, her gaze grew unexpectedly sympathetic. "I am not known for my candor, Mrs. Verney, but you may trust that I speak from experience when I say that all men are not alike. Their needs are similar, yet the way each man translates that need into being can be as individual as the man himself. Many men have not the least understanding or interest in what we females need or want, but there are some who do—and others who are willing to learn."

Embarrassed, Diana's eyes lowered, yet her desire to *know* overcame her reticence on the subject. "And is it possible to feel nothing at all with one man, and . . . and something with another?"

Mrs. Clement nodded slowly. "It is not only possible, it is inevitable. *If* you are lucky enough to find a man who will give of himself, then my advice is to cherish him . . . *love* him, if you can. With such a man as that, you will not find the marriage bed distasteful, I assure you."

The ensuing conversation was no less frank, and when Diana rose to leave, it was with the knowledge that she would always recall this interview with mixed feelings. Mrs. Clement was both candid and encouraging—but she also laid bare her scarred past to the possibly censorious eyes of a woman she scarcely knew. In times to come, there would be moments when something would jog Diana's memory, and she would remember Mrs. Clement's courage and compassion, and from whence was born the sage advice she offered.

But it was not this which made Diana's spirits soar as she headed back to Aunt Serena's house. Her thoughts were only of Geoffrey and the future, a future suddenly gleaming with the promise of happiness. However, a rude shock awaited her back in Arlington Street. It seemed that Aimee and Mary had never returned from their walk in Green Park. In fact, they had vanished without a trace.

Chapter Seventeen

"*What do you mean Aimee is missing?*" Midway into Aunt Serena's Yellow Saloon, Diana came to a frozen standstill, her heart lurching as the first and worst possible explanation leapt into her brain.

"I mean exactly what I said!" bellowed the dowager from where she sat, swaddled in shawls. "She told me she'd return in an hour, and it's been nearly three! She ain't here, and she ain't in the Park either! So where the devil is she?"

Diana pulled off her bonnet. "Well," she said, after a stunned moment in which she denied her initial fear, "she must have decided to return home, or—"

"Do you take me for a fool?" There was a heavy, ominous quality to her aunt's voice. "Hang it, girl, Jermyn Street was the first place I sent 'em to look! I didn't cut my milk teeth yesterday, y'know! And where have you been all this time? I was beginning to think you'd disappeared too!"

"I had a call to pay," Diana answered shortly. She moved to the nearest chair and perched on its edge, frowning.

Aunt Serena thumped her cane. "You've got more things to worry about than paying calls," she said in a grim tone. "Not only is your sister missing, but something else is afoot. I suppose you've been too damned preoccupied to notice that the gossipmongers are on the attack again?"

"No!" Diana's eyes widened in dismay.

"Oh, yes! You've done it to me again!" the dowager informed her. "It's beyond me why other women can manage to be discreet, but *you* have to start a scandal every time you come to town. They're saying he sleeps under your roof every night. Is it true?"

Diana gasped. "Good God, of course not! Who on earth would say such a spiteful thing?"

Aunt Serena did not mince words. "Lady Edgerton, for one," she retorted, "along with a handful of other hens with nothing better to do than flap their beaks together." She made a sweeping, rather irritable gesture. "It's time to end this namby-pambying around with Lucan. I'm going to send the announcement of your engagement in to the newspapers, and drop word of it in one or two appropriate ears. Better yet, we'll say you've married him already—that'll clip their wings!" She cackled gleefully. "We'll steer the gossip the way *we* want it to go! We did it once, and we'll do it again—"

"No, you will not!" interrupted her niece, springing to her feet. "Don't you dare meddle, Aunt Serena! I must speak to Geoffrey about this at once, and *we* will decide what must be done!" Though she did not notice, the decisiveness in her voice brought a hint of approval to the dowager's expression. "Never mind that," she went on with an air of decision. "Right now we must discover where Aimee is! Could she have gone shopping, perhaps?"

Aunt Serena glanced at her clock. "Hrumph . . . not likely at this time of day. It's near five, now. And she'd have come here first so that one of the carriages could be sent for, wouldn't she?"

"I suppose so." Diana's forehead creased with thought. "I don't like this at all, Aunt Serena." She began to retie the strings of her bonnet.

"Where the devil are you going?"

"I'm going to consult with Lord Lucan," she said unevenly. "I've a dreadful suspicion Sir Henry is behind this. Do not ask me to explain, but . . . Geoffrey will know what to do!"

In the event that Aimee had returned home in the interim, Diana went first to her own home in Jermyn Street. She had been making use of Aunt Serena's landaulet, and it was this which conveyed her, less than ten minutes later, to her own front steps. Leaping from the carriage, she hurried forward, and was about to throw open the door when a folded slip of paper tucked into the crack attracted her attention. She snatched it up, and seeing it addressed to herself, unfolded it with trembling fingers.

As she read, the color drained from her face. "My God," she whispered. "Oh, Aimee, Aimee!"

Whirling, Diana lifted her skirts and dashed back to the landaulet, instructing the coachman in a harried voice to drive immediately to Bruton Street. As they rolled through the cobbled streets, she reread the note several times more, then shoved it into her reticule with a small moan. Please, she prayed silently, please, *please* let Geoffrey be at home!

It seemed to take forever to reach the earl's residence, for it was the fashionable hour, and a plethora of vehicles were beginning to clog the streets. Strictly speaking, it was improper for her to visit an unmarried man in his own home, but Diana could hardly allow such considerations to weigh with her at such a moment. As before, she ordered the coachman to wait, and sped up the steps of the earl's house to bang the knocker repeatedly.

Like any worthy member of his profession, Lord

Lucan's butler allowed no vestige of his surprise to show when he opened the door to discover a beautiful but highly agitated Lady of Quality demanding to see the earl on a matter of Great Urgency. He ushered her ceremoniously into the drawing room, but when she very prettily begged him to hurry, he did allow himself to wonder what could occasion such turmoil in so lovely a female breast. None of this, he hoped, was visible in his demeanor as he bustled up the stairs to the floor above.

Lord Lucan, as it happened, was expecting a guest, and had just donned his coat when the astounding intelligence that Diana was below reached his ears. It caused him to utter a stifled oath, and to head for the drawing room with such swift strides that both his valet and butler were to form some rather interesting conclusions about his visitor.

Diana was pacing up and down the carpet when he entered. "Oh, thank God you are here!" she cried, moving toward him with something very like a sob. When his arms opened automatically, she threw herself into them without reserve. "Oh, Geoffrey, Geoffrey," she wept, "It is all my fault! I should have told you the complete story last night, and now he has taken his revenge. He wants the Torrington diamond!"

With her soft body pressed so distractingly against his, the earl found it difficult to think, or indeed, to make any sense at all out of what she said.

"Diana," he replied shakily, pressing his lips to her hair, "I don't know what you're talking about. What are you doing here? You should not be here at all." Somehow, he forced himself to push her away. "You're pale," he added with concern. "You'd better sit down before you explain."

He led her to a chair, but he himself remained standing, his alert gray eyes fixed on her face.

Blinking back her tears, Diana fumbled to draw out the

ransom letter. "It's Aimee," she blurted. "She and Mary left Aunt Serena's for a walk in Green Park and never came back! And then—"

"Not again!" he cut in roughly. "After that Cheltenham tragedy last night I'd have thought your sister would have had enough of pranks—"

"This is not a prank!" Diana thrust out the note with its carefully printed, chilling message. "Read this!" she said wildly. "I found it on my own doorstep not a quarter of an hour ago."

The note was brief, and Lord Lucan took in its contents in seconds. "Your sister's life for the Torrington diamond," he commented, glancing up. "And you think you know who sent this?" His voice was cool and steady, full of common sense.

Diana struggled to mirror his calm. "It's got to be Sir Henry!" she said. "You see, it was he who . . . who waylaid Aimee in Vauxhall Gardens. I was afraid to tell you last night because I knew you'd be angry . . . perhaps say something cutting to her when she was already feeling so wretched."

The earl's dark brows snapped together. "Oh, really? Dammit, I wish you'd learn to trust me a little more, Diana. And I wish to God you'd come to me last night, instead of dashing off on your own—"

"But I do trust you," she protested in a watery voice. "I came to you now, didn't I?"

"True," he conceded, after a pause. "So Harry has still not learned his lesson, eh? It seems I underestimated him." Abruptly, he glanced toward the door. "A damned good thing your cousin is due at any moment—this is as much Charles's concern as mine! I rather think that choking the truth out of Sir Henry Neyle should be his privilege, though I daresay I would enjoy it even more."

He did not elaborate, and in the moment of silence which followed he was obviously thinking hard. Conscious that half her panic had subsided the moment she was in his company, Diana fell to studying the hard planes of the earl's face. His sensual lips were set in a forbidding line, yet she was sure he was not unsympathetic of her sister's plight.

Then suddenly, she remembered. "Aunt Serena says the gossips are talking about us," she said without preamble.

"*What?*" The roar in his voice took her by surprise.

"I said . . . people are saying you and I are . . . lovers." Her voice was low, but somehow she managed to keep it unwavering, her tone matter-of-fact. The earl's reaction was far less controlled.

"That tears it, then," he growled, cursing beneath his breath. He began to pace the room, his athletic frame moving with the taut grace of a jungle animal—or so Diana thought. The comparison rang true, yet seemed odd when one considered that he was elegantly garbed in the civilized clothing of a London gentleman.

Before Diana could summon the courage to say anything more, footsteps on the stairs heralded the arrival of her cousin.

Charles Perth did his best to hide his surprise at finding her in the earl's drawing room. "Why, hullo, Diana," he said, bowing politely. "Uh, what brings you here?"

Charles's face darkened as the earl, in cool, precise terms, furnished him with a summary of recent events, To her approval, he did not forget his promise to her sister, and looked to her to contribute what specifics she wished about the Vauxhall incident.

Before the story was finished, Charles Perth's green eyes were blazing. "God blast it!" he exploded. "That pretty-faced scoundrel ain't going to be so dashed pretty when I'm through with him! Rascally, lousy, little cur! I'll kill him so help me God if—" He ranted on for a bit longer, and finished with, "Hang it, what are we waiting for? Let's go find the worthless bugger!" The words were flung over his shoulder as he plunged from the room.

"I'll be with you in a moment," called the earl after him. Taking Diana's arm, he guided her firmly toward the door. "Go home," he ordered, "and wait for me there. You have a carriage?"

Diana nodded, her fingers clutching his sleeve. "Aunt Serena's landaulet. But I want to come with you and Charles!"

"Don't be ridiculous. We can't take you to Harry Neyle's house. And if he is not there, lord only knows where we may track him down."

"Aimee may be there," she said stubbornly. "She will need me."

"And she may *not* be there," he returned. "Don't argue, Diana. If, as you say, your reputation is once again under fire, then for God's sake let's not feed the tabbies any more food! Go home! I promise I'll come there the instant I learn anything."

She heard the steel in his voice, and though she did not like it, she knew there was sense in what he said.

"Oh, very well," she said crossly. "But do not forget that Mary is missing, also. You have two females to rescue you know."

For the first time, he smiled, a reassuring smile that warmed his eyes and held a teasing glint. "Don't look so put out," he murmured. "I won't forget you while I'm gone." He raised her chin with a finger and planted a firm kiss on her lips. "You just stay home like a good girl," he added, "and leave the rescuing to us."

It was positively infuriating. No woman of spirit could fail to appreciate the maddening aspects of the situation, thought Diana pugnaciously. Flouncing to the window, she peered out for what must surely be the dozenth time since she arrived home half an hour before, but there was as yet no sign of the earl. Of course she loved him immeasurably, but still, she reflected, it was extremely arrogant and superior and thoughtless of him to expect her to wait while *he* got to go and watch her cousin plant Henry Neyle a facer. At least, she believed that was the phrase the sporting gentlemen used. It certainly had a satisfactory ring to it.

Just stay home like a good girl . . . In retrospect, it sounded positively condescending, and she wished she'd had the wit to tell him so at the time. Something warned her that being married to Geoffrey Trevelyan was going to have its challenges, that she would have to be sure not to let him have his way too often. Not, of course, that he would do so intentionally, but he obviously had a dictatorial streak. Diana had a sneaking suspicion he'd been trying to conceal it from her, but she was not fooled in the least. Did she love him anyway? *Dear God, yes.*

Nevertheless, he needed to be taught a lesson. Surely if she put her mind to it, there was *some* way she could contribute to Aimee's rescue. Tapping her fingers on the windowsill, Diana cudgeled her brain in an effort to think logically. Well, if they were unable to find Sir Henry . . . or if they *did* find him and he refused to talk— an unlikely contingency, of course—then Aimee would still be missing. Of course, Geoffrey would find her, but in the meanwhile, no whiff of scandal must be allowed to drift to the gossipmongers. How many of Aunt Serena's servants knew what had occurred, she wondered uneasily?

Well, Aunt Serena would naturally tell them to—good heavens! She had forgotten the dowager completely! Aunt Serena would be practically foaming at the mouth by this time, she reflected, rushing up the stairs to fetch her cloak and bonnet.

"Diana? Is that you?" called Miss Tilden from her bedchamber.

Diana suppressed a flash of impatience. "Yes, Tildy? Is anything wrong?"

"No, my dear. It's just that it's so quiet here, I've been wondering where everyone was. I could do with a spot of tea, if you would care to join me."

Diana groaned. "I'm sorry, Tildy, but I cannot. I have to go to Aunt Serena's immediately. I'll send Meg up with tea and cakes, if you like."

She gave her abigail the instructions, adding, "When Lord Lucan arrives, tell him I went to Aunt Serena's house, if you please. Keep a sharp ear out for him, now. Where is Lawrence?" she asked, glancing around for the butler.

"'Tis his afternoon off, ma'am. He should be back any minute now, though."

Diana nodded. "Very well. See that he knows where I am, too."

Her abigail curtsied, and Diana hurried from the house, indifferent to the promise of rain hanging heavily in the air. As she walked, intermittent gusts of wind whipped her gown against her legs, reminding her of that first encounter with Geoffrey. How greatly she had changed since that day, she mused. Her whole outlook was no longer focused inward, no longer distorted by a brooding lack of faith in the entire male sex. Thanks to Geoffrey, her ability to trust a man had been completely revitalized; she knew now that Edmund had been but a bad apple, while Geoffrey—and for that matter, Cousin Charles—where men upon whom a woman could rely, men who would protect and value a woman instead of wounding and scorning her. Surely they would be able to find Aimee soon, she thought, as she reached the end of the street.

Jermyn Street ran perpendicular to St. James's Street; while directly across, Bennet Street led from St. James's to Arlington. Diana did not normally care to cross St. James's at this hour of the day—particularly without a maid—but she had long since sent the landaulet back to the mews, and it was simpler and faster to walk. She had not forgotten that Ladies of Quality did not visit St. James's in the afternoon, but in her view, *crossing* it was hardly a fracture of that rule. Thus it was not propriety which made her hesitate upon the curb but the vast number of swiftly moving vehicles bowling along without any apparent regard for the safety or existence of pedestrains. Twice she stepped out, and twice she was forced to leap back or risk being run down, which made her wonder whether she would be able to cross at all.

She almost did not notice the hackney coach until it slowed to a stop beside her, and then she was startled and a little apprehensive until she recognized its sole passenger, his round, good-humored face peering out at her with doddering geniality.

"Oh, Lord Hervey!" she cried, moving eagerly forward. "Thank goodness it is you! Would you mind terribly if I joined you? I must get to Aunt Serena's at once!"

His lordship pushed open the door, and reached out a pudgy hand. "Climb right in, m'dear. Here, let me help you. There! Always pleased to oblige a lady." He took in her slightly disheveled appearance. "In a hurry, you say?"

Diana nodded. "Yes, the most dreadful thing has happened. I must speak to Aunt Serena at once."

Lord Hervey looked at her intently. "Nothing serious, I hope?"

Diana hesitated. "Well, yes, it is serious. I suppose

304

Aunt Serena will not mind my telling you. You see, my sister has disappeared."

"I said, *where is she?*"

Of his two uninvited guests, Sir Henry Neyle considered Lord Lucan to be the most dangerous; however, it was Charles Perth who had led the charge into his bedchamber, and it was Charles who appeared the most irate. The earl merely blocked his escape by propping his broad shoulders against the closed door, leaving it to Mr. Perth to shout wild, incomprehensible accusations and wave his doubled fists at the startled baronet. Keeping his wary gaze on them both, Sir Henry beat a strategic retreat behind his washstand, his celestial blue eyes regarding the intruders with considerable alarm.

"I really have not the least idea what you mean, old boy," he quavered, trying to sneer. "I haven't seen Miss Farington in ages. Sweet little gal, isn't she? Not my style, of course . . ."

Lord Lucan snorted, and Charles stepped forward in a menacing fashion, which had an oddly stimulative effect upon Sir Henry's memory.

"Wait now, ahem, er, yes. Now that you mention it, I *do* seem to recall seeing her at Vauxhall Gardens last night." When Charles made a savage gesture, Sir Henry's voice grew a trifle shrill. "I swear the chit did nothing but talk my ear off!" he insisted. "I never heard such a little prattlebox in my life! For hell's sake, I never even got a kiss for my pains!"

"I'd break his nose if I were you," offered the earl in contemptuous accents.

Sir Henry gave a horrified gulp. "Egad, Geoff, such violent inclinations you have! Every feeling is offended, I assure you! Think of what *ma mère* would say—she would never forgive you if you spoiled my face, y'know." Licking his lips, his eyes darted nervously between the two men. "Anyway, now that the little chit is so thin, she isn't nearly as appealing as before," he added unwisely.

The washstand did nothing to save Sir Henry; it tipped over with a crash as Charles dove forward to grab him by the neck. Cursing furiously, Aimee's raging suitor rammed the baronet's head against the wall.

"Just one more word," he grated, "just one more word about Miss Farington and I will personally change the shape of your nose! Better yet, I'll wring your scrawny neck, you complacent little turkey cock. Now, for the last time, what the devil have you done with her?"

"Nothing!" screeched Sir Henry. "You're both mad! Let me go! Ouch! You're choking me!"

"I don't think he knows anything," said the earl suddenly.

"The devil he doesn't! Look at the lily-livered coward. The fellow's positively shaking in his boots! He's hiding something, sure as check."

"I think he's only worried about his face. It's his only hope of winning a rich wife." The earl's tone was sardonic. "Buck up, Harry. We won't damage that spectacular countenance if you cooperate. Have you seen Aimee Farington since last night?"

"No!"

"You did not write a ransom note, by any chance, and address it to Mrs. Diana Verney?"

Sir Henry goggled. "Ransom note?" he echoed, a shade squeakily. "Why the devil should I do that? Diana Verney hasn't any money. At least not the kind I want."

The earl exchanged looks with Mr. Perth. "I suppose we could take him with us," he suggested. "Knowing what he does, I wouldn't trust him out of my sight, and he might be useful."

Charles released his captive with a derisive snort. "Useful? This fellow's never done a useful thing in his life."

Sir Henry was edging toward the mirror. "So sorry to disoblige," he protested, "but I really do have other plans." His head craned forward in an attempt to get a clear view of his mangled neckcloth.

"What plans?" said the earl, his lip curling. "Don't worry, Harry. You look fine."

"Personal plans," retorted the baronet, his voice resuming its normal tenor. "With a lady who is none of your concern, old boy."

"Dammit, *who?*"

Sensing that further dissembling would only result in damage to his person, Sir Henry lifted a petulant shoulder. "If you must know, Lady Uxbridge. She and I have struck up a bit of a friendship just lately."

The earl's voice altered abruptly. "Ah," he said, an unpleasantly soft edge to his voice. "And does this 'friendship' include the friendly practice of spreading malicious gossip?"

Sir Henry started guiltily. "How the dev—?" Knowing he had betrayed himself, he cried out, "Devil take it, Geoff, it was Sophia's idea. I swear I had nothing to do with it!"

"I see." Lord Lucan's face was cold with contempt. "For this, Harry, you are going to pay, unless you can tip the scales in your favor very quickly. As you must have already guessed, Aimee Farington has been abducted and is being held for ransom. She must be found as quickly as possible, and if you can think of some way to expedite the process, I strongly suggest that you do so."

*　　　*　　　*

"Disappeared!" repeated Lord Hervey in a thunderstruck voice. "Why, how can that be?"

"I fear the whole story is a long one, my lord. She appears to have been abducted, for the nefarious object of extorting money from my aunt. Or to be more precise, it is the Torrington diamond that this . . . this person wants"—Diana's lips trembled—"in exchange for my sister's life."

"The diamond," he echoed. "Yes, I s'pose it is worth a fortune, ain't it? But not as much as a human life, eh? Never fear, Serena will give it up," he told her, patting her hand comfortingly. "She don't have a selfish bone in her body, y'know."

Diana cast him a quick glance. "Yes," she agreed, a shade uncertainly. "But I think it wrong to yield to an extortionist, don't you? My hope is that we can catch whoever did this vile thing before any real harm befalls my sister."

"We?" inquired her portly companion in an odd tone.

"My cousin, myself, and . . . Lord Lucan," she explained, coloring slightly. "You see, we think we know who is responsible."

Under her startled gaze, Lord Hervey's complexion grew queerly mottled, and his hamlike hands began to open and shut until one, as of its own accord, shot across to close around her wrist. "Who?" he uttered, almost hoarsely. "Whom do you suspect?"

"I think it better if I do not say," she replied, with new wariness. "It is quite possible that we are mistaken. Pray, release me, my lord. You are hurting me."

He did so at once. "Beg your pardon, m'dear. I'm just sick about this whole terrible thing, y'know. Can't bear to think of your aunt being upset about this. And that pretty little sister of yours, too! She must be sick with fright! Well, at least she has her maid with her. I daresay you'll

308

get them both back right and tight once the ransom is paid."

"How did you know Mary was with her?" asked Diana bluntly.

"Eh?"

"I asked you how you knew the maid was with my sister," she repeated.

Lord Hervey's mouth gaped open. "Why, you said so, m'dear. I heard you . . ."

Diana's head shook. "On the contrary, I said nothing whatever about Mary. What have you done with them, my lord? What have you done with my sister?"

Chapter Eighteen

During the heavy silence which followed, Lord Hervey seemed to wilt before Diana's eyes. A faint, staccato tapping on the roof marked the beginning of the rain, and this, combined with the oppressiveness of the air inside the coach, somehow added to her sudden fancy that the scene was unreal, a vivid nightmare conceived from her own wild imaginings. Yet the perspiration beading on Lord Hervey's brow was only too real, as was the ugly transformation of his complexion, which had turned quite muddy. He looked, she thought, as if he were going to be ill.

"What have you done with my sister?" she asked once more, her eyes pinned to his. The insistent question hovered between them, its silent echo begging for an answer.

When he finally spoke, there was a choking edge to his voice. "If only Serena had let me have it reset. I was going to have a copy made, a good one, so that no one would ever notice it was not the original. If only she had let me do it . . ." His fumbling fingers dragged a handkerchief from his pocket.

To Diana's dismay, his lordship's eyes were brimming with tears. "I am so sorry," he sobbed. He swabbed his upper lip and brow with the small square of white linen, then blew his nose on what remained. "So very, very sorry," he added, his mouth quivering like a child's.

He sounded so despairing that Diana was seized with terror. "My God, do not tell me you have *killed* her—!" she cried, going quite white.

"Oh, no." His head shook. "No, course not. I wouldn't hurt a pretty little gal like that," he insisted with pathetic dignity. "Even for the Torrington diamond." Another large tear rolled down his cheek.

Unburdened of this dreadful fear, Diana collapsed against the squabs, one hand pressed to her breast in an effort to still her own shaking. Within seconds, however, this relief gave way to an anger so powerful her hand itched to slap him across the face.

Resisting the impulse, she said sternly. "Well, being sorry is all well and good, my lord, but you must stop crying and tell me where Aimee is. Now look, we have reached Aunt Serena's. Do you wish to talk inside, or—?"

"No, no!" he whispered, shuddering visibly. "Serena mustn't see me like this. Tell the coachman to keep driving—please! Tell him to take us to Covent Garden."

"Covent Garden! What on earth for?"

"That's where she is," he said simply. "Her maid, too. Tell him Maiden Lane, near Covent Garden."

Hearing the hackney driver's impatient shout, Diana pushed open the window and gave the order; she then sat back and fixed the plump little man in front of her with an unwavering stare.

"I hope you mean to explain what my sister is doing in such a place," she said. "If she has suffered any ill, I can asssure you that Aunt Serena will—"

"Promise you won't tell her!" he interjected in a panicky voice. "I don't want her to know. We'll get little Aimee back, but for God's sake promise you won't tell Serena!"

"I can make no such promise, Lord Hervey. What you have done is wicked and dishonest and—"

"Aye, aye, but you don't understand. I was desperate," he explained, looking shamefaced. "Y'see, I'm rolled-up . . . ruined. I've got a pile of debts as high as St. Paul's—gaming debts, most of 'em. Serena despises gamesters, but I ain't a gamester, really. I just had a run or two of bad luck. Still, she'll despise me if she finds out!" He regarded her earnestly. "Y'know, I was pretty well up in the stirrups five or six years ago, but now—! Now, I'm a fair hop into Dun territory. My own fault, of course. I admit it. If I could do it all over, I'd do different."

"But you can't," she pointed out.

He sighed deeply, his hands resting atop his big stomach. "No," he agreed in a sad tone. "The Torrington diamond would've solved all my problems, though. It was either that or go to a shark, but I figured that wouldn't fadge. I'd have to be insane to get myself caught in the toils of a moneylender." He paused for an instant, and when he spoke again, his voice shook with emotion. "Y'know, it hurts a man's pride to depend on a woman for his blunt, and it's worse when other people start to suspect. They gossip about you, call you a parasite behind your back. And, by God, it's true!" He lifted his hand, ticking off a list on his fingers. "I sold my curricle. I sold my traveling coach. I sold my carriage horses. Did it quietly so Serena wouldn't know. Private sales, all of 'em." His hands spread. "And what's left? Not much! Now I hire a hackney or take one of Serena's carriages when I need to get about. And people notice," he nodded. "People notice."

"But, my lord, *stealing* is no better—in fact it is much, much worse!"

"No, it ain't," he retorted. "That big old rock ain't

312

doing nobody any good lying around in a locked box. S'pose you think I'm selfish and evil. *I* don't think so. But like as not I'll have to flee the country like that poor devil George Brummell. Ten to one I'll die in some cold, dirty French garret, instead of spending my old age with the woman I love. Serena won't marry me, but I know she loves me. Wants me to visit her every day, and how can I do that if I'm wasting away in some filthy garret or debtor's prison?"

Diana's brow furrowed in thought. "Well," she said slowly, "there must be some solution, and I daresay we shall think of it if we set our minds to it for a bit. But before that, my lord, it is of the first importance that we bring Aimee and Mary back as quickly as possible. Where are they exactly?"

Once again, Lord Hervey looked uneasy. "It was my manservant's idea," he said defensively. "*I* didn't like the notion, but Jacob said they'd be safe. He said that sort of place knew how to keep its females away from its customers—when it chose. He's the sort who should know."

"What kind of place do you mean?" Diana looked at him blankly.

"Well, I guess you could call it a fancy house," he said, rubbing his head, "but it ain't one of the better ones. I didn't like it, but it was the only one where Jacob knew the abbess well enough to ask a favor."

Diana stared in appalled comprehension. "Do I understand you to mean my sister is in a . . . a *brothel?*" she exclaimed, both face and voice awash with indignation. "An innocent young girl of gentle birth?"

Lord Hervey looked ashamed. "Aye. When you put it like that, it does sound wicked. I admit it, and I'm sorry for it."

Again, she almost slapped his face. "Yes, I do think it wicked!" she flashed. "And you had better hope that

313

neither girl has suffered any harm, for if they have, I, for one, will not rest until I see you brought to book for this outrage. And as for Aunt Serena, I will not even venture to guess what she will say, but you can be very sure it will be unpleasant."

She might as well have struck the man, for he flinched just as much. "Your sister is safe and well," he insisted, but his voice was laden with such doubt that she could not be reassured.

Trembling with fury, Diana merely turned her head away, for she could think of nothing civil to say, and railing at the ineffectual little man certainly did no good. Instead, she directed her gaze toward the rain-splattered streets, and wondered suddenly what Geoffrey and Charles would say when they discovered she was not at Aunt Serena's. She rather thought Geoffrey was going to be annoyed, for not only had she gone off without him again, she had left not a trace of a clue to tell him where she might be found. Suppressing her qualms on this count, Diana forced herself to stop worrying and relax. At best, it would teach him to leave her behind, wouldn't it? And at worst—well, she would not think of the worst.

Geoffrey, as she would eventually learn, *was* a little annoyed to find Diana gone from her home, however as she had most thoughtfully left a message providing him with her destination, he was not unduly perturbed. He therefore betook himself, along with Charles and the ever-reluctant Sir Henry, off to Arlington Street, it being his intention to reexamine the ransom note, in case he had missed some subtle clue as to the writer's identity.

The three men arrived at the dowager's residence just short of half-past five, a time when the dowager was normally enjoying a light repast with Lord Hervey. Today, however, she was eating alone, a circumstance

314

which did nothing to improve the surliness of her disposition. It grew worse at their entrance, for it was at that moment that she inhaled a crumb, and spent the next minute coughing while her well-meaning grandson pounded her on the back.

"Let be, Charles, let be! Are you trying to kill me, for God's sake?" she shouted, launching into a tirade about people who jumped into rooms and startled defenseless old women. At length, she said, "And what the devil do you want, anyway? And what did you bring *him* for?" she added, pointing at Sir Henry Neyle. "I don't like the fellow, and I don't want him in my house."

"Now, Grandmama—" began Charles. He rolled an expressive eye at the earl, who quickly came to his aid.

"I would think you'd know why we are here," he said, ignoring the majority of her speech. "May I speak to Di— Mrs. Verney, please?" He glanced around in obvious puzzlement. "She *is* here, isn't she?"

"Diana?" repeated the dowager viscountess, scowling at him. "Of course she ain't here! The silly girl ran off to find *you* over an hour ago. Took a notion that you would know how to—" She broke off, and favored Sir Henry with an imperious stare. "Does he *really* have to be here?"

"I'd be more than happy to leave," offered Sir Henry with a well-bred bow.

"You can speak in front of him, ma'am," said the earl ironically. "Unfortunately, he already knows about Miss Farington's disappearance. Well, where is Di—Mrs. Verney, then? Her message said she was returning here." He glanced down at the dowager, his forehead creased with disquiet. "You see, ma'am, we had some reason to believe Sir Henry might have been responsible for the entire business. So far, it seems we were wrong," he added. "Diana assured me she would remain at home while we went to Sir Henry's lodgings, but she apparently

315

changed her mind." He paused. "I suppose you know nothing about the ransom note?"

"Ransom note?" Aunt Serena sat up straighter and reached for her cane. "Confound it, man, what ransom note? No one bothers to tell me anything!"

"Someone wants the Torrington diamond," put in Charles angrily, "and when I find the miserable swine I'll kill him. If he's hurt one hair on Aimee's head, I'll kill him, so help me God."

Aunt Serena looked stunned. "The Torrington diamond . . ." she repeated in such an odd tone that all three males looked at her curiously.

"Yes, ma'am?" prompted the earl in an urgent voice. "You have an idea that might help us?"

Slowly, the dowager shook her head in disbelief. "I wouldn't have believed he'd go that far . . ."

"Who?"

It was the first time the earl had seen her falter. "Thurstan," she finally answered. "So that's why he ain't here."

"You mean Lord Hervey?" he said. "Are you serious?"

"Well, personally, *I'm* not surprised." The remark came from Sir Henry, who had taken up a negligent attitude against the wall. "The fellow's up to his ears in debt—debt he can't possibly pay."

The earl looked skeptical. "How do you know that?" he asked. "The man must have assets—property he can sell, investments he can tap into. I've heard nothing about him being that far under a cloud."

Sir Henry gave him a superior smile. "That's because you don't move in my circles, Geoff, old boy. You've all the blunt you need, but some of us don't. Some of us," he emphasized, flashing his teeth, "can hardly be blamed for taking advantage of the circumstances. By George, I rather admire the fat little fellow. The Torrington

316

diamond, eh? Well, well. I wish I'd thought of it myself."

"That man," said the dowager emphatically, "is starting to give me palpitations. I wish you'd get rid of him."

"Why the devil did we bring him anyway?" inquired Charles, who was pacing the floor in frustration. "I can't see any use for the fellow at all."

The earl shrugged. "It was just a hunch."

Sir Henry sidled toward the door. "Does this mean I am free to, uh, make my departure?"

"*No.*"

A clap on his shoulder could not have been more effective than the one clipped word. Sir Henry stood in a frozen posture, regarding Lord Lucan with fresh alarm. "Why not?" he whined. "What do you want with me?"

"You seem to know a great deal about Lord Hervey's financial circumstances," continued the earl, in a hard voice, "and I don't find your reason all that convincing. I'm beginning to think you're hiding something, Harry."

"*I?* Hide something from *you*, Geoff, old boy? You cannot honestly think that—" The sentence ended in a squeak as the earl bore down on him. "Beg your pardon, old boy. It's merely that I've an agile mind. Don't know anything for certain, of course, but I *can* add two and two."

"What the devil are you trying to say?"

Sir Henry affected a languid smile while backing cautiously away. "Life is full of the oddest coincidences, don't you know? Let me tell you an amusing little story, old boy. One day I was strolling along Bond Street and I spied my own manservant walking ahead of me. Well! As far as I knew, Isaac was at my lodgings, and I was curious as to why he should have abandoned his duties. I called out to him, naturally. He turned, and after speaking with the fellow, I discovered that he was not my Isaac at all, but his brother, Jacob. His *twin* brother, I should say.

317

Isaac and Jacob . . . *so* biblical, don't you think?"

"Get to the point, Harry."

Sir Henry licked his lips. "The point is, old boy, that Jacob is Lord Hervey's servant. And the two brothers sometimes go out carousing together when they have the chance. Apparently they share a common interest in, er, debauchery. Rather charming, what? So the full sum of my story is that upon occasion Isaac has some rather interesting stories to tell. And that's all I know!"

"But what has this to do with Aimee's disappearance?" exclaimed Charles in disgust. "It's a sheer waste of time listening to this silly fellow's babblings."

"On the contrary," said the earl grimly, "he has provided us with a lead. I think we had better have an interview with this Jacob immediately."

Not to be outdone, Aunt Serena began spewing directives. "You find my nieces, Lucan!" she bellowed, brandishing her cane. "You bring 'em back safe—both of 'em, and you tell Thurstan I want a word with him! And then you marry Diana, do you hear me? No more namby-pambying around with my niece, do you hear me?"

Lord Lucan bowed. "There's nothing wrong with my hearing, ma'am," he responded. "I beg you will not shout."

"Impertinent!" sputtered the dowager with a gleam of appreciation. "Insolent, impudent young devil! My God, if I was forty years younger—!"

Maiden Lane proved to be a dark, constricted street, its narrow houses crammed uncomfortably together, its inhabitants shabby and ragged in appearance. Ill at ease, Diana made sure Lord Hervey bade the hackney coachman to wait, since it seemed the height of folly to be trapped in such a place without a means of transportation. She stepped daintily over a pile of refuse and

318

glanced around, suddenly conscious of silence, of foul smells, and of numerous pairs of eyes watching from the shadows. Four or five urchins had been splashing in the gutter puddles, but their activity had ceased when the hackney rolled into the lane. They all gaped, and one ginger-haired lad crept cautiously forward, his bright, black eyes fixed on Diana, his grubby hand raised as if to seize her skirt.

"Back with you, now," growled Lord Hervey, shaking his fist at the boy. "Get back! Haven't you ever seen a lady before? Get back!" He added, in an undervoice, "Hope you ain't too shocked, m'dear. Once you get into these smaller streets, it's all pretty much the same."

"Oh?" It was all Diana could think to say, but her heart was torn with pity for the wretched youngsters. "And this is where my sister is?" she asked, and found herself wishing that the man beside her was tall and powerfully built, rather than short, elderly, and portly.

"Aye," he mumbled, taking her by the arm. He led her to the largest house in the street, and pounded on the door.

The girl who admitted them was not at all what Diana expected. True, she was young and uncommonly pretty, but she was also clean, and the simple gown she wore was modest in its cut. Furthermore, she displayed no vulgar curiosity at their purpose, but invited them in with a respectful curtsey, her soft brown eyes downcast. If all was as it seemed, and this sweet, unaffected girl with her cultured accent was representative of the inhabitants in this house, then perhaps, thought Diana, just perhaps there was nothing to fear.

Lord Hervey gave the girl his hat. "I need to speak with Mrs. Creech as soon as possible. Is she available?"

The girl curtsied again. "I will go and see, sir. If you and the lady will follow me?"

She left them in a small salon, which, though not elegant in the true sense of the word, had a distinguished appearance, as if it had been furnished with the desire to make a visitor feel secure. Lulled by these surroundings, Diana's apprehension receded; then her pleasant illusion shattered as somewhere above them a door slammed, and a shrill, cockney-accented voice screeched a long stream of obscenities.

Diana's eyes flew to Lord Hervey. "Why didn't you ask her about Aimee?" she said nervously.

"She ain't the one to ask, m'dear. Mrs. Creech's the abbess of the place. It's her domain."

Ten agonizing minutes passed before the door opened, and a woman of approximately fifty years of age came into the room. Mrs. Creech was small and round, with shrewd gray eyes and a complexion so pale it gave her a bloodless look. Coarse yellow curls clung to her head, her neck was incongruously long, like a goose's, and her lips were tight and hard and smiling.

"Ah, Lord Hervey," she said smoothly, "I was not expecting you. How can I help you now?" Her eyes flicked briefly over Diana, then attached to his lordship's face.

Lord Hervey coughed. "I've come for the girls—both of 'em. Apologize for the inconvenience and so forth, but I've, uh, changed my mind and want 'em back."

For a few seconds Mrs. Creech did not speak, then all at once her smile broadened. "Unfortunately, my lord, this is not the way I conduct business. Our arrangement was somewhat different, if you recall. If you now desire the return of your merchandise, you must pay for it."

An involuntary protest ripped from Diana, but Lord Hervey only swallowed resignedly, and said, "How much?"

Head tilted, Mrs. Creech folded her arms. "I think the quality must be taken into account. Two such attractive young girls, both probably virgins. I think two hundred pounds might cover the cost of my trouble so far today."

"Two hundred pounds!" Lord Hervey's face went pasty white.

Diana could no longer keep silent. "But this is preposterous!" she cried, stepping forward. "You have no right to refuse us! You are holding those girls here against their will, and I demand that they be—"

"You demand?" interrupted Mrs. Creech in amusement. "You come into my house and dare to make demands?"

In an unconscious imitation of Aunt Serena, Diana's expression turned haughty. "Certainly," she replied, with Olympian coolness. "I not only demand, but I promise that I have no intention of leaving here without my sister or the maid, Mary. Be advised that I am not without connections, Mrs. Creech. If you prefer to be brought before a magistrate—"

"And now you dare threaten me!" Mrs. Creech was still smiling, but her eyes had narrowed to icy slits. "I can think of uses for you, my fine lady, where such threats will earn you nothing but the beating you deserve." She was moving sideways as she spoke, and too late Diana saw her hand snake out to drag open a small drawer. "Don't bother to scream," she continued, raising a pistol. "In this neighborhood, no one will bother to take notice."

Lord Hervey moaned and dropped shudderingly into the nearest chair. "Oh, God, God! Serena'll never forgive me for this! Never!"

Mrs. Creech's lips curved in a contemptuous line. "Men! They're all fools. Weak, helpless fools, useless save for one thing only. I've changed my mind," she went on, her eyes running over Diana in an assessing, insulting manner. "There's a market for young women like you, and as for him"—she waved the pistol at Lord Hervey—"if he's found floating in the Thames come

321

tomorrow morning, who's to connect it with me? Neither Jacob nor Isaac will say anything." Her smile spread. "My sons will not betray me."

Mrs. Creech would doubtless have been enraged to know that one of her sons was not as encumbered with filial allegiance as she believed. In fact, several well-placed blows to various portions of his anatomy had persuaded Jacob Creech to become quite voluble. Bruised and sullen, he now lay against the wall of Lord Hervey's drawing room, glaring balefully at his persecutors.

Even with his back to the scene, Sir Henry Neyle had winced at every sound. "*Are* you quite finished, old boy?" he inquired, finally daring to peer over his shoulder. At the earl's curt nod, he reached for his quizzing glass. "Good heavens," he drawled, surveying his manservant's twin with a shudder of distaste. "You know, I never would have thought to associate *my* Isaac with *that* Mrs. Creech. So your mama runs a bawdy house, eh, Jacob? How bloody convenient."

"Only you would think so," was the Earl of Lucan's dry comment. "Do you accompany us there? Or would it be too much for your sensibilities to handle?"

"Let's leave the tiresome fellow," spluttered Charles. "What the deuce do we want him for?"

"I tend to agree," said Sir Henry languidly. "Surely I have been adequately, er, helpful?"

"Helpful?" Lord Lucan's face hardened. "You've barely begun to scratch the surface, Harry." He took a threatening step forward. "Very well, you may go—on one condition. You and your friend Lady Uxbridge will oblige me by spreading another rumor as fast as possible. The rumor is this: that Diana Verney is a lady of unimpeachable virtue and that I have been courting her with marriage in mind. You may add that there is likely to be a formal announcement at any moment. Do you have it?"

Sir Henry smiled. "Oh, to be sure. Anything you say, Geoff, old boy."

The earl pointed to Jacob Creech. "If you fail to do as I bid, or if that other rumor you started does not die a swift and permanent death, then you, Harry, are going to look far worse than he does. Do you understand?"

"Perfectly," responded Sir Henry, the smile wiped from his face. "Sophia will know just how to go about it."

"See that she does," said the earl coldly. "You have twenty-four hours to do it, and after that, Harry old boy, it is you who will pay the forfeit."

Sir Henry fled.

Diana shifted her body, and struggled once more against the cruel ropes that held her prisoner. Where on earth was she? Vaguely, she remembered that Mrs. Creech had struck her with the pistol, which accounted for the strange floating sensation in her head. She remembered, too, that Lord Hervey had cried out, but beyond that it was all a sickening blur.

She decided she must be directly under the roof, for the beat of the rain came through distinctly, and the room was cold and dank. Vaguely, she knew she was shivering, either with shock or cold or fear, or some ghastly combination of the three. The straw upon which she lay was damp, and she wriggled sideways, hoping to locate a dryer spot. Instead, she managed to roll directly under an area where the roof leaked and the floor was drenched with water.

Sobbing with frustration, Diana inched her way back to her original position. The whole left side of her gown was soaked, and her wrists and ankles throbbed from where the bonds cut into her flesh. Exhausted and disoriented, she lay gasping, her mind spinning with pain. Whoever had tied the knots had not been gentle, nor had they intended her to escape.

Oh, Geoffrey, help me . . . please, please, come quickly . . . where are you? . . . oh, my beloved, please come . . . hurry . . . I love you so . . .

For the next little while, Diana slipped in and out of consciousness, a tangle of dreams and half-formed ideas drifting through her head. Despair had driven everything from her heart but the earl; he was her obsession and her hunger, and she focused on him as her only sane thought.

He would find her. Somehow he would find her and bring her out of this awful place. He would find Aimee, too, she thought hazily. She had been foolish to come here without him, and no doubt he would rant and rave and scold, but he *would* find her, and if he would only hurry, she would gladly bear his tongue-lashing. And when he was done, she would make very sure he knew how pleased she was to see him . . .

For a while, Diana's dreams were only shifting patterns of bizarre colors, then they faded to something far more agreeable, a marvelous dream wherein a door opened and the earl came into the room. He was calling her name, over and over, with such a queer, passionate intensity that it banished the colors and patterns for good.

"I knew you would come," she croaked, suddenly certain it was no dream, and that the Earl of Lucan really *was* there. And from the unspeakable things he was muttering under his breath, Diana knew also that her Geoffrey was in a black rage, which somehow seemed so completely right that she merely gazed at him and reveled in his curses.

"Thick-skulled female!" he growled, sawing through her bonds with something she could not see. "Empty-headed, *obstinate* woman! Do you know what a fright you gave me? I don't know whether to kiss you or strangle you! Brainless, *stubborn* girl!"

Diana eyed him lovingly. "You forgot maddening," she quavered, her voice small and cracked.

"There's several words I forgot," he responded, with tender asperity. "I'm saving them for a more appropriate moment."

Then he was rubbing her wrists and ankles, massaging the sensation back into them until she cried out from the pain.

"There, darling, I . . . I think you'll be all right," he said, his voice shaking oddly. "Don't cry now, there's a brave girl."

With a final sob, Diana flung her arms around the earl's body and pressed her dirty, tear-stained face to his chest. She hugged him with all her strength, and in turn, received the most crushing embrace of her life, a hug so forceful she thought her bones would crack.

Later, she would try to understand what there was about the moment that made it the right time to tell him. Somehow the entirety of her inhibitions had vanished, peeled away by shock, by the earl's tenderness, and by her own raw emotions. When he would have taken her away she begged him to wait, and to listen, while in a little voice, she spilled out her long-kept secret. It was time he knew the truth about the Edgerton ball and what it was that Edmund had caught her doing. It was time to unload the burden for good.

"—so you see, Geoffrey, I really am not as . . . as good as you think. I crept up those stairs intending to . . . to spy . . . to eavesdrop upon Sir Henry . . . and I was guilty of vanity because I believed that I was . . . the one he should have been walking with . . . and . . . why are you smiling?"

"Because you are such a goosecap," he said, kissing the tip of her nose. "Oh, Diana, my sweet, sweet love, you can't really believe you did something terrible? Do

325

you mean to tell me that all these years you've been—"
He saw her expression and stopped, and when he spoke
again, it was a trifle unsteadily. "So because you, an
innocent young girl, formed a *tendre* for a handsome man
and behaved in a human manner, did you really believe
you deserved to be . . . to be mauled and humiliated and
socially ostracized? Did you really believe you deserved
to be forced to marry a man you loathed, and be
mistreated by him?"

When she gazed up at him mutely, he swore under his
breath. "If it takes me the next thirty years, I will make it
up to you," he promised, his arms tightening about her
slim body. Then he kissed her once, hard on the mouth,
and scooped her into his arms.

"No more talk," he said. "I'm getting you out of this
hellhole."

Chapter Nineteen

"And Charles says that if Papa gives his consent—which I know he will!—we can be betrothed at once, but that we must wait a year before we marry. He does not want it said that he married a girl just out of the schoolroom, you see. He thinks I should be given the chance to grow up a little more." Aimee's voice was half-rapturous and half-wistful. "Also, he says he wants to be sure my affections are genuinely engaged, but I think I have succeeded in convincing him that they are!" She giggled. "Kissing Charles is such fun, Diana. You can have no notion!"

"Is it, my dear?" Diana smiled absently. "I am very happy for you."

Diana was still in her nightdress, and at everyone's insistence, had been in bed ever since the earl had brought her home from Maiden Lane the previous evening. Dr. Hatfield had examined her then, and again this morning, and in the end pronounced her injuries to be very minor. Indeed, except for a few bruises and a lump on the side of her head, she felt quite her usual self, and had been chafing to get up for some time.

"What time did Lord Lucan say he would be here?" she inquired for at least the third time that hour.

Aimee hid a smile. "About one o'clock or thereabouts. Charles is coming back too. They had to deal with certain things pertaining to our misadventure, as well as Aunt Serena, of course. Charles says she is taking the whole thing amazingly well. She refused to press charges against Lord Hervey, which one might have predicted, but what surprises me, Diana, is that she seems willing to forgive him." Aimee's expression was solemn. "I think she really does love him, don't you?"

Diana sighed. "I suppose so. I myself find it very hard to forgive him, but perhaps in time I will feel differently." Her mind very much occupied by private matters, she gazed pensively at her ringless fingers, then pushed back the bedcovers with decision. "And speaking of time, I think it is past time I got up. What a sluggard I am! I must decide what to wear to see Geoffrey and—oh, my goodness!" she exclaimed, catching sight of herself in the mirror. "Something must be done with my hair!"

By the time Lord Lucan was due to arrive, Diana was looking her very best. She was wearing one of her most alluring gowns—its color a shade of blue she had reason to know he particularly admired—while her hair, newly washed and golden as a new-minted guinea, cascaded over her shoulders and down her back in soft, shimmering waves.

When he first entered, Geoffrey Trevelyan's eyes were both unsmiling and possessive, concern for her welfare as yet the reigning emotion in their gray depths. Indifferent to the presence of Charles and Aimee (who were deeply involved in their own greeting), he strode forward and caught up her hands, as ever giving the gesture an intimate flavor by raising them to his lips.

"You are well?" He said it tersely and his look was more critical than complimentary.

Diana nodded. "Beyond a few bruises, quite well," she said, reassuring him with a smile. "But I hope you do not

328

plan to be as cross as you look, my lord, or you will send me into a fit of the dismals."

She basked in the way his eyes flashed and changed to something warm and deeply amused, something that made her feel a little breathless, and sent strange shivers racing over her flesh.

"I had no notion my moods affected you so," he replied, a teasing glint in his eye. His gaze ran over her anew, this time with an air of masculine appreciation. "You look beautiful," he murmured.

They were simple words, spoken without embellishment, yet laden with such a wealth of meaning that Diana blushed with pure pleasure.

"Thank you," she said quietly. "Thank you for everything."

He sat beside her on the couch, while Aimee and Charles pushed a pair of chairs together for themselves. Lawrence brought in hot tea and freshly baked scones, and while the butler was in the room the conversation remained desultory. The moment he was gone, however, the talk immediately shifted to the subject occupying all their minds.

"On the face of it," explained the earl quite seriously, "a daylight abduction such as Lord Hervey planned seems an utterly mad scheme, almost impossible to carry out successfully—at least in this section of London. It worked for two reasons. First, because he had access to the Dowager Lady Torrington's coach, and second, because he had managed to obtain two sets of livery almost identical to that used by the servants in her household. One was for Jacob Creech and the other, of course, was for his brother, Isaac. It was Isaac who was driving the coach."

"*Was* it?" Thinking back, Aimee's head shook in perplexity. "I was completely taken in. When the footman came up to me with a message from Aunt

Serena, it never even occurred to me to question him. I had never seen his face, but the livery was familiar, so . . ." She gave a little shrug. "When Aunt Serena sends a summons, one tends to listen. Mary told me afterward that she did not know him, but of course, she assumed he'd been hired since she came to work at our house. Until the carriage took off down Piccadilly, of course. Then we both knew something was wrong."

Diana gazed at her sister. "And you thought Aunt Serena sent the carriage out of consideration for your health, I expect. But you did not notice the coachman?"

"No." Aimee still looked a little uncertain. "I don't recall even glancing at him. And his back would have been toward us, wouldn't it?"

"But, good lord!" exclaimed Diana, with a startled glance at the earl. "Where *was* Aunt Serena's coachman, then? Surely he would not just hand over the coach to a pair of strangers?"

"Stunned by a blow, just as you were," he answered tightly. He reached for her hand, holding it firmly so that it rested between both of his. "Apparently, the two brothers simply walked into the mews and took the coach. Thanks to an order sent down from Lord Hervey, the horses were already harnessed and ready. I suspect the Creech brothers must have bribed one or two of the stableboys to absent themselves at the crucial moment, but more investigation will have to be done before we know for sure."

"We're dashed well going to find out," said Charles grimly. "I'll have no disloyal servants in my grandmother's employ."

The coach was found abandoned near Leicester Square," added the earl. "They were too shrewd to steal the horses, of course. It would have been much too dangerous."

Diana sipped pensively at her tea. "So Lord Hervey

knew that Aimee would be in the Park—Aunt Serena told him, I suppose—and sent the order. Then the two brothers must have been ready to act at any moment."

Lord Lucan nodded. "Yes, he admitted as much to your aunt. They had been ready for some weeks, it seems. His lodgings are very close to hers, so it did not take him long to return there, apprise Jacob that it was time, and send Jacob to fetch Isaac."

Aimee sighed. "I keep thinking what a pea goose I was to be so easily duped. And even after I was in the coach, I could not conceive of what was happening. And then Mary went into a fit of the vapors, and by the time I had calmed her down, I no longer recognized what street we were on." She frowned suddenly. "Oh, yes, and the handle to the door was jammed. I tried it, because I was wondering whether we ought to try and jump out."

"Well, it's a dashed good thing you didn't!" retorted Charles, looking startled. "You might have broken your neck!"

Aimee gazed coyly up at him from under her lashes. "It's quite plain I need someone to look after me," she complained. "Someone tall and forceful and very, very ardent—"

"Now, Aimee," chided her future husband, very hastily. To Diana's amusement, he turned a trifle pink. "S'pose she told you I made her an offer," he said in a gruff voice. "Ought to have waited to speak to her father first, but—"

"—but I made it *dashed* difficult," finished Aimee with an irrepressible smile. She reached for the teapot and refilled each of their cups, saying, with dancing eyes, "Oh, Diana, you should have seen Charles come dashing to my rescue! I swear he cast Lochinvar completely into the shade! We must ask Sir Walter Scott to compose something in his honor."

The tips of Charles's ears went even pinker. "Well, I'm

glad you can joke about it," he said with extreme feeling. "I know *I'm* going to have nightmares for a twelve-month! The whole business was deuced unnerving."

"Gracious, yes!" agreed Diana with a shiver. "I was utterly terrified, especially when I knew what—" Her voice fluctuated with emotion and the earl's tanned fingers tightened while for a few seconds she fought back the fearful memories. Drawing strength from him, she looked up, her gaze connecting with his in a contact more comforting than any words.

"Should we tell her?" she asked him in a low voice. "She does not yet know the whole of it."

"You mean what Mrs. Creech really intended?" the earl shrugged, and leaned forward to select another scone with his free hand. "Perhaps it would be best," he said, addressing Charles. "It might induce her to cultivate a little more caution."

Aimee was beginning to look indignant. "What are you two talking about? What should I know?"

Charles cleared his throat. "I ain't at all sure she ought to know—"

"Of course I ought to know!" she cried. "Tell me at once, Charles!"

"Well," he said uneasily, "it seems that Mrs. Creech had connections with the criminal underworld of which Lord Hervey was unaware. I ain't exactly sure why he thought he could trust her, but it's devilish clear he couldn't. *His* plan was simply to get as much as he could for the Torrington diamond and the rest of the jewels in the tiara, pay Mrs. Creech a small fee for holding the girls, and have them released. He ain't exactly what you call awake on every suit," he added disparagingly. "Only a Johnny Raw wouldn't have known the woman would try to stab him in the back."

Aimee's eyes grew round. "You . . . you mean she did not intend to release us? That is what she told me. That is

332

why I was only a . . . a little afraid."

"Unlikely," put in the earl harshly. "From what she said to Diana, and from what she told Lord Hervey before she had him trussed up and tossed into her cellar, it seems clear that her plans were more ambitious. She does not admit it now, of course."

Charles patted Aimee's hand. "Hate to tell you this, kitten, but you had a dashed narrow escape. The Creech woman was going to take Hervey's blunt, and then, er, toss him into the river, so to speak. You and Mary were destined for something . . . worse."

The earl nodded. "When Diana arrived, Mrs. Creech was forced to alter her plans. I imagine she still hoped to get her hands on the Torrington diamond, but she now had Diana, too. Three healthy English girls, all well-looking in appearance, two of gentle birth . . . and apparently someone who was willing to pay dearly for them. Much as I hate to say it, there are still illicit markets for such women—particularly in some of the eastern countries."

"Edmund mentioned something about that once," put in Diana slowly. "I thought he meant it as a sick jest or . . . or said it only to disgust me. I could not believe such things were true. But when Mrs. Creech said . . . what she did . . . then I remembered." Once more the earl squeezed her fingers, and just as before, it helped.

"But could they really hope to get away with such a wicked scheme?" asked Aimee in a constricted voice.

"Probably not," said the earl, observing her white face. "In any case, Mrs. Creech has broken enough laws to be transported. In particular, any form of slave-trading has been a criminal offense in this country since 1811, and if it can be proved—" He broke off at the sight of Aimee's expression. "But we need not go into that any further just now. The important thing is that Mrs. Creech has been caught. Unfortunately, both her sons have eluded the authorities thus far."

"We should have tied the fellow up," exclaimed Charles, clapping a hand to his brow. "Why the devil didn't we think of it before?"

Lord Lucan looked equally rueful. "It was incredibly stupid of us, I agree. All I can say is that I, at least"—he cast an inscrutable look at Diana—"had something far more important on my mind."

"And what might that have been?" Diana made a strict effort to keep the question casual, and if there was a slight huskiness in her voice, she blamed it entirely on the earl, whose thumb had begun to caress her wrist in a most disturbing manner.

He gave her an amused look. "Why, I fear I cannot call it to mind at the moment," he replied, with a smile that made her heart thud.

"So Sir Henry was not involved in this after all?" said Aimee suddenly. Her eyes flew inquiringly to Charles.

"No, dash it! And I was sure the fellow was guilty!" His vexation evident, Aimee's betrothed popped the remainder of his fourth scone into his mouth and chomped on it savagely.

"In fact, he was actually instrumental in achieving your release," added the earl, reluctantly dragging his eyes from Diana's. "I would have questioned Lord Hervey's servant, of course, but without Sir Henry's information, I'm not sure I would have thought to, er, offer him physical violence—at least not to quite such a degree." His gaze returned to Diana, who was looking dismayed. "I'm afraid it was the only way we were able to get anything out of the man," he explained, with a faint air of apology.

Charles snorted. "His nose'll never be quite the same, and who cares? I'm devilish sure I don't!"

"Speaking of noses," remarked the earl in an altered tone, "do you agree that Sir Henry has earned his reward?"

Charles stared at him. "Reward? What sort of reward?"

"I thought we had both expressed an interest in rearranging certain of his features?"

"Oh!" Charles sat back with a grin. "Aye. I s'pose we ought to let him keep his nose," he stated, with careless magnanimity. "As long as he continues to mind his manners!"

After this, the conversation wended its way into more general channels, and when it turned eventually to horses, Aimee began to beg Charles to take her riding. Mr. Perth was not entirely sure that his beloved was ready for such strenuous exercise, but he found himself completely unable to resist her coaxing, and since she very meekly agreed to tell him the moment she began to feel fatigued, he finally yielded to her entreaties. He was, after all, only human, and there were a number of rather private sentiments he wished to impart (again) into her ear. A ride in the Park would offer them a chance to continue one particularly interesting discussion that had begun just after he had slashed the ropes which bound her prisoner in Mrs. Creech's house. And perhaps, he reflected, if he was very lucky, and they found themselves in an unoccupied area of the Park, they might be able to exchange another kiss. He therefore took himself off to his lodgings to change into riding clothes, while Aimee scurried upstairs to do the same.

Grateful to be alone at last with the earl, Diana turned to him eagerly, but was shocked to realize that he, too, was rising to his feet.

"But . . . but you are not leaving *now*, are you?" she faltered.

Observing her forlorn expression, he immediately sat down again and pulled her into his arms. "Don't look so wounded, love," he said, raising her chin with his finger. "I don't *want* to leave you, "—there was a queer flicker in his eyes—"but I have several important matters to

335

attend to this afternoon and if I stay another minute I won't be able to drag myself away at all." Diana's unconsciously provocative pout nearly changed his mind. "You want me to kiss you, don't you darling?" he murmured. "Well, and why not?" His lips came down to brush hers lightly, hovered for an instant, then withdrew before it ever became a real kiss.

"On second thought, I think you are crediting me with more willpower than I possess," he said, expelling a jagged breath. Her topaz eyes were wide and doubtful, and he pulled back enough to look down into them for a long moment.

She stared back, seeing something that was at once hard and soft, candid and enigmatic. "You don't want to kiss me?" she whispered in confusion.

"Dammit, of course I do, Diana. But the next time I kiss you,"—he said it roughly, deliberately—"I don't intend to stop before we're finished."

The words were suggestive enough to make Diana's mouth go dry. "I'm sure I don't know what you mean," she lied, her heart knocking against her ribs. Fearing he might explain, she added quickly, "And I don't know what could possibly be so important that you could not stay a short while longer." She did not care if she sounded pettish, and neither did the earl, apparently, for he merely grinned and ruffled her hair.

"Oh, can you not?" he retorted rather lazily. "Well, you soon will, my love. I'll take you for a drive tomorrow morning, how about that? Do you think you can be ready by eleven o'clock?"

"As to that, my lord, I shall have to consult my social schedule," she replied with spirit. "It is quite possible that I am engaged to drive out with some other gentleman. Someone with enough courtesy to request—"

"I *did* request!"

"—the pleasure of my company. Someone who inquires

336

whether I am feeling well enough for such exertion—"

"My dear Diana, if I thought for one moment that you were not—"

"Someone," she continued in deeply piteous tones, "who does not run off and abandon me only hours after I have sustained a severe shock—a shock, I might add, which would have sent *most* females into repeated fits of hysterics! Which reminds me, my lord, I should like to know just why my companion is not here. Aimee informs me that you descended upon us this morning while I was still asleep and *abducted* poor Tildy!"

"Miss Tilden," he responded, without remorse, "was not abducted. In fact, she offered to go and help sustain your aunt in her Hour of Need. Your Great-aunt Serena evidently took a liking to Miss Tilden, for she specifically requested her attendance."

"Oh. I—I see," said Diana, abandoning her theatrics. "Very well, then. If it is as you say—"

The earl's patience was dwindling rapidly. "My dear Diana, I am still awaiting your answer with bated breath. Dare I hope that you will accord me the honor and pleasure of your charming company for a leisurely ride in my carriage tomorrow morning? At approximately eleven o'clock?"

"My dear Lord Lucan," she said, her eyes cast demurely downward, "since you phrase it so gallantly, how can I possibly refuse?"

Though she would not have liked him to know it, Diana was wearing a track in the drawing room carpet more than thirty minutes before the earl was due to arrive. Over and over, her fretful gaze swerved to the clock upon the mantelshelf, then moved to the mirror above, where she anxiously inspected her appearance. Why hadn't he come early? Wasn't he as eager to see her as she was to

337

see him? Was he actually going to be *late?*

It was ten minutes past eleven before she heard the bell ring, and by then, Diana had worked herself into a fume. It was outside of enough for him to have deserted her yesterday, just when she'd been about to blurt out all her feelings for him, but now, *now* when she was positively languishing over him, he had to go and be late! How could he be so infuriating?

When Lawrence announced the earl, however, Diana was seated in a chair with her back to the clock. "What, is it eleven already?" she remarked, feigning an airy little start of surprise as she twisted around, "Gracious, I had no notion of the time! Where *has* the morning gone?"

Moving toward her with long strides, the earl grinned his appreciation. "Miffed again, Diana? Lord, what a scolding little fishwife you are going to make me!"

Diana's brows arched. "Why, what can you possibly mean? Simply because you are ten minutes late, does not mean—" The sentence ended in a small squeak as he reached down and pulled her manfully into his arms.

"In reality, my dear delight, I am as punctual as always. I told you that blasted clock was wrong, didn't I?"

The heat of his nearness made a clever response impossible. "Well, I was hoping you'd be early," was all she could manage, on a shred of reproach.

"I would have been but for your aunt," he said wryly. "She sent me an early morning summons, and what could I do but obey? Come, are you ready?"

"What?" With difficulty, Diana focused on the latter question. "Oh, yes, of course. No, wait—I must put on my bonnet." This delectable confection of feathers and flowers lay beside her gloves atop a nearby table, and as she tied it under her chin, she said in some bewilderment, "But what on earth can have possessed Aunt Serena to send for *you?* Especially at such an hour?"

"She likes me," replied the earl, shepherding her toward the door with determination.

"Yes, but that hardly explains—"

"Can you wait until we're outside?" he demanded. "I'll explain it all to you then."

It seemed judicious to do as he desired, but the moment they stepped out of the house, Diana's curiosity received a startling new stimulus.

"But . . . but this is a traveling chariot!" she protested, staring at the light, yellow-bodied chaise-and-four standing in the street.

"So it is, he agreed, urging her forward with his hand. "I purchased it only yesterday so there are no crests on the door panels as yet. I did not think you would care about that."

"But, Geoffrey, there are *trunks* strapped to the boot. Are you—we—going out of town?"

"Clever girl," he approved, as the postilion hurried to let down the steps. "I usually hire a post-chaise, but I thought it high time I bought my own conveyance. Do get in, love."

For some unfathomable reason, Diana found she lacked the will to refuse. In fact, an unexpected, heart-jarring excitement was rushing through her, so that all she could do was say, in as blithe a tone as she could manage, "I presume you mean to tell me where we're going!" and climb into the coach.

The earl did the same, settling himself beside her with an air of intense satisfaction. "That was certainly easier than I expected," he remarked. "I envisioned having to sling you over my shoulder and—"

"What was easier?" she interrupted, her voice rising a little. "Geoffrey, I really must insist you explain what this is about."

"I have every intention of explaining," he retorted. "You see, my dear delight, I'm abducting you."

"*What?*"

"I said I'm abducting you." Both his tone and expression strongly suggested that he was uncommonly pleased with himself.

"Geoffrey," she said, after a brief struggle with her emotions, "this is quite unnecessary. I am perfectly willing to marry you."

"Ah, but you see, I'm no longer asking you to marry me," he replied, to her utter astonishment. "The offer is withdrawn."

Diana was almost certain she saw his lips twitch, but to her, it was hardly a laughing matter. "I'm afraid I don't understand," she said, rather shakily. "If you don't want to marry me, then why . . . go to all this trouble?"

"I do wish you would pay attention, Diana," he complained. "Did I say I do *not* want to marry you? No! I said I have withdrawn my offer of marriage." He reached for her hand and carried it to his chest, holding it where she could feel the steady thud of his heart. "I'm still determined to have you, Diana, but the fact is, I have proposed—or tried to propose—marriage to you three times, and each time have had the infelicitous experience of being turned down! First," he said in an aggrieved tone, "you made false assumptions about me, then you hemmed and hawed over the whole business until I was ready to tear out my hair with frustration—"

Diana's conscious-stricken expression vanished. "I was not hemming and hawing!" she said indignantly. "I was simply considering—"

"—and considering and considering," he went on, growing wrathful. "I never met a woman so given to thinking things over! Then you said you loved me—"

"And it's true!" she protested.

"Yes, thank God, I'm aware of that. But then you gave me some cock-and-bull story about how you were not a normal woman with normal responses—"

"Well, how do you know it's not true?" she inquired

340

in a small, breathless voice.

The earl's expression was laughing and tender—but it was also mixed with a hint of steel. "I know," he said firmly, "because I've held you in my arms. I know because I've kissed you, Diana, and I can tell a quiver of desire from a shiver of revulsion. There is nothing wrong with you, and I intend to prove it before the day is out."

His meaning was more than plain. "You would really take me without marriage?" she whispered.

"If that's the only way," he told her bluntly. "One way or another I intend to show you that your fears are misplaced! However, I just happen to have a special license in my pocket, only inches from your fingers, my sweet." Her hand jerked, but he recaptured it and carried it to his lips. "You know, as much as I enjoy kissing these pretty fingers," he teased, "there are a number of other parts of you that I'm even more anxious to kiss."

Diana was too upset to be diverted. "But, Geoffrey," she objected, "you are making no sense. Either you do wish to marry me or you don't—"

"Oh, didn't I explain?" He made a pretense of looking surprised. "*You* must ask *me* to marry *you*."

Diana's mouth fell open. "But—that's absurd!" she said, finding her voice at last.

"Why?" He grinned. "I should like it above all things, you know."

She thought this over. "Then you *do* love me?" she asked hesitantly. "I mean, *love* me . . . not just *care* for me?"

He stared at her in astonishment. "For the love of heaven, Diana, haven't I made that clear? Of course I love you! I'm mad with love for you, darling!"

His arms reached out to crush her against him, an embrace which ended with her snuggled cozily upon his lap, and what remained of her bonnet shoved into the opposite corner.

"Lord, what a clunk I am not to have said it!" he

murmured, stroking her hair. "Love was just a meaning-less word until I met you." He kissed her ear, then the tip of her nose. "Oh, granted I loved my parents, but . . . the love I feel for you transcends anything I have ever felt. You have taught me to love, Diana. I adore you, every blessed inch of you, and I plan to spend the rest of my life proving it. And I'll love you just as much when we're old and fat and all our teeth have fallen out!"

Diana saw no purpose in hiding her delight. "That is absolutely the most romantic thing anyone has ever said to me," she remarked, sighing dreamily. "In that case, Geoffrey, will you please, please marry me? For I *do* love you so very much!"

Her words were simple and sincere, and as far as he was concerned, the sweetest words she could have spoken.

"In a very short while," he promised, his voice unnaturally husky, "we will find a clergyman and attend to the matter."

His broad shoulder offered an enticing spot for her head, but too many unanswered questions still crowded Diana's mind. "But, Geoffrey," she said, after a few moments, "I still do not quite understand why we are leaving London. And you've not told me where we are going, either!"

"We're on the Bath Road," he said, "which I'm sure you know takes us eventually into Wiltshire. I seem to recall you telling me about a certain set of parents and siblings in that area, who have, by the way, been apprised of our imminent arrival. And the reason we're leaving, dear delight, is because there are too many blasted rumors flying about London for my comfort!"

In reply to her look, he grumbled, "The first, of course, you already know. Then there's a second rumor which suggests the we are *not* currently engaged in a liaison of a passionate nature, but that a formal an-nouncement of our approaching nuptials is expected at any moment. That one, by the way, is being circulated by our dear friend Sir Henry at, er, my suggestion. And now a *third* version has sprung up!"

Diana blinked. "A third?" she echoed. "What is it?"

"An unnamed personage," he said sardonically, "has started a rumor that we are already married, and in fact have been so for a great many weeks! And as of this morning, it seems to be the most prevalent of the three!"

"Aunt Serena!" A variety of emotions swept over Diana, but the strongest—mirth—won out within seconds. "Oh, Lord, I might have known!" she said, between giggles. "I wonder what reason she invented to account for it? Why are you scowling? Her story scarcely does any harm, does it?"

He smiled reluctantly. "Oh, I agree it's the best of the three, for it cancels out the stench of the first. However, when every gossipmonger in town feels free to bandy my future wife's name about, I find it puts me in a devil of a temper."

Back in March, Diana would have been horrified by the notion, but now she merely leaned up to kiss his chin, her eyes dancing with laughter. "Never mind, I daresay it will all soon die down. In fact, I can think of a few other details I am more concerned about."

"Oh? And what are they?" he inquired, one dark brow rising quizzically.

She traced the line of his jaw with her finger. "You, my dear Geoffrey, may have had the foresight to bring every stitch of clothing you own, but I have brought nothing. And if you mean to tell me I can purchase more, it seems to me a shameful waste when I've so many things, and *furthermore,* we have brought neither maid nor valet with us, which is going to look rather peculiar, don't you think?"

The earl's chest shook with laughter. "Have you no faith in me, my little pea goose? Thanks to your abigail,

343

one of those trunks up in the back is filled with your clothing—although I confess I added a few items of my own choosing. The weakest part of my plan, you see, was that you might notice half your gowns were gone."

"Well, I didn't!" she said, with new asperity. "Indeed, how could I? Everyone made sure I lay about like some sort of vaporish invalid and did nothing for myself! And how shockingly *high-handed* of you to persuade my abigail to go behind my back! How did you manage it?"

He smiled wickedly. "You could say it was a combination of your aunt's influence and my own personal charm."

"Oh, really?" she retorted. "So Aunt Serena knows about this, does she?"

"And totally approves—except about the business of a church wedding, for I don't expect to find a clergyman before the noon deadline. But I *won't* wait another day Diana, so don't ask! Your aunt and I had that out already, both yesterday and again this morning. I only got away by promising we'd be married a second time *in* a church, *in* her august presence!"

"This seems to be getting rather complicated," Diana complained.

He looked amused. "No, it's actually quite simple," he said, gently pinching her chin. "We will be married once today, most likely in Reading since we are due to change horses there shortly. That will enable us to live as man and wife in *your* house, Diana, rather than in your parent's. Yes, I thought you might see the advantage of that. By sometime next week, your aunt will have arrived, along with Aimee, Charles, Miss Tilden, my valet, your abigail and her, er, husband—"

"Meg is married?" interrupted Diana in surprise.

"Yes. To your footman, it seems. Their romance appears to have taken place under your very nose, my dear, but that is another story. Now, to continue: I

344

dispatched a letter to my own mother this morning, whom I hope will also be able to attend our, ah, second wedding. She ought to be able to arrive by next week also, but if not, we will wait until she does."

Diana regarded him with near astonishment. "Oh, this is all very simple, indeed! And then what?"

His eyes glinted. "And then, my darling, we shall go anywhere you like and do anything you like. As long as you do it with me."

They were married in Reading by a stout, elderly clergyman with three chins and a fatherly manner. The earl had not forgotten to purchase a ring, and when he slipped this—a large sapphire surrounded by diamonds and pearls—onto Diana's finger, the fit was as close to perfection as anyone could wish. When the ceremony was over, the Earl and Countess of Lucan shook hands with the clergyman, signed the register, and proceeded to *The George* for what they jestingly called their "wedding breakfast"; they then returned to the chaise and recommenced their journey through the Berkshires. An hour and a half later they had crossed into Wiltshire and were skirting the Savernake Forest, the edge of which, Diana informed him a trifle absently, was but three miles from her home.

At this point in the journey Diana fell abnormally silent, and when she frowned suddenly, her concerned husband was quick to demand the explanation.

"Geoffrey," she answered in a serious tone, "I have been thinking."

"Have you, my darling? What about?"

"Now that we are married, it has just occurred to me that I no longer have any need of Edmund's money." She turned anxious eyes to his face. "Do you have any need of it? For if you do not, I should very much like to give it

345

to my parents, for they *do* need it, you see. They would not accept my help before, but I think perhaps that under the present circumstances they might."

He was conscious of a profound feeling of relief that her frown had not arisen from second thoughts about their union. "A capital notion, my love," he approved heartily. "They are welcome to every penny of it, for I have more than enough for our needs." He did not add that he wanted nothing of Edmund Verney to remain in their lives, for she very likely knew that.

Diana's frown vanished. "You are so very good," she said, emotion creeping back into her voice. "Oh, but now I have recalled another favor I must ask you."

"Here it comes!" he groaned, in mock despair. "The never-ending list of wifely demands."

Diana poked her husband in the ribs. "No such thing! I merely wanted to ask if you have any objection to Tildy living with us. She is getting old, and has no family of her own, and while she *could* live with my parents, of course, I think she would be happier with me. We are very close, you know."

"Miss Tilden is welcome to live with us for as long as she pleases," he stated. "From what I have observed, she is very much like my own mother in disposition. In fact, my mother is also a knitter, so I daresay they will form a lasting friendship. You will like my mother, by the way. She is not at all high in the instep."

"And do you think she will like me?"

He smiled. "She will be in transports about you. She still blames herself for allowing me to make a loveless marriage the first time around. Not that she could have prevented me, of course. At that time I did not believe in love, so I did not seek it."

He sounded so rueful Diana reached up to touch his cheek. "Your first wife ran away from you. Did she hurt you, my dear?"

346

His head shook. "My pride, perhaps," he said honestly. "But to be hurt, I think, one must love—and I loved Laurette no more than she loved me." His arm tightened around her. "One must come to terms with one's past, Diana," he added meaningfully. "The future is what concerns me. *Our* future."

She nodded. "It is the same for me," she told him quietly. "Edmund is truly gone for me, now. The future is what counts."

Diana did not argue when her husband insisted they go first to her house rather than her parents', for she had sensed his growing impatience to make love to her ever since they left Reading. The woman she had left in charge of the house greeted them warmly, as did her burly husband, who hurried to unload the trunks and take charge of the chaise and horses. Seeing the way Mrs. Piper's eyes kept darting to the earl, Diana hastily informed her they were married, and with a blush which deepened as she spoke, went on to say that they intended to take a short rest and must upon no account be disturbed. The journey was quite exhausting, she explained in an increasingly flustered voice.

The earl's face was very bland during his wife's speech, but when they were mounting the stairs to the second floor, he chuckled and whispered. "You did not deceive her in the least, you know!"

Any reply she might have made was trapped in her throat, for his hand was caressing her hip in a manner which drove away her voice.

Within her bedchamber, Diana turned to her new husband with confidence. She knew no apprehension, nor dread, nor even nervousness, for no shadows from the past lingered to sully the moment with doubts. This was *excitement* she was feeling, a pure, restless sort of excitement, an unguarded yearning to give all of herself to the man she loved. And deep down inside, she knew she was going to make him a very good wife.

To Geoffrey, Diana still looked as vulnerable as ever, but though he studied her carefully, he saw no hesitation or fear in her face. Complete trust was shining in her brown-gold eyes—trust in him, along with the first stirrings of knowledge, a half-awakened awareness of her own feminine needs. Reassured, he held out his arms to her, and she went into them with a choked little laugh that meant more to him than a thousand words of affection.

As his lips sought hers, Diana went up on her toes, pressing herself against him with an abandon she had never known. She wanted him as much as she loved him, and the two mingled within her to form something more powerful and potent than she had ever dared imagine. How strong, how splendidly, solidly *male* he felt beneath her hands! Her eager fingers stroked the nape of his neck, dragged through his raven black hair, then almost of their own accord went down to grip the top edge of his waistcoat, where the pounding of his heart reminded her that this was only the beginning.

"My beautiful wife," he whispered against her upward tilted lips. "My beautiful, wonderful wife."

Then he was claiming an even more demanding kiss, a blending of mouths that took Diana into an entirely new, compellingly fundamental arena of sensation. Before her reeling mind could comprehend her own delight, his tongue was sliding down her neck, then up again to her mouth with a hungry, thrusting movement that sent a stab of pleasure to her very core.

His hands were fumbling at the ties of her gown, then she felt him pulling it up and off so that she stood before him in nothing but her undergarments. Trembling a little, Diana bent to remove her shoes and stockings, aware that her husband's eyes were devouring her, scorching her with the intensity of their gaze. Then she

348

straightened, and, pushing away the last remnants of self-consciousness, took off her chemise.

"Diana—!" Geoffrey's voice caught in a throat grown thick with desire. She was just as he'd imagined, only better because she was really here and she was finally his. Her rosy-tipped breasts were perfect, just the size to fit into his large hands, while the rest of her was even more heavenly. But he would go slowly, he promised himself. He would court her senses so that she would feel everything, so that she would never again doubt that she was anything but the most flawless, the most exquisite, the most vital of women. In turn, he wanted to witness her pleasure, to know that every sigh and tremor was for him. With iron control, Lord Lucan lifted his new wife and placed her tenderly upon the bed.

"I adore you," he said, raking her with possessive eyes. "And if I can get this damned thing off"—he yanked impatiently at his neckcloth—"I mean to prove it! Unfortunately, gentlemen's garments are not so simple to remove," he added, with a lopsided grin.

Diana forgot her nakedness in the joy of watching him undress. His body was hard and lean and utterly masculine, so unlike Edmund's that it was ridiculous to compare. Moreover, Geoffrey's love for her seemed as solid and tangible as his body, and it was partly this which made it impossible to look away or be afraid.

To her surprise, his lovemaking was almost too leisurely at first, his caresses featherlight and teasing when some unreasoning part of her longed for haste. Then, once or twice, he did something which startled her, but each time this happened, he whispered something so outrageous that instead of tensing, she giggled and yielded to his mastery. He wooed her with consummate skill, slowly building their hunger until it reached a new summit where nothing existed but the fierce interdependence of the masculine and the feminine. And when he finally entered her, she opened to him like a flower to the sun, welcoming his thrusts into her body with soft, gasping cries that spoke of a pleasure as great as his.

Afterward, they did not talk at once, but lay with limbs entwined as lovers do. At length, however, the earl rose up on his elbow, and regarded her with a mischievous grin. "I told you it was a cock-and-bull story."

He sounded so smug Diana hit him with a pillow. *"Oooh*, you! Impossible man! I suppose you will tease me about that for the rest of our lives!"

He gave a mock yelp as she swung again. "No, no, I promise I won't! On one condition, that is."

Since he was still grinning, Diana eyed him with suspicion. "And what is that?"

"That you never wear a corset!" he replied, grabbing the pillow away from her. "I cannot abide the things, and I want to be able to do this—"

"Geoffrey!"

"—and this—"

"Geoffrey!"

"—without unlacing you for half an hour!"

"I don't even own a corset," she informed him with dignity. "In the meantime, if you can possibly attend to something serious, I wanted to tell you where I would like to go for our wedding trip."

He pulled her closer, so that the full length of their bodies touched. "Where?" he whispered in her ear.

Trying not to be distracted by his nibbling kisses, she replied, "Cornwall. I want to see your home, Geoffrey. It is a part of England that has long intrigued me, and—will you stop doing that?"

His lips rose from her neck long enough to say, quite fervently, "I am glad you desire to go there, for it is the one place above all others on earth I wish to show you. There is more beauty in Cornwall than one could absorb in a lifetime! Just thinking of it, I can taste the salt air and

350

hear the pound of the sea." He dropped a kiss on her chin, his harsh face growing animated. "I will take you to visit the fishing, farming, and mining communities so you can hear their superstitions and legends for yourself. You'll be highly entertained by their stories, my love. And we'll ride the moors together, Diana, the miles and miles of moorland stretching far as the eye can see. There is nothing like it, I promise. And we can still come up to London whenever you like." He said it eagerly, as a small boy offering to share his candy with a friend.

She smiled at his enthusiasm. "I'm sure I will, my dear. I would love any place in the world if I could live there with you."

"And when we're done with riding, we will find a private place and work on producing the next generation of Trevelyans," he added roguishly.

Diana's arm slid around his waist. "Shall we, indeed? I think I would like that very much."

"On second thought," he murmured, nuzzling into her neck, "why wait?"

This was obviously not the time, reflected the new Countess of Lucan, to reprimand her husband for his high-handed tactics. It would have to be done, of course, but on this particular occasion, she could not help but feel that it was wiser to let him have his way. Husbands had to be humored, didn't they?

It was the easiest decision of all.

Julie Caille welcomes letters from readers and invites you to write to her c/o Zebra Books, 475 Park Avenue South, New York, NY 10016